Praise for *The G*

"*The Good Part* left me buried und___ _____ __ ____ emo-
tions and with a new appreciation for life's small, beautiful
moments. This is a book to read twice—once to feverishly tear
through the pages and a second time to savor."
—Annabel Monaghan, author of *Same Time Next Summer*

"Warm, funny, joyful, and wise . . . With a brilliant premise,
The Good Part explores the 'grass is greener' concept through
a wonderfully loveable heroine. If you want to giggle and feel
all the swoony feels do pick up a copy of Cousens's latest."
—Cesca Major, author of *Maybe Next Time*

"A charming look at the road not taken, *The Good Part* delves
into both the ooey goodness and the messy realities of growing up and landing on both feet."
—Allison Winn Scotch, author of *The Rewind*

"Delightfully zany and full of heart, [it's] the perfect read for
anyone who has ever felt a little lost in their own life. (And
who among us hasn't?) . . . [My] favorite Sophie Cousens
book."
—Becca Freeman, author of *The Christmas Orphans Club*

"This charming and poignant timeslip story had me considering my own experiences from a new perspective and with a
renewed sense of gratitude. Sophie Cousens is one of the few
authors I will happily allow to break my heart again and again,
because it's just such a pleasure to find out how she'll mend it."
—Sarah Adler, author of *Mrs. Nash's Ashes*

"A delight . . . With characters that are full of heart, this book is the reminder we all need to stop and relish all the moments along the way to whatever our dream life looks like. I couldn't put it down!"

—Betty Cayouette, founder of
Betty's Book List and author of *One Last Shot*

Praise for *Before I Do*

"A thoughtful and romantic story about the moments and choices that change our lives in unexpected ways . . . Cousens has created something special with this lovely tale."

—*Washington Independent Review of Books*

"Witty and heartfelt, *Before I Do* takes a familiar trope and turns it on its head, and readers will find themselves tearing through this book to find out how it ends." —*Booklist*

"A charming and surprising take on a classic love-triangle formula." —*Kirkus Reviews*

"[W]itty and emotionally rich . . . Readers will be especially drawn to Audrey, a woman unafraid to chase her own happiness and face challenges head-on. This is sure to charm."

—*Publishers Weekly*

"The perfect feel-good book." —*Reader's Digest*

Praise for *Just Haven't Met You Yet*

"Endearing, sparkling, and hilarious."

—Josie Silver, author of *One Day in December*

"A perfectly charming escape. I laughed, I teared up, and I smiled my way through."

—Helen Hoang, author of *The Kiss Quotient*

"A delightfully romantic tale of one woman's search for her happily ever after in the form of the owner of a swapped suitcase."

—PopSugar

"[F]iction slowly becomes truth in this highly enjoyable, delectable tale."

—GoodMorningAmerica.com

"Sweet [and] funny . . . It's just the story to offer a little romantic escapism during the holiday season."

—CNN

"Hilarious moments, heartfelt charm, dynamic character . . . this rom-com has it all."

—*Woman's World*

"Cousens imbues the entire story with an uplifting sense of hope. . . . The Jersey setting creates a cozy, windswept background to the deliciously slow-burn romance. A warm, witty, and absolutely charming seaside holiday that's perfect for fans of Sophie Kinsella."

—*Kirkus Reviews* (starred review)

"Humor and poignancy keep the pages turning. Fans of Sophie Kinsella and Josie Silver will find plenty to enjoy."

—*Publishers Weekly*

"A wonderfully layered story of love and loss."
—Shelf Awareness

"For the friend who loves curling up at home, pick up *Just Haven't Met You Yet*, a fun meld of drama and romance."
—*Parents*

"Reading Sophie Cousens is like meeting a new best friend. She makes you laugh, she makes you cry, you feel like you've loved her forever, and you don't want to let her go."
—Clare Pooley, author of *The Authenticity Project*

"This book is pure, unbridled joy."
—Rachel Lynn Solomon, author of *The Ex Talk*

Praise for *This Time Next Year*

"A funny, pull-at-your-heartstrings read . . . It's a hug in book form." —Josie Silver, author of *One Day in December*

"[A] second-chance romance that makes you feel unabashedly hopeful." —Refinery29

"The characters in this page-turning novel are richly drawn and transform substantially, especially Minnie, and all suggest that maybe happy ever after is up to us." —NPR Books

"If you make time for just one holiday read this year, make it Sophie Cousens's *This Time Next Year*." —PopSugar

"Cousens's debut is ripe with both emotional vulnerability and zaniness."
                                                    —*Publishers Weekly*

"A brilliantly written story about love, redemption, friendship, and self-empowerment . . . This book is an absolute delight . . . [and] a feel-good tale to cozy up with."
                                    —*San Francisco Book Review*

"Rom-com readers will revel in Cousens's wry, lively story, which probes themes of self-discovery, acceptance, and forgiveness, and the abiding nature of friendship."
                                                    —Shelf Awareness

"Sparkling and uplifting."
                —Mhairi McFarlane, author of *If I Never Met You*

THE
GOOD
PART

THE

A NOVEL

GOOD
PART

Sophie Cousens

G. P. PUTNAM'S SONS
New York

PUTNAM
— EST. 1838 —
G. P. PUTNAM'S SONS
Publishers Since 1838
An imprint of Penguin Random House LLC
penguinrandomhouse.com

Library of Congress Control Number: 2023036295

ISBN 9780593539897 (trade paperback)
ISBN 9780593539903 (ebook)

Printed in the United States of America
1st Printing

Book design by Ashley Tucker

This is a work of fiction. Names, characters, places, and incidents
either are the product of the author's imagination or are used
fictitiously, and any resemblance to actual persons, living or dead,
businesses, companies, events, or locales is entirely coincidental.

To my twenty-six-year-old self.
Hang in there, hun.

THE **GOOD** PART

TODAY

MY BED IS WET. NOT DAMP, BUT PROPERLY SOAKED, AS though my pillow has been used as a sandbag during a flood. Looking up, I see a small stream of water dripping through the yellow stain on my bedroom ceiling: the source of my current dampness. The bedside clock tells me it's five AM, which is the worst of all the AMs—not early enough to guarantee getting back to sleep, but not late enough to contemplate starting your day.

Jumping out of bed, I navigate the obstacle course that is my cluttered bedroom floor and run down the corridor, out of the front door, and up the cold stone stairs to the top-floor flat.

"Mr. Finkley! Mr. Finkley! Your bathroom is leaking again," I shout while beating on the door with two fists. There's no response. He'd better not have died in the bath with the tap running, because then the whole ceiling might fall in, and I'll have his dead body to contend with on top of everything else. "Mr. Finkley!" I call again, with more urgency this time, trying to banish the mental image of my bed crushed beneath a pile of rubble and bubble bath. Finally, the door opens a crack, and Mr. Finkley peers out at me. He's in his sixties and has wispy blond hair that sticks out vertically on either side of his bald pate. His face is all angular features, and he wears brown-rimmed glasses permanently smeared with grease. Every time I see him, I need to remind myself not to call him Mr. Stinkley, which is what my flatmates and I call him in private.

"Bathwater is leaking through the ceiling again," I tell him sternly.

"I was having a bath," he says, winding a wisp of wet hair around his index finger, then removing the finger, leaving behind a hair horn.

"It's the middle of the night," I say wearily. "And remember the plumber saying you can't have baths, not until you've sealed the floor tiles properly? Any overflow comes straight down into my bedroom." My voice is measured, as though I'm explaining this to a toddler.

"I don't like showers," he replies, twiddling a symmetrical horn of hair on the other side of his scalp.

"Nor do I—especially when I'm asleep, *in bed*." I stomp down the stairs, calling back as I go, "Just put some towels down, please."

There's no point trying to reason with the bath-loving lunatic. I'll have to call our landlord, Cynthia, *again*. All any of us know about Cynthia is that she lives in Spain, is allergic to cat hair, and is a horribly negligent landlord. She often berates me for "vexing her with our domestic concerns," but I am vexed, Cynthia, I am extremely vexed.

Back in my bedroom, I remove my beloved books from their plastic storage box, then place the box on the bed to catch any remaining drips. Surveying the books, I feel like a mother who's failed to provide for her children. They deserve a decent bookcase; they deserve to be displayed, spine out, sorted by genre, not heaped in a pile on the floor of my damp room. *One day, books, one day.* After changing my sodden bed shirt, I crawl into the dry end of my bed, desperate for a couple more hours, but it's hard to sleep when your mind is racing and your toes are damp. I must drift off, because I wake to my alarm, confused as to why I'm sleeping upside down.

My room looks completely different from this perspective. Out of the window I see the promise of another gray spring day, and the spider plant on my windowsill looks even browner and sicklier than it did yesterday. The plant was a gift from my dad, along with the now-drooping yucca in the corner. He's convinced that indoor plants help stave off depression and anxiety. Ironically, keeping them alive until his next visit has become a major source of anxiety for me. Dad assured me, "You can't kill spider plants, they thrive on neglect," but I seem to have managed it. These plants feel like canaries in a coal mine, a litmus test for inhospitable living conditions.

Wrapping a towel around myself, I head to the bathroom, which I find occupied. It is *always* occupied.

I tap, then call through the door, "It's Lucy. Are you going to be long?" If it's Emily or Zoya, they'll be quick, but Julian might be hours. I want to know if it's worth waiting or if I should go make myself a cup of tea.

"Just having a shave," Julian calls back. Great. That means the sink will be full of tiny bristles, and there'll be shaving foam all over the hand towel.

"The ceiling in my room is leaking again," I tell him.

"That's annoying," says Julian lightly, his tone failing to

convey the true scale of quite how annoying it is, especially for the person who sleeps beneath said ceiling. As I'm standing in the corridor having a conversation with the bathroom door, a man emerges from Emily's room. He's tall, with peroxide-blond hair and a huge tattoo of an eagle in the middle of his chest.

"Hi, I'm Ezekiel," he says, giving me a sheepish wave. "Friend of Em's."

"Hi," I say, hurriedly pulling my towel up to make sure it's adequately covering my chest.

"Is the bathroom free?" he asks with a yawn, slowly stretching his long, pale arms above his head. He has the languid manner of a man who is not in a rush to be anywhere—unlike me, who has a job to get to.

"Bit of a queue, I'm afraid."

Making small talk with one of Em's random shags is not my favorite thing to do in the morning, so I head through to the kitchen, where I find Betty, Julian's on-off girlfriend, boiling three different saucepans on the stove. Whatever she's making, it smells like a horse died in a ditch, then someone brewed up the ditch water with a few herbs. I have nothing against Betty as a person, but she's *always* here, *always* batch cooking, and the flat is hardly big enough for four of us, let alone Betty and all her mason jars.

"Morning, Betty! What's cooking?" I ask brightly. One of my greatest qualities is that I can be polite and jovial even when I'm feeling grumpy and furious. Hiding how you really feel is an essential skill, especially when you live in a busy flat share. No one wants to live with a Moaning Mary. Before Betty can answer, I hear the bathroom door click open, and I dart back into the corridor to get in there before Em's conquest. He's still hovering outside Em's door, but I manage to launch myself into the bathroom first. "Sorry, desperate," I say, crossing my legs and giving him an apologetic eye-roll.

As predicted, the sink looks like an army of miniature hedgehogs molted in it, and there is no loo roll, again. Luckily, I have a secret tissue stash, hidden in my wash bag for just such emergen— *Oh. Someone found my secret tissue stash.*

When I draw back the moldy shower curtain, I find the bath full of very large, very real bones and stagger back in horror, thwacking my head on the towel rail. "Ow!" *What the hell?* Is someone is trying to dissolve a body in acid? As if this flat weren't sordid enough.

"You okay?" a voice calls from the corridor. Backing out of the nightmare-inducing scene of death and decay, I hurry back to the kitchen.

"Why is there a body in the bath?" I demand. "Did you two murder someone?"

"Oh, it's not a body," Betty says with a tinkling laugh. "Julian and I are doing a broth fast this week. I needed to blanch the bones for the next batch, but I didn't want to monopolize the kitchen sink. The butcher gave me a whole cow for next to nothing. Do you want to try some? Does wonders for a leaky gut." Betty holds a ladle toward me.

"No, thank you," I say, swallowing my urge to gag. While I'm glad that no one has died, I'm perturbed that my first instinct was to think my flatmates might have killed someone. It's possible I've been watching too much *Poirot* again. It's my go-to comfort TV, but maybe it's breeding a suspicious mindset. "How am I supposed to have a shower?" I ask Betty as calmly as possible. "I can't be late for work, not today."

"There's no hot water anyway, we used it all blanching the bones," Julian yells from his bedroom.

"I'll move them in a mo," Betty says sweetly.

Em's one-night stand has now taken ownership of the bathroom, and I'm vaguely concerned that I can hear the shower running. *Is he standing in the bones to shower? Why am I the only one disturbed by this?* Emily's door is ajar, so I pop my head in to see if she's awake.

"Good night?" I ask the mop of red dreadlocks emerging from beneath her duvet.

"Oh, Lucy, can you find out his name?" she whispers at me. "I can't remember."

Before moving into the Vauxhall flat, Emily lived in a houseboat community in Shoreham. She abhors "the capitalist system" and makes a point of trying to barter for things people expect her to pay for. Impressively, she got most of her bedroom furniture by swapping it online for homegrown cacti. On principle, she insists we "share everything," which translates to her sharing my cereal, my bread, and my face wash and moisturizer. When I first met her, I thought she was a hippie loon. Now, having lived with her for two years, I've decided my assumption was entirely correct.

"It's something biblical. Jeremiah? Zebadiah?" I whisper. "Where did he come from?"

"Poetry jam in Shoreditch," she says, slapping a palm to each cheek. "Hot, isn't he?"

"He's certainly got a presence," I say tactfully. Emily and I do not have the same taste in men. I tend to gravitate toward men who prioritize wearing clean underwear every day, for instance. "My ceiling is leaking, again," I tell her.

"How tedious," she says, then pulls her nice dry pillow back over her head. Sometimes it feels like I'm the only one here who cares about my ceiling issues. As if answering my self-pitying call, music starts to pulse from Zoya's room at the far end of the corridor. Hopefully my best friend will be more sympathetic to my plight.

"Hey," I say, knocking on her doorframe. She's dancing to the new Taylor Swift album in tights and a bra.

"Morning, Lucy Lu," she says in a singsong voice. I know Zoya was out partying until three AM, and yet here she is, just five hours later, looking fresh and flawless, with her mane of glossy black hair, sparkling bright eyes, and enviably svelte figure. She's the kind of person who falls out of bed wearing last night's eye makeup but it looks like an effortless "smoky eye." When that happens to me, I just look like a conjunctivitis-ridden badger.

I've known Zoya since we were twelve years old, though if I met her now, I'm not sure if we'd be friends—I'd be too intimidated. She grew up in India, then moved to England via America. When she arrived at our school, with her stylish American clothes and this glamorous East Coast accent, it felt like a movie star was walking among us. But once I got to know Zoya, I discovered that underneath it all, she was just a geek like me. We bonded over our collections of Snoopy memorabilia and a mutual love of Stephenie Meyer novels.

"Can I drag my mattress in here tonight?" I ask her, sitting down on the end of her bed. "Stinkley flooded his bathroom again. My bed is soaked."

"Of course, poor you! Do you want me to help hair-dryer your duvet?" she asks.

"No, don't worry. I'll do it later."

"What the hell is that smell?" Zoya asks, grimacing and holding her nose.

"Julian and Betty are batch cooking bone broth. There's a

pile of bones in the bath." Zoya makes a suitably horrified face. "Of all the flat shares in all the towns in all the world, why did we have to walk into this one?"

"Because it was the only one within budget that had two rooms available," says Zoya.

"Emily's got another random guy here."

"Hide your cash. I'm pretty sure the last guy she had over stole a twenty from my wallet and a pair of knickers from my drawer."

"Lucky I have nothing to steal then," I say. "Unless he wants a dying spider plant."

"I don't know where she finds these sketchy men."

Zoya turns down her music and sits at her dressing table to straighten her hair. Standing behind her in the mirror, I'm reminded how terrible my own hair looks—mousey brown and asymmetrical, the result of an online tutorial on how to cut your own hair. Maybe I didn't have the right scissors. Maybe I didn't have the right hair.

"Look at this," I say, tugging at the shorter side.

"It's not that bad," says Zoya. "Come on, I'll put it up for you." She stands up and motions for me to sit down, then sets to work, pinning it into a stylish messy bun. "You've got to look smart for your first day in the new job."

"Yes," I say, touched that she's remembered today's the day. "Finally, I'm going to get to do more than print scripts and clean up after everyone."

"I'm so proud of you, Luce," she says. "My best friend, the big-shot TV researcher."

"*Junior* researcher," I correct her, feeling myself flush at the compliment. "And I didn't get a pay rise, just a new title, but I will have more responsibilities now. Hopefully I'll be able to pitch ideas, maybe even brief the guests."

"You've worked your little butt off," Zoya says, picking up a sparkly hair band and laying it on my head like a crown. "You'll be queen of TV in no time. Which reminds me—" Zoya reaches to pull a card out of a drawer and hands it to me. On the front is a sketch she's drawn. It's of me wearing a crown, holding a TV, surrounded by books and badgers. It says "Congratulations!" in perfect calligraphy across the top.

"This is amazing," I say, laughing. "A Zoya Khan original. This might be worth a fortune one day."

"It's to put on your desk at work, to remind yourself where you're headed."

"I love it. What's with all the books and badgers?"

"You like books and you like badgers," she says with a shrug.

I reach up to squeeze her hand and mouth "Thank you" in the mirror.

Zoya has always been a stalwart supporter of my stuttering TV career. My parents were open-minded when I got my first job in production, but eighteen months later, when I was still a runner on minimum wage, they started to question what I was doing with my life. All my friends were moving up their respective career ladders, making good use of their degrees, while I was still languishing on the bottom rung, making coffee.

On the dressing table is a framed photo of our group of friends from school: me, Zoya, Faye, and Roisin. The four of us talked about living together when we first moved to London, but then Faye's parents bought her a studio flat, and Roisin, as a trainee lawyer, had a far bigger budget than Zoya and me.

"How perfect would it be if we could swap Emily and Julian for Faye and Roisin," I say quietly, meeting Zoya's eyes in the mirror.

"Roisin wouldn't be able to handle the lack of en suites," Zoya says, laughing. "And Faye would probably make it her mission to tackle Stinkley's antisocial behavior with reflexology and herbal tea."

"Maybe we should set them up," I say, and we both burst out laughing.

Zoya's room used to look like mine, posters Blu-Tacked to the walls and a clothes rail held together with duct tape. But now, looking around, I realize something has changed. Her room looks like the "after" photo in an Instagram makeover reel. She has procured several lamps, a blue velvet armchair, scatter cushions, matching bed linen, framed art on the wall, and the biggest source of my envy—a dark wooden bookcase that's not even IKEA. So this is what a decent salary looks like.

"You've made it so nice in here," I tell her, trying not to sound jealous.

"Thanks, you can come and sit in my reading chair whenever you like."

Zoya used to be a penniless creative like me, but then a few months ago, she dropped out of art school and got herself a job as an estate agent. It seems a shame because she's an incredible artist, but then again, that bookcase is a work of art.

Squeezing my shoulder, she says, "There, done," as she puts the final pin in my hair.

"Thank you. I don't know how you do that."

In the corridor, I hear a door open. "Bathroom's free," Em yells as her door closes. I dash back into the hall, only to see Betty sneaking in there before me.

"Sorry, just need to grab my bones," she yells, and I turn back to Zoya and make a murderous expression. Surprisingly she doesn't laugh, but only says, "Luce, I need to talk to you about something. Walk to the tube with me?"

"Sure. I don't have time to shower now anyway. Give me five minutes to get dressed."

My room feels even more depressing after being in Zoya's. No one wants to live in the "before" photo. My parents say I'm "living like a student," but it's actually worse than that. As a student I had furniture and a dry bed, I had access to a student loan and subsidized accommodation. Now, after tax, rent, bills, loan repayments, and my travel card, I'm left with thirty-five pounds a week for everything else: food, booze, clothes, tampons, you name it. If I could only get promoted to researcher, I'd earn an extra eighty pounds a week. With that kind of money, I could eat, I could buy a nice big bookshelf, I could go back to using normal tampons rather than the two-sizes-too-big moon cup I got free in a party bag at my cousin's hen party. But there is no point fantasizing about such heady luxuries.

After passing a wet wipe beneath each arm and rolling on some deodorant, I throw on a pair of black jeans and a fitted T-shirt. I apply a lick of mascara and a dab of blusher. It's enough to make me look passably fresh and professional. If only my life could be so easily rectified.

Zoya is waiting for me by the front door. In the hallway, she takes an exaggerated gulp of clean air, which makes me smile. Once we're down the stairs and out on the street she says, "So, I wanted to tell you first."

"What?" I say, immediately worried.

"I think I'm going to move out, Luce."

"What?" I can't hide the horror in my voice. "Why?"

"Because we live in a dump, and I'm earning money now." Her face contorts into an apologetic wince. "You know I adore living with you, but I can't handle the others anymore. Julian has had wet washing sitting in the machine for three days. *Three days.*"

"So you're abandoning me?" I say, making loud cartoon sobs to hide the fact that I genuinely feel like crying.

"Oh come on, you can take my room, it's drier than yours."

"I can't afford your room. It's twenty quid a week more than mine."

"I'll sub you the difference."

"No, don't be silly. I'll be fine. I'm happy for you, genuinely." I try to swallow my intense misery. This is not about me—Zoya's worked hard, she deserves this.

"Thanks, chick." Zoya looks relieved. "And you know you can hang out at my new place whenever you like. I promise there will always be loo roll and never any dead cows in the bath."

"Maybe a hot Frenchman will take your room," I say, forcing a goofy smile, while inside I'm struggling to quell a rising tide of panic. *I'm being left behind. The flat will be unbearable.* Who will I crawl into bed with on a Sunday morning and watch reruns of *Friends* with? Who will I swap books with? Who will I complain about the others to? Who will care enough to dig me out of the rubble if the ceiling really does fall down?

WHEN WE REACH the turnstile at the underground station, I realize with a sinking feeling that my weekly travel card has expired, and I don't get paid until tomorrow. I don't want Zoya to know how broke I am, so I try swiping my bank card, offering up a silent prayer to the gods of the turnstiles. Luckily, they let me through.

The board tells us there's a train in one minute.

"Come on, let's run," I say, grabbing Zoya's hand.

"Can't we just get the next one?" she groans. "You're always rushing me."

We make the train and, luxury of luxuries, we even get seats, though there is a woman and her annoyingly loud baby sitting right next to us.

"So, are we all meeting for a drink after work to celebrate your new job?" Zoya asks.

"I don't know. I didn't get much sleep last night. I could probably use an early night."

When the train pulls into Oxford Circus, my stop, Zoya gets up to give me a hug. Looking around the carriage, I notice all eyes are on her. At a guess, all the men are wondering what she looks like naked, while all the women are wondering what product she uses to get her hair that bouncy and shiny. (The answer is a mayonnaise hair mask once a week.) As I get off the train, she sticks her head out of the carriage and hollers down the crowded platform.

"You can sleep when you're dead, Lucy Young. We're celebrating your promotion, end of. Drinks on me."

I can't help grinning as I turn to walk away.

2

AS I'M WALKING FROM OXFORD CIRCUS TOWARD SOHO, my stomach rumbles and I realize in all the commotion of the morning, I failed to have breakfast. My route to work takes me past numerous delicious-smelling cafés and eye-wateringly expensive clothes shops. I allow myself a moment's pause in front of a minimalist shop window, gazing up at a slim-cut red suit. It is feminine and powerful, fashionable yet timeless. *One day, Lucy, one day.*

As I'm daydreaming about wool-blend blazers, my phone rings. Home is calling.

"Hey, Dad," I say as I answer. It is always Dad. Mum will be in the background, shouting out things to say. They haven't gotten to grips with the concept of speakerphone yet.

"We know you're busy, we just wanted to wish you luck on your first day."

"Tell her good luck!" I hear Mum shout. "Ask her what she's wearing."

"What are you wearing?"

"Said the actress to the bishop," I say in a silly voice, and Dad bursts out laughing. It's a childish joke between Dad and me. We race to say it whenever there's even the hint of a double entendre.

"What's so funny?" asks Mum in the background.

"Tell Mum I'm wearing M&S court shoes and a sensible hemline." He repeats this back to Mum and I hear her say, "Very good."

"Thanks for calling, but I've got to run," I say, dragging myself away from the shop window and hurrying down the street.

"Okay, darling. Just remember to have fun. You're only young once," says Dad.

"Have fun? Why are you telling her to have fun, Bert?" says Mum. "She needs to apply herself. Remember Eleanor Roosevelt—'I am who I am because of the choices I made yesterday.'"

"Mum also says to have fun," Dad says before hanging up.

By the time I reach the office, I'm so hungry, I'm beginning to regret saying no to Betty's broth. Hopefully there'll be some leftover biscuits in the communal kitchen. Someone brought a proper tin in last week, though all the chocolate ones had already been eaten.

"Lucy." A sharp voice snaps me out of my reverie about biscuits. It's my boss, Melanie. She has a phone to her ear but holds out a finger, indicating I should wait until she's finished her call.

Melanie Durham is everything I aspire to be in the world. She's in her midforties, whip-smart, and impossibly stylish. She's one of the executive producers at When TV and she exudes a steely confidence that instills respect and fear in equal measure. She once shouted at me in a meeting for not opening a window fast enough and I ever-so-slightly peed my pants. Sometimes I go to sleep fantasizing about what it must be like to be Melanie. She buys hardback books as soon as they're released, not even waiting for the paperback. Every day, she buys a takeaway coffee on her way in to work, then she has lunch from one of the expensive Soho delis. She sometimes sends me to get her lunch and her salads cost thirteen pounds. *Thirteen pounds!* Can you imagine? That's my entire weekly shop. Apparently, she's married to a tech entrepreneur called Lukas (with a k) and they live in a detached house in Islington. *A detached house, in London.* They don't have to share a single wall or ceiling with *anyone*.

But the biggest source of my Melanie envy is her wardrobe. She has twenty-six different pairs of heels. I know this because I've counted them. Today she's wearing my second-favorite pair—her black Louboutin ankle boots. If I owned those boots, I don't think I could be anything but deliriously happy all day long. Anything could happen—I could get pecked by a pigeon or hit by a truck—and I'd just look down at my perfect ankle boots and feel that everything was right with the world.

"We've got the channel coming in for a pre-show meeting this morning," Melanie says, and I realize she's finished her call and is now talking to me. My eye line snaps up from her boots and back to her face. "Can you nip to the bakery on the corner and pick up some pastries?" She pauses. "Get a dozen. Since it's show day, I'll treat the team."

The thought of a delicious pastry from the posh bakery makes me want to weep with joy. Then I remember, I'm a junior researcher now—maybe I should ask Coleson, the new runner, to go for pastries so that I don't miss the production meeting. Then again, I don't want Melanie to think this mini promotion has gone to my head. As I'm having this internal debate, Melanie walks off toward the lift, and I cringe as I'm forced to call after her, "Sorry, Melanie, please can I just get some cash, for the pastries?"

"Just bring me the receipt," she says, looking annoyed that I've troubled her with the practicalities of pastry purchasing. She's in the lift before I can explain that I don't have enough on my credit limit to spend thirty pounds on pastries.

By the time I've tracked down Gethin, the production manager; begged him for a loan; legged it to the bakery; then run all the way back, the production meeting has started without me. After I offer around the pastries, there are six left in the box—cinnamon swirls, chocolate croissants, and the almond ones with icing sugar on top. I don't even mind being the last to choose, they all look incredible, and the smell of delicious warm, flaky pastry is making me light-headed with anticipation. Just as I'm about to take one, Melanie says, "Lucy, can a few of you hold back? I want to make sure there's a choice to offer the channel commissioners. You can have what's left after the meeting."

THE PRODUCTION MEETING is full of important information about the show recording this afternoon, but I can hardly concentrate. All I can think about is the unfairness of the croissant distribution and the smell of sweet, flaky pastry that still fills the room. Near the end of the meeting, Melanie asks, "So, who's got new ideas? We need segment suggestions for next week's show."

Hands fly up, including mine. The show we're working on, *The Howard Stourton Show*, is a prime-time chat show full of celebrity interviews, sketches, and games with the guests. All the A-list stars love Howard. They're happy to come on his show and juggle jelly or get pranked because he's chat show royalty, and the humor is always inclusive rather than mean.

"Tristan." Melanie points to one of the producers.

"Everyone loves it when Howard's dog, Danny, comes on the show," Tristan says. "What about a segment called 'Date with Danny'? We set up a restaurant scene and the guest has to date the dog."

Everyone laughs. It's a stupid idea, but those are often the ones that work. I wonder if it would be funny for Howard to voice the dog's internal monologue. He's brilliant at that kind of improvised comedy. I start to suggest it: "Maybe Howard could do the—"

"I like it," Melanie says, cutting me off. "We could get Howard to voice the dog's internal monologue."

"Yes! That's so funny," Tristan enthuses.

"Maybe Danny is really picky," Melanie goes on. "He finds Miley Cyrus's table manners off-putting, the way she eats with a knife and fork and discards all the tasty bones on the side of her plate."

Everyone's laughing at the idea, and I kick myself for not speaking up faster or louder. I have more ideas though, so I thrust my hand higher. I've spent every evening this week working up segment ideas, just waiting for the chance to pitch them, to show Melanie I can contribute creatively. But Melanie doesn't ask me and eventually my arm is too weak from lack of croissants to keep in the air. Once, I emailed Melanie a few of my ideas. She sent a one-line reply saying, *Printer out of ink. Stationery cupboard a mess. Please rectify.* I took this to mean, "Stop sending me ideas when there are runner's jobs to do." It's so frustrating, because when I see what the producers do—talking to guests, briefing Howard, coming up with content—I know I could do it just as well as they do, maybe better even, if only someone would give me a chance.

At the end of the meeting, Mel asks me to plate up the remaining pastries for her meeting with the channel. Perhaps this is how they tortured people in the olden days? Did they have croissants in the olden days? I google "when were croissants invented?" *Eighteen thirty-eight.* I'll tuck that little fact away just in case I'm ever on a quiz team and one of the questions is "When were croissants invented?"

"Lucy, are you busy? Can you photocopy some scripts for me?" Linda, the production secretary, calls across the room. I want to tell her that photocopying tends to be the runner's job and remind her I'm a junior researcher now, but Coleson is nowhere to be seen and I don't want to appear precious when there's so much to be done.

Having photocopied, stapled, and distributed the latest scripts to everyone on the team, I'm about to ask the producer if there's any research I can help with, when Gethin asks me to do a tea round. This time, Coleson is sitting right there, twiddling his thumbs.

"Maybe Coleson could do it?" I ask lightly, trying to sound amenable.

"If you supervise," Gethin says, without looking up from his computer. Coleson once made Gethin tea in the microwave and evidently has not been forgiven. He's not had the best start, poor guy. It didn't help that Melanie called him "Coleslaw" in a meeting and no one corrected her. Now everyone's confused about what his name is and will only ask him to do something if he's looking directly at them.

"Thanks for showing me the ropes," Coleson says, standing uncomfortably close to me in the kitchen. "I feel like I'm not doing a great job."

He bites his lip, scuffing his shoe against the kitchen floor, and I feel a pang of sympathy. I remember what it was like to be the new kid.

"Coleson, I'm going to lend you my book," I say, handing him the small leather notebook my parents gave me for Christmas. "In here, I write down everything I might ever need to know—how everyone takes their coffee, that Melanie likes scripts presented with a chunky paper clip but Gethin likes his stapled. Everything important anyone tells you, you write down, then you never have to be told twice. You can borrow mine until you get your own."

"Wow, thanks, Lucy," Coleson says, flicking through my notes, then reading, "'There are no traffic jams on the extra mile.'"

"Melanie said that in a meeting once."

By the time I get back to the room, Melanie's meeting is over, and I'm greeted by a sight that makes me want to throw my head back and howl. THERE ARE NO CROISSANTS LEFT. Not one. *I don't understand how this happened.* There were only three people in that meeting, and there were six croissants on that plate. Did someone get here before me?

That's when I see it.

The abomination.

Two and a half croissants, languishing in the wastepaper bin. *In the bin!* Who would do that? Who would only eat half of one of those delicious, flaky, expensive pastries? Who would throw perfectly good croissants away? Especially when there are people in the world waiting for those croissants, *counting* on those croissants.

"Lucy?" Melanie's voice buzzes somewhere on my periphery.

"Sorry?"

"I said I'd like you to be the runner in the studio gallery today." I turn to see Melanie standing at the meeting-room door furnishing me a benevolent smile.

"Thanks, Mel, um . . . you remember you promoted me, though? I'd hoped going forward, I might have the chance to take on a more creative role. I—"

"Teach Coleslaw to be as good a runner as you, then we'll see about expanding your responsibilities."

"It's just—" I pinch my mouth closed as one of Melanie's perfectly shaped eyebrows rises to silence me.

"Ambition is like perfume, Lucy. A little goes a long way."

And just like that, my optimism about today, about ever escaping the bottom rung, vanishes.

3

"I ATE A CROISSANT OUT OF A BIN TODAY." ZOYA, FAYE, Roisin, and I sit in the Blue Posts on Newman Street later that evening. I've been putting a brave face on it all day, but now, among my closest friends, I can be honest about my mortification.

"Oh, Lucy, why?" Faye asks, leaning across to put an arm around me.

"Because I didn't have breakfast and I was hungry. I only had to pick off a few pencil shavings." I hang my head in shame. "Do you think I'll get lead poisoning?"

"They don't make pencils out of lead anymore. You can eat as many pencils as you like," says Roisin.

"Well, Bin Muncher, we're still proud of you, of your promotion," says Zoya, reaching out to clink her glass with mine.

The four of us have been there to support one another through everything: exams, breakups, Faye's parents separating, Roisin losing her mum. We've celebrated one another getting driving licenses, degrees, first jobs, first loves, first flats. But now, four years out of university, I never seem to have as much to celebrate as the others. Roisin is killing it at one of the big law firms, and she and her boyfriend, Paul, are talking about moving in together. Faye is a chiropractor, working in a thriving practice in Hampstead, and she's already a homeowner. As for Zoya, well, she's about to move out of our gross flat share and get a place of her own.

"I don't know," I say, slumping back into the pub's worn leather seat. "Everyone's still treating me like the runner. Maybe I'm deluding myself that I'm getting anywhere at all."

"TV is one of the most competitive industries there is," says Faye, rubbing my back, "and you're working on *The Howard Stourton Show*, for goodness' sake. Eighteen-year-old you would be pinching herself."

"You're right, she would," I say, twirling the stem of my wineglass. Faye always thinks of the perfect thing to say.

"Maybe you need to be bolder with this Melanie woman," says Roisin. "When I started at my law firm, people always left it to me to pour tea and coffee in meetings. Even if there were several other junior associates in the room, everyone turned to me as the woman. I ended up talking to one of the partners about it. I said I thought it made the firm look misogynist and old-fashioned if junior female lawyers were always left holding the teapot. You know what he did? He made it firm policy that if there was tea to pour, it would always be the most senior person in the room who poured it."

"Wow. Go, Roisin," says Zoya. "Modern-day Emmeline Pankhurst right there."

Roisin kicks her under the table.

"Ow! I was being serious!" Zoya laughs.

"You tell this Melanie, 'I'm not being your tea bitch anymore. Find some other sucker,'" says Roisin, jabbing a finger at my chest.

The very idea of saying this to Melanie makes me choke on my wine and Faye pats me on the back until I regain my composure.

"Unfortunately, I think 'tea bitch' is in my job description," I say. "I can handle it. It would just be nice to know it's all going to be worth it, that it will work out eventually."

"This coming from the person who reads the last chapter of a book first, because she needs to know how it ends," says Zoya, putting her arm around me.

"I did that *once*."

"And you ruined it for yourself, didn't you?" Zoya says, tutting.

"I did."

"I hate the thought of you going hungry, Luce. If you can't afford to eat, I can give you money for breakfast," says Faye.

"I will buy you a bed of croissants," says Zoya, "and a duvet of jam."

"No, thank you, but that's my point. You guys are always buying me drinks and bailing me out. I don't want to be a freeloader all my life." My lip wobbles, and everyone stops trying to find words to make me feel better and instead leans in for a group hug.

"I'm fine, honestly, just having one of those days. I'm sure I'll wake up tomorrow with a whole new perspective."

"Blame the moon, it's a waxing gibbous moon tonight, always challenging," says Faye, raising her hands in the air and stretching.

"Ah, so it's the moon that's to blame for Zoya abandoning me," I say.

"What? Are you moving out?" Roisin asks Zoya, who shifts awkwardly in her chair.

"It's time for me to have my own space. That's why I took the job at Foxtons—I want to live in a nice place, I want to have money to go out, to travel. There's so much life I want to live, and everything costs money."

"I want to do all those things too," I say, then immediately regret the note of self-pity in my voice.

"If TV's not making you happy, maybe it isn't worth the long hours and the terrible pay?" Zoya says. "I could get you a job at Foxtons tomorrow, you'd be brilliant. How fun would that be, Luce, us working together? Then we could both move out!" Zoya bounces up and down in her seat, nearly upending her wine.

"I don't want to be an estate agent, Zoya," I snap, my wine-softened brain letting out the words before I can filter them. There's a heavy pause, and I sense Faye physically brace, her hand tightening around her wineglass, while Roisin makes an audible intake of breath.

"Oh, sorry to propose something as mercenary as working for money," Zoya says tightly.

Why couldn't I just say, "Thanks, Zoya, I'll think about it," like any normal person?

Faye and Roisin take slow sips of their drinks in perfect unison.

"I didn't mean it like that. You're brilliant at it and I know you love it, but I just don't think it would be for me."

"It's a means to an end, so I can do fun stuff, so I can travel."

"And that's great, for you. I just . . . I feel too young to give up on my career just yet."

"You mean like I did, giving up on art school?" Zoya asks, pursing her lips, arms crossed in front of her chest.

"No, I didn't mean that at all."

"You're in a different situation to me," Zoya says, her face serious. "If I don't earn my own money, my parents will pressure me into marrying some nice Indian boy from a good family. You know they always viewed my art as a hobby, something to do before I got married, that I'd give up when I had kids, but I'm not going to live a small life." She thumps the table with her fist, her eyes brimming with emotion. "I *will* paint, on my own terms, in my own time."

"I know you will, Zoy, and I don't want you to think I'm blaming anyone else for my situation," I explain.

"Well, stop whining about it then," Zoya says. "Or get a side hustle or something." She pauses and then pushes her chair back from the table.

"Oh no, Zoya, please don't go. I'm sorry," I plead, reaching out a hand to her.

"I've got to do an early viewing tomorrow. All part of my soulless, cop-out job." She slaps a twenty-pound note down on the table, more than enough to cover the wine we've drunk. Then, before I can stop her, she's walked out of the pub.

"Wow, the moon is being a real bitch tonight, huh," Roisin says, but when I don't smile, she puts a hand on my arm and adds, "She'll be fine. You know what she's like."

"I was just venting, none of that was about her," I say glumly.

"We know you were," says Faye.

"I just . . . I don't know what I'm going to do without her."

AN HOUR LATER, I'm at the tube station saying a wobbly good-bye to Faye and Roisin. Faye is cycling home, and Roisin is getting a cab.

"Are you sure you're going to be okay?" Faye asks, her face creased with concern. "If you're really worried about this ceiling situation, you should sleep in Zoya's room."

"I know, I will, and thanks for tonight, I appreciate you all coming out."

It's only when they've both left, and I've swiped my empty travel card, then my even emptier debit and credit card, that I realize I don't have enough money to get home. Damn. I could call Faye, ask her to cycle back and lend me a fiver, but it's too humiliating. The map on my phone tells me it will only take forty-five minutes to walk from Soho back to Kennington Lane, which feels like a long way at ten o'clock at night, but then distance is relative. Hannibal walked over the Alps, didn't he, and the Roman army walked all the way from Rome to Britain. Everything's walking distance if you have enough time and the right footwear.

It turns out I don't have the right footwear. I'm thirty minutes into my epic walk across London when my cheap, black ballet flats start to hobble me with blisters. I'm guessing the Roman army didn't cross Europe in ballet flats. I'm trying to conserve my phone battery by not checking my map all the time, but now nothing looks familiar, and when I sit down on the pavement to consult my phone, I realize I've walked too far east.

As I'm zooming in on the road names, a notification flashes up on my phone from LondonLove, a dating app I signed up for because it was offering a thirty-day free trial. Some guy called "Dale29," who I must have swiped right on, just matched with me. The app lets you know when matches are within a half-mile radius, so you can meet up on a night out.

Lucy26. You're in my hood! Fancy a drink? writes Dale29.

His profile picture looks good. He has blond curly hair and a tan, and there's a picture of him holding a surfboard.

Just passing through. Maybe another time, I reply. If I had any money to buy a round, I might meet up with him, if only to give my blistered feet some reprieve.

One drink, on me? I love your profile, it made me laugh out loud on the tube. Everyone looked at me. It was awkward.

Flattery will get Dale29 everywhere. After a little more back-and-forth, Dale suggests meeting at a bar on the parallel road—the Falkirk. I suppose I could go for one, recharge my feet and my phone. Even if this guy's nothing special, I'll have only wasted half an hour of my life.

When I get to the pub on the next road, I find it closed and someone who looks like Dale29's less handsome brother waiting outside. He's heavier and paler than his profile picture but not entirely hideous. He gives me a friendly wave as I approach.

"I'm sorry, I forgot they're closed for refurbishment and there's nowhere else around here. I'm Dale, by the way." Dale holds out his hand and gives me a firm handshake.

"Lucy," I say. Even though he's less attractive in real life, I'm still disappointed about the bar because now I won't be able to charge my phone.

"I live right here," Dale says, pointing to the flat next door. "If you want to come up for a drink, I have some dodgy Slovakian gin and flat tonic." He shoots me a broad smile. "You might be wary of going into someone's house who you've just met online, but I promise I'm not a murderer."

"That's what a murderer would say," I tell him, smiling politely.

"You're right." He puts a hand to his chin in a purposeful

pose of contemplation. "There should be some kind of 'Decent Guy' ID card I could show you. It might not attest to my gin-making skills, or the quality of my conversation, but it would guarantee I'm not a threat to life."

"Let me see your wallet," I ask, holding out my hand. He gives it a little too willingly, considering he only just met me.

"Are you robbing me?" he asks.

There's something I like about his manner and I feel myself smiling as I rifle through his cards. Among the usual bank cards, I find a Southwark Libraries membership, which I take a photo of with my phone. "I'm going to send this to my friends. If you murder me, everyone I know will take books out using your membership number. You'll have library fines following you around for the rest of your life."

Dale lets out a full-bodied belly laugh. He has a library card, and he thinks I'm funny, which eases my reservations about going back to his. Sometimes you need to be guided by your gut and your phone-charging requirements.

Dale's flat is unremarkable. He tells me he lives with a girl called Philippa, but she's away in Spain this week. He puts on some music while he fixes us drinks—something Spanish and acoustic that suggests he knows more about music than I do. Once he's handed me a charger and a gin and tonic, I find my-self relaxing into his low, beige sofa. Dale tries to tidy up the living room as he talks to me, throwing an old pizza box out into the hall, moving a laundry rack, and hiding a messy pile of post. Maybe Dale is a decent guy, maybe we'll see each other again and start dating and this will be the story of how we met. Could I seriously date someone called Dale, though?

"So have you met many people through LondonLove?" I ask him.

"You'll be my fourth," he says. "I prefer it to the other apps. I don't like talking to someone online for weeks only to meet up and find there's nothing there."

"Completely." I nod. *Forget the name, could I fancy Dale? He might not be as slim and tanned as his profile picture, but if I squint, he could pass for a short Chris Hemsworth, if Chris Hemsworth had a hangover and a dad bod.*

"I met this one girl; she was a personal trainer." Dale smiles at the memory and then sits down next to me on the sofa. "She seemed normal, but we ended up in bed, and she wanted me to count, you know, as if I was doing reps in the gym."

"That's a lot of pressure," I say, laughing.

"So much pressure! I hit twenty and lost count and then I was paranoid she thought I couldn't count to more than twenty."

"I once met up with a guy who brought a Tupperware pot full of his own nuts to the bar. He said he didn't trust the hygiene of bar nuts."

"Ah, Squirrel Man, he's a mate of mine," says Dale with a grin.

We laugh at each other's shared confessions, and I sense the early ember of attraction. I like how easily he laughs, how animated his face is when he does. He puts a tentative hand on my leg, and I don't move to brush it away.

"So, Lucy26, what do you want to be when you grow up?"

"Good question." I take another sip of my drink, enjoying the warm sting of it in my throat. "I always wanted to be a TV producer, but I'm twenty-six and I'm still at the bottom of the TV food chain. I'm not sure how much longer I can handle being plankton. How about you?"

"I'm impressed you've reached the heady heights of plankton. I'm still a student so I'm not even in the food chain."

"What are you studying?" I ask.

"I'm doing a master's in machine learning."

"Ooh, what does that involve? Teaching robots how to take over the world?"

He laughs again. *Maybe he laughs too easily. Maybe he laughs like this with everyone.* "Ha, no. More like computer programming."

"I'm terrible with technology," I tell him.

Dale pulls out his phone and now I wonder if I'm boring him.

"I have some questions about your profile," he says, putting on a voice, as though this is a serious interview. "You have some interesting things on your 'likes' list."

"Do I? I can't remember what I wrote."

"You say here you like badgers. Why badgers?"

I shrug. "They're feisty and I like their monochrome vibe."

"Fair enough. You've also put *Poirot* here under 'likes.' Isn't that old-lady TV?"

"Sacrilege, no!" I say, giving him my best indignant face. "I used to watch it with my parents growing up. I find the theme tune immensely comforting." Dale waits for me to say more. "It's the original cozy crime, isn't it? Poirot always catches the bad guy, everything gets explained in a satisfactory way. In the world of Agatha Christie there is balance and order and resolution."

"Unlike real life, you mean?" Dale asks.

"I guess so, I think that's why I love TV in general. When the world outside doesn't make sense, TV usually will." I pause, catching his eye, worried I'm coming across too earnest now. "I'm probably overthinking it. Most likely I was just a lonely only child who was allowed to watch way too much

TV." I reach out to take Dale's phone. "Anyway, enough about me, let's look at your profile. You like pizza? That's like saying you like breathing, Dale."

Dale laughs and I begin to relax again. "I think you'll find I wrote sourdough pizza. Which is entirely different and very niche."

We share stories, and more gin, and our bodies move closer on the couch. The more we talk, the more I'm starting to like Dale. He's self-effacing and he asks questions. You wouldn't believe the number of dates I've been on where a guy doesn't ask you a single question before, "So do you want to come back to mine?" Though come to think of it, that was in fact the first thing Dale asked me. I don't know how much time has passed before he leans in to kiss me, and then it all goes wrong.

The kiss is not good.

He sucks my tongue. I'm not just talking about a kiss with traction, I mean he genuinely sucks my entire tongue into his mouth, like a Dementor in *Harry Potter* or the facehugger in *Alien*.

When the suction relaxes enough for me to free myself, I try to catch my breath and then excuse myself to go to the loo. He gives an awkward laugh and says, "Good idea."

Good idea? What does that mean? It's my bladder, Dale, I'm the one to decide if peeing is a good idea or not. Sitting on the loo, the familiar curtain of disappointment falls. There's always *something*. Dale seemed normal, Dale listened, and he liked my joke about being plankton. So why does kissing him have to feel like being inhaled? Before I leave the loo, I roll up a wodge of toilet roll and stuff it into my bra just in case there's still none in the flat when I get home. Hello, new low.

Bracing myself for the awkward good-bye and making of

excuses, I come back into the living room to find Dale standing in the middle of the room, naked.

"Oh Jesus, Dale, I don't think I'm ready to see that," I say, my voice calmer than I feel.

"I like you. You like me. Our time on the planet is short. Let's not overthink this." He laughs again. Okay, he *definitely* laughs too much.

"Good-bye, Dale," I say, retrieving my phone and my bag.

"Can you at least suck me off before you go?"

And once again, my desire to date has been tempered by the depressing reality that is 99 percent of men.

CHAPTER 4

BACK IN THE STREET I KICK MYSELF FOR BEING SO STU-pid. *Clearly*, Dale29 was going to be a weirdo. Every man I've dated since uni has been a weirdo, or a misogynist, or harbor-ing some secret fetish for eating crisps off my thighs. (I went with it but could never get the vinegar smell out of my sheets.) Where are all the normal men? As I cross the road, rolling my poor bruised tongue around my mouth, the sky cracks wide open—releasing a sudden downpour. The sole of one ballet flat gives way, the cheap glue dissolving at the first sign of wa-ter. When I woke up this morning, I wasn't aware of how long my tether was, but now, I realize I'm at the end of it. I allow myself one melodramatic groan, two foot stomps, and one fist shake at the sky.

How am I going to get home? Maybe I should call Zoya, apologize, beg her to come and meet me with a pair of trainers. But my phone is dead—after all that, it didn't even charge. So, I start running, hoping to see somewhere familiar. Soon, I'm out of breath and my feet are too sore to go on. Turning right down Baskin Place, past an old red telephone box, I notice a twenty-four-hour newsagent's a few doors down and race toward it, hoping I can wait out the worst of the rain. It's a small, tired-looking shop with a blue and white awning and shelves full of dusty cans. The elderly lady behind the counter smiles at me. She's wearing a tartan beret with a matching waistcoat and playing a game of solitaire on the counter with a faded pack of playing cards.

"Can I help you, duckie?" she asks in a broad Scottish accent, putting down the four of diamonds. "Looking for anything in particular?"

"A new life," I say, smiling so she thinks I'm joking, though at this point, I'm not. My tongue aches, and I decide then and there I am deleting all the dating apps from my phone. I'll have to find love the old-fashioned way—drunk at a bar. As I'm wondering how long I can lurk in this tiny shop without buying anything, leaving wet footprints across the lino, I come across a curious machine tucked away at the back of the store. It looks completely out of place. It's the size of a large ATM and across the top, in faded gold writing, are the words Wishing Machine.

"You need a penny and a ten-pence to make a wish," the old lady explains, following my gaze.

My hand moves to the coin slot. There's something tactile and pleasing about the worn metal. It feels like a machine from a different era, like a 1950s fairground attraction that has toured the country for decades and finally come here to retire.

"Why is it here?" I ask the woman.

"People need wishes as much as they need bread and milk. Maybe more so," she says, smiling at me, and there's a kindness in her soft, lined face. Something tells me she won't mind if I wait out the rain without buying anything. "You look like you could use a wish, duckie."

"I don't have a penny," I say, pulling wet hair off my neck as I glance back at the torrential rain and listen to the drum of water beating down on the awning outside. The woman holds out a shiny penny and a ten-pence piece to me.

"Here you go, duckie. Best make it a good one."

It's only eleven pence, but after the day I've had, the kindness makes me want to cry with gratitude. She moves away, as though wanting to give me some privacy. Though I'm under no illusion that a wishing machine is going to solve my problems, I'm curious and it's still pouring outside, so what the hell.

The coins clunk into the slot, and the old machine lights up a ring of warm orange bulbs. A tune starts to play, something like "Camptown Races" with several notes missing. The ten-pence disappears into the bowels of the machine, but the penny rolls along a narrow wire track, round and round toward a central metal plate. At the back of the box, neon yellow words illuminate—Make Your Wish—and even though I know it's just a toy, I find myself holding the sides of the machine and channeling all my frustrations into it.

I wish . . . I wish I could skip to the good part, where my life is sorted. I'm so tired of being broke and single and stuck. I wish I could fast-forward to when I know what I'm doing, when I have some semblance of a career, when I've met my person and I don't need to go on any more soul-crushing dates. I just want to live somewhere nice, with a sturdy ceiling and a shower with no bones in it. If the love of my life is out there, I want to get to the part that he's in. I just want to get to the good part of my life.

It's as though the machine knows when I'm done, because the moment I finish my thought, there's a grinding of gears and a second plate comes down to press the penny. Then it falls into a separate slot, below my left hand. It has been crushed flat with new writing layered on top: YOUR WISH IS GRANTED inscribed in small, swirling capitals. Turning the pressed penny over in my palm, I do feel marginally better—maybe it's therapeutic to vent to a machine, cheaper than a therapist anyway.

"Be careful what you wish for," the old woman says, and I look up to see her watching me from her seat behind the till. "Life is never quite sorted, whatever stage you're at."

It's only when I'm halfway home, wearing plastic bags over my feet, that I pause, confused, because I don't remember saying any of that out loud.

5

I WAKE UP WITH A HEADACHE. NOT A NORMAL HEAD-ache; this feels like someone took out my brain, sautéed it, flambéed it, rolled it in barbed wire, and then slopped the whole mess back into my skull. Holding my head with one hand, I try to open my eyes to look for water, or paracetamol. That's when I notice the curtains, the navy blue, beautifully textured, heavy linen curtains. *Those aren't my curtains.* Then I look down at the cream-colored, soft cotton duvet. *This isn't my duvet.* Above me, there is no sign of the damp yellow stain on the ceiling, only a large rattan light shade. *This is not my bedroom.*

The searing pain in my head makes me wince as I turn and find a man in the bed beside me. The shock of seeing another person makes me freeze, and I pull my lips closed to stop myself from squealing in alarm.

Why is someone in bed with me? Did I sleep with Dale? I know I didn't sleep with Dale . . . Unless I did. How much did

I drink last night? Three glasses of wine in the pub and then two gin and tonics an hour or two later with the face sucker, so drunk, but not so drunk I wouldn't remember going home with someone. Looking at the body beside me, I quickly conclude it does not belong to Dale. This man's shoulders are broader, his hair is darker. Could I have picked someone up between Dale's house and mine? What if I had my drink spiked? Maybe this guy spiked my drink and then kidnapped me to his perfectly furnished house.

Cautiously, I lean over to get a better view of my potential abductor. He's lying on his front, his face away from me, with one arm draped over the pillow, obscuring my view. He has a nice back. Even in the disorientating fog of a killer hangover, I know a nice back when I see one. His skin is smooth and tanned, his muscles clearly defined, and he can't be flexing because he's asleep. Unless he's fake sleeping while flexing, but that feels like a lot of effort to impress someone you've kidnapped.

My need to know where I am and who he is outweighs my desire to lie down and concentrate on the pain behind my eyeballs. I need to get a proper look at this guy before he wakes up. He could be planning to tie me up in his basement and feed me nothing but dog food for the next six months. A cold chill tingles across my skin—I shouldn't have watched so much true crime, it's much more harrowing than my usual Agatha Christie. Zoya tried to reassure me that statistically I am probably more likely to marry a member of One Direction than end up in a dog food/kidnap situation, but I'm not sure she gets her statistics from peer-reviewed publications.

Creeping from under the duvet as quietly as I can, I glance

down at my legs. What am I wearing? These aren't my pajamas. I don't even own pajamas, I usually just sleep in a baggy
old T-shirt. These are soft cream silk with cute tiny zebras.
Did this guy lend me his flatmate's pajamas? Maybe he's got a
thing for nice pajamas and dresses all his victims in high-
quality nightwear before killing them? They'll make a Netflix
series about him called *The Pajama Killer* or *My Nightwear
Nightmare.*

As I tiptoe around the bed, trying to ignore the pulsing
pain in my temples and the racing in my chest, I notice again
how tastefully furnished this bedroom is; there's a gray-linen-
covered ottoman at the end of the bed, a lime-washed oak
chest of drawers, and—oooh, is that a walk-in wardrobe? This
bedroom is nice, too nice. It feels like the bedroom of a
grown-up, someone with enough money to buy furniture that
doesn't come flat-packed.

This guy must live with his parents. *Is this his parents'
bed?* I creep around to his side. Now that I can see his face, my
new theory goes out of the window because the man looks to
be in his forties.

On the plus side, if we're looking for plus sides, this man is
hot. Not just attractive, I mean Bradley Cooper–in–his–heyday
beautiful. He has a defined jaw, a little stubble, impossibly
dark eyelashes, and shaggy, chestnut-colored hair. My headache, disorientation, and fears about dog food lift just long
enough to congratulate myself on going home with a man this
gorgeous. Even if he is older than I'd usually go for, I can see
why me of last night thought this was a good idea. Unless this
was a drink-spike situation, in which case I need to stop thinking about this man's beautiful eyelashes and call the police.
Maybe I should do a urine sample now in case I need it for

evidence later. Would it be weird to pee into a pot and hold on to it, just in case?

As I look around the room for something appropriate to pee into, I see the man's hand on the pillow and notice he's wearing a gold band: a wedding ring. *He's married.* His attractiveness rating just fell through the floor. There's a door leading to an en suite next to his side of the bed, so I dart in and lock it behind me. I need to wash my face, get my head straight, try to remember anything about how I got here. But as I turn and see my reflection in the mirror, I slap a hand across my mouth to stop myself from screaming, because looking back at me with terrified eyes is . . . me, but not me. Me, but different. My skin looks sallow and blotchy, my face is puffy but narrow—I can't compute what I'm seeing. Is this the worst bathroom mirror ever invented? It looks like someone removed my skin, washed it on the wrong wash cycle, then tried to stretch it back over my skull. The shadows beneath my eyes are like a thousand hangovers rolled into one. The first signs of crow's-feet fan out from their corners, and there are crease lines on my forehead that don't spring back when I stop frowning. I can't stop frowning.

I look . . .

I look *old*.

Stepping closer to the mirror, I see the reflection definitely is me, but not the me of yesterday. It's not just my skin that's changed, my hair is different too. My hair is . . . better? It looks like I've had highlights done, several shades of honey and gold, and I've got a proper haircut with layers around the front. *I've got fucking Jennifer Aniston hair.* How was I able to afford this kind of haircut? And where the hell did I get highlights done south of the river in the middle of the night?

Sitting down on the toilet seat, I rub my face with my palms, reluctant to look at my alarming reflection any longer. This must be some messed-up prank show—a new reality TV idea where they knock you out and make you over to look ten years older. There could be cameras behind that mirror, recording my reaction. But who would watch this? It feels mean-spirited and not at all good television. I tug at my skin to check, but it hurts, so it can't be a prosthetic.

Pulling down the silk pajamas, I go to the loo before realizing that with all the shock of the mirror, I forgot to find a pot to pee in to keep as evidence for the police. Damn. Will it work if I take a sample from the loo? As I'm mulling pee dilution, I notice my stomach. *What has happened to my stomach?* It's fleshy and baggy and—ahhhh! There's a weird scar across the top of my pubic hair! Did someone cut me? Oh God, I'm a drug mule. It's like that Scarlett Johansson film where she wakes up and finds she's had loads of mind-altering drugs sewn into her stomach. Though I don't understand why that would make my stomach bigger.

Standing up, I pull off my pajama top to inspect my body in the mirror. *What have they done to me?* My boobs are bigger too, but lower, and there are little white lines all over them, as though they've been blown up and deflated. I'm probably the same size I was before, but my skin is less taut, like the middle-aged women I see in the changing rooms at the public pool. Then I lift my arms and notice a small, firm ridge of definition along the top. *I have biceps.* Where did they come from?

"Lucy?" calls a voice from the other side of the door. *The man's awake, and he knows my name.* Quickly, I throw the pajamas back on, my head scrambling with pain and growing bewilderment. If this really is some messed-up reality show, I intend to sue the production company for intense emotional distress.

The knob jiggles, then, "Why have you locked the door?" the man asks.

"Just a sec!" I call back. I'm going to have to talk to this guy. He's the only one who can tell me what's going on. My hand shakes as I unlock the door, and when I open it, I find the man standing there in his boxer shorts; his hair is bed tousled and his eyes are the most piercing cobalt blue I've ever seen.

"What's going on? Where am I? Who are you?" I ask him, my voice panicked and unfamiliar.

"Big night, was it?" he says with a smile, then gives me a brief kiss on the cheek as he walks past me and picks up a slim electric toothbrush from a wireless charging pod by the sink. I didn't even know you could get wireless charging pods.

"What am I doing here? Why do I look so old?"

He laughs, as though I've made a joke. "You don't look old, darling, you look gorgeous."

Darling? "Did someone put drugs in me?" I ask him, holding my stomach across the small white scar.

"I doubt it, Luce. You were at a Thursday night work party. Why? Did it all get a bit messy?"

Messy? Work party? "I don't know who you are." My voice is serious, but my lip trembles.

"I know, I know, I don't recognize myself either," he says, turning back to the mirror. "Too old to imagine getting drunk midweek." He frowns at me in the mirror as he takes in my expression. Then he turns and puts a hand on each of my shoulders, his toothbrush resting between his teeth. "Don't worry, there's always coffee."

"But how did I get here?" I ask. He really doesn't seem to understand the seriousness of the situation.

"Taxi. I heard you get in around one. I was surprised you stayed out so late when you're pitching to the channel this morning."

Pitching to the channel? Why would I be pitching to the channel? I'm not getting any answers here, just more questions. This man is not acting like someone who's abducted me, he's acting like someone who *knows me*. As I open my mouth to quiz him further, he takes off his boxers, right in front of me, and I lose all power of speech.

"I'm going to jump in the shower," he says, walking into the rustic blue, gloss-tiled wet room and turning on the water. Somewhere close by, a baby starts to cry. "Can you grab Amy?"

Amy? Who the hell is Amy? This flat might have nice furnishings and the most stunning shower I've ever seen, but it does not have good sound insulation. It sounds like the neighbor's baby is literally *in* the flat with us. Backing out of the bathroom, away from the alarmingly naked man, I look around for my phone. My phone will have the answers—phones always have the answers. It's my best hope of piecing together this brain-melting trip of a hangover.

Stumbling around the bedroom, I search for my battered gray handbag, but I can't see it anywhere. I can't even see my clothes from last night. Venturing out into the hall, I'm faced with another bedroom. Through the open doorway I can see a cot, and standing up looking at me—a baby. *Jesus!* This guy has a *baby?*

"Mama!" says the baby, holding out its arms.

My head darts around, checking to see if some other woman has miraculously appeared behind me, but no, the baby is holding its arms out to *me*. Cautiously, I take a step toward the child's room.

"Not your mum, I'm afraid," I tell the baby. "I'm sure your dad will be out in a minute. I'm just looking for my handbag." Why am I talking to this baby? It probably doesn't even speak yet. I've got no idea how old it is, could be six months or two years for all I know about children.

"Mama!" it says again, grinning at me. As far as babies go, I'll concede it's a cute one. From the pink bears on its romper suit, I'm guessing it's a girl. She's got a wild mop of curly blond hair and piercing blue eyes just like her father.

"Are you Amy?" I ask her.

"Aim-eee," she says, holding the bars of her cot and jumping up and down. I'm about to go back to the bathroom to tell the guy what a nerve he's got, asking me to watch his kid, but then I remember his nakedness and the weird scary mirror. I might be better off just finding my bag and getting the hell out of Dodge. Quietly backing out of the baby's room, I carry on down the corridor, looking for signs of a living room, a kitchen, anywhere I might have left my phone, my clothes, and my sanity. But as soon as I'm out of the baby's sight, she starts to howl.

"Oh, for fuck's sake," I mutter to myself.

"Mummy said a bad word."

Spinning around, I see a small boy standing behind me in the corridor, appearing like some freaky child apparition.

"Jesus Christ! You made me jump," I say, pressing a hand against my chest to fend off a heart attack.

"Mummy swore *again*." The boy slaps both hands over his mouth, his eyes bulging like he's a fish out of water. Baby Amy is still howling, rattling the cot barriers like a prisoner desperate to escape.

"I'm not your mum, kid," I say to the boy. "How many children live here?"

"Two," the boy says, narrowing his eyes at me. At least this one can speak; he might be able to help me.

"Do you know where I can find my handbag? I need my stuff, my phone."

"Amy's crying," the boy says, looking at me with such abject disapproval that I feel compelled to walk back toward the baby banshee. The boy follows me.

"What does she want?" I ask him.

"Milk, nappy change, I dunno," he says, leaning against the doorframe. Amy's face is streaked with tears and her little cheeks are now red with rage. Whoever invented babies, they did a great job of making their cries completely unignorable. I'm forced to pick her up just to stop myself from clawing out my own eardrums. As soon as she is in my arms, the noise stops, but now it's my nose that's being assaulted.

"She's done a poo," the boy tells me.

"What's your name?" I ask him.

"Felix," says the boy. "What have you done with my mummy? Are you an alien? Did you eat her brain?"

"I didn't eat anyone's brain and I don't know where your mum is. Are your mum and dad, um, divorced? Separated?"

"Divorced?" he asks.

"Does your mum usually live with you?"

"Yes," he says slowly.

Great. I'm no child-rearing expert, but I'm pretty sure I shouldn't be the one to break it to this kid that his father is a douchebag.

"Can you help me with this?" I ask Felix, pointing at the

baby. He screws up his face and shakes his head. "How old are you? Eight? Nine?"

"Seven," he says. "Where did you put Mummy? Have the aliens taken her back to their planet?"

Have I been abducted by aliens and put back in the wrong body? At this point I'm not discounting any possibilities. As I contemplate the logistics of an extraterrestrial body swap, the man appears at the door to the baby's room. I'm relieved to see he's no longer naked and is now wearing a pair of worn blue jeans and a white linen shirt. He's so effortlessly attractive, it's distracting, and I briefly forget to be freaked out that his kids are calling me "Mummy."

"Morning, buddy," the man says. He ruffles Felix's hair, walks over and kisses baby Amy on the head, then leans in to kiss me, *on the lips. The lips*! I freeze, too stunned to move, looking up at him with wide, unblinking eyes. The gall of this man. I'm holding his child that smells of literal shit, and he just kissed me like it was the most normal thing in the world.

"Ben's sick, so I said I'd take his tai chi class this morning," the man says. "Maria's coming early to do the school run, so you should still be fine to get the eight fifteen. Sorry, I've got to run. See you tonight. Oh, and good luck with your pitch. They're going to love it." Then he waves and turns to walk away.

"Wait, what? You're leaving me here, with your children?"

He stops, turns, then frowns, annoyed with me for some reason. "I know, they're as much my responsibility as they are yours, but it's not like I do this all the time, Luce." He rolls his eyes. "Ben is always covering for me. Come on, it's not my fault you went on a midweek bender last night. You really don't think you can cope for twenty minutes until Maria gets here?"

This line of argument, that I'm being unreasonable not wanting to stay here and babysit, is so preposterous that before I can even fathom how to respond, he's gone. Putting the baby down on the landing, I stagger after him, only to discover we're not in a flat at all, but an entire house, and it's all just as tastefully decorated as the bedroom. There's a vintage wooden sideboard on the landing with two Jo Malone candles, a framed photo of the children, and a gloriously verdant yucca plant. Further on, along one side of the landing, there's a huge built-in bookcase, neatly filled with hundreds of books. *I always wanted a bookshelf just like that.* A thick, plush-pile carpet leads all the way down a wide, curving staircase, framed by polished mahogany banisters.

Momentarily distracted by the beautiful house, by the time I've gotten downstairs and located the front door, a car is pulling out of the driveway. Upstairs, the baby is howling again. Was it bad that I left her on the floor? What if she crawls to the stairs and falls down them? Even if this guy is *insane* thinking I'll watch his children, I don't want to be responsible for anyone getting hurt. Racing back upstairs, I find the boy sitting on the floor, trying to comfort his sister. They both look up at me with wounded eyes.

"What's that guy's name, the one who just left?" I ask the boy.

"Daddy?"

"Yes, but apart from Daddy, what's his real name? Like I'm Lucy, you're Felix, and he's . . . ?"

"Sam."

"And how do I know Sam?"

Felix narrows his eyes again and then glances to the left, to the wall beside me. Instinctively, my eyes follow the direction of his gaze to a large framed photo mounted on the wall. It's of a couple on their wedding day, standing in a field. The man in the photo is a younger version of their dad, Sam, and the bride is . . . the bride is . . . *me*.

6

"HOLY FUCK!" I SHOUT. FELIX CLAPS A HAND OVER HIS mouth. "How is that me? How is . . . Is this Photoshopped?" I lift the frame off the wall so I can inspect it more closely. The woman looks *just* like me, the real me, not this weird, haggard, great-haired, drug-mule version of me. Do I have amnesia? Did I hit my head and forget twenty years of my life?

That's when I remember, the wishing machine. *The wishing machine.*

"No way," I say as my mind contemplates the idea that just presented itself. "No, no, no. This couldn't be that." *What did I wish for? To be sorted, to have found my person, to skip to the good part of my life.*

The nausea comes on suddenly, and I rush to the bathroom before I throw up all over this ridiculously plush carpet. When I'm done, I look up to see Felix standing in the doorway, his little face puckered into a grimace.

"Mummy says better out than in. You wanted this," he

says, holding out a blue leather handbag. "Will you put my mummy back when you've finished your alien experiments?"

"Thank you," I say, wiping my mouth with a tissue, then taking the bag from Felix. Rifling through it, I find a phone, a far larger, slimmer handset than my thirdhand iPhone. The screen saver is a photo of me, Sam, Felix, and Amy. The date on the lock screen says Friday, the twenty-second of April, which is the day after yesterday, but there's no year.

"What year is it?" I ask Felix, who is still standing in the doorway, a pensive look on his face.

Felix answers, but I must mishear, because I think he says a year that's sixteen years later than it was yesterday. I need to be sick again. The doorbell rings; Amy is still crying. Staggering out onto the landing again, I pick her up, making "shhhh" sounds and hugging her against me. That's how you comfort babies, right? A feeling of guilt envelops me, like a scratchy blanket against my skin. Guilt that I might have caused this, that I might be responsible for taking this child's mother away from her. Carrying Amy down the stairs, I open the door to a platinum-blond woman in her fifties.

"What's wrong? You look terrible," she says to me, immediately reaching out to take Amy. "Are you sick?" This must be Maria.

Shaking my head, I manage to say, "I'm fine." Why is that such an ingrained response? Clearly, I am a very long way from fine.

"Who's a stinking lady?" Maria says, and I cover my mouth self-consciously but then realize she's talking to the baby. She tickles Amy's chin. Amy gurgles and *finally* stops crying. "You go, get dressed, don't miss your train. I'll sort the children out."

Thank God for Maria—I want to hug her. Should I tell her

what has happened? What would I say? What has happened? Something tells me I need to get it straight in my own head before trying to explain it to anyone else. Felix is sitting on the top step watching me as I head back upstairs.

"I'm fine, I just get a little confused when I drink gin," I say, reluctant to traumatize this poor boy any more than is necessary. I don't want him going to school and telling everyone that his mother has been abducted by aliens. Though now he might go to school and tell everyone his mother is an alcoholic. He widens his eyes at me but says nothing.

Back in the bedroom, I shut the door and find the phone the boy gave me. My face unlocks it. Scrolling through my contacts, I search for Zoya. I need to apologize about last night, tell her about the messed-up situation I've found myself in. But when I try her number, it won't connect. I try calling Faye, but that goes straight to answerphone, and Roisin's number rings and rings with an abroad tone but no one picks up. Why is Roisin abroad? Something is going on with the phones. Whatever's happening, I just need to get home, back to the flat, back to my own bed—give myself time to come down from this hallucination. I take a long, deep calming breath but inhale an array of uncalming odors. Maybe I should have a shower before I go.

The shower helps, mainly because it's the best shower I've ever had in my life. There are three different showerheads, all at varying heights and with exceptionally well-distributed water pressure. Nothing like the crappy micro-shower in the Vauxhall flat that is so clogged with limescale it sprays in every direction except down, or my parents' shower, which is so narrow you can't move your elbows once you've closed the door. So this is what I've been missing all my life? The warm water starts to ease my headache, and I begin to feel more myself.

Clean and dry, I investigate the walk-in wardrobe; I'm going to need to borrow some clothes. Suit jackets and men's shirts line the left-hand side, while a huge, perfectly ordered selection of women's clothes lines the right. My hand skims the delicate fabric on a row of blouses. At the far end of the wardrobe a wall of shoes is illuminated like the altar in a church. *So many shoes!* Kurt Geiger, Russell & Bromley, Hobbs, every heel, boot, wedge, or sandal a girl could ever want or need. If this really is a glimpse of my future life, then something's gone right, for my feet at least.

After choosing jeans, a silk blouse, and some black suede ankle boots, I open the drawers of the dressing table to find a shallow tray of perfectly organized high-end cosmetics. My hand pauses on an eye shadow palette. Putting makeup on doesn't feel like a priority right now, but then I'm reluctant to go out into the world looking quite this terrible. My flatmates might not recognize me, they might be scared. *Are my flatmates even going to be there if I really have skipped sixteen years?* I can't think about it, I just need to get out of here. I need to get home.

DRESSED AND MADE UP, I feel slightly calmer when I look in the mirror. After the initial shock of seeing this reflection, I have to concede I don't look bad for forty-two, if that really is how old I am. My figure is still decent enough, in clothes anyway, and my face is, well, it's still my face. It was just a shock seeing the effect of sixteen years all at once, like that scene in *Indiana Jones and the Last Crusade* where the guy chooses the wrong cup and ages a hundred years in five seconds.

Grabbing a worn, brown leather biker jacket and the handbag Felix gave me, I head downstairs, where I find Maria giving the children porridge. It looks messy, with Amy's high chair already covered in oat mulch and berries. I take a step back to protect my nice clothes from all the goo.

"Ah, so much better!" says Maria.

"Thank you," I say, attempting to smile. Felix turns to look at me, and I see a flash of myself in his face. The shape of his eyebrows, his full lips. *He looks like me.* The realization fills me with wonder and horror in equal measure. Part of me wants to just sit down and stare at these children, to find more familiar traces, proof that they came from me. The scar on my stomach must be from a C-section. Did they both come out that way, or are there more scars, unseen, inside of me? If I dwell on the lunacy of this, my head starts to spin. I don't have the capacity to examine these thoughts right now, so I look away.

"How do I get to the tube from here?" I ask Maria, realizing I have no idea where I am.

"In your spaceship," Felix says, eyes wide and unblinking.

Clearly, he's joking, but then . . . what if he's not? Maybe in the last decade and a half, someone did invent mini spaceships to replace cars. It doesn't seem like the most cost-effective solution to traffic congestion, but hey, it's the future, so what do I know?

"To the station? You drive or get a cab," Maria says, the spoon she's holding pausing midway between the bowl and Amy's mouth. "Why?"

"Right, yes, of course," I say. "Just checking." Looking around for car keys, I find some on a hook by the door, conveniently marked "Keys."

"Okay, I'll see you later then," I say, though as I say it, I realize I'm hoping I won't see them later, that I'll wake up from this nightmare before any kind of later comes.

"Bye-bye, Mumma!" Amy babbles, before reaching hungrily for the porridge spoon and sloshing it all down her front.

"You need to come back and look after us when Maria goes," Felix tells me.

"Right, remind me when that is?"

"Six thirty on Fridays," Maria says. "I have a facial booked, so don't miss your train again."

"Yes, ha. Got it. Silly me."

Felix narrows his eyes at me again, and I feel compelled to leave before Maria realizes I'm an imposter.

Outside, in the driveway, I look around at the quiet cul-de-sac. This doesn't look like London, no part I've ever been to anyway. *Where the hell am I?* My phone will tell me. When I open what looks like a map app, a 3D projection rises out of my phone screen. *Wow, that is incredible.* It's like I'm a giant looking down on a miniature landscape. Peering into the map, I see a tiny digital version of me, standing in a tiny version of this driveway. "I've a feeling we're not in Kansas anymore, Toto," I say to my little map self. Zooming out, I establish I'm in Farnham, a town in Surrey, forty-five miles from London, which might as well be Kansas.

Clicking the key in my hand, the sleek silver estate car on the drive beeps. This car is a different beast from the rusty old Nissan Micra I drove at university. It's about eight times the size and . . . oh, doesn't appear to have a steering wheel. As I sit down in the driver's seat it moves and shifts, adjusting to my frame. Wow, comfy. There's no gear stick, no visible hand brake, not even a hole I can find to put the key in.

"Drive," I try telling it, but nothing happens. "Please drive?"

Nothing. With no buttons to press, I put a hand on the

smooth dashboard, and with a low beep, something starts to happen. A control panel lights up, then the dashboard opens, and a steering wheel slowly folds out toward me. *Whoa, that is so cool.* Putting my hands on the wheel, I feel the low hum of an electric engine. *It's palm activated.*

Then the car starts talking to me.

"Good morning, Lucy," it says in a sexy male American voice that sounds just like Stanley Tucci.

"Hi?" I reply.

"Lucy, your alcohol reading is too high to drive safely. Please seek another form of transportation." I think that *is* Stanley Tucci. The car powers down and the steering wheel retracts. It's not going to let me drive. The way my head is feeling, I probably am still over the limit from last night.

Cab it is then.

Fortunately there's a taxi app on my phone.

Minutes later, a sleek, black electric car arrives. As I climb into the back seat, a voice says, "Lucy, you have not eaten breakfast. Your energy levels will dip midmorning if you don't start your days with a nutritious meal." *Wow. How does the cab know I haven't had breakfast?* But when the voice starts again, I realize it's coming from my phone. "You have only done TWO UNITS of exercise this week. Consider fitting in a high-intensity workout during your lunch break to stay on track with your goals." The phone pauses. "NATALIE is attending a yoga class at SOHO GYMNASIUM at ONE FIFTEEN. Would you like to join her?"

"Oh, that is, wow . . ." *I don't even know a Natalie.* "Did my phone just tell me I'm fat?" I ask the cabdriver.

"Welcome to the future, love," he says, shaking his head.

"Thanks," I say, before realizing he was probably being

sardonic. "Do you know how I turn this voice off?" I pause. "It's a new phone."

"You'll lose all your points if you turn it off. My wife's well into it, she hit Gold Level Fitbulous last month." The driver glances at me in the rearview mirror. "You can switch it to text updates if you like, I can show you how, but then you won't get any Listen and Learn bonus points."

"I will happily forgo the bonus points," I tell him.

When the car pulls into a station car park, the driver waves his hand for me to pass him my phone, then changes the settings for me.

In the station, there's a coffee bar. Looking up at the price list, I see a latte is twelve pounds forty. *Twelve pounds forty?* What fresh hell is this? That's four times what I would expect to pay. Maybe I'm in a coma, or dead. Maybe my ceiling fell in on me and this is purgatory—suburban living with extortionate coffee. At the ticket barrier, some people are swiping cards, while others are simply scanning their palms on the machine. There's a wallet in my bag full of bank cards, but I try my palm first and the barrier pings me through.

Four minutes later, I'm sitting in a window seat on my way to London. Safe, familiar, glorious London. The train carriage feels reassuring—same ugly seat covers, same faint smell of bleach and overflowing bins. I imagined trains in the future would look like those slick bullet trains they have in Japan. So either the rail network is still chronically underfunded, or I'm not in the future after all. Then I remember the events of this morning and my body gives an involuntary shiver.

Pulling out my phone, I try Zoya's number again. It still won't connect. As I'm contemplating who else to try, Office flashes on my screen. Then an alert from Fit Fun Fabulous informs me my heart rate and stress levels are higher than normal. Would I like to engage in a guided deep-breathing exercise? No, I would not. I push the phone to the bottom of my bag and turn to look out of the window, focusing on the trees and houses zipping by. I just need to get home, back to my bed, go to sleep, and wake up from whatever this is. *Train, home, sanity. Train, home, sanity.* I repeat the words in my head like a mantra. If I start to think about anything else, like how I got here, or where and when *here* is, my brain is liable to implode.

CHAPTER 7

LONDON DOESN'T LOOK LIKE I REMEMBER IT. THERE ARE
no ticket barriers at Waterloo, just gateways that let out a low
ping when you walk through. There is a new brightness to
the concourse, and when I look up, I see the vaulted ceiling
has gone and there is only blue sky above us. This feels archi-
tecturally impossible, and then I notice advertising banners flying across the sky, which makes me think it must be a giant
screen or projection. At my feet, there's a purring noise, and I
look down to find a sleek Roomba-style machine polishing
the concourse floor. This all feels too detailed to be a dream.
I can't stop to think about what it all means, I just need to
get home.

But home doesn't look like I remember it either. When I
emerge into daylight at Vauxhall station and walk beneath the
bridge onto Kennington Lane, everything feels subtly different. The yellow and white road markings are gone, replaced
by shimmering electronic markers that change with the traffic

lights. Our beloved Vauxhall Tavern has been torn down, and there is a column of shiny glass-fronted flats where the pub should stand. *How can they have torn down the Vauxhall Tavern? It's an institution, a London landmark.* If I didn't have more pressing priorities, I would write a sternly worded email to my MP. I start to run, desperate to see if my flat is still there, to find out if my former life has been completely erased. All I want to do is crawl back into my damp, uncomfortable bed and for this whole hallucination to be over.

Thankfully, number eighty-three is still standing. The building looks unchanged, if a little worse for the wear. A small sign on the placard next to the third-floor buzzer reads Graham rather than ZoLu JuEm, but I buzz anyway. There's no reply and I clench my hands around the doorframe. It's as though everything I have seen so far, I can rationalize as a delusion, but my flat, my home, the place I went to sleep—if that's not there, then . . . then what? I should call Emily. Emily is always home. On my phone, there are now three missed calls from Office. Emily picks up after two rings.

"Hello?"

"Emily, oh, Emily, thank God. Something completely insane has happened, I really need your help. Are you at home?"

"At home?" she repeats. "Who is this?"

"It's Lucy. Lucy Young."

"Oh, Lucy. Hi." *Why doesn't she have my number in her phone?*

"Look, Em, this is going to sound insane, but I think I've traveled through time. Either that or I'm having a full-on psychotic delusion. I need to get into the flat."

"Right," she says slowly, in that way people talk to children or men wielding knives.

"Yesterday we were flatmates in Vauxhall, berating old Stinkley upstairs. You'd just slept with someone called Ezekiel or Zebadiah, something like that. Do you remember?"

Emily makes a strained "hmmm" sound.

"Then today, I woke up in some random house in Surrey with a husband and two children." I say it with a little laugh, to illustrate how crazy I know I must sound.

"Right," she says again, then after another long pause, "have you taken drugs, Lucy? Where are you?"

"No, not that I know of, and I'm outside the flat, our flat. I just told you."

There's a beep on the screen; she's requested to switch our call to video. I click accept and Emily's face fills the screen, only she looks nothing like the Emily I know. Her red dreadlocks are gone, replaced by a sleek bob. Instead of her usual dungarees, she appears to be wearing a collared shirt and a gray suit jacket. She looks like Shiv from *Succession*.

"Emily?" is all I can say.

"I needed to look you in the eye, to see if you were joking or high," she says, and as she holds my gaze, her face softens. "If it's neither of those things, then it sounds like you need to see a doctor, Lucy. Have you had a knock to the head?"

"I don't think so, but maybe." I pause. "I know it sounds nuts, but it feels more like an intensely realistic hallucination . . . or . . . or time travel."

"Right," she says again, her voice loaded with skepticism.

"You look so different from how I remember," I say. "What happened to your dreadlocks?"

The hint of a smile plays at the corner of her mouth. "They went a long time ago." She tucks a loose strand of red hair behind an ear.

"And are you still lino printing?"

Emily closes her eyes briefly, as though indulging me. Then she says, "I work in executive search now. I live in Kent, I have three children."

"Oh, wow, that's crazy."

"Listen, Lucy, I'm sorry, but if you're serious, I think you really do need to see a doctor." She pauses. "Do you have a history of mental health issues? Has this happened to you before?"

"I don't need a doctor, Em, I just need a friend."

"Lucy, we haven't spoken in fifteen years."

"We haven't?"

"No. We didn't stay in touch when we gave up the flat." She drops her gaze.

"What about Julian? Where's he?"

"I think he lives in America now." She bites her lip. "Look, is there someone I can call for you? Family? Your GP? One of your old school friends? I'm about to go into a meeting, but I feel a duty of care now that you've called me."

Duty of care? She sounds nothing like the Emily I know, and I don't want her calling people, telling them I'm on drugs or that I've lost my mind.

"No, no, thank you. I'm fine, look, I'm probably just hungover. I was passing the flat and thought of you and . . ." *And what? I thought she might still live here? I thought she might be able to help me?* "Just a bad case of nostalgia, I guess. I'll be fine. Good luck with your meeting."

Hanging up the phone, I lean my shoulder against the front door. Of all the unbelievable things I've been faced with this morning, that hippy-dippy Emily now wears a suit and works in executive search is one of the least fathomable. A feeling of intense loneliness crawls over me. Something about Emily's reaction—she was never going to believe me. Who *would* believe me? If I put myself in her shoes and someone called me with this story, wouldn't I give them the exact advice Emily just gave me—to see a doctor? Maybe I am ill. I open my phone again, clutching it like a lifeline.

Fit Fun Fabulous Alert—Your stress levels are highly elevated. Why not engage in a leisurely walk?

"Fuck off," I tell the screen, deleting the app. I think about calling my parents, but as I scroll to Home a new queasiness sinks in. If I'm really in my forties, both my parents would be in their seventies by now. What if they don't answer? What if . . .

As I'm holding it, my phone flashes in my hand. Office is calling again, and I find myself answering it, if only to distract myself from the horrible thought that one or both of my parents might be dead.

"Lucy, it's Trey, where are you?" says a loud male voice.

"Vauxhall," I say.

"Did you have train issues? The channel execs are here. I've given them coffee, but we don't want to start the pitch without you. How soon can you get here?" Whoever Trey is, he sounds stressed.

"Um, yes, about that, I'm . . . sick."

Though I am curious to see where Future Me works, clearly, I can't attend any kind of meeting right now, I wouldn't know anything. I assume from what Trey's said that I still work in TV, but TV production could be completely different now. It might all be made by robots with 4D cameras and

Smellovision. Though given the lack of improvements on the trains, I might be giving the future too much credit.

"You're sick?" echoes Trey in alarm. "I thought you were in Vauxhall."

"I'm so sick. Something I ate for breakfast. Bad kippers." *Kippers? Why did I say kippers? Only eighty-year-old men who wear handkerchief sun hats and live in boardinghouses in Margate eat kippers.* "Can you do the meeting for me?" I ask hopefully.

"Me? You want me to deliver the pitch? Surely Michael should do it?" says Trey, his voice rising an octave.

"Yes, yes, Michael, of course. Kippers remorse is messing with my head. Um, got to go, I think I'm going to be sick again. Good luck!" *It's not a total lie. I have been sick today.*

That was stupid of me to answer the call.

So, if I can't go home and I can't go to work, where do I go now?

The newsagent's. The wishing machine.

That's where this started, I'm sure of it. If I can find the machine, maybe I can wish myself back. If that's really what this is—some supernatural wish fulfillment? But where was it, the newsagent's? After leaving Dale's, I remember running in the rain, though I'm not sure how far or in what direction. Getting home from the newsagent's is a complete blur. Is that because I never made it home, or because it happened sixteen years ago?

Closing my eyes, I try to visualize what I'm looking for—a blue awning, a street name beginning with B; it can't have been far from the pub, the Falcon? What was it called? I highlight Southwark on my phone, then search "pubs." Several dots appear on the screen. The Rising Sun, the Huntsman and Hound, the Falkirk. *The Falkirk*, that was it. It's still there.

Following the map, I feel a renewed optimism. Find the pub, find the newsagent's, wish myself home, and all this will be over—a surreal story to tell my friends in the morning. When I get to the pub, it looks entirely different; it's now a brutalist glass and steel box. It must have been demolished and rebuilt but retained the same name. *What is it with people demolishing all these perfectly good buildings?* Following some instinct, I head down one road, then another. Then in front of me, a familiar street name, Baskin Road; an old red phone box on the corner; a feeling I have been here before. *This is the place.* Turning onto the street, I hold my breath, hoping to see a blue and white awning. But there is nothing— only a building site, bannered Schwarz Construction, and three or four flattened plots on the side of the street where the newsagent's would have been. And as quickly as my hopes for a way home were raised, they are dashed to oblivion.

8

I'M ONLY A FIFTEEN-MINUTE WALK AWAY FROM VAUX-hall, and I don't know where else to go, except back the way I came. Should I get the return train to Waterloo? Find my way back to this Farnham place? Ask that man I woke up with to help me? As I wander along now familiar streets, I realize I'm already on Kennington Lane. Like a concussed homing pigeon who doesn't know where else to go, I find myself pausing once more at my front door. In desperation, I press all the buzzers in a last, hopeless bid to be admitted back into my old life. This time a male voice responds. "Yes?"

"Hello?" I call into the speaker.

"Who is this?" asks the voice.

"It's Lucy, Lucy Young, I live in flat three—I *used* to live in flat three."

"Hmmmm," comes the voice, and it's a familiar-sounding "hmmm." *Stinkley?*

"Mr. Finkley? Is that you?"

"It might be," he says.

Before this morning, I wouldn't have been able to imagine a scenario where I was glad to hear Mr. Finkley's voice, but here it is.

"Oh, Mr. Finkley, you still live here? I can't tell you how happy that makes me. Do you remember me? Lucy, I used to live in the flat below, we had the bathroom issue, leaks through the ceiling?"

"Lots of people have lived below me," he says. "Lots of them had issues with my bathroom."

"Would you let me in? I'm having a strange day and I'd love to see a familiar face."

There's a pause, a sigh, then, "Are you going to rob me?"

"No, I'm not going to rob you."

"Because I've got nothing worth nicking, 'cept my stamps."

With a buzz and a click, the front door opens before I can offer reassurances about not stealing his stamps. Racing up the stairs two at a time, I pause at the door to flat three—my home for two and a half years. On the floor by the door are a pair of small Wellington boots, a child's bike, and a mat with "Welcome to the Madhouse" written in twirling, cheerful font. I press a hand against the door, as though this proximity to my old life might have some talismanic, calming property. It does not.

Mr. Finkley is waiting on the landing above, peering down at me. My first impression is that he hasn't changed. He has the same angular face, the same gravity-defying hair.

"I remember you. You gave me the plants." *Plants?*

"Who lives here?" I ask, pointing at the door to flat three.

"A couple with a loud child." He narrows his eyes at the

door. When I slump back against the wall, sliding down to sit on the floor, he asks, "Are you all right?"

"This is going to sound crazy," I say, "but yesterday I was twenty-six and living in this flat, then this morning I woke up somewhere else and I'm sixteen years older."

Mr. Finkley nods, as though this is a perfectly normal explanation for why I'm here. He opens his front door and says, "You'd better come in then. I don't have any coffee or tea to offer you, though."

Mr. Finkley's front room is a riot of greenery. There are plants *everywhere*. Ceramic pots pepper every surface, hanging baskets overflow with leaves, and there are tendrils of foliage climbing the doorframes. Hidden within this jungle are boxes and boxes of junk, piled high around dusty brown furniture. The air smells of wet laundry, moth-eaten carpets, and garden center.

"I can offer you water or ham or both," he says, moving a plant from the sofa to take a seat opposite me, then picking up a cup, which looks and smells suspiciously like coffee.

"I'm good, thank you. You have a lot of plants," I observe. When I'm nervous, I'm prone to stating the obvious.

"You started my collection. Don't you remember?"

"Me? I'm terrible with plants, and no, I don't remember anything, that's kind of why I'm here."

We sit in silence for a moment. I'm not sure how I expect Mr. Finkley of all people to be able to help me, but there is something comforting about sitting with someone who looks and sounds the same as I remember them, someone who is not looking at me like I'm completely deranged.

He frowns. "So, you've lost a few years."

I nod. "There has to be a logical explanation, but it feels like I jumped ahead somehow," I tell him.

"There's not always a logical explanation. Some things don't make sense, like wormholes and nanotechnology." He pauses, raising his index finger in the air and peering at me over his coffee cup with unblinking eyes. "Did you ask for this? Did you wish your life away?" His tone is so serious that I find myself bursting into tears.

"Yes, I think I did," I say, and then I'm howling, tears streaming down my face. "But I didn't mean to, I didn't want to be old, I just wanted to eat croissants and to stop going on terrible dates."

Mr. Finkley stands up, and for a moment I'm worried he's going to try to hug me, but he simply hands me a box of tissues. All the tissues in the proffered box look to have been used and replaced, but I take it to be tactful, then subtly wipe my tear-stained cheeks on my sleeve.

"Quite the predicament." Mr. Finkley sighs, drumming his fingers on the arms of his chair as he waits for me to stop crying. "And this future life you've found yourself in. What does it look like? Is it any good?"

"I don't know. I haven't had a chance to think about it. There's a good-looking man, two children, lots of nice shoes." I shake my head, aware how foolish I sound.

"Doesn't sound too bad then—if you like that sort of thing. Wouldn't be for me. I don't tend to like children or shoes." Mr. Finkley stands; picks up a small, rusty watering can; and starts to water his hanging baskets. Only now do I notice he's not wearing shoes or socks.

"But if this is real, then I've missed *years* of my life. I don't know my children or the man I'm married to, or even who my friends are now. Plus, not to sound vain, I'm sure aging isn't so bad when it creeps up on you gradually, but it's terrifying when it happens all at once." I pause to wrap both my palms around the back of my neck, which is aching with tension. "The worst part is, no one's going to believe me if I tell them what's happened. Frankly, I'm amazed you believe me."

"Did I say I believe you?" Mr. Finkley asks, raising a gray, wispy eyebrow at me. "If I've learned anything in life, it's that it's best to keep an open mind and a closed toilet seat."

"So, what would you do, if you were me?" I ask, rubbing my face between my palms.

"You didn't like your old life." He shrugs. "I'd enjoy the upgrade. If you can't get off the bus, you might as well enjoy the ride. I saw that on a poster in the prison library."

"Did you *work* in a prison?" I ask nervously.

"No, spent a few nights in the clink." He pauses, then adds, "It was mainly a misunderstanding." He pauses again, takes off his glasses, and wipes them on the corner of his shirt. "I'd give anything to be forty-two again. The places I would go." He points to a dusty map of the world, propped up against the mantelpiece.

"You like to travel, Mr. Finkley?"

"In my youth, I went everywhere. Not anymore." He taps the side of his head. "Too many people watching. All this face-recognition technology—it's how the shape-shifting reptiles get you."

Riiiiight. Mr. Finkley's eyes dart around the room, as though, even now, someone might be listening in on our conversation. Maybe I shouldn't be seeking life advice from a man with a criminal record and paranoid tendencies.

"Thank you for listening, Mr. Finkley. I won't take up any more of your time. It's been, um, nice to see you again."

He nods. As he moves to escort me back to the front door, he takes a piece of ham out of his pocket and rubs it between his fingers, before popping it into his mouth and chewing slowly.

"You're the first visitor I've had in six years. Come back sometime if you like. I could show you my maps."

"That's kind, thank you," I say, while knowing it's highly unlikely I will ever come back to see his maps.

WHEN I'M ALONE in the hallway that looks like mine, I concede that however eccentric Mr. Finkley might be, he could be right. I don't know how to get back, so what else can I do but go out and explore?

Before I do anything, I need coffee. Given how expensive they are here, I should check my bank balance first. I can't face the indignity of having my card declined on top of everything else today. Across the street, there's an ATM. I find a debit card in my wallet and slot it into the machine. It doesn't even ask me for a pin, but simply scans my face with a green light. "Face ID accepted." When I tap "See balance" a number flashes up on the screen.

"Holy bejeezus!" I exclaim, blinking my eyes in disbelief.

Yesterday I had minus money, my overdraft was maxed out. Peering down to check the number again, I can't quite believe it. Future Me is *rich.* And whoever said money can't buy you happiness hadn't been living off thirty-five pounds a week for the last four years.

CHAPTER 9

WHERE DOES A WOMAN EXPERIENCING AN EXISTENTIAL life leap, with money in the bank and a wallet full of credit cards, go? To Selfridges, of course. Personal shopping, with a quick detour via the croissant department. Okay, so it might not be called the croissant department, it's called the Food Hall, but it boasts a mouthwatering selection of the biggest, flakiest, most expensive croissants I've ever seen. I buy myself one, along with a double-shot latte, and eat it right there at the counter. Then I buy another and eat that one too. Then I feel a bit sick and regret eating the second one. That was completely unnecessary. Also, I just spent thirty-seven pounds on coffee and croissants, and even though I'm rich now, that still feels obscene.

On the women's clothing floor, I promise myself I'll show greater restraint.

"Can I help you?" asks a wisp of a girl wearing an Hermès scarf and a name tag that reads "Linda."

"Yes, Linda. Yes, you can," I say, my voice full of confidence. "I want you to imagine a scenario where someone who adores clothes, who daydreams about shoes and was pretty much born to shop, has never had the chance to buy anything before. Ever." Linda frowns. "She's only ever had access to charity shops and discount racks." Linda looks suitably horrified. "Now, imagine that person has recently come into some money. She'd have some catching up to do, don't you think?" Linda nods, as though she knows exactly what I'm talking about. "Can you help me catch up, Linda?"

"I think we're going to need some champagne," Linda says with a conspiratorial grin. I've never felt more seen by another human being and all my vows of restraint go straight out of the window.

What follows is a shopping montage Carrie Bradshaw would be proud of. I try on everything. *Everything.* Linda orders more champagne. I discover, to my relief, that even in this new body, well-designed clothes look great on me. And I know, I know, I'm shallow and vain, but honestly, nothing fixes a bout of existential depression like a pair of killer heels and a fitted purple suit with epic shoulder pads.

"It looks amazing on you," Linda says as we both admire my reflection in the enormous changing-room mirror. It's a bold statement suit by a designer whose name I don't recognize. With its elegant cut and soft silk lining, it feels wonderful to wear.

"It does, doesn't it? It's also making me feel better about how old I look."

"You don't look old," says Linda, her eyes sparkling with the unmistakable glow of day drinking.

"How old do I look?" I ask, and her eyes grow wide in fear.

I know it's a mean question. It's like asking someone if they think your boyfriend is hot—you can't win.

"Midthirties?" Linda is being kind, but I'll take it.

Looking at myself in the statement suit and heels, I know I'm going to buy them. Who knows when I'll wear them, but since this whole experience could well be a hallucination, it's easy to rationalize anything. Dorothy got new sparkly red shoes, why shouldn't I have a new purple suit?

"How much is it?" I ask Linda.

"It's on sale," she says excitedly. "So only two thousand and eighty pounds."

After briefly choking on my own tongue, I quickly calculate that there's probably been some inflation I'll need to account for here. Since coffees and croissants cost roughly four times what I'd expect to pay, two thousand pounds is probably the equivalent of only five hundred pounds in old money. Which is still a lot, I know, but it's like when you go to a festival and you get drink vouchers, you can't think of it as real money or you'd never buy any drinks. Besides, if you can't buy yourself a ridiculously expensive suit to make yourself feel better about time traveling through half your twenties and your entire thirties, then when can you buy one?

"I'm going to take it, and these shoes . . . and these boots," I tell Linda, handing her the black ankle-length boots that feel soft as butter. At the till Linda rings up the suit and shoes, plus a top and jacket I like, plus a sparkly brooch, because what's a little more when you're spending this kind of cash? The total when I hand over my bank card makes me feel physically sick, but that's probably the residual croissant binge. I reassure myself that there is still plenty in my account, and that it's not even real money, because none of this is real. Probably.

Linda holds a card reader toward me, but there's no pin pad or eye scanner.

"It's a palm reader," she says, sensing my confusion. Cautiously, I lift my hand to the reader, which instantly flashes green. "You have twenty-four days to return anything, as long as it hasn't been worn and still has the tags on."

Watching Linda carefully wrap the purple suit in crêpe paper, I realize I feel so much worse now that I'm not wearing it. Maybe this clammy, guilty feeling will go away if I put it back on?

"You know, I think I'm going to wear the suit home," I say.

"O-kay," says Linda, enunciating each syllable, in a way that makes me think maybe she doesn't think it is okay.

"If a tutu was good enough for Carrie Bradshaw to walk the streets in . . ."

"Who's Carrie Bradshaw?" asks Linda.

And just like that, I feel incredibly old again.

AS I WALK down Oxford Street in my new I-might-have-lost-a-decade-and-a-half-of-my-life-but-I've-gained-a-phenomenal-suit suit, I realize I have no idea what time it is. I switched my phone to silent hours ago to stop it from beeping and ringing and offering me stress-busting suggestions. Sitting on a bench, I retrieve it from my bag and see it's two o'clock. There's a message from Emily: Are you okay? I'm worried about you.

I quickly reply that I'm fine and she doesn't need to worry. I think about sending her a selfie of me in my new suit but then think better of it. Expensive shopping sprees might not be everyone's definition of "fine."

There's also a text from Sam: Deal on tiles at Tanbury's if you want to get those blue ones you like for the downstairs bathroom? Then he's attached a photo of some beautiful hexagonal tiles, with a geometric turquoise pattern. I might not know much about Future Me's life, but I know she would want me to say yes to those tiles.

Yes! I reply. Do I leave a kiss? He didn't put a kiss on his message to me. Scrolling back through our chat, I see that I do usually add a kiss. There are messages about Felix's swimming bag, about picking up the mild cheddar he likes for his lunch box, what train I'm going to be on, and whether Sam needs to ask Lenny to look at the dripping tap in the kids' bathroom. In short, it's all incredibly dull. I imagined marital WhatsApp might contain a bit more flirting, a few more dick pics, but the only recent photo on the chat between Sam and me is of the aforementioned leaky tap and more close-ups of the Tanbury tiles. *Ooh, they are nice.* I follow up my initial text with a more enthusiastic, Love these tiles! xx

My phone starts to ring as I'm holding it. Michael Green is calling, whoever Michael Green is. It might be the new suit or those two glasses of champagne, but I now feel equipped to take a call from anyone.

"Michael, hi," I say, full of confidence.

"Are you feeling better?" he asks. If he thinks I'm ill, he must be Michael from work, the one Trey mentioned.

"I am, thanks."

"I didn't want to disturb you when you're sick, but I thought you'd want to know that the pitch went well. Sky loved your idea. They've committed to giving us development money for a pilot."

They loved my idea. I feel a swell of pride. Even though it wasn't really *my* idea, it was still some version of me, and that counts for something. "That's great!" I say.

"You focus on getting yourself well," Michael says. "Everything else can wait until Monday, I just knew you'd want to hear the good news."

I quickly assess my options. I could head to Waterloo, get a train back to that house in Farnham, and hide under the luxuriously soft duvet until all of this goes away. Or, like Mr. Finkley said—I could explore this new world while I have the chance. This might be my only opportunity to see what my future life looks like. I don't know the rules; for all I know this could be a twenty-four-hour thing and I could wake up in my old reality tomorrow. If I am being offered a chance to see what my future holds, maybe I should embrace it. Besides, the dopamine hit from shopping is beginning to fade and this Michael guy sounds friendly enough. I already look the part, what have I got to lose?

"Michael, I'm feeling better. I'm coming to the office."

10

THE MINUTE I'VE HUNG UP, I REALIZE I DON'T KNOW where it is I work. I can hardly call Michael back and ask him. Then I remember, Trey called me from a landline number. I call the number and a male voice answers, "Good afternoon, Badger TV." I hang up straightaway. Ha, I am a detective extraordinaire; Poirot would be proud of me.

Google informs me that Badger TV is based on Beak Street, just off Carnaby Street. How would anyone navigate a life leap before phones or the Internet? Jumping in a cab (two cabs in one day, what decadence), I spend the journey reading up about Badger TV.

"Incorporated eight years ago by TV executives Michael Green and Lucy Rutherford." Lucy Rutherford? Is that me? Is that my married name, Sam's name? I try saying it out loud, "Lucy Rutherford," but it sounds alien and wrong. I am Lucy Young, I will always be Lucy Young. Shaking my head, I keep reading. "The independent production company has gone from strength to strength, carving out a specialty in innovative children's television." *Children's television?* I never imagined myself working on kids' shows, though I suppose children need good TV as much as anyone. A news article tells me Badger TV was acquired a year ago by Dutch media giant Bamph and is slated for "significant structural changes," whatever that means. Then my cab arrives at the address and that's all the detective work I have time to do.

Walking through revolving doors into a brightly lit reception area, I know I must be in the right place because the walls are decorated in badger wallpaper. The reception area is sparsely furnished with low silver sofas, a long white desk, and a glass-walled meeting room along one side. At the far end of the room there are lift doors and a staircase, presumably leading to an office above. A blond receptionist wearing horn-rimmed glasses looks up from his paper-thin computer screen as I walk in.

"Oh, hi, Lucy. Wow, great suit. Where are you off to?"

"Nowhere special," I say, slightly thrown that this person knows my name.

His eyebrows crease into a confused frown, but he continues to smile.

"So, I work here . . . ," I say, hoping he might volunteer some information about what it is I do, but alas, he does not. "Is there a runner or someone you could call to come down here and talk to me?"

"You want me to get Callum?" the receptionist asks.

"Great, yes. Get Callum."

The receptionist makes a call, and I pace up and down in front of his desk. I don't have a plan here. Well, my plan was, "Just go, see what happens!" but that doesn't seem like much of a plan now that I'm here and I've sobered up. I wasn't going to tell my colleagues the truth. I'd just be pitied, sent home, or told to see a doctor. They'd look at me the way Emily did, as though I've lost my mind. If I'm going to see what my future life is like, I need to experience it as Lucy Rutherford, not as a lost Lucy Young.

A few minutes later, a slim man in his early twenties with spiky brown hair and a nose piercing bounds down the stairs. He's cute in a "probably plays the ukulele and brews his own ale" sort of way.

"Hi, Lucy—" he says, eyes widening as he takes in the purple power suit. "I thought you were off sick today."

"I was, but I'm better. Can I have a word?" I step into the glass-walled meeting room to our left and beckon him to follow. "Look, Callum—can I call you Callum?"

"Yes," he says, eyeing me warily.

"It's always the runners who know everything in a production company. So how do you feel about being my eyes and ears this afternoon?"

"Okay," he says, staring at me with wide, unblinking eyes.

"It's a concept for a new show," I say, thinking on my feet. "Can you guide an imposter through a job they don't know? Just follow me everywhere and discreetly tell me who everyone is and what job they do."

"Isn't that already a show? *Job Blag* on ITV," Callum says, pressing his palms together in a nervous prayer.

Who would make that into a show? It's a terrible idea.

"Yes, yes," I say, unbuttoning my jacket. "But I have a different version in mind."

"Oh?" Callum asks.

"The format's not quite there yet, I'm just stress testing the principle. Look, do you want to help me or not?"

He nods like an overeager puppy, so I open the door to the meeting room, and he follows me out. "Just give me a rundown on all the people who work here, the whole hierarchy of the office, a who's who of Badger TV."

"Even Ravi?"

"Who's Ravi?"

"Him." Callum points to the receptionist, looks at me in confusion, then grins. "Was that a test?"

"Yes, that was a test. Assume I know *nothing*."

I realize I'm still holding all my Selfridges bags, so I ask Ravi if he'll look after them for me and he kindly stows them beneath his desk. At the top of the stairs, we emerge into an open-plan office full of clean white desks and impossibly trendy-looking people. There's one man wearing a blouse with a prominent neck ruff so outlandish, it makes Harry Styles's wardrobe look positively conservative.

"We've only got the development team in the office right now, since we're between productions," Callum tells me. "But there's Dominique, the AP"—he points at a girl wearing a leather onesie—"Trey, the producer"—neck ruff man—"Leon, the researcher"—glasses, impossibly vertical hair. "Is this what you mean?"

"Perfect," I say, which only makes Callum more eager. He reminds me of my parents' old dog, Apple, who was always jumping up excitedly.

"In there you have Michael, BTV's cofounder." Callum points to a closed door with "King Badger" written on a silver placard. People nod or wave to us as I follow Callum across the office floor. Everyone looks surprised to see me. On the walls are framed posters of programs Badger TV must have produced: How Does Your Garden Grow?, with images of children planting vegetables; Busy Lizzy's Gruesome Mysteries, with a young girl holding a magnifying glass.

"And my desk is . . ."

"In there." Callum points to a huge corner office with "Queen Badger" written on the door.

"And the pitch this morning was for . . . ?"

"*Rainbow Bear and Friends*," Callum says, looking more confused by the minute. "It's a preschool show. Rainbow Bear makes a new friend in every episode. Someone with a problem or insecurity that Rainbow Bear can solve with love and understanding."

"Sounds a little twee," I say, grimacing.

Callum laughs, then covers his mouth, unsure whether I'm joking. The chair at my desk is one of those huge ergonomic ones, with multiple levers for maximum comfort. On one side of my computer is a framed photo of Sam and the kids, and on the other, the 'Congratulations' card Zoya drew with the sketch of me holding a TV. *I framed it, I kept it all this time.* Picking it up, I find a photo behind it of me and Michelle Obama.

"I met Michelle Obama?" I squeal, examining it to check it is real.

Callum looks ever more perplexed. "I think that was taken at the Women in Business Awards. She was hosting."

I met Michelle Obama, I run a production company, I have my own office and a chair with multiple levers. This is so much better than I ever could have imagined.

With a knock on the door, a man I assume must be Michael lets himself in. He's older than everyone else, possibly late forties, with a graying Afro and wise, gentle eyes. He is impeccably dressed in a waistcoat and shirt, with trousers that have a sharp crease down the front. He looks like the Great Gatsby, if the Great Gatsby was being played by a younger Danny Glover.

"I thought you were ill," he says.

"Turns out it was just one of those two-hour things. Puke your guts out in a train station toilet and then you're fine. Better than fine."

"I don't think you've taken a sick day in four years, not about to start now, huh?" he says, shooting me a knowing smile. "What's with the suit? That's a very different look for you."

"I have a thing . . . later," I say, suddenly feeling less confident about my ability to pull off this outfit. Maybe it screams cartoon villain, like the Joker, rather than fashion-forward professional with her shit together. "So, the pitch went well?"

"We knocked it out of the park, Luce." Michael swings an imaginary baseball bat and makes a "glock" sound in his throat, like a ball hitting a bat. "They're looking to commission more diverse programming, so it's right on message for them." He claps his hands. "They've even asked for a budget for twenty eps rather than twelve. Do you want to run some numbers now? We can get them an updated projection."

Budget? I wouldn't know where to begin doing a budget. As I try to think of a valid excuse for not doing that, the rest of the team have moved from their desks and are now loitering in the doorway behind Michael.

"We just wanted to say congratulations," someone says. "You're on a roll."

Then they all start clapping. Wow, Future Me is brilliant. I am Queen Badger, TV producer extraordinaire, with a team of people who will give me a round of applause without even being prompted.

"Well, it was a team effort," I say graciously. Even if it wasn't a team effort, people in teams usually like to think that it was.

"Lucy, while we're all here, would now be a good time to update everyone on the Kydz Network situation?" Michael asks. I look for my translator, Callum, but he's at the back of the crowd and can't help me. With all these expectant eyes upon me, the blagging radar on the Lucy submarine starts beeping a frantic alarm. Then I have a flash of inspiration.

"Or, since it's Friday, we could clock off early and go for a celebratory drink?" I say, clapping my hands. If Melanie Durham can buy everyone a croissant, I can go one better and buy everyone a cocktail. Besides, it will be far easier for me to work out the company dynamics over an informal drink. People glance around at one another, then back to me. "What's the point in being the boss if you can't knock off at"—I check my watch—"three thirty occasionally?" The team whoops and cheers. I am the best boss ever.

As people disperse to pick up bags and coats from their desks, abuzz with excitement about my drinks plan, Michael stays behind and takes a seat on my desk.

"I'm glad you're feeling better, Lucy, but don't you think we should take some time to talk about Kydz Network? I know you're confident, with good reason, but it's not far off."

My source of intel, Callum, is still loitering by the door, unsure whether he should stay or go. "Callum, what are your thoughts on the Kydz Network situation?" I ask, and Michael looks back and forth between us in confusion.

"Um, I think it's bad," Callum says, but then sees me frown

at how unhelpful he's being and adds, "or good, obviously. It could be good."

"A profound insight. Thank you, Callum," I say. Callum takes this as his cue to leave, which I did not mean it to be.

"Look, the sooner you share what you're thinking with the team, the more time we'll have to prepare," Michael says.

"I know there's a lot to do. Maybe I got carried away with your good news. I just think a bit of team bonding might be beneficial for morale."

Michael stands up, the concerned look receding. "You're right, we should treat the team occasionally. We can deal with Kydz Network on Monday."

"Monday, great." *Ha! I'll probably be back in my real life by Monday.* And if I'm not, I certainly won't be coming to work, at least not until I'm up to speed on whatever this mysterious Kydz Network situation might be.

FIVE HOURS LATER, we're in a cocktail bar on Carnaby Street and I'm having the best night of my life. My company card is behind the bar *(Yes, I have a company card, I don't even need to spend my own money)* and I am bonding with my brilliant team. I must be great at employing people, because everyone who works at Badger TV is whip-smart and hilarious. Unless the lens of afternoon cocktails is distorting reality.

Leon has been telling me a funny story about some celebrity I've never heard of who was dating another celebrity I've never heard of. Even though I don't get any of the references, I laugh along because the way he tells it is hilarious. Michael started off a little uptight, but after a few beers he relaxed into the idea of the team bonding and has been regaling everyone with his thoughts on "why baseball is a superior spectator sport to football." From the looks on the team's faces, I suspect it's a topic they've heard before.

It's been happy hour for the last five hours, and I am feeling pretty darn happy. I'm certainly feeling a lot better about this life leap than I was this morning.

"Lucy, I wanted to ask your advice," Trey says, sliding into the booth beside me. Trey is in his late twenties and good-looking in a feline way. His hair is a little too perfectly gelled for my taste, the neck ruff a little too out-there, but he has soulful eyes and cheekbones you could cut cheese with.

"Advice?" I ask, unable to fathom what kind of advice I might be able to offer anyone.

"Yes, I was thinking about proposing to Clare." His eyes are earnest as he looks to see my reaction.

"Well, do you think she's the one?" I ask.

"Oh yes, she's everything to me," he says.

"And remind me how long you've been together?"

"Six years, since college."

"Then yes, what are you waiting for?"

"It's just with my job being so up in the air, you know? Her parents are old-fashioned about job security, getting a mort-gage and stuff. I was worried it might not be the best time to ask." *Why would his job be up in the air?* "My sister thinks I should pay off my debts first, wait until I've got a staff contract."

"Wait schmait," I say, tilting my head from side to side in a way that makes me think I might be slightly drunker than I realized. "Just buy a smaller ring. Love is all you need." I know nothing about Clare, her feelings on jewelry, or her relationship with Trey, but these cocktails are making me feel pro-romance, pro–throwing caution to the wind. Trey looks like he's trying to tie a knot in his eyebrows as Michael comes to join us in the booth.

"I'm afraid I'm not going to stick around, Cardinals are playing tonight," says Michael.

"Baseball," I say, taking an educated guess.

"You know me, three things in life I care about: my wife, my work, and my baseball, though not necessarily in that order." He grins and leans over to squeeze my shoulder. "Well, adieu to all," he says, waving an arm to everyone in our little corner of the bar, then he taps his stomach. "Jane's game-night fritters wait for no man."

Those within earshot say good-bye to Michael, while Trey turns to me and whispers, "Jane," in a dark, conspiratorial tone.

"Jane," I repeat. My French teacher at school once said, "If you're ever stuck in an oral exam, mirror the examiner." But this still feels like trying to solve a murder without knowing who's been murdered and not being able to ask any questions.

"Jane," Trey says again, with even more venom, this time punching a fist into his other hand. Before I'm forced to embark on a long game of "Jane" tennis, I'm saved by Dominique, who comes over with another round of cocktails, and Trey excuses himself to use the bathroom.

"I love your outfit, Lucy. It's so gene you come to the office dressed like that," Dominique says, sitting down beside me. *Gene? Are there new words I don't even know?*

"Thanks," I say, taking the drink she offers me. "I've never owned something this nice before, so I thought I might as well wear it."

"What do you mean? You have an amazing wardrobe,"

Dominique says, then pauses. "Don't take this the wrong way"—her pupils roll to the ceiling, and she flings a limp arm around my shoulder—"but I'm usually a little intimidated by you. You're so great at what you do, and you're always so, I don't know, together." She turns to look at me, and sees I'm surprised by what she's saying. "Sorry, I'm drunk." She shakes her head and laughs.

Something in her mannerisms reminds me of Zoya and I instantly want to be friends with her. She's got a glitter tattoo on her shoulder, which is the coolest thing I've ever seen. *Maybe I should get a glitter tattoo?*

"We don't usually socialize together?" I say, half question, half statement.

"At wrap parties, sure, but you usually leave early."

"Sounds like I'm super lame," I say, then burst into a fit of giggles. I feel really drunk, which is strange, because I've only had three of these martinis and I can usually have at least four before I start to get silly.

"Let's dance!" I say, suddenly feeling the urge to move. I grab Dominique's hand and pull her up to the dance floor. Callum and Ravi are standing by the bar, and as we're dancing, I ask Dominique, "Is it me, or is Callum quite hot?" I have to shout to be heard over the music.

"Callum?" She shakes her head. "What, for me?"

"No, for me," I shout back. "I'm going to ask him to dance."

He's completely my type, all dark hair, long limbs, and puppy-dog eyes. He's looking at me like he likes me too. At least I think he is, it's hard to be sure when everything's starting to blur. I stride across to the bar and lunge for Callum's hand.

"Dance with us?" I say, grinning, pulling him to join us. He blushes, embarrassed, but follows anyway. I feel like I'm thirteen, at a school disco, as we dance side by side. Dominique has disappeared, so it's just the two of us now, and I turn to dance with him face-to-face. Our eyes meet. *He looks like he wants to kiss me. Maybe this is an excellent idea. A really gene idea.* Just as I'm leaning a little closer, I feel Callum's hands on my wrists, pushing me away. Then he's leading me back to the booth, making me sit down. He looks mortified. *Did I almost kiss an employee, on the dance floor, in front of everyone?*

"Aren't you married?" Callum whispers, his eyes wide in surprise and embarrassment.

Oh shit. I *am* married, I completely forgot. Here I am acting like I'm on some great night out with fun, hot new colleagues, but I'm not—I'm not me anymore.

"What time is it?" I ask, swallowing a wave of martini-flavored nausea.

"Nine o'clock," says Callum. "Shall I get you some water?"

The twenty-year-old runner is trying to sober me up. This is bad. This is so bad. Maybe I was supposed to be back to look after those children hours ago? *Shit.* Maybe Future Me doesn't have the same tolerance for alcohol that old me did.

"Do you want me to put you in a cab, babe?" Dominique asks, patting my arm sympathetically, and I manage to nod my head up and down.

IN THE CAB, I finally check my phone again. I have a lot of messages and missed calls, mainly from Sam. As I'm looking at my phone, he calls again.

"Where the hell are you?" he asks, his voice sharp.

"Um, I had a work thing. I lost track of time." I wince, wondering if I'm going to throw up all over my beautiful suit.

"You didn't tell me you were going to be out. I got a call from Maria saying you never showed up. I've been working from Reading today, no one could get hold of you. She had to stay until I could get home. She missed an appointment."

"Zorry," I slur.

"You're drunk," he says, his voice stern and unimpressed.

"A little," I admit. Having a husband feels a lot like having a parent. Maybe I don't want a husband. Maybe I'd rather be rich and single, picking up men half my age like Brigitte Macron. Then I remember how hot Sam is, and how valid his annoyance, given the situation. At least when you're married your husband has to love you unconditionally.

"Just get on the nine forty train, and I'll send a cab to pick you up," Sam says, sounding very little like someone who loves me, unconditionally or otherwise.

CHAPTER 11

WHEN I WAKE UP, I SEE THAT I'M IN THE GROWN-UP BED-room with the fancy curtains and the super-soft duvet. I'm still wearing the purple suit trousers, and I have a headache almost as bad as yesterday's. Reaching a shaking hand beyond the safety of the bed, I find a glass of water on my bedside table and gulp it down.

The fact that I've woken up here, rather than Kennington Lane, makes me suspect this flash forward/life leap, whatever it is, might be more permanent than I'd hoped. Not that I did a degree in time travel or wrote a thesis on the space-time continuum, but going to sleep here and waking up again makes it feel less likely to be a dream. A fussy fog of remorse tells me that I might owe Future Me an apology for acting inappropriately with her work colleagues. Did I . . . did I try to kiss Callum? Oh, I can't think about it, it's too awful.

There's no sign of Sam or the children upstairs, so I have a quick shower and find a fleecy beige tracksuit to change into.

At least it's Saturday; a morning of hangover food and mindless TV will sort me out. Downstairs, I pause by the kitchen door, observing the scene. Sam is playing peekaboo with Amy from behind a cereal packet and she's giggling in delight. Felix is wearing a shiny red cape over his dinosaur pajamas and has lined up mini-Weetabix like dominos across the kitchen table.

"Hi," I say with a timid wave. Sam looks up and responds with the coldest "Hi" I've ever heard. It's arctic. No, colder than arctic, it's the temperature of one of those planets at the furthest edge of the solar system where it's minus four hundred degrees.

"I'm sorry about last night," I say, walking into the kitchen and taking a seat. "Yesterday was a bit of a strange day for me."

"I don't want to talk about it in front of the children," Sam says. A muscle pulses in his jaw, and he turns away from me to switch on the coffee machine. *Hmmm, I could murder a coffee.*

"Are you Mummy again?" Felix asks me.

"Morning, Felix," I say, sidestepping the question. There's a loud whirring, crunching sound as coffee beans are pulverized into delicious submission. Amy covers her ears.

When the noise finally stops, Sam asks Felix, "What do you mean, 'Are you Mummy again?'"

"Yesterday Mummy wasn't Mummy. She was an alien," Felix explains.

Sam looks at me, and I shrug as though I have no idea what he's talking about. Right now, with him radiating all this freezing-cold Neptune energy toward me, doesn't feel like the right moment to try to explain wish-based time travel.

"Sometimes grown-ups have too much to drink, and it makes them act differently. It doesn't mean they've been possessed by aliens," Sam says, handing me a coffee. Then he picks up a banana, which he peels and passes to Amy in one motion.

"Thank you," I say, hugging the cup in my hands.

"If I drink too much, will I act differently?" Felix asks.

"No, it only happens with alcohol, which you don't drink," Sam explains.

My coffee smells so good I want to cry, and I take a long, slow breath. When I look up from the mug, I see Felix observing me.

"What's my middle name?" says Felix.

"Huh?"

"I'm trying to think of questions only Mummy would know the answer to, that the aliens wouldn't."

Damn, this kid is bright. How old did he say he was again?
"Funny boy," I say, putting my cup down, then ruffling his hair in the way I've seen people ruffle kids' hair on TV. Sam turns back to the coffee machine to make a cup for himself.

"I'd be surprised if Mummy can remember her own name this morning."

"What's your favorite number?" Felix is not giving up.

"Um, eight," I say, plucking a number out of thin air.

"Ha! Mummy's favorite number is eleven!" Felix holds his arms out wide, as though this proves his point.

"Do you even remember getting home?" Sam asks me. His tone is light, but he won't look at me.

"Maybe not every element," I admit.

"Felix, do you want to put the TV on for your sister?" Sam says, lifting Amy out of her high chair and putting her down on the floor. She immediately toddles toward me and tries to hug my leg with her sticky banana hands. I move away so she can't smoosh banana goo onto my nice, clean, fluffy jogging bottoms.

"Can you wipe her hands?" Sam asks, throwing me a wet dishcloth, which I miss, and it hits the wall behind me with a thwack.

"Mummy would have caught that," Felix says, his voice an awed whisper.

Picking up the cloth, I try to clean the baby's hands as best I can, but she's still trying to hug me, so I end up holding her at arm's length with one hand, while trying to clean off the goo with the other. When I look up, Sam and Felix are both watching me with the same suspicious expression.

"Told you," Felix says, shaking his head, then he takes his sister's hand and leads her into the next room.

As soon as they are out of earshot, Sam hands me a plate of buttered toast, and I wonder if I'm out of the woods in terms of everyone being annoyed with me. Sam's wearing a gray T-shirt and faded navy-blue jeans, while his wavy brown hair is slightly mussed up at the side. He really is incredibly attractive. If I can shake this hangover, I wonder if sex might be on the cards. Surely that's one of the perks of having a husband—you don't need to get all dressed up, faff about with liquid eyeliner, or even leave the house, you can just get it on in your pajamas. *Would sleeping with Sam involve cheating on myself somehow?* The thought hurts my brain.

"So, you don't remember falling asleep on the train? Me having to put the kids in the car and come fetch you from Alton station?" he asks in a tone that makes me think hot morning sex might not be on the menu.

"Oh, shit. Did I? I'm so sorry."

"What happened yesterday, Luce? Let's put aside the state

you came home in, I got a notification on our joint account that you'd spent nearly three thousand pounds in Selfridges. Have you lost your mind?"

"I, um . . . I wanted to treat myself. I never get to go shopping."

"Never get to go shopping—Lucy, you have a wardrobe full of clothes! We can't afford to spend that kind of money, you know we can't."

"We look to be doing okay," I say, waving my arm to indicate the beautiful house complete with shiny coffee machine and fridge the size of a small country.

"Yes, we're incredibly fortunate, but you know we're overextended. We need every penny we earn to cover the mortgage, the loan on the car, Maria's salary, the new loft cladding, our pension contributions. You were having a go at me last week for buying new running trainers when we're trying to pay off the eco-boiler, then you go and blow ten times that on one shopping trip?"

When he puts it like that, it does sound pretty irresponsible. Maybe I miscalculated how rich we are. "You're right. I'm sorry," I say, sinking down in my chair. This conversation is depressing me. To think: you finally get a decent salary and money in the bank, but then you have to spend it all on boring stuff, like boilers and loft cladding, so there's nothing left for fun shopping trips.

"What's going on with you?" Sam asks, taking a seat at the kitchen table, his annoyance shifting to concern. I need to tell him the truth. Honestly, if I'm worried he's going to think I'm insane, he's already looking at me like I've lost the plot.

"Sam, there's something I need to tell you. Something strange."

AT FIRST SAM'S eyes grow wide in disbelief, but as I go on, he hunches forward, eyebrows furrowed in concentration, hands clasped so tight his knuckles start to go white. I tell him about going to my old flat and then to Badger TV despite not remembering where I worked or what I did there. He listens attentively, not saying a word, the crease in his forehead deepening with every new admission.

When I'm done talking, he gets up from the table and draws me into a hug. *Does he believe me, or does he think I'm making all this up to distract him from the spending spree?* When he pulls away, I see the blue in his eyes has melted into pools of compassion. He believes me, and he isn't cross with me anymore.

"We'll get this sorted, don't worry," he whispers, pulling me close again.

There's something incredibly comforting about the feel of his arms around me, the oaky, clean smell of his neck. I could happily stay like this for hours. Good hugs are underrated; I don't think any of my past boyfriends have been great huggers, it always felt perfunctory or transitory. With Sam, it feels like his arms are creating a force field around me. It's as though his body is telling me that if he could, he would absorb my every worry or pain. When he finally pulls away, he picks up his phone from the table and says, "I need to make some calls. Stay here, relax, don't exert yourself." Then he disappears into the next room.

Well, that went better than I could have hoped. I was sure Sam was going to think I'd lost my mind, that he'd rush me to the doctor to have my head examined. Maybe in a marriage you just believe each other, no questions asked.

While he's gone, I scan the front page of the newspaper, open on a tablet on the kitchen table. There are pictures of a war somewhere, a headline about drought, stories about an American politician I don't recognize, and an interview with Harper Beckham about her new role as UN ambassador. Reading these headlines makes my skin prickle with some new fear, and I quickly close the screen and push the tablet away. My brain is having a hard enough time catching up on what I've missed in my own life, I'm not sure it's ready to absorb what I've missed in the rest of the world. If I open those floodgates I might drown.

When Sam comes back, he shoots me a sympathetic, wary smile, as though he's worried that if he says the wrong thing I might spontaneously combust, right here in the kitchen.

"I feel fine, I'm not ill. Honestly, it's as though I've time-traveled here. Did you ever see that movie *The Time Traveler's Wife*? Maybe it's like that."

He leans down and kisses my forehead. "Why don't I make you a real breakfast?"

As soon as he says it, I realize I'm ravenous. I didn't have a proper meal yesterday. The buttered toast has helped, but I could definitely eat something more substantial.

"That would be lovely, thank you."

I watch as he busies himself cracking eggs and unwrapping pancetta from wax paper.

"Poached eggs, just the way you like them," he says, putting a pan of water onto the stove. He's right, poached eggs are my favorite. How strange that he knows. As I watch him getting plates from the cupboard, I realize he hasn't asked me any questions about my story. If the situation were reversed, I think I would have plenty of questions.

The eggs are incredible, the best I've ever had—solid whites, with perfect runny yolks, sprinkled with a delicious spicy seasoning and flakes of crispy pancetta. Sam insists on doing all the washing-up, he won't let me lift a finger. *Maybe I could get used to having a husband*, I think, just as the doorbell rings. Sam jumps up to get it and returns with a worried-looking Maria.

"I asked Maria if she'd watch the kids for a few hours," Sam says, looking at me with those "please don't spontaneously combust" eyes again.

"Hello, dear," Maria says, her face set in a sympathetic grimace. "How are you feeling?"

Sam must have told her I had a terrible hangover and wouldn't be able to look after the children today.

"Not too bad, thanks. I'm sure I'll be fine in a few hours."

"We're going to nip out for a bit," Sam tells me. "I got us an emergency appointment with Dr. Shepperd."

"A doctor?" *Oh.* Sam and Maria exchange looks.

"We need to get you checked out. Memory loss can be a symptom of something else."

So much for Sam believing me. Maybe he's planning on having me committed. Or he'll make me live in the attic like Mrs. Rochester, then get himself a new, younger, Jane Eyre-ier wife.

"Better safe than sorry," says Maria, patting me on the arm.

Fine. I'll go to the bloody doctor. But I'm not going to mention time travel or the wishing machines, or how much money I spent in Selfridges. Whatever's going on here, I do not intend to get Mrs. Rochestered.

12

SAM OPENS THE PASSENGER DOOR FOR ME, THEN GETS into the driver's side.

"Stan, please take us to the doctor's surgery on Lodge Hill Road," Sam tells the car as our seats adjust to our respective bodies.

"Why is our car Stan?" I ask him.

Sam looks across at me and laughs, as though I've made a joke. Then he sees in my face that I'm serious.

"'STAN' stands for 'Self-Taught Auto-Navigation,'" he explains. "The car can learn your regular routes and drive you semi-autonomously."

"Oh, right, I thought it was called Stan because he sounds like Stanley Tucci."

"That's what you said when we first got this car," Sam says. "You really don't remember any of this?"

I shake my head and watch Sam's face crease with concern, as though each new thing I don't remember makes this all the more real to him. He catches me looking at him and forces a smile. "I take it you don't remember this feature then," he says more brightly. "Stan, what can I cook for my gorgeous wife tonight?"

"You have the ingredients for Thai soy salmon, which you and Lucy both rate FIVE. Grocery note—you are almost out of JAM and BABY WIPES."

"Can you order more of those, thanks, Stan," Sam tells the car, then glances across at me.

"Wow. What else can it do?" I ask, my curiosity piqued.

Sam demos the car's "daily words of affirmation" feature. Stanley Tucci telling me, "I am proud of you and all you do," might not solve my current predicament, but by the time we reach the doctor's surgery, my mood does feel as though it's lifted.

DR. SHEPPERD LOOKS around Sam's age, and the two men seem to know each other. From the small talk they exchange, I conclude they play sports together, maybe mountain biking or mud wrestling, something involving mud guards in any case.

After some extensive mud guard chat, I get to tell my story, *again*, this time leaving out any mention of time travel, wishing machines, magical Scottish ladies, or any other elements that belong in the "fantasy" section at the library. I stick to the facts. I woke up and I don't remember the last sixteen years of my life. Dr. Shepperd says he wants to run some tests. He books me in for an MRI, a CTH, and an FYD. I don't know what any of those letters stand for, but it feels like a lot of letters.

"This all sounds expensive," I say, trying to impress Sam

with my money-conscious thinking after Suitgate. This is a private doctor's surgery, and in a world where a coffee costs over a tenner, I can't even imagine what a brain scan might set you back.

"Don't worry, your insurance will cover it," says Dr. Shepperd.

"Did they dismantle the NHS?" I ask nervously. *Please don't tell me they dismantled the NHS.* I'm not sure I could handle discovering anything too bleak about the future, like the end of universal healthcare, sea level rises covering half of Britain, or Piers Morgan being prime minister. If I'm going to get my head around being married with two children and missing a third of my life, I'm not sure I can handle a dystopian hellscape too.

"No, but you get private coverage through work," Sam explains.

"Did they cure cancer yet?" I ask Dr. Shepperd.

"I'm afraid not. Are you worried about cancer?"

"No. I just hoped they might have cured it by now."

Sam and the doctor exchange concerned looks.

By the end of the brain scans, reflex tests, blood tests, urine samples, an eye exam, an *extensive* mental-health survey, plus some strange nostril swab, I feel like screaming because I know they're not going to find anything, and sure enough, they don't. A second doctor, a woman called Dr. Flynn, is called in to look at my brain scan results.

"We can't see anything to worry about, Mrs. Rutherford," she tells me. "There's no signs of a bleed or any suspicious growths. You appear to be in excellent health."

Dr. Shepperd nods sagely. "There are no signs of trauma, and given your otherwise clean bill of health, we can only assume transient global amnesia, a sudden, temporary loss of memory and inability to recall the recent past." Dr. Shepperd looks to Dr. Flynn, who nods in agreement at this prognosis. I raise my hand.

"Sixteen years doesn't seem *that* recent though, does it?" I say. "Maybe in the grand scheme of tectonic plates shifting and dinosaurs roaming the earth, but in the scale of my life, it feels distinctly un-recent."

"Every case is different. I'm afraid there's still a huge amount we don't know about the brain," Dr. Flynn tells me, tapping a pen against my scan results. "The good news is, it's probably not permanent."

Probably?

WHAT IF THEY'RE right and I do have amnesia? I wonder on the car journey home. It would be a more rational explanation, but then the timing of all this, with it happening straight after I made that wish . . . and something about the machine, that woman, her knowing eyes.

Sam reaches across from the driver's seat and puts a hand on my knee. "I'm sorry this is happening to you. I can't believe how measured you're being."

"Well, I did spend thousands of pounds in Selfridges and get so drunk I fell asleep on the train, so not *that* measured." Sam smiles. "Do you think my medical insurance will cover expensive suits bought while under the influence of memory loss?"

"I don't think so," he says, glancing across at me, his eyes warm with affection. It's the same look my parents' dog, Banana, used to give me whenever I walked through their front door; he was always so pleased to see me. It makes a weight in my stomach shift because I can't remember ever being looked at like this by another human.

"How did you and I meet?" I ask Sam.

"I'm sure it will come back to you," he says, returning his gaze to the road.

"Maybe, but tell me anyway?"

He bites his lip, then runs a palm up his neck. "I could tell you anything and you wouldn't know if it was true. I could tell you we met hiking Kilimanjaro, or that you were my pole-dancing instructor."

"I don't think I've had a personality transplant. I would never willingly climb Kilimanjaro; I hate hiking—" And then in unison we both say, "Unless there's a pub at the end of it," which makes us both laugh.

"We met in a karaoke bar off Shoreditch High Street on your thirty-first birthday. I was thirty-three, on a horrible stag party, and it was the only bar that would let a bunch of guys in matching T-shirts through the door."

"I was doing karaoke?" I ask in surprise. "That feels almost as unbelievable as me climbing Kilimanjaro."

"Why? You have a beautiful voice. You were out with Zoya, Faye, and Roisin, and you got up on the stage, wearing this incredible gold minidress, then you sang 'The Promise of You' in this perfect, husky voice. It was love at first sight and first sound, on my part anyway."

"And for me?" I ask, finding myself smiling at the story, trying to imagine the scene.

"At first, you didn't want to talk to me because you were out with your friends, but you gave me your number and I called the next day. We met for enchiladas at Borough Market. Eight months later, I asked you to marry me."

"That was a bit keen," I say, making a face of mock disapproval.

"When you know, you know." He looks at me again, and in his eyes I feel the history between us, even if my mind doesn't know it. A warm hum resonates within me. I wanted to get to the good part—is Sam the good part? From what I've seen, I'd be lucky to end up with someone like him. He's handsome and kind, a hands-on father. Now, if I could just go back in time and tell twenty-six-year-old me that it's all going to be fine and she just needs to chill the fuck out, delete all the apps, and wait for him to show.

At the house, we pause in the driveway for a moment, neither of us rushing to get out of the car. "Thank you," I say, not sure what I'm thanking him for—for taking me to the doctor? For being so understanding? For marrying me? All the above? Sam reaches for my hand, then looks down at it.

"You're not wearing your wedding ring," he says.

"Oh," I say, following his gaze, seeing a lighter band of skin around the ring finger of my left hand.

"You keep it on your bedside table at night," he says, turning away from me.

"Right, I didn't know," I say.

Sam squeezes my hand. "Temporary, she said. Hopefully you'll be yourself again tomorrow."

I nod, wanting to be optimistic, but I can't help thinking that my "being myself again" means something very different to him than it does to me.

As we walk through the front door, Amy waddles toward me with outstretched arms. She's not covered in banana goo or drool now, so I don't mind picking her up. She's kind of sweet when she's not crying, with her pink flushed cheeks and her wild, curly hair.

"How did it go?" Maria asks, peering into my eyes as though she might be able to see what the problem is.

"Good. I'm fine," I tell her. *I don't remember giving birth to these children, but apart from that, perfectly fine.*

"Are you going to be all right with the kids? I'll be half an hour taking Maria home," Sam says.

"Sure. We'll be fine," I say in an overly cheerful voice.

"They had spaghetti Bolognese from the freezer for lunch, and we took Felix's scooter to the park, so they've had their fresh air and exercise."

"Great, thank you," I say, but now I feel panicked about being left alone with them. Would I have a clue what to feed them or how much exercise they need? What if Amy poos again? Can Felix go to the loo by himself? What if *I* need the loo? Can I leave them alone for two minutes or will I need to take Amy to the bathroom with me? Will they listen to what I tell them to do? What do I do if they don't? I don't feel like these are questions I can ask without alarming people.

As Sam is about to leave, he kisses me, on the lips. It's only a quick peck, but my body must have some muscle memory because I find myself closing my eyes, leaning into him, my lips following his as he moves away. Maria gives me a strange look, as though I've forgotten how to give an appropriate good-bye kiss and she's marking this down as a sure sign of insanity.

"I'm fine. I'll be fine," I reassure them, pressing my lips together.

Once they've left, Amy tugs on my hair with her plump little fists. It's annoying, so I put her down. "What do you want to do?" I ask Felix, who's looking at me like I'm ET.

The living area is one long room, with sliding doors that partition it down the middle. One side is all scatter cushions and elegant table lamps, and the other is a playroom lined with shelves full of puzzles and toys. Above the fireplace is an eye-catching watercolor of a multicolored mountain, properly mounted in a thick, gilt frame. Amy crawls off in the direction of the playroom. Compared to the cramped living area in my flat share, this room feels decadent. Kennington Lane was always cluttered with laundry racks and bicycles. It often smelled of rubbish bags waiting to be taken out and damp washing that had sat in the machine too long. Maybe middle-aged people rarely go out because their houses are too nice to leave.

I sit on the floor beside Amy, and we play a game of stacking cups. It's a simple concept that involves me stacking colorful cups on top of one another and Amy knocking them over. The way Amy purses her lips in concentration as she swipes at the cups reminds me of my mum.

"Hey, Amy, how about we make this more interesting," I say, grabbing a pen lid and hiding it under one of the cups. "Find the pen lid!" I say, muddling up the cups. "Best of three." But Amy doesn't like this game, she only wants to knock them over. As I'm looking around for something else we can play, Felix appears in the doorway wearing a colander on his head and a body shield made of kitchen foil.

"Ooh, are we playing knights and dragons?" I ask.

"It's not a game. It's to protect me from your alien brain waves."

"Right," I say slowly. "Look, Felix, the doctor thinks it's likely I have temporary memory loss. I'll probably be myself again tomorrow." Whether I believe this or not, it feels like the responsible thing to say to a freaked-out seven-year-old who's covered himself in several rolls of aluminum foil.

"What do doctors know about aliens?" Felix asks, his face puckered in confusion.

"I'm not an alien. I'm . . . I don't know what's happened to me."

Felix pauses, adjusting the colander as it's slipped down over his eyes.

"But you want to go back to where you came from?" he asks, pointing a wooden spoon toward my chest.

Do I want to go back? Yes, of course I do. However interesting this glimpse of my future life might be, I can't *stay* here. Sure, this house is amazing and my job seems incredible and that bookshelf upstairs is beyond dreamy, but I can't miss the rest of my twenties, my entire thirties; I can't just *be* this grown-up version of myself forever.

"Yes, I do," I hear myself telling Felix.

"Then we need to find the portal," he says, sitting cross-legged opposite me on the playroom floor while Amy bangs a doll against the toy basket in an alarmingly violent manner.

"Portal?"

"How you got here. What portal did you come through?" Felix walks across the playroom and takes a science fiction book from the shelf. He turns to a page and points to a big white hole. "Space is too big to travel anywhere by regular rocket, even the massive ones. If you want to travel a long way, you need a portal, or a wormhole, but they're hard to find."

"I already thought of that," I admit. "I don't think I came from outer space, I think I might have time traveled here from the past." Something in Felix's intense expression makes me want to be honest with him now. "There was this machine, a wishing machine, in this newsagent's in London. I made a wish to skip to the good part of my life, and then I woke up here."

"That will be it then, that will be the portal!" Felix says, taking the colander off his head.

"But it's gone," I tell him.

"Gone?"

"I looked for it yesterday. The shop isn't there anymore, it's a building site."

Felix slaps his book shut just as Amy falls over and bangs her head on the toy bucket. She starts to howl, so I jump up and try to comfort her. She flails her arms like an angry octopus, her little face puce with pain and frustration.

"Oh, poor Amy, are you okay?" I ask, trying to distract her with a cuddly toy, but she bats it away.

"Maybe you were looking in the wrong place," Felix suggests.

Amy is still yelling and it's such an intense sound, I can't think about anything except making her stop. I try patting her on the head like you'd comfort a dog, but that only aggravates her further.

"She likes it when you swing her from side to side and blow on her nose," Felix says, rolling his eyes. I do as he suggests, and sure enough, Amy immediately calms down enough to let me cuddle her. "Or, just because the shop's gone, it doesn't mean the machine has gone. They might have moved it. What did it look like?" Felix jumps from side to side as though preparing for a race.

"Felix, I looked. It's gone, and . . ." I pause, worried about lending too much credence to this portal theory when I don't even know the truth myself. "Just because the wishing machine is the last thing I remember, it doesn't necessarily mean it's a portal."

Felix looks deflated, and his wooden spoon drops to the floor. "But I need my mummy back. I need her help with my school project."

"Maybe *I* can help with your school project? What do you need me to do?"

But before I can coax him further, there's a warm feeling beneath my hand and an unpleasant smell fills the room.

"She's pooed *again*!" I say in disgust.

Amy gurgles in response, then says, "Poo poo," in that cute baby voice that makes it sound charming when it is anything but.

"She does that a lot," Felix tells me, a note of resignation in his voice.

Of all the things I don't feel equipped to deal with in this brave new world, wiping another human's bottom is right up there.

Armed with a clothes peg on my nose, washing-up gloves on my hands, and an apron to protect my clothes, I manage to extract Amy from her leggings, dismantle her vile-smelling nappy, and wipe up the mess with copious amounts of wet wipes. Suffice to say, it's one of the most disgusting things I've ever done, and I once sifted through a bag of week-old rubbish at work looking for a ring Melanie thought she'd lost. (It turned out it was in her ring drawer at home.) How do people bring themselves to do this nappy thing five or six times a day? Do they not realize how gross it is, or do they just get used to it, in the way prisoners must get used to prison food and sleeping with one eye open?

Having triple-bagged the offending stench bomb, I take Amy back to the kitchen, where she immediately starts crying again. "Oh, what now?" I ask her, exasperated. The emotional journey of a toddler looks like one of those balls in a pinball machine: up, down, bam, ping! Happy, sad, bam, ping, laugh, cry, bam, ping! It's exhausting, and I could really do with some downtime, a chance to regroup without anyone crying or needing me to do things.

The doorbell rings. Amy in my arms, I hurry to answer it, but when I open the door, I get such a fright I almost drop her. Hovering at my eye level is a flying robot. It scans my face with a beam of light, like something out of *Minority Report*, and my first thought is that it's been sent here to kill me. Ducking for cover, I scream, then throw a protective arm over Amy's head. But the robot simply drops a small package on the doorstep, then flies away. I turn to see Felix standing behind me in the hall. "Why are you screaming?"

"There was a flying robot!"

"A delivery drone," says Felix, shaking his head. He walks past me to pick up the package from the doorstep and hands it to me. It's a small Amazon box with "Jam and Baby Wipes" written on the contents label.

"Oh," I say, feeling foolish. "I thought it was a bad robot, not a good robot."

"You're so weird," says Felix, walking back through to the kitchen.

While I was changing Amy, Felix set himself up at the kitchen table with a tray full of loo rolls, tissue paper, and other craft items. I put Amy in her highchair so I can unpack the delivery box. Felix gets up from his chair and hands Amy a soft giraffe from the sideboard. "Neckie. He's her favorite."

"Neckie," I repeat. "Thank you, Felix." Amy starts chewing its ear.

"She loves giraffes," he says with a shrug. This detail feels important somehow, and I tuck it away in my list of what children need—food, fresh air, clean nappies, special toy giraffes called Neckie.

"So, what are you making? Is this the project for school?"

"A human heart," he says, biting his lip in concentration as he cuts out a piece of cardboard.

"A human heart, out of loo roll? Wow."

"You can use anything," he says with a shrug. "Mummy's usually great at craft stuff."

Am I? I can't help but feel proud. Then I remember he's seven—his bar for what constitutes artistic skill is probably quite low. I take a seat beside him.

"So, how I can help? Shall I look up a picture of a heart on my phone? What do you need me to do?"

Felix is quiet for a moment. Then he bows his head and says, "I need you to find the portal. I need my mummy back."

CHAPTER 13

WHEN SAM GETS HOME, HE COOKS THE CHILDREN'S dinner, then takes them upstairs to bed. I offer to help, but Sam insists I "take it easy" and "relax." It's as though he thinks if I exert myself, I might start shedding more memories. Today has been exhausting, though, so I'm grateful for the chance to retreat to the living room sofa and finally sit down.

I can't find a remote for the enormous, wall-mounted television. I don't want to bother Sam, so I occupy myself by perusing the shelves that line the living room wall. On the lowest shelf I find a wedding album, *our* wedding album. It's a curious feeling, seeing pictures of yourself doing something you don't remember, especially when all your friends and family are in the photos too. The wedding looks like such a joyful, happy day. People are beaming in every shot, especially me. *Ooh, they had the ceremony outside, beneath a tree full of fairy lights—cute.* I've never created a wedding mood board, but if I had, it would look just like this.

In one photo, Sam sits behind a piano, on a terrace, wearing a straw Panama. I am leaning on the piano looking down at him adoringly while he gazes up at me, hands on the keys. It's an arresting image because it captures this look between us, a spark that fizzes out of the photograph. I always did have a thing for musical men. I haven't seen a piano in the house, though; I wonder if he still plays. Then I realize that besides the fact that he's devastatingly handsome, that we met in a karaoke bar, and that he cooks great eggs, I know next to nothing about this man I am apparently married to.

When Sam comes downstairs, he finds me looking through a holiday album, a trip to Portugal when Felix was a toddler.

"This looks like a great trip," I say, almost guiltily, as though he's caught me snooping through his things.

"The album makes it look that way, doesn't it?" he says, running a hand through his thick, disheveled hair. "You didn't put any photos in of the two nights we spent in the hospital because Felix picked up a vomiting bug, or you on hold with the airline for three hours because they lost your bag."

"I guess photo albums never show the whole picture," I say, closing the book and looking at the perfect little family on the front cover. "Is our wedding album a curated highlights reel too?"

"Now, that was a great day. No curation required." Fondness flashes in Sam's eyes as he says it. "I'm going to make us something to eat. You hungry?"

I nod, then follow him into the kitchen, watching while he throws things into a pan. He's soon whipped up a delicious-smelling bowl of Thai vegetables, chili salmon, rice, and soy sauce. *So he can cook too.*

"Strange day, huh," I say as he hands me a bowl and we sit down at the table.

"Yes," he says with a wry smile. "Though I've probably had stranger."

"Stranger than this?" I ask, and he nods.

"When I was fourteen, I was out walking, alone. I fell over and fractured my ankle in a peat bog, miles from anywhere. I couldn't walk and it was eight hours until my dad came and found me."

"Ow," I say, wincing in sympathy.

"That was fine. It was when a grouse hen started talking to me that things got weird. Her name was Sheila. She told me at great length about all her family problems, her overprotective father and fear of guns. It went on and on." Sam bites back a smile. "I must have been hallucinating from dehydration, or exposure, but I've never looked at grouse hens the same way since."

"I have no idea if you're joking or not," I say, laughing.

"You've always said you can tell when I'm lying. I have an obvious tell, makes me a terrible poker player."

"You're not going to tell me what it is?" I ask, holding his gaze.

He leans over toward me and I'm not sure what he's about to do, but then he taps me gently on the head. "I think it's in there. I'm going to wait for you to remember that one."

The gentle confidence of his voice is so reassuring.

"What if I'm not fixed when I wake up tomorrow?" I ask, my voice suddenly quiet and serious. Sam takes my hand, but I can't read his expression. "I was thinking of calling my parents, but . . ." I trail off, biting my lip. "I wanted to check, that they're . . ." I can't even ask the question.

"They're fine," he says, moving his hand to stroke my cheek. He's so tactile with me, his tone so familiar. This sort of quiet intimacy is something I haven't been privy to before. Despite my earlier thoughts about sleeping with Sam, now even an inconsequential cheek stroke puts me on edge. I am an imposter, taking cheek strokes that are not meant for me, cheek strokes I haven't earned. Looking through all those albums hasn't helped, it's only made me feel more removed from this life I am occupying.

"Your dad had some heart issues a few years ago," Sam tells me. "He had a pacemaker fitted. Your mum's got cataracts. Other than that they're both in good health." He pauses, then adds softly, "Call them if you want. Though your mum will be in the car on her way over here before you've even hung up the call."

"Maybe tomorrow then," I say, shifting back in my chair. "Yesterday, when I spoke to my old flatmate Emily, she said we weren't friends, that we hadn't stayed in touch."

"You've never mentioned her to me." Sam frowns. "I still can't believe you went to London and tried to carry on as normal, Luce. What did you say to your colleagues?"

The memory of getting drunk and lunging at the twenty-year-old runner flashes through my mind, making me physically cringe.

"Who am I friends with now? Tell me I'm still close to my school gang—Faye, Zoya, Roisin?" Sam's eyes drop to his lap. "What?"

"Let's just see how you are tomorrow, the doctor said—"

"The doctor doesn't know what's wrong with me," I say, my voice cracking with emotion. "I went along with all those tests today because, well, it's the only logical explanation, isn't it, but nothing about this feels logical. Please, just tell me I have some friends left."

"You have plenty of friends. Faye lives twenty minutes away; you see her all the time. We could invite her over tomorrow if you like."

This is a relief. "What about Zoya, Roisin? I couldn't get through to anyone." Sam braces both hands against the edge of the table before saying, "How about we sit down in the morning, and I'll catch you up on everyone. We'll work out how to tell people what's going on." His face darkens, all the levity gone. "Today has been a lot to take in. I don't think you should try anyone tonight."

I'm not sure if he means a lot for me, or a lot for him, but I nod. I suppose I can't expect to be caught up on sixteen years in just one day.

"Will you tell me more about you?" I ask.

"Me?" Sam looks coy suddenly.

"Yes. I don't know anything about you. What do you do for work? Where are you from? Do you have siblings? Any weird hobbies or predilections I should know about, apart from a strange relationship with grouse hens?" He smiles. "I see from the wedding album you play the piano."

He shakes his head and puffs out his cheeks, perhaps still unable to compute that I really don't know any of this. Then he takes a long, slow breath, as though gearing up to respond.

"Well, I'm from Scotland originally, a small village called Balquhidder. I have two sisters, Leda and Maeve. Leda's still in Scotland, Maeve moved to America, we don't see them as often as we'd like. I work as a composer, so yes, I play the piano every day. I used to have hobbies, but now I spend my weekends running around after the kids and picking up my drunk wife from train stations." This last part makes me reach out and gently tap my fist against his arm.

"A composer? That sounds impressive. What do you compose? Where's your piano?"

"This is so nuts," Sam says beneath his breath. Then he turns to face me and says, "I used to write songs, now I mainly do scores for film and television. I have a studio at the end of the garden. You and I built it together when we first bought this house."

"I don't know what I'm more surprised by," I say, "that I helped construct a studio or that I'm married to a pop star."

"Definitely not a pop star," Sam says firmly. "I wrote songs for other people; I never performed them myself."

"You never wanted to?"

"No, I don't enjoy performing. You think it's because I'm shy, but it's not. I love writing music; that doesn't mean I have any compulsion to get on a stage."

"There's a photo of you playing at our wedding."

"That was different. That was for you, for close family and friends." He drops his gaze to the table. "Plus my leg was shaking so much I could hardly press the pedals."

"We look very in love in that photo," I say, feeling my cheeks heat as I say it.

"We were. We are." His eyes meet mine, causing the heat to spread through my entire body.

"Have you written anything I would have heard of?" I ask briskly, unnerved by this new energy between us. He pauses. "What? Why are you smiling?"

"I wrote the song you sang in the karaoke bar eleven years ago, the night we met."

"So, it was 'love at first sight' because I was singing *your* song?"

"That's not why," he says, biting his lip.

"I bet you use it as a line all the time—'Hey, you hear that song on the radio? I wrote that.'" *Am I flirting with him? It feels like I'm flirting with him.* He crosses his arms in front of his chest and it's endearing, this coyness. He clears his throat.

"That's not my style, no."

"That's what I would do if I wrote a famous song," I tell him.

"I know." Sam's eyes are dancing with amusement. "You go up to people in bars all the time and yell, 'My husband wrote this song!' It's embarrassing."

We share a look and then I laugh, because that does sound like something I would do. "I want to hear it, this song—the reason we met. Will you sing it for me?"

He pulls out his phone and searches for something. "Better you hear it sung by a professional." After a few taps, music spills out of unseen speakers that must be built into the walls. I'm about to object, to insist I want to hear him sing it, but the beat captivates me, and I pause to listen. A deep, soulful male voice is accompanied by an electronic beat and the rousing swell of classical strings—it's a unique combination.

"When did you write this?"

"Years ago. I haven't written anything as good since."

The chorus kicks in:

Like an imprint on a slept-in bed
Like words that are felt but never said
Somehow I always sensed, I always knew,
That I had the promise of you.

My skin prickles with goose bumps as the words get straight beneath my skin. Then the beat kicks back in and the violins swell, lending an ethereal, almost religious quality to the song.

"I love it," I say, and when my eyes meet his I get goose bumps again. There's something in his gaze I can't translate; sadness that I don't remember, pride that I like his song, something else intangible that makes me prickle with desire.

"Was it a huge hit? Did it make you rich?"

"It was a hit for the singer, Lex." Sam shakes his head. "I was young and naïve, I signed a contract I shouldn't have signed, so sadly no, not rich."

"Did you write more songs when you were older and wiser?"

He stops the music with a tap to his watch. "I don't write that kind of music anymore." He stands up, reaching to take my empty bowl. I was enjoying our conversation, but I sense I've said something wrong, because then he says, "It's been a long day. Shall we go to bed?"

Go to bed? Does he mean together? Talking to Sam this evening has felt like a perfect first date, and I haven't had one of those in a long time. I like Sam, I know I'm attracted to him, but now the thought of sleeping with him, even beside him, feels more complicated than I'm ready for.

"Um, do you have a spare room?" I ask tentatively.

"Sure," he says. His voice is kind, but I see the injury of rejection in his eyes. "I can sleep in the spare room."

"I'm happy to. I just, I need to get my bearings, a good night's sleep. This is all so . . . different."

"Of course. The doctors said you need to rest, avoid stress." He shoots me a smile, but now there's an awkwardness between us, the playful, flirty energy gone. Until now he was treating me like his wife, a wife who's lost her memory. Now it's as though he's finally understood the possibility that I am not her.

We go upstairs, and Sam follows me into our shared bedroom to collect his toothbrush and book. Then he gives me a tentative kiss on the cheek. As he leans in, I inhale the oaky, warm smell of him and my hands lift, almost in reflex, as though they're used to wrapping themselves around his back. But I catch them just in time, pulling my hands tight behind me.

"Good night then, Sam," I say, my voice catching in my throat.

"Good night," he says, heading out onto the landing and closing the door softly behind him.

Finally, I'm alone. Falling back on the bed, I stare up at the clean, white, dry ceiling and remember what the old lady from the newsagent's said: "Be careful what you wish for." Nothing in this life feels like mine—the nice clothes, the clean house, the attractive husband and sweet children, they all belong to someone else. I know, metaphorically, that walking in someone else's shoes is meant to be a good thing, but in reality it feels a bit icky, like chewing someone else's gum. Isn't this what I asked for? But I can't shake the feeling that I have been tricked somehow, that this is poetic justice for all my complaining. Despite the many comforts of this life, right now, all I want is to wake up back in my old bed, with my old, manageable problems. Lying alone in the dark, I find myself whispering a prayer to whoever might be listening.

"I get it, I've learned my lesson. If I could go back now, please, that would be great."

14

WHOEVER IS UP THERE DOESN'T LISTEN, BECAUSE I WAKE to the sound of Amy crying. Stumbling out of bed, I go to her room to comfort her. She needs her mother, and for now, I guess that's going to have to be me. However clueless I am about children, I need to learn how to do this, because the look on Felix's face yesterday when he said he wanted his mummy back cracked something inside me. Opening the door to Amy's room, I find Sam already there. He's wearing nothing but boxers, cuddling Amy over one shoulder and singing to her quietly.

"Oh hi, I . . ."

"I've got this. You go back to bed," he whispers.

Turning to go, I pause in the doorway to watch them for a moment. Sam is whispering a song, his Scottish lilt more pronounced when he sings. His strong, tanned arms so gentle around her tiny body, the rhythmic dip of his chest as he bobs her up and down. He instinctively knows how to soothe her in a way that I wouldn't. "Go back to bed, it's fine, she's almost asleep," he says again.

Lying in bed, listening to the sound of Sam in the next room, I feel disturbed that I found that whole scene slightly arousing. "Man holding baby" is not something I would have put on my list of things that do it for me. Man in uniform, sure. Man jumping out of his car to stop traffic so an old lady can cross the road, definitely. Man running from burning rescue shelter with a dog under each arm, yes, yes, a hundred times yes. But man holding baby? No. Never. Not once has this come up in my internal image library of things I find hot.

Trying to distract myself from these confusing thoughts, I turn to my bedside table. Two rings sit in a silver, leaf-shaped dish. They are both gold, one with a band of tiny diamonds all the way around, and the other a simple diamond solitaire. Picking them up, I admire how tasteful they are. I slip them onto my ring finger—they fit. But then an old superstition niggles—you should never wear someone else's wedding ring. Besides, it feels wrong, these weren't given to me. I quickly take them off and banish them to the bedside drawer, picking up my phone instead.

There's a new message from Michael Green.

Hope the team bonding went well, sorry I had to slip away early. I've put a meeting in your diary for Monday to discuss the Gary/Kydz Network email. I know you're confident we're doing the right thing, but if I'm honest, I've been feeling a bit sick about it all week. M

Whatever this email from Gary is about, it sounds important. I'm going to have to come clean with my colleagues. But the thought of telling them deflates me. I loved being at work on Friday, seeing what Future Me had built. Unlike the role of wife and mother, being a TV producer is not such a stretch for me to imagine. I *want* to be Queen Badger, producer extraordinaire. As soon as my colleagues know the truth, they will know I don't belong.

Despondently, I scroll through various WhatsApp chats until I come across one that I recognize: Fairview Forever. After seeing Emily's transformation, I'm nervous about discovering how much my school friends might have changed. Cautiously, I scan through recent messages. Faye sent something a few days ago, recommending a long-sleeved swimsuit for wild swimming. Before that, there was a conversation I was involved in, about whether it was acceptable for Roisin to be invited to her ex Paul's wedding. *Paul and Roisin broke up?* Though it's currently five in the morning I tap out a message to the group. I know Sam said to wait, that he would catch me up on everyone in the morning, but the lure of being less alone is too strong.

Lucy: Is anyone awake? Having a strange couple of days. Could do with seeing you all.

Faye: Of course. Barney DOES NOT SLEEP.

Who's Barney? Her child? The idea of Faye doing all this nappy-changing, banana-goo parenting stuff makes me smile. With her relaxed, earth mother vibe, she'd be so great at it.

Roisin is typing.

Roisin: I'm awake. In LA. Work trip. Drunk.
Gawwllaladshifuhf.

The message is so reassuringly Roisin, it feels like a hug
through the phone from my old life.

Faye: Why strange few days? How did your pitch go for the
bear show? Barney smashed my phone screen again so I'm
catching up on messages.

I don't plan on telling them what's happened by text at five
in the morning, it's just nice to feel their voices through the
phone.

Lucy: Pitch went well, thanks. Nothing major, just need to
see you all. Any chance you could come to my place one
night this week?

Roisin: Sounds cryptic. Last time I called a mysterious
group meet it was to tell you I was getting divorced. Tell me
it's not that, Luce?

Lucy: No! Nothing like that. Just need to see you all.

Roisin: I'm in LA until next weekend I'm afraid. Legal
conference, blah blah.

Faye: Not blah blah—you're the keynote speaker! I miss
work, I miss travel, I miss wearing non-elasticated trousers.

So many questions, none of which I can ask.

Faye: I can come over whenever—if you don't mind me bringing the sprog. Alex is away on an abseiling weekend. I know. Who the hell did I marry?

Who the hell *did* she marry? Alex. I want to know all about Alex. A new ache of loss hits me as I realize it's not just my own life I've missed, it's all my friends' lives too. Roisin got married and divorced and is now giving a keynote speech in LA; Faye is married and has a child. Who knows what Zoya is up to? There's nothing I would be shocked to hear. She could be the CEO of a huge corporation, or a barefoot painter living in the Himalayas.

Lucy: What are the chances of Zoya being able to come?

I don't know where anyone lives, whether it's too much to expect them to come to Surrey for the day, or if it would be easier to meet in London. When no one replies, I wonder if they've gone to tend to children, or in Roisin's case to the bar, but then my phone flashes: **Faye calling**. I answer with a whispered, "Hello."

"That's not funny," Faye snaps down the phone at me. "Why would you say that?"

"Say what?"

"About Zoya." Her voice breaks, and I realize I must have made a major misstep.

"Faye, I didn't want to say over text, but"—I opt for the rational explanation—"I'm having some memory issues. I know this will sound dramatic, but I woke up yesterday and I don't remember anything about the last sixteen years." Silence. Faye doesn't respond. "I'm fine, I don't have a brain tumor or anything, the doctors checked. There's just this huge chunk of time I know nothing about. I'm told it's likely to be temporary."

"Are you kidding me? What?" Faye says, her voice now laced with concern. "Why didn't you call me?"

"I did try. I spent most of yesterday having tests." I pause. There's something not sitting right about this conversation. I want to know why Faye had that reaction to my mentioning Zoya. Pulling the phone from my ear, I go back to the Whats-App group and flick to the list of members. There are only three: me, Roisin, and Faye. What could Zoya have possibly done to get excommunicated from Fairview Forever?

"Why isn't Zoya in our group anymore?" I ask Faye, my voice unsteady.

"Because Zoya is dead, Lucy." Faye takes a long, emotional-sounding breath. "And now I'm really worried about you. Are you serious with this?"

"Zoya is dead?" I ask, covering my mouth with a hand to stop a loud sob from escaping.

"You are serious. Okay, I'm coming over right now."

My hands are shaking as I hang up the call. *Zoya is dead. Zoya is dead?* It crossed my mind that I might find out one of my parents had died in the last sixteen years, but not my best friend. It can't be true, there must be some mistake.

SAM FINDS ME crying in the kitchen.

"What's wrong?" he asks, sitting down beside me.

"Zoya."

"You remember?" he asks, his voice laden with both sympathy and hope.

"No. I spoke to Faye. She's on her way over."

"I'm so sorry, Lucy. I was working out how best to tell you these things. There's already so much for you to get your head around, without—"

"How did she die?" I ask.

Sam takes both my hands in his. "A brain aneurysm, eight years ago. It came out of nowhere." He reaches to rub one hand in a circular motion on my back, as though he's soothing a child. My body slumps in the kitchen chair, and I pull my hands away to wipe my eyes.

"Did you know her?" I ask.

"Yes, I did. I got to see why you all loved her."

I think of the last thing I said to her, the last thing I *remember* saying to her, our stupid argument about being an estate agent. *This can't be how it ends.* There's a tight pain in my chest, as though my heart is folding in on itself. I can't believe it. I won't believe it. I bite down hard on my bottom lip.

"Where . . . how . . ." I grasp for something to ask. "What did she end up doing, with her life?" I ask Sam.

"She ran a travel company—taking artists abroad to paint. The landscape above the fireplace is one of hers."

Pushing my chair back, I hurry through to the living room, as though I might find her in there.

"It's Rainbow Mountain in Peru," Sam says, following me. Looking at it now, I see a small familiar signature in the corner, ZKhan. "Her first group expedition outside Europe. You were always her most devoted customer."

I hate that he knows all this and I don't.

There's a knock on the door and I brace myself to answer it. What if Faye has changed? What if I don't feel close to her anymore? What if everything I loved has gone?

But as soon as I open the door, there is Faye, holding a car seat with a sleeping baby inside. She puts it down, then envelops me in a huge hug. After squeezing her back, I pull away to get a proper look at her. There's a rush of relief when I see she is just the same. Her face is a little more lived in, there's a hint of gray at her temples, but she is intrinsically still Faye. The same ballerina posture, the same light in her eyes. If anything, the light seems only brighter.

"So, what's this all about?" she asks, picking up the car seat and walking past me, through to the kitchen. "You really can't remember anything?"

I shake my head.

"I was trying to call you," Sam tells Faye, crossing the room to give her a kiss on the cheek.

"Sorry, Barney strikes again with my phone," says Faye, then turns back to me. I'm staring down at her baby now. *I can't believe Faye has a baby.* "Don't worry, he sleeps through anything when he's in his car seat."

Looking back up at Faye, I blurt out, "Tell me about Zoya, what happened?"

"I'll go check on the kids," Sam says. Faye pats him on the back, then rubs her hand down his shoulder. There's an easy affection between them, as though they've known each other for years.

Once Sam's gone, Faye asks, "What do you want to know?"

"Was there anything anyone could have done?"

She shakes her head. "No. They said it was a massive bleed, even if she'd gotten to the hospital sooner . . ." Faye trails off. "We were in France. We all went to Cannes to celebrate her engagement. You, me, and Roisin flew home after the weekend. She stayed out there with Tarek, her fiancé. Two days later, he called to tell us what had happened. He could hardly get the words out."

Faye's eyes are welling with tears now, and I feel bad for making her relive this.

"They said it happened so fast, she wouldn't have known anything about it." Faye squeezes my hand, then reaches for her bag. "I brought some ginseng and chamomile tea, shall I make us a pot?" I nod, reassured that Faye still thinks the right tea can fix anything.

"I don't know if I really have memory loss," I confess quietly, pressing my palms against the kitchen table. "It feels like I time traveled here. I know that sounds nuts, but I made this wish to skip to the good part of my life and then I woke up here."

Faye looks at me, and it takes a minute to identify the look in her eyes—pity.

"That might just be something you remember, Luce. It doesn't mean it's cause and effect." She pauses, head tilted. "The newsagent's in Southwark?" she asks, and I nod. "I remember you telling us about that night. When you lived in Kennington Lane—the date who got naked, your shoes dissolving in the rain, the mad old Scottish lady who offered you a free go on her wishing machine. You dined out on that story for months. It was a classic Lucy caper."

A cold, numbing sensation creeps down my neck, along each limb, all the way to my fingers, and I crunch my hands into fists. *She remembers me telling her about Thursday night.* I feel nauseous. The logic of my narrative is starting to crumble, because with Zoya gone, how could this possibly be the good part of my life? And if these years happened and I forgot them, then I won't be going back. Falling in love, getting married, having children, I'll never experience any of them. Worst of all, Zoya will really be dead, I will never see her again. I won't get to say good-bye. I won't get to say, "I'm sorry."

15

GOOGLE LAYS OUT THE FIVE STAGES OF GRIEF FOR ME.
One: denial. Done. Clearly this isn't happening. Two: anger.
Have I done anger? I don't think I have. ARRRGGGHH. I
must have skipped that stage. Perhaps I'm too confused to be
angry and the anger will come later. Three: bargaining. Done.
I lay in bed last night swearing to any deity who would listen
that I would never complain about my shitty damp flat or Mr.
Finkley or not having any money, *ever* again, if only I could go
back to my real life, back to Zoya being alive. The fourth is
depression. I guess that's where I am now because I've been in
bed for three days, hiding from this scary new Zoya-less world.
Five, acceptance, feels a long way off.

I confine myself to bed, and days and nights start merging
into one long, continuous landscape of time. I sleep a lot. Sam
and the doctors think I need "time to recuperate," as though
I'm recovering from a concussion and my brain simply needs
quiet time in a dark room to heal. But it is my heart, not my
brain, that is broken.

I WAKE FROM fitful bouts of sleep, my chest contracting with a tight panic, my sheets damp with sweat. I need to call Zoya. I need to find her. Where *is* she?

My phone is the only place I can look. Scrolling back through the years, I find the very first video I have of her—it is of the four of us at sixteen, getting ready for the end-of-year social at my house.

I'm filming. Zoya is doing Faye's makeup on the bed, and Roisin is pinning up her minidress in the mirror to make it even shorter. Roisin has feathers in her hair, which makes me muster a smile, because I'd forgotten hair feathers were ever a thing.

"Guys, I'm filming. We've got to record this moment," comes my sixteen-year-old voice from behind the camera.

"What is so important about this moment?" Faye asks. She looks so young, with her round face and chunky braces. She's wearing a side fringe, which she was always fiddling with, desperate to grow out.

"Us, finishing our GCSE year," I say from behind the camera, moving toward Zoya, who waves.

"Our graduation into womanhood," Roisin says in a mockingly dramatic voice. "Our last night of purity before the virgin sacrifices." When the camera moves to Roisin, I see how much more mature she looks than the rest of us. Her body developed first, and she was taller than we were. No wonder she was able to get served in a bar at fifteen. Out of everyone, it is Zoya who looks most unchanged. Same big hair, same small body. Her skin has a few pimples, her cheeks are a little rounder, but otherwise, she looks just as I remember her.

"Who's doing a virgin sacrifice?" Faye asks, frowning, always prone to take Roisin too seriously.

"Hopefully Will Havers will be sacrificing mine," Roisin says, running toward the camera and trying to lick the screen.

"Gross, stop it, this is my dad's phone!" I squeal.

"Stop filming then," Roisin says, holding her hand up against the lens. "Pervert."

"Oh, let her," says Zoya. "She's got to practice for her big career in show business. You can interview me."

Roisin moves aside, and the camera travels across to Zoya. She stops doing Faye's makeup and sits down on the bed.

"Okay, yearbook questions," I say in the tone of a serious interviewer, and the camera wobbles as I consult the yearbook in my other hand. "When we're old, like thirty, we'll watch this back and see what we got right. First question," my voice goes on. "Which of us is most likely to be rich?"

Zoya thinks for a moment. "Faye. She'll be one of these good witches who makes her own potions. They'll blow up online and become cult products."

"I made my own perfume once," says Faye, leaning across the bed and draping her long arms around Zoya in a clumsy hug. We were always hugging one another back then, climbing on one another, sitting on one another's laps. There was zero sense of personal space.

"A *good* witch, I said, good witch," says Zoya, kissing her cheek.

"Most likely to get married?" I ask, the camera wobbling as I consult the yearbook again.

"Zoya," Roisin and Faye say at the same time, then both shout, "Jinx."

"No way," says Zoya. "I guess you, Luce, you're the most romantic."

"I might have to kiss someone first, but okay. Ooh, most likely to get divorced."

"Roisin!" Zoya says with a smile, and the camera moves to Roisin, who gives Zoya the finger. "What? You'll be like Elizabeth Taylor."

"Most likely to be a nun?" comes my voice again.

"Faye!" shouts Roisin.

"So, I'm a nun *and* a witch? I don't like this game," says Faye.

"Most likely to become prime minister," I ask.

"Zoya," Roisin and I both say together. This question hits me hard because she could have been, she could have been anything she set her mind to.

"Most likely to have kids first," I ask, and the yearbook creeps back into frame.

"You," Zoya says, her eyes intent on the person behind the camera, and it feels as though she's talking to me, here, now. "You'll marry a nice man and have two point four children. Then split your time between a quiet cottage in Devon and your glam pad in Hollywood."

"Where are you in all this?" I ask her. "I don't want to live in Hollywood if none of you are there with me."

"Don't worry, we'll all go off and do our own thing for a bit. I'll be an artist, traveling the world in a camper van. Then, when we're old, we'll dump our men and the four of us will live in a commune," Zoya says, her smile lighting up the screen.

Then my dad's voice shouts from somewhere far off, "Lucy, girls, are you ready to go?" and the camera view drops to my shoes. "Coming!" I yell. That's the end of the video.

Hindsight can be so cruel. Seeing my childhood bedroom, I think of all the hours of my life spent with Zoya—at school, at her parents' house, at mine, on nights out, hanging out at Kennington Lane. How can all that shared life just end? Where have all *her* memories gone?

As I'm scrolling through more videos, from times I can remember, Sam's face, furrowed with concern, appears around the bedroom door.

"Can I get you anything? Coffee, company?"

I shake my head and turn over in bed to face the wall. I can't face talking.

I text Michael: I'm sick again. I can't come to work.

I sleep. Sam brings me food like I'm an invalid. Downstairs, I hear life going on without me.

I DECIDE TO call my parents. There's no answer on the home phone, so I call my mother's mobile. As I wait for her to answer, a thought takes hold—I could ask them to come and get me, to take me home to my childhood bedroom. Mum could look after me, make me chocolate semolina like she did whenever I was ill as a child. Dad could light the fire in the living room while filling me in on the daily waxing and waning of his vegetable plot. The thought brings on such a wave of nostalgic longing, I clench my jaw to stop myself from crying out.

"Hello, Lucy." My mother's voice sounds distant. "You know we're in Scotland? We're out and about, if it sounds windy. Does it sound windy?"

"Scotland?" I ask, the urge to sob receding.

"We won that voucher, remember? We're staying at the

Balmoral. It's terribly smart. The Scots do know how to do a hotel."

I hear Dad's voice in the background. "We're being treated like royalty. Tell her we'll bring her back some of that rum-and-raisin-flavored fudge she likes."

"She doesn't like rum-and-raisin fudge, Bert, it's you that likes it," says Mum. "Honestly. Oh, the bus is coming. No, that one, Bert, the fifty-seven. Yes! Yes, flag it down! Sorry, Lucy, we're on the fly. Is everything okay? We're seeing you soon, aren't we?"

"Yes, I'm fine. Don't miss your bus. I'll catch up with you later."

Hearing their voices was enough.

FAYE VISITS OFTEN. She brings homemade herbal teas and my favorite Rich Tea biscuits. Mostly, we sit on my bed and watch Poirot together.

"You must have watched all these so many times, there can't be any mystery left," Faye says. I remind her that for me, that's the point.

SAM IS GIVING me space, sleeping in the spare room, occasionally coming in to get clothes, to let daylight in, and to ask if I want clean sheets. This might be a tactful, grown-up way of telling me I stink and that I should get up and have a shower. I ignore it.

Roisin video-calls me from LA. Faye must have filled her in on what's happened.

"Are you faking this to get out of something?" she asks, a

familiar teasing tone in her voice. "I remember you always faked period cramps to get out of swimming at school."

"Yes. I'm faking amnesia to get out of work," I deadpan.

"And childcare." She laughs, and I want to reach down the phone and hold her. Her laugh is just the same.

"I'll come and see you as soon as I'm back," she says, her voice softer now. "I'm sorry this is happening to you, babe." I wish she'd stuck to teasing because when Roisin starts taking something seriously, you know it really must be serious.

DURING THE DAY, when everyone is out and I have the house to myself, I spend hours inspecting my face in the mirror, looking for signs that this might be temporary, that the real me might still be in there somewhere. These hours in front of the mirror don't help my state of mind, especially when I find several chin hairs. *Chin hairs!* We're not talking downy cheek fuzz here, we're talking centimeter-long, wiry hair, like I'm a wizened old crone. Where did these come from? My neck is also upsetting me. The fine lines and wrinkles I can cope with, but my neck resembles a tent without enough tent poles; the tautness is gone. I experiment with pulling the skin up and back, searching for the familiar contours.

A youthful body, where everything looks fine without trying, is something I realize I took for granted. I've never done regular workouts, or eaten particularly healthily, but in my twenty-six-year-old body, I could always jump out of bed, even with a hangover. My face looked fresh enough without makeup and my muscles all worked exactly how I needed them to. Now when I wake up, it's not pain exactly, but there's a feeling of needing to "get myself going." There's a stiffness in my back; my brain takes a minute to fully engage with the day. Being constantly in bed is probably not helping, but the thought that I might never feel young and sprightly again makes me want to cry. I do cry, a lot. For Zoya, for the years I've lost, for the contours of my jaw.

And I know, if this was a film, I'd be complaining, "I *did not* like the main character, she was self-absorbed and defeatist and spent far too much time crying in bed. I was looking for more of a get-up-and-go heroine." And even though no one, not even Sam or Faye, is privy to the level of self-pity I have sunk to, I judge myself and my lack of resilience. Yet I can't stop. All I want is to be left alone to eat Twix bars in my pity cave.

Twix bars are now smaller, which is also upsetting me.

I THINK IT'S the fifth day of my bed-bound pity party when Faye comes into my room and opens the curtains.

"I think you should get up, Lucy. This isn't helping, you need daylight." I respond by putting a pillow over my head and groaning. "Alex and Barney are downstairs. Why don't you come and say hello? They want to see you."

Meeting Faye's husband is the last thing I feel capable of.

"I don't think I'd make a good impression," I mumble, head still beneath the pillow.

"Hey, Lucy," says a voice at the door, and I look up to see a woman with long black braids and large dark eyes standing in the doorway with a baby in her arms.

"Who's this?" I ask Faye in confusion.

"Alex, my wife," Faye says, dipping her head.

"Your *wife*? You're a lesbian? Since when?" I throw away the pillow and sit bolt upright in bed.

"Oh right, you don't remember that part," Faye says.

"I'll give you both a minute," Alex says, shooting me a sympathetic look before heading back down the corridor with her gurgling son.

Faye sits on the end of my bed, her eyes downcast, her hands clasped in her lap.

"Since when did you like women?" I ask, and she looks to the ceiling.

"Part of me always thought I might, but I never met a woman I wanted to be with," Faye says, her eyes crinkling into a smile. "And then I met Alex on this upholstery course, and it was like everything that had been missing in my life just clicked into place."

"Why didn't you ever tell me that you were into upholstery?"

Faye gives me an amused look. "I don't know. Everyone discovers themselves at different times." She frowns. "She's going to be upset that you don't remember her. I should go see if she's okay."

"Should I come and apologize?" I ask, but Faye shakes her head. "I'm happy for you, Faye. I'm sorry I didn't say the right thing. Just when I think I understand how everything is different, something else changes." I wave an arm in her direction.

"I haven't changed, Lucy. I just met someone and fell in love." Faye reaches out to stroke my hair. "Why don't you have a shower, get dressed. We could all go for a walk together. The crocuses are out, it's a glorious day."

"Maybe tomorrow."

"You can't hide up here forever. You're going to have to face life eventually." She turns at the door, then says more firmly, "People need you, Lucy."

Once Faye has gone, I try to quell a nagging sense of guilt by picking up my phone. There's a new message from Michael.

> Lucy, I know you're not well, but we really need to talk. The pitch-off is only three weeks away, and I haven't even heard your idea. Is there anything you can send over? Anything the team can be working on in your absence? M.

Pitch-off? A new hum of anxiety sets in. I shut my phone in the bedside drawer and pull the duvet back over my head.

SOMEONE NUDGES ME awake, and I open my eyes to see Sam sitting on the bed beside me, picking up my book, which has fallen on the floor. "Lucy, come on. The doctor said you needed rest, but this isn't healthy. At least come downstairs for a meal with the kids." He pauses, his eyes full of concern. "Do you even know what day it is?"

"Wednesday?"

"It's Friday, Lucy."

"I'm just so tired. I've got this terrible headache." Both these things are true. Though mainly because I stayed up all night reading *Breaking Dawn* and googling "When did Twix bars get so small?" so I'm out of sync with the world.

Sam's jaw clenches as he reaches out to feel my forehead.

"Please just let me sleep," I say, already exhausted by this conversation.

––––––

IT MIGHT BE the following morning when I wake to a small knock on my door.

"Hello?" I say, squinting toward the light coming from the corridor.

"Can I come in?" Felix asks, hovering at the threshold.

"Of course," I say, sitting up and pulling my T-shirt down to make sure I'm decent. Now when I'm not wearing a bra, my boobs droop. They're not always where I think they should be, so in company, I double-check they're fully sheathed.

"Why are you in bed? It's teatime," Felix asks, turning on the light. My eyes squint against the unwelcome glare.

"Mummy's not very well," I say, channeling Beth from *Little Women*.

"You don't look sick," he says.

"Well, it's not something you can see, it's an inside illness. Do you know what 'mental health' means?"

"Yes. We have a mental health coach at school." He pauses. "Don't you want to find the portal and go home?"

"Felix, Mummy was confused when she said that. She doesn't think there is a magic portal." I attempt a maternal smile, now channeling Marmee from *Little Women*. *Why is* Little Women *my only reference point for facial expressions? And why am I speaking in the third person? I hate it when people do that.* I try again. "I'm still me, Felix, I'm still your mother. I've just forgotten a few things."

"I've been thinking," Felix says. "If you tell me what the machine looked like, we could find out who made it. People collect these old machines, don't they? There could be more than one."

Before I can reply, he's thrust an iPad into my hand, and the screen animates with multiple-choice questions, under a golden banner than reads "Portal Quest." "You made this?" I ask, impressed.

"I do coding club at school. We're studying flowcharts and visual problem solving. Mummy said it wouldn't be hard for me, and it's not."

His confidence is contagious, and I feel a brief rush of hope. Maybe the machine *is* out there. Maybe we *could* find it. But then my rational mind kicks in.

"Even if I still *believed* there was a portal, which I'm not sure I do, the chances of me finding it and somehow being able to wind back time—it's all so improbable," I say with a sigh. Felix scuffs his shoe on the carpet, one arm swinging limply at his side.

Besides the shock of learning about Zoya, I think the reason I haven't been able to get out of bed these last few days is that doubt about how I came to be here has set in. If I no longer believe there is a portal . . . then I have to accept there's no going back.

"So you're just going to stay in bed for the rest of your life?" Felix asks, his little voice angry.

"No, I'm . . ." But I trail off because I don't know what to say. "I'm just sad, Felix."

He turns and heads for the door, hugging the tablet to his chest. Then he stops in the doorway and says, "Remember when I didn't want to go to school because Tom Hoskyns was picking on me for still liking *Corn Dogs Adventure Planet*?" He shakes his head. "*You* said, 'You have to get up and face the day, because every day is a gift, and you can't let Tom Hoskyns or anyone else steal a single one from you.'"

"I said that?"

"Yeah, you did," Felix says with a sigh. Then, before I can say anything else, he stomps off down the corridor, his shoulders hunched up on his narrow frame.

Unexpectedly, this is the pep talk I needed to push me out of my depressive funk. He's right. I'm not going to fix anything by lying here feeling sorry for myself, scrolling through old photos, watching endless Poirot episodes, and lamenting the size of chocolate bars. However I got here, here I am. I've missed a huge chunk of my life, one of my best friends is dead, and I'll never be able to go braless in public again, but it is what it is. With aching clarity, I realize that however alien this life might feel, it is more of a life than Zoya will ever get to live. That little boy needs a mother, even if it's one who's completely unqualified, who doesn't know anything about him or even what *Corn Dogs Adventure Planet* is, but I guess that's what the Internet is for.

So, I get up. I have a shower. I wash my hair and I change my bedsheets. Then I draw back the curtains and open the windows. Maria is downstairs when I emerge looking clean and almost human. She crosses the room to give me a hug.

"Oh, Lucy, you poor thing. How are you feeling?"

"Like it's time to get up."

Amy reaches for me from her high chair. "Mama!"

"She needs a nappy change," Maria says, crossing the room to get her.

"I'll do it," I say.

"You sure?"

"I'm her mother, aren't I?"

Then I thank Maria for all her help, and I send her home. She's already worked plenty of overtime this week and I'm sure she has her own life to get back to. If I'm going to learn how to do this, I need to be able to do it on my own. Maria looks torn but then admits she has a microneedling appointment she'd rather not postpone.

Once she's gone, Amy wriggles in my arms and looks up at me expectantly.

"Well, Amy, as my granny used to say, 'Life's a shit sandwich,' so best to get it over with."

CHAPTER 16

AS I FINISH CHANGING AMY'S NAPPY, ONLY GAGGING twice this time, my phone lights up. The name Coleson Matthews flashes on the screen. Coleson? Runner Coleson from When TV? Did we stay in touch? Are we friends? My thumb hovers over "decline" but then I pause, my curiosity piqued.

Answering with a tentative "Hello?" I set Amy down on the floor and watch her toddle off toward Neckie across the living room. She might do revolting things in her nappy, but she does have a cute little waddle—like a drunk penguin, swaying from side to side on slippery ice.

"Lucy, Lucy, Lucy," says Coleson. It's a knowing "Lucy," but I don't know what it is he knows.

"Coleson, Coleson, Coleson."

"You know what I've been thinking about this morning?" he asks.

"What have you been thinking?"

"How good my name is going to look on the door of your office."

His tone is gently menacing, so I stay silent, hoping he'll keep talking and give me more clues about the nature of our relationship. After an awkwardly long pause, he says, "Word on the street is that you have a *big* idea for the pitch-off. Or is this all part of your game plan to psych out the competition?"

"Word on the street?" I say, wondering how long I can get away with this echoing technique.

"Well, the shared workspace in the Caffè Ritazza next to London Studios." Coleson laughs, a slow chuckle that sounds nothing like the meek, skinny boy I used to know. "Big gamble you're taking with this 'all or nothing' approach, Rutherford. You should have accepted a merger. Look at the stats, we had eight new commissions this year. What are you at? Four? You really want to gamble your whole company on the strength of one idea?"

I'm gambling my whole company on the strength of one idea? That does sound rash.

If Coleson is my competition, I can't let him know that Badger TV is currently a captainless ship. So I try my best to match his cocky tone.

"I'm pretty confident, Coleson. This big idea of mine is pretty darn big."

"Just because I was your runner all those years ago, you think you've still got one up on me," he says, a note of bitterness creeping in. "I'm not Coleslaw anymore."

"I never called you Coleslaw."

"You didn't correct people though, did you?" He spits out the words. "Now I'm going to take your job, your team, and your office too. All that badger décor is getting covered in ferrets."

"Not if I wallpaper your office first," I say, riled by his aggressive tone.

"Well, you can't, because I don't *have* an office," Coleson declares smugly. "Ferret Productions operates a hot desk system for all staff. Ha."

"Oh really? You like working like that? Isn't that really annoying, not being able to put your stuff anywhere?"

"Yes, it is quite annoying. I have my chair set at a certain height and people keep messing with the back support."

"I hate when people mess with the back support."

We both pause, aware our rivalrous repartee has stalled somewhat.

"So did you just call for a little verbal sparring, or is there anything else I can help you with, Coleson?"

"Just the verbal sparring, thanks. Byesy-bye."

He hangs up and I shake my head in incomprehension. Coleson Matthews is my rival and work nemesis? Coleson Matthews, who barely knew how to work the photocopier, made tea in the microwave, and wasn't even aware you could pause live TV? I frown at my reflection in the bathroom mirror, then Amy's high-pitched whine slices through my ear canal, forcing me to rain-check this meeting with myself and dart off to find her.

Amy, I'm learning, is not very good at entertaining herself. Sitting on the playroom floor, I use one hand to help her with a farmyard puzzle while using the other to scroll through emails, trying to piece together a puzzle of a different kind. Searching "Gary" and "Kydz Network," I find an email from a few weeks ago. There's no text, just an attachment. When I click on it, I almost drop my phone as a lifelike, three-dimensional hologram of a man shines out of my handset. The unexpected brightness and incredible realism of the technology takes me by surprise, and I let out a gasp. Amy abandons her puzzle in favor of swiping her hand through the air, trying to grab hold of the hologram's leg.

"Morning, Coleson, Lucy," says the man, and a flashing "Gary Snyder—CEO," illuminates on the floor beside him. "As you know, since incorporating both your companies into our wider Bamph family, we've been looking to streamline development budgets. Two teams competing for the same slots is, as I'm sure you can understand, not optimally efficient. I've spoken to you both independently, and neither of you were keen on a merger. So we're going to go with Lucy's suggestion of a good old-fashioned 'pitch-off.'" My heart beats faster in my chest at the mention of my name. "Kydz Network needs a new show for their prime-time Saturday slot—it's a high-value commission. You'll both pitch directly to the channel, and the team with the best idea will get to keep their department intact. Best of luck to you both."

The hologram vanishes. Below this email from Gary, there's an exchange between Michael and me.

FROM: Michael@badgertv.com
TO: Lucy@badgertv.com

L
Do you really think this is the way to go? It's a lot of people's livelihoods to gamble on one idea. Kydz Network are re-staffing their commissioning team, we won't know who we're dealing with.
M

FROM: Lucy@badgertv.com
TO: Michael@badgertv.com

I don't want to lose a single member of my team, and I won't
work with Coleson's numpties. Don't worry—I've got a big idea
that's perfect for this slot. Trust me.
L

Trust me.

Great. So, Future Me has gambled the jobs of my entire
team on some "amazing big idea" that no one else knows about,
least of all me. I'll need to call Michael and break it to him
that however screwed he thinks we are, we're infinitely more
screwed because there is no idea, big, small, or even medium
sized. As I'm mulling the unfortunate timing of all this, a small
thought takes hold. *Isn't this what I asked for—to have my
ideas heard, to be taken seriously?* If Coleson Matthews can
do this job, surely I can—memory or no memory. How hard
can it be to come up with one great idea? These last few days,
grief has knocked me into neutral. But now, with the prospect
of doing something useful, something inside me notches into
gear. I always loved a challenge.

FELIX IS IN his room doing homework. I offer to help, but he
says he's not doing alien studies right now. Rude. He does ask
what we're having for tea though, and with Maria gone, I
guess that's now my responsibility. *Ooh, I could make my signature dish—risotto balls, everyone loves my risotto balls.*

But cooking with a toddler in tow turns out to be signifi-
cantly harder than regular cooking. I end up throwing one
batch in the bin because I burned them, then resort to letting

Amy watch cartoons on my phone to get the second batch in the oven. By the time I'm done, it feels like I've used every pan in the kitchen, and both my and Amy's patience has been thoroughly tested. Abandoning all the dishes in the sink, I take her into the hall to roll a ball back and forth, which delights her for all of two minutes before she decides she'd rather chew the ball.

"You're not in bed." Sam's voice takes me by surprise, and I turn to see him standing in the hallway watching us, a huge smile on his face.

"Yes. Sorry I've been so out of it," I say, getting to my feet.

"It's fine," he says, walking across the hall to pick up Amy, who gurgles in delight as he lifts her above his head. "Do what you need to do to get well."

"I'm not sure bed rest was helping. I think I should try and get back into my normal routine, if you could just tell me what that involves."

"Well, on a Saturday, we'd usually have friends over for a game of jetpack polo in the garden," Sam says, swinging Amy from side to side.

"Really?"

"No," he says, his expressive eyes flashing with mischief.

"Okay, some ground rules, no jokes like that—not fair on the woman with amnesia," I say, pretending to frown. "Do we really have jetpacks, though?"

"No jetpacks. Sorry," he says, then puts Amy on the floor and walks across to pull me into a hug. "It's great to see you up."

He leans forward to kiss me, but he must feel me tense because he pauses, then kisses me on the head instead. "Sorry. I keep forgetting I'm a stranger to you."

I shake my head, feeling awkward. "It's fine, sorry, it's just—"

"Don't apologize," he says, covering the sting of rejection with an overblown smile.

"I know this must be difficult for you too, and for the children," I say, then pause, pulling my hands behind my back, not sure where to put them. Seeing Sam again in daylight, I'm reminded how tall he is, what a presence he has, how perfectly his jeans fit, sitting at just the right level on his hips. "Can I ask, do you know anything about a pitch-off, something happening at my work?" I ask, drawing my eyes up from his hips.

"You can't worry about work now," Sam says with a frown. "Your health needs to take priority."

"So, I didn't happen to mention some amazing 'big idea' to you?"

Sam shakes his head. "Afraid not. If you'd written something down, it could be in your office."

"I have an office?"

"Second door on the right." He points down the corridor toward the back door.

"Okay, thanks. I might take a look later," I say, smiling up at him, resting one hand on my hip, then switching it up to put one hand behind my back. How does a normal person stand? I feel like I've forgotten.

"I'll make the kids dinner then, shall I?" Sam asks, reaching out to brush a strand of hair away from my face.

"I already made food," I tell him. "Risotto balls; they just need warming up."

"Risotto balls? Wow. That's a first." Sam looks impressed and I shrug, as though it was nothing. Then he looks me in the eyes and says, "Hello, stranger." It takes me a moment to realize he means it as a joke about the fact I don't usually cook, but the way he says it makes me feel as though he's talking to me—*the real me.*

"Hi," I say, holding his gaze. Then my stomach flutters—a spark, some kinetic burst of energy. I sense he feels it too, because his body stills and he doesn't look away. Whatever this feeling is, it's both unnerving and oddly familiar. I don't know what to do with it, or how to respond, so I turn to walk away.

"Um, I just need to talk to Felix, if you're okay to watch Amy," I say, heading for the stairs, suddenly self-conscious about how I'm walking. *Am I strutting? Is this my normal walk?*

"Sure," says Sam, exhaling heavily, before picking Amy up off the floor.

As I walk up the stairs, I need to hold the banisters to steady myself, because my whole body now feels charged with an undefinable tension. Why am I being so awkward and weird? Then it dawns on me. *This is how I get when I have a crush on someone.*

17

FELIX IS SITTING ON HIS BED, READING AN ENCYCLOPE-dia. I know I've upset him, and I need to fix it.

"I'm taking your advice—I'm not letting Tom Hoskyns or anyone else steal a day from me," I say, and he gives me a grudging smile. "There's food downstairs if you're hungry."

"Will you look at my Portal Quest now?" he asks.

"Sure," I say, humoring him. I sit down on his bed and he eagerly hands me his tablet. The first screen asks, "What does your portal look like?" It then takes me through a series of questions about the machine's size, color, lights, and functionality. Once I've answered the final question, a graphic appears—a rudimentary digital sketch of the wishing machine. It looks like it's been drawn by a child, which, of course, it has.

"Is that what it looks like?" Felix asks, bouncing his bottom up and down on the bed.

"Yes, that's it," I say, trying to be diplomatic.

"Now we just need to put it online. Someone will see it,

someone will know where we can find one." He pauses. "I made a list of possible websites, forums that arcade game collectors use." He opens another tab on his tablet. "You have to be over eighteen to post on them, though."

"Thanks for doing all this, Felix, but could I look through the list tonight, when I have time to research it properly?" I don't want to rain on his parade, but I doubt even the most avid collector would be able to identify the machine from this sketch. "Do you want me to help you with your school project?" I nod toward the cardboard heart sitting on his desk.

"I want it to work. How would you make it work?"

"I'm not sure you're going to be able to make a beating heart out of loo roll, but we can probably make it look a little more heart-like." My eyes cast around the room, falling upon a red squishy ball by the door. "Look, this could be the center, then we could cut and glue the loo rolls to make the tubes narrower, then they'd be more in proportion."

Pulling up a bean bag, I sit down beside his desk.

"There needs to be a pulmonary artery, the aorta, the superior vena cava, and the inferior vena cava," Felix says, pulling out his child-sized desk chair.

"I'm impressed you know all those words."

"They were in the encyclopedia you gave me for Christmas."

Searching through a jumble of craft material in his desk drawer, I pull out some glue and blunt-tipped scissors. Felix watches as I get to work, cutting the tubes in half and rolling them smaller, then shaping the ends so they'll sit flush against the ball.

"Do you get a lot of homework like this?" I ask him. He

shrugs again but now he is watching intently and doesn't object when I take scissors to his red ball.

"There's an end-of-year project fair," he tells me. "The best projects go on display for the whole school to see. There are judges and everything. Last year, me and Mummy made this epic volcano, but when I took it in to show my class, I couldn't get the lava to bubble up the way we made it do at home." He pulls the sleeves of his jumper down over his hands.

"Well, we can only try our best," I say, then realize I've just used a phrase my dad often said to me. Do these phrases sit dormant in our minds, just waiting to be deployed when we become parents ourselves?

Felix follows my instructions and helps glue all the component parts back together. When we're done, I wipe my sticky hands on my jeans and stand back to admire our handiwork. It's a jumble of ball and cardboard, but I think I could identify it as a heart if I had to guess. "There. What do you think?"

Felix stares at it, and I can't read his expression at all. When he finally looks up at me, I imagine he's going to fling his arms around me, thank me for not having lost my amazing crafting abilities, and tell me it's exactly what he wanted it to look like. But he doesn't. He doesn't say anything. He just stands up, picks up my heart, and throws it into the wastepaper bin on his way out of the room.

MY COOKING SKILLS go equally unappreciated. Felix deigns to try a risotto ball, then proclaims it "tastes weird" and is "too spicy," and asks, "Why can't we have fish fingers?" Amy won't even try the risotto balls. She squishes one in her tiny palm, then flings it across the room, where it lands with a splat on the floor by the fridge door.

"Those took me ages," I say despondently. I once made fish cakes for my flatmates; they were dry and full of bones, but everyone at least had the decency to *pretend* to like them.

"Delicious," says Sam, taking a risotto ball from the plate and popping it into his mouth.

"Do they usually like my cooking?" I ask him quietly.

"Sorry to break it to you, but no. Amy will usually try things, but Felix is pretty committed to beige freezer food right now. His journey into food exploration has stalled on the foothills of Mount Birds Eye."

A squabble breaks out between Felix and his sister because Amy wants the green mug that Felix is holding. The tussle sends the contents of the mug spilling all over the table.

"I'll get you another mug, Felix," I say, rolling my eyes.

"You always take her side!" Felix yells, watching Amy chew on his now empty mug.

"I'm not taking anyone's side. She's slobbered all over it, do you really want it back?" Wow, children fight over the most ridiculous things.

"You always let her take my stuff!" Felix wails. *Maybe he's right, it was his mug.* I try to take it back from Amy, but she clings on to it like a freakishly powerful giant pink leech.

I try negotiating with her. "I'll get you another mug, Amy, a better mug." Then there's a sharp pain in my finger that forces me to let go. "She bit me!" I cry indignantly, clutching my index finger.

"Amy—don't bite," Sam says, trying to intervene, but then Amy starts wailing at his stern tone and he picks her up, trying to comfort her with a shushing noise. Inspecting my finger, I can see *actual* tooth marks in the flesh.

"Dad *always* takes her side," Felix says, patting my arm in an unexpected display of sympathy.

The sink is still full of pans, the floor is covered in smashed risotto balls, and Amy won't stop howling. How can one meal create so much drama and mess?

As I'm lamenting the failure of my first afternoon parenting, there's a noise outside and Sam walks across the room to look out of the kitchen window.

"Someone's here," he says. "Shit, it's your parents."

"Daddy!" says Felix.

"Sorry. I mean, shoot, it's your parents, Lucy."

"My parents?" I ask.

"Yes," he groans. "With everything going on, I forgot—they're staying the night with us on their way from Scotland to some literary festival." He glances at the digital family planner on the wall, where, beneath today's date in a large font, are the words "M&D to stay."

I'm going to see my parents. Sam stands beside me at the sink and we watch Dad emerge from the passenger side. He looks smaller, more stooped. He's wearing a cap, so I can't see his face.

"Margot will be upset I haven't called to tell her what's happened," Sam says, biting his lip.

"I called them a couple of days ago. I didn't want to worry them."

"You know your mum will want to move in if she thinks you're having a major life crisis."

"I *am* having a major life crisis," I say.

Mum gets out of the driver's side. She's got her anorak

hood up, but she's got the same gait, the same ramrod posture. My heart swells with gratitude that they are both still here, still healthy.

"I know." Sam rubs his chin with the heel of his palm. "I just don't think I can handle your parents staying with us for more than one night, not right now."

"Let's not tell them, then. I don't want them to cancel their trip. We'll tell them when they get back—if I'm still . . . you know."

Sam puts an arm around my shoulders and kisses me on the head. I feel a brief, heady rush at the firm clasp of his hand, then hear the familiar voice of my mother calling "Cooeee!" through the letter box.

MUM MARCHES INTO the kitchen and waves an arm in greeting before heading straight for the kettle. "Hello, hello, don't mind me, you know I like to make tea my own way. Goodness, what a mess in here. Feeding time at the zoo, is it?"

Her hair is short, and I can't stop looking at it. She always said she'd never cut her hair, that it was "terribly aging," that cutting it would "feel like giving up." Practically her entire life, she's worn her hair long, salon highlighted, set in curlers each night to retain the volume. Now it's short and gray and sticking out in wild tuffs. There is something so familiar about her new look, and then it dawns on me—she looks just like her mother, my gran.

"You cut your hair," I can't help saying as she takes off her anorak and greets me with a firm kiss to each cheek.

"Have I? No, it's a haystack. I haven't been to the hairdresser's in months," she says.

"You cut it short, I mean." But she's distracted by the children now, leaning down to greet Amy and finding Felix hiding underneath the kitchen table.

Part of me is waiting for her to look at me, to notice the change and then scream. But she doesn't, she doesn't see me at all. Glancing out of the window, I see Dad showing Sam a scratch on his car bonnet. Sam nods in sympathy, then reaches out to give Dad a pat on the back.

"Have we arrived at an inconvenient time?" Mum asks. "I told your father we should have left earlier, we hit the M25 at the worst time. He's impossible to get out of the house these days, we had to go back twice to check he'd turned off the car port."

Dad comes through to the kitchen and takes off his cap. I allow myself a moment to absorb the changes in him. His hair has gone from salt-and-pepper to entirely white. His face looks ever more lived in, softened and worn. He looks like a granddad, and then I realize that, of course, he is one now. Despite all the subtle changes to his physical appearance, his voice and smile are the same and he radiates a familiar, comforting sense of "Dadness."

"We brought you some tablet from Scotland," he says, handing me a brown paper packet.

"I'll get the kids into their pajamas," says Sam, scooping up a child in each arm, making them squeal in delight as he spins them around on his way to the door. "Then maybe Granny and Granddad can read you a story."

Now that they're both here, I lunge across the room and wrap an arm around each of my parents. "It's so good to see you. I'm so glad you're here, I love you both so much."

As a family, we're not prone to overt displays of affection.

My flurry of emotion causes Mum to pull away and eye me with suspicion.

"What's wrong? Are you sick?" she asks.

"I'm not sick. It's just nice to see you both," I say, wiping an eye with the back of my hand.

"Are the children sick?" Mum asks, her voice now an urgent whisper. "You're not getting *divorced*, are you?" She clutches her chest, and I shake my head.

"You sounded like you are about to tell us bad news. I'm not sure I can take any more bad news this week." She presses her fingertips together, making a spire with her hands, a gesture I must have seen her make a thousand times. "Yesterday, the gardener told us that the beech hedge is dead, the whole thing will have to come out. Then we found out the Grievesons are moving. 'Downsizing' apparently, though I'm sure they wouldn't need to if only they went on fewer cruises. Such a disruption, moving at our age. If you're going to downsize, you do it in your sixties, everyone knows that. Quite extraordinary behavior."

"Extraordinary," Dad says, giving me a sly wink.

Dad excuses himself to use the bathroom, and as soon as he's out of the room Mum starts talking in a whisper.

"It's blow after blow. I'm *extremely* worried about your father."

"Oh?" I whisper back.

"Memory issues," she says, tapping her head. "My side of the family were all sharp as tacks well into their eighties, but your father's side has a history of early mental decline. He's forgetting everything, Lucy—he left his car keys in the vegetable aisle of Tesco's last week. It was lucky someone didn't drive off with the Peugeot. They would have found a lovely topside of butcher's beef in the boot. Then on Thursday I asked him where the book I was reading had gone—the twentieth Richard Osman, special edition, no less. Bert tells me he's taken it back to the library. It wasn't even a library book for goodness' sake! What am I to do? You know how he is about doctors. There are things you can do these days, supplements, electroconvulsive therapy, but he won't acknowledge he's going doolally."

"None of that sounds too major, Mum," I say tentatively. "I think it's normal to be a little absentminded at your age."

"Will you talk to him? He listens to you." We hear the shuffle of Dad's footsteps in the hall, and Mum quickly changes the subject. "The gardener thinks we should put a fence up, says it will be easier to maintain, but you know my feelings on fences. What would the neighbors think? It would lower the tone of the village. No, no, we'll have to replant the whole hedge at vast expense. We'll be dead and gone before anyone sees the benefit, but at least we won't be letting the side down."

"Are you *still* talking about hedges?" Dad asks. "Honestly, you'd think it was a person who'd died, the wailing and the gnashing of teeth this beech hedge has caused."

"When you live in an area of outstanding natural beauty, you have an obligation to maintain certain standards," says Mum. "Our garden can be seen from the road. Remember when Tilda Stewart-Smith started experimenting with garden gnomes? It was a most delicate situation for the village committee. Poor Tilda, so sensitive, so lacking in taste and judgment."

"I don't see the issue with a fence," Dad says. "I found a cheap one online. I could erect it myself."

"Said the actress to the bishop," I say, leaning into Dad

with an expectant grin, but he only looks at me blankly. *He can't have forgotten, surely?*

"Dad? Our silly joke, remember?"

"Ah right, very good." Dad smiles back at me, but his eyes look blank. Mum tilts her head at me, as though to say, "See what I mean," and now I know I really can't burden her with my situation too.

As I take them both through to the living room, I'm half expecting them to comment on the house, on the décor, how stylish it is, what an upgrade on Kennington Lane, but of course they don't.

"Now, darling, are we still planning on doing an . . . event?" Mum pauses, her face suddenly somber. "For Chloe, next month." *Who's Chloe?* I don't know, so I give a noncommittal nod. "Because we're keen to help mark the occasion, however difficult it may be." Mum pauses, reaching out a hand to touch my knee.

"Who's Chloe?" Dad says, and I want to kiss him for asking the question I can't.

I look to Mum to answer, then I see that she's tearing up. Mum never cries.

"I'm so sorry, Lucy. He's awfully muddled."

"I am not muddled," Dad says, scowling at her.

"Look, I know no one likes to talk about these things, but I think it's better to have things out in the open. If you can't recall basic information—that's going to have a knock-on effect on all of us," Mum says, just as Sam walks down the stairs with an armful of laundry.

"You told them?" Sam says in surprise, and before I can respond, Mum is sitting bolt upright, head darting from left to right like a meerkat on high alert.

"Told us what?"

"About Lucy's memory," Sam says.

"Lucy's memory? I was talking about Bert. What's wrong with Lucy's?"

"Oh," says Sam sheepishly, giving me an apologetic look.

"Lucy?" Mum asks, splaying her fingers and pressing them to her lips.

"We didn't want to worry you unnecessarily—" I say, but Mum interrupts me.

"I knew it, I knew you were ill! Your skin is so sallow, your cheeks are all puffy. You're on steroids, aren't you? Is it cancer? Tell me it isn't cancer."

"I'm not ill," I say, holding up a palm to stop her from talking. "I've just had some trouble remembering recent events. Temporary amnesia, the doctor says—"

"Amnesia? This is your side, Bert," Mum says sharply to Dad. "We'll have to cancel our trip. We'll have to stay and help. Sam can't be expected to cope with all this alone. Just look at the state of the kitchen!"

Sam bites his lip, but I can see the agitation in his hands as he slowly clenches and unclenches his fists. "We're managing, honestly, Margot."

Mum is pacing now, wringing her hands like a character in a Jane Austen novel who's just learned the regiment is about to leave town.

"There must be something we can do to help," she says.

Sam looks at me, a glint in his eyes as he says, "There might be something."

CHAPTER

18

"DATE NIGHT. YOU'RE A GENIUS," I SAY AS WE SLIDE ONTO two barstools in a dimly lit pub called Polly's on Farnham High Street.

"Your mother's biggest fear, after illness, is marital discord. She's a firm advocate of date nights to stave off a relationship's decline."

"She is?" *This is news to me.*

Sam had a shower and changed into a clean shirt before we came out. The hair at the nape of his neck is still slightly damp and I resist an inexplicable urge to reach up and sweep it away from his collar.

"Your mum and dad went to couple's therapy a few years ago," Sam says. "Now they do date night twice a month and we get regular updates in the family WhatsApp."

"My parents went to a couple's therapist? I can't compute them spending money on something like that."

"They won vouchers in a raffle," Sam explains while scanning the bar menu with his watch. "Do you want a French martini? That's what you usually have here."

I don't even know what a French martini is, but I nod, deferring to my future self's taste in alcoholic beverages. As Sam orders, I look around the bar, reassured by how familiar this pub seems. Pints are still pints, pub carpets are still inexplicably hideous, and drunk old men are still there, still trying to chat up the disinterested barmaid.

"Bars haven't changed much, have they?" I say.

"What were you expecting, robot bartenders?"

"Yes," I say, laughing, "I want robots and anti-hangover drinks."

"Oh, we have anti-hangover drinks," Sam says.

"Really?"

"Yes. They're called soft drinks."

"Oh, ha ha," I say, elbowing him gently while the barmaid passes our drinks over the bar. "That's a real dad joke."

Sam lifts his pint to my cocktail glass. "My specialty. Cheers."

There's something about Sam's posture, his body language, that tells me he's comfortable in his own skin. I wonder if he has always been this way, or if this stillness is something people grow into.

"I'm sorry I've been so out of it this week."

"There's been a lot for you to get your head around. I'm just glad you're feeling better now. Oh, before I forget, Amy's got this rash, so you need to put cream on after every nappy change, it's the blue tube on the changing table. Felix has got an away game at school on Monday, so he needs—"

"Do you mind if we don't talk about the children tonight?" I ask, gently resting my hand on his arm. "I want to get to know you, Sam. I hardly know anything about you . . ."

"Right." Sam lifts his eyebrows, tilting his head to one side. "Well, this might be one of the strangest conversations I've ever had, but okay. What do you want to know?"

"Everything," I say, hearing a flirtatious note in my voice that I didn't plan on being there.

"*Everything* might take a while."

"The headlines, then."

"On our first date you asked me a series of quick-fire questions. You said it was the most efficient way of uncovering any red flags."

"Sensible," I say, feeling myself smile. "And did I uncover any?"

"A few orange ones. I smoked at the time and you hated that. You didn't like that I was a musician either."

"Oh? Why not?"

"You'd dated a drummer and sworn off us for good."

"But you won me over."

"I won you over."

His mouth is so expressive, I can't help watching it as he talks. He's got this broad smile that shows in flashes. When he grins, it's like a chain reaction spreading out across his face as the smile ripples into dimples in his cheeks, then creases around his eyes. He rubs his stubbled cheek with a hand, as though conscious of my gaze.

"Tell me more about your family, where you grew up in Scotland," I ask him.

"Well, we lived on a farm, four miles from the nearest village. My dad was a farmer, my mum was the local postie. My best friend was a mangy sheep called Patrick."

"Who's your best friend now?" I ask.

"You. Luckily you smell better than Patrick."

"I should hope so," I say, feeling myself grin as I twist a piece of hair around one finger.

"I only ever told you about Patrick because you told me about Lisa."

"I told you about Lisa?" I swivel my barstool around toward him. Lisa was my imaginary friend, who lingered far longer than imaginary friends are supposed to. "I must really like you. I've never told anyone about Lisa."

"You really like me," Sam says. He catches my eye and now it feels as though he is flirting with me. I force myself to sit on my hands to stop myself from fiddling with my hair.

"Apart from my obvious sheeplike qualities, what did you like about me then, when you first saw me in that karaoke bar?"

"Well, I thought you were gorgeous, that goes without saying. But there was the way you held yourself, how you were with your friends, the way you sang my song. You sang it the way I always wanted it to sound." We bump knees, and when he looks at me, I feel a warm pull, like an invisible elastic band drawing me in. The woman he's describing doesn't sound like me. Shifting on my seat, I realize I'm fiddling with my hair again, so I reach for my drink instead. This French martini really is delicious, and I congratulate Future Me on her taste in both men and cocktails.

"And what did I like about you?" I ask, looking up at him from beneath lowered lashes.

He leans in slowly, then says, "I don't know. Maybe when you remember, you'll tell me." As he gets closer, I sense his warm, oaky smell, the hint of minty shower gel and freshly pressed linen.

"Okay, some quick-fire questions, then, for old times' sake,"

I say, clasping the bar to stop myself from leaning into his neck. "Favorite place?"

"Our garden."

"Favorite song."

"'Giuseppe' by Grange."

"That means nothing to me. Did we sleep together on our first date?"

Sam clears his throat, and I realize how attractive I find him when he gets slightly embarrassed. "That depends on what you define as our first date. Plus, I don't think it would be gentlemanly of me to say." I look up at him now and catch the flush of pink rising up his neck.

"I'll take that as a yes. Why don't you write songs anymore?"

While I was wallowing in bed, I googled Sam. I listened to all the songs he's ever been credited with writing and discovered he hasn't written anything with lyrics in over five years. He shifts in his seat. "That's not a quick-fire answer. Can I pass on that one?"

"Fine, you get one pass. What's your favorite memory?"

"With you, or from life in general?" Our knees are touching again, and his forearm skims my hand on the bar.

"Either," I say, and he ponders this for a moment.

"Do you want one of my favorite childhood memories?" he asks, and I nod. "It's not a quick one."

I press an imaginary button in the air between us. "Pausing quick-fire round."

He takes my hand and moves my finger to another point in midair.

"Here's the fast-forward button if I'm boring you." My cheeks begin to ache, and I realize I've been grinning since we sat down. "Okay, so I'm four years younger than Maeve, so for most of my childhood my sisters just saw me as the little kid they didn't want tagging along. Most of the time when they went out to play, I was left behind, but the summer I was six, there was this brief window of time where they let me be in their gang. They built me a den in the woods. Sam's Shack, they called it. Leda made a wooden sign with a soldering iron. Maeve hung a tire swing and cooked corn fritters on the camping stove. We played out there every day of the holidays. Then Maeve went to secondary school and neither of them wanted to play in the woods after that. But I had that one perfect summer."

Picturing Sam as a little boy, playing with his sisters in the woods, being so happy to be included, makes my heart swell for him.

"Are you still close with them, your sisters?" I ask.

"Leda more so—we speak on the phone most weeks." He shifts in his chair, then takes a sip of his pint. "What's your favorite childhood memory? You know, I don't think we've ever had this conversation."

"Me?" I try to think. I'm an only child, so I don't have any sibling memories to call upon. "I don't remember a lot of details about my childhood, but I remember it being happy. Summers sitting on the grass making daisy chains, watching my dad endlessly tend to his vegetables." I pause, remembering Dad's blank face when I told him our joke. "Do you think my dad's okay? Mum's worried he's forgetting things."

Sam reaches out to squeeze my knee. There is something so reassuring in the gesture, beyond anything he might be able to say.

"Okay, I have one," I say, keen to steer us back to lighter

conversation. "It was coming up to my tenth birthday. Every day on the way to school, Mum and I would walk past this fancy bakery. There was this cake in the window, and I would stop and point it out every time we passed—it was the cake I wanted for my party. It was a rich mocha gâteau with liqueur icing, totally inappropriate, but I just loved the look of it. I wanted it *so* much. It looked like a cake from a picture book, something you might draw. Mum said, 'No, that's not a cake for children.' I kept asking, saying I'd forgo all other presents if I could only have this cake, but still she said no. Then, on the day of my party, she walked out of the kitchen with it, this cake from the bakery. None of my friends would eat it—they thought it was disgusting, she actually served this alcoholic cake to all these ten-year-olds." I laugh. "But I loved it. I was the best birthday cake I've ever had."

Sam reaches out and takes both my hands, knitting his fingers between mine.

"You've never told me that story before."

"Haven't I?"

"No." Our knees meet again, and now I am sharply aware of every part of my body that is in contact with his.

We talk for hours, telling each other stories from our lives before, from the times I can remember. Sharing these stories, I can be myself, I don't have to try to hide what is missing. We order more drinks and move to a booth near the back of the bar. Sam is funny, interesting, and attentive. This has to be the best date I've ever been on. Unlike all the weird, self-involved twentysomethings I've been out with recently, Sam is delightful company. He's mature, handsome, and engaging. He really listens when I talk, and the way he looks at me, with this unfiltered affection—it ignites something inside me I didn't even know was there. As an added bonus, I can be confident he's not going to suddenly admit to having a crisp-eating fetish, or holding any alarming political views, because he's already been thoroughly vetted, *by me.*

When I tell him the story about the bones in the shower, he lets out a deep, unfiltered laugh that makes everyone in the bar turn to try to see what's so funny. Sam's eyes settle on mine as he says, "We never do this anymore, just the two of us."

"Why not?" I ask. Then I feel him reach for my hand beneath the table and slowly circle a finger around my palm. It's sexy as hell.

"I don't know. We're always so busy, or we're socializing with friends, making plans, doing admin. We never make time to just chat and tell each other stories. I love your stories. I have always loved the way you tell stories."

His finger on my palm feels exquisitely torturous in its limitations, and I can't focus on what he's saying. I lean in and kiss him, right there in the bar. At first, I feel his surprise, but then he responds, moving a hand up my neck into my hair, kissing me back. His lips are firm yet soft, hot and—

"Let's get out of here," he says, his voice now a husky whisper.

We stumble out onto the street, laughing like teenagers. His hands are on my waist, but I need them to be all over me. Pushing him against the wall of the bar, I lean in to kiss his neck.

"You're so hot," I say into his warm skin, running a hand down his thigh. "How did I end up with someone like you?"

"We're in the street, Lucy. Someone will see us," he says, his deep voice rasping slightly, and I can feel he wants me too.

Sam orders us a cab, and one arrives in minutes.

"I really thought we'd have driverless cars by now," I tell him between kisses as we make out like teenagers in the back seat.

"We did have them," Sam says. "But then there was a legal battle over this patent, and they were all taken off the roads until—"

"Okay, never mind," I say, needing him to kiss me more than I need him to explain why driverless cars aren't part of the future yet. As soon as we get back to the house, I grab Sam's shirt collar and lead him upstairs. We're trying to be quiet, but we're drunk and giggling loudly as we kick the door closed behind us.

IT'S A STRANGE experience, sleeping with someone who knows my body, someone who knows what I like—who knows things I didn't even know that I liked. I'm drunk enough not to care that my parents are in the house with us, and at one point Sam has to cover my mouth and say, "Lucy, shhhh," in this stern voice, which, honestly, only turns me on more.

Afterward, I sit astride him in a heady daze, running a finger down his broad, firm chest. "Is that how we usually do it?" I ask.

"Not usually that loudly," he says, putting a hand on either side of my hips. I rock my pelvis against him, unable to stop smiling. "What's gotten into you?" he asks, staring up at me and slowly shaking his head.

"I woke up and found I was married to a complete hottie."

He flips me over so I'm lying on my back and he's on top of me, which makes me squeal with laughter.

"Maybe there are some advantages to you waking up and thinking you're twenty-six again, Mrs. Rutherford," he murmurs in my ear.

Twenty minutes later, as I'm lying in our big, beautiful bed, with Sam's strong arms wrapped around me, I feel an overwhelming sense of contentment. Sure, it's not ideal that I've missed sixteen years of my life, but this situation certainly has its advantages. I'll never need to have bad sex ever again or wear cheap footwear that dissolves in the rain. The shower pressure in the bathroom is to die for. Zoya would scream if she saw the size of it. *Zoya.* All my contentment dissolves, like a hand gently shredding a spiderweb. *How could I be happy when she is not here? How could anything in my life be good when she is not there to share it?* I wonder if Future Me felt this way too, or if she had learned to live with this gaping absence.

Sam strokes my hand, and I try to think of something else.

"Did you find your rings?" he asks.

"Oh yes, I'm keeping them safe in there," I say, pointing to the drawer.

He leans across me to open it, feels for the rings, then holds up my hand and gently threads them onto my ring finger. "Safest place for them," he says, turning his head to kiss my neck. I close my hand, trying not to mind. My eye darts to the dresser, where there's a framed photo of Felix and Amy sitting on a picnic blanket in a woodland glade. I think back to the story Sam told me about playing with his sisters in the wood. There's more than a six-year age gap between Felix and Amy, so I don't expect they'll ever be close in that way.

"Why did we wait so long to have a second baby?" I ask Sam, and his hand stops stroking mine. "Six years feels like a long gap."

Sam's whole body goes rigid.

"Oh, love," he says, and his voice is full of so much unexpected emotion it makes me sit up in bed.

"What?"

"Let's not talk about that now. We've had such a lovely evening . . ." He trails off. "Can we save it for the morning?" There's a finality to his tone, and he swiftly scoops me into a spooning position, wrapping his arms around me. It's a novel feeling to be held so close, to be so warm and entirely cocooned by another body. I don't think I'll be able to sleep like this though, I'm too used to spreading out, to sleeping alone. "I love you, Lucy," Sam says in my ear. I feel I should say it back, to recenter whatever tonal shift I created, but I don't. Even though we've had the most wonderful evening, I've only known him a few days. How could I possibly love him?

As soon as he's asleep, I quietly slip out of his arms, take off the rings, and return them to the bedside drawer. Then I crawl into the other side of the bed, more comfortable sleeping alone than in someone else's arms.

CHAPTER 19

"WELL, I THINK WE CAN ALL ASSUME 'DATE NIGHT' WAS a success," my mother says tightly over breakfast, shooting me a disapproving look. "I'm surprised you didn't wake the children."

"Mum, please," I hiss, hearing Sam on the stairs.

"I suppose it's reassuring. If your marriage is strong, you can survive anything. You've been through worse."

Have I? Before I can ask her what she means, Sam appears at the kitchen door.

"Morning, Margot," he says. "Sleep well?"

Mum clears her throat, then takes a loud sip of her coffee. "Adequately, thank you."

Sam has been in a strange mood since he woke up. Maybe, like me, he's a little hungover. He opens the fridge, closes it, opens it again, stares at the contents for a minute, then closes it one final time before turning back to Mum and me. "Something has come up," he says, his face serious. "There's this recording session in Manchester tomorrow, with a full orchestra, it's been scheduled for months. What with everything going on here, I'd asked a colleague to stand in for me, but he just messaged to say he's sick." He pauses. "There's no one else, and I'd be letting a lot of people down if I don't go."

"Of course you should go!" Mum says. "We can stay and help Lucy."

"I don't want you to miss your festival, Mum, I'll be fine," I say.

"Maria will be here to help first thing tomorrow, but I wouldn't be back until Tuesday morning," Sam says, looking at me hopefully.

"We'll stay until the morning," offers Mum. "Most of the talks don't start until midday anyway."

"What do you think, Luce?" Sam asks me.

"Of course I can manage," I say, feeling insulted. "Honestly, you don't think I can cope for less than forty-eight hours with the help of grandparents, a nanny, school, and nursery?" Mum and Sam exchange glances. "I am a competent adult, I'm not thirteen."

Mum clears her throat. "You seem entirely compos mentis to me."

Sam combs a hand through his hair, his face serious.

"Fine. If you're sure you don't mind staying, Margot? There's a list on the fridge of anything you might need, Maria knows it all anyway." He pauses, looking at me again. "I'll need to get the train up there this morning so I have time to prepare."

"On a Sunday?"

Mum is sitting right here, so I don't expect Sam to be all over me, but I can't help feeling that he's being slightly off this morning. His body language certainly isn't saying, "I got laid last night and it was pretty awesome." Does he regret how drunk we got? Is he embarrassed by how loud we were? I try to convey in a smile that I don't regret a thing. I want that delicious buzz of flirtation back, but then Amy toddles in, chased by my dad holding a puppet badger, and when I look around, Sam has left the room.

Amy grabs my legs for safety, and I lift her onto my lap, where she snuggles into my chest, her whole weight falling against me. She pushes a hand up beneath each of my arms, nuzzling her head into my chest like a baby koala. It's a unique feeling, being hugged by a child—my lap her refuge from everything scary. It feels like a big responsibility to be that to someone. I wonder what age I stopped crawling into my mother's lap for comfort. Inhaling Amy's sweet, milky smell, I hug my arms around her soft little thighs and bury my face in her hair. It's calming, the gentle pressure of her, this unhurried cuddle that has no agenda, except a desire to be as close to me as possible.

Dad volunteers to drive Sam to the train station, but I manage to grab Sam alone at the door before he leaves.

"So, last night was fun," I say, shooting him a cheeky grin while reaching for his hand.

"Yeah, it was," he says, a brief, guilty look crossing his face. Does he feel bad we haven't made time to talk, to discuss whatever it is he hasn't told me? My mind jumps to what it might be—did they, we, have a miscarriage, multiple rounds of IVF? Maybe we had a bad patch in our marriage and more kids were off the table for a while. Whatever it is, I'm not sure I want to know right now.

"I don't need to be told everything all at once, the stuff I've forgotten," I tell him. "Can we just enjoy this bit for now, catch up on the rest later?" I search his face—does he understand? I just want to hold on to this glorious feeling for a little longer, where everything about the other person is ahead of you, yet to be discovered. I don't need the crib notes on our whole relationship history before it's even started.

I lean in to kiss him on the lips, but he moves his head and plants a kiss on my cheek.

"Sure," he says. "You're really going to be okay without me?"

"Of course." I reach out a hand to catch his waist, but he's already turned to go.

"And you will call me if there's anything, with the kids?"

I nod.

ONCE SAM AND Dad have left, I end up confiding in Mum about my work situation. She insists I spend the afternoon hunting down this "big idea" while she fields the children. Ushering me off to my office, she says, "Lucy, when the world is spinning, work tethers us with purpose," which sounds like a misquote from a throw cushion, but I take her point. After my extended absence last week, wouldn't it be great if I could stride into work tomorrow, Big Idea in hand, and save the day?

My office is tucked away at the back of the house. Opening the door gives me a Virginia Woolfish thrill. A wide wooden desk sits in front of an expensive-looking swivel chair, and tasteful framed prints hang on the walls. On the left-hand side is a bookshelf lined with awards: Best Independent Production Company—Badger TV; BAFTA Children's Award, Best

Animation—Underwater Sam. On the bookshelf are books covered in Post-it notes, written in my handwriting. On one, *Fairies Aren't Real*, I've written, "Potential stop animation?" On another, *Space Camp*, "Eight-part series, one episode per planet." This whole room is *full* of ideas.

The laptop unlocks with my fingerprint, but after skimming through various folders, I can't find anything obvious. I do find an up-to-date CV, listing every show I've ever worked on, and a thought takes hold—if I watch all these, I could fill in the gaps, catch up on what I've missed. Soon I'm lost in a rabbit hole of research. In each new program, I see some element that might have come from me. I'm also burning with a new sense of pride—I worked on these shows, these good shows, there's my name in the credits. A familiar creative spark ignites, as new ideas vie for my attention, and I look for a pen to jot them down.

On the desk, there's a photo of me and Sam. He's standing with his arm around me in a garden. I whisper to myself, "You did it." You stuck at it, you weathered the terrible pay and the fierce competition, and you got your ideas made. You got what we always wanted. The thought puts a new fire in my belly— I've been left in charge of Badger TV, for how long, I don't know, but I'll be damned if I'm going to let Coleson Matthews, or anyone else, take it away on my watch.

I shoot a text to Michael:

Apologies for the radio silence. I'm finally feeling better— have lots of ideas to discuss. I'll be in the office tomorrow first thing. L

He replies straightaway:

Wonderful. So glad you're better. You had me sweating
there. M

Ideas I can do. Ideas are my forte. I used to think of them
sitting on my bed, scribbling down titles for shows in dog-
eared notebooks. Here I have a massive desk, a fancy computer, and a bookshelf full of inspiration. Plus, I don't even
need to think of loads of ideas, I just need one. How hard can
it be to come up with one brilliant show idea?

20

"YOU'RE REALLY FINE WITH US GOING?" MUM ASKS later that evening when they're finally packed and ready to go. I've insisted they leave tonight. The children are in bed, Maria will be here early in the morning, and I have everything under control. Mum's friend Nell is expecting them in Wales, and I know they want to beat the morning traffic.

"I'm fine. You'll have a clear run up if you leave now," I reassure her.

She dithers at the door while Dad rearranges the contents of the boot for the umpteenth time. As I watch her run a hand through her short gray hair, it strikes me that this style suits her better than wearing it long ever did. Before, she was always checking her hair in the mirror, constantly smoothing it flat with her palms. This short style has her much more at ease.

"Will you still be okay for next month?" Mum asks. "I'm having my cataracts operation. You said you would come and stay for a couple of days, I might need a bit of help." She flushes slightly. She has never asked me for help with anything before.

"Yes, of course I can, just tell me when," I say, and the tension in her face relaxes as she nods, then pats me on the arm.

"Remember, we're only ever a phone call away," says Dad, coming back for his coat while Mum goes to the car.

"How about you, Dad?" I ask gently, helping him into his coat. "Mum's been distracted by my news, but I know she's worried about you."

"My forgetfulness aggravates your mother far more than it aggravates me," Dad says, patting me on the arm just as Mum did.

"You don't think you should talk to a doctor?"

"I had a look at your veg patch, propped up some sagging tomato vines for you. Make sure you keep watering them, there's not been much rain of late," he says, ignoring my question completely.

"I didn't even know I had a veg patch, so, thanks," I say, flattening one of his coat lapels.

"You know what I've always loved about gardening?" he asks, and I shake my head. "Plants don't mind who you are, what you've done, or what you've forgotten. If you visit them frequently and look at them properly, you'll sense what they need. People are the same—you don't need to know someone's entire history to know when they need a hug." Then he pulls me into his arms.

"Oh, Dad," I say, sinking into him.

"If I'm going doolally, I'll go doolally on my own terms, love." He pauses, then gives me a questioning look.

"I'll be fine," I say. "Don't worry about me. I've got this."

IT TURNS OUT, I have not got this. Not by a long shot.

Amy wakes four times in the night. Once for a nappy change, once because she's thrown Neckie out of the cot, and the other two times, I don't even know why, she just grizzles until I pick her up. The only thing that will make her stop is walking around and around the room with her, which is the last thing you feel like doing when you're shattered yourself. *How do people survive off this little sleep?* Then Felix wakes up distressed because he doesn't have Hockey Banjo.

"Am I looking for a real banjo?" I ask him.

"No," Felix wails, "my armadillo."

"I'll help look. He must be somewhere," I say.

"She's a she, and she doesn't like the dark," Felix sobs, crawling on the floor to look beneath his bed.

"She won't be lost."

"How do you know? You don't even know what she looks like because you're not real Mummy!" Felix cries. He's right. I don't know what his toy looks like. Maybe she is lost. Maybe Hockey Banjo went through a portal and is now living my old life, drinking bone broth and tequila with Julian and Betty.

Eventually, at four AM, after pulling apart the playroom, I find a cuddly armadillo that fits Felix's description and Felix, placated, finally manages to get back to sleep. I do not. I am too wired, too primed for the next disturbance. I resort to un-muting the Fit Fun Fabulous app on my phone and asking it to play me a sleep meditation.

"I let go of the waking world," comes a breathy female voice, accompanied by soft chiming bells. "I relish this feeling of stillness. I cherish my journey to sleep."

Nope. No relishing or cherishing happening, just an intense new hatred for this woman, who sounds incredibly smug about how well-rested she is. I check the time again. I just need to get through to seven fifteen. As soon as Maria arrives, I can make coffee, I can go to work, I can get my head together.

But at seven I get a call from Maria saying she's developed an infection from her routine microneedling appointment and isn't going to be able to come to work. *Shit.* I'll need to get the children up, dressed, fed, and to school and nursery all by myself, then catch a later train to London. I was planning to wear something nice for my first day back at work, to do my hair, try to look professional. But with two children now shouting for breakfast, I have to make do with throwing on the first outfit I find and pulling my hair into a messy bun.

"Did you look at the forums? Did you upload my drawing yet?" Felix asks. *Bollocks, I completely forgot about that.*

"Um, not yet, sorry, I got distracted," I say while trying to find "the shapey cereal" he has requested for breakfast.

"But you're going to London, aren't you going to look for the portal?" Felix asks.

"No, I'm going to work—to my job."

"Do aliens know how to make TV?"

"I am *not* an alien. This one?" I hold up a box of Captain Crisp and he shakes his head. "This one? This one? This one?" I pull all the cereals out of the cupboard, and Felix picks the packet of Weetabix. "How are those 'the shapey ones'?" I ask, exasperated. He holds up an oblong wheat biscuit to illustrate how obviously shapey it is.

"What should I make you for your packed lunch?" I ask him, pausing to pick up Amy's milk cup, which she's lobbed across the room for no reason.

"Cheese sandwich, please," says Felix. *Well, at least that was easy.* "But only if you have the white cheese. I don't like the yellow cheese anymore. And only if we have the long rolls? I don't like the bread with the green man on the packet, he's got scary eyes. And if there's no white cheese, ham, but only if it's the ham with the edge."

I should not have consulted him. Grabbing a packet of crisps, a bag of nuts, and an apple from the cupboard, I throw a piece of what might be cheese into the only bread I can find and stuff it all into a yellow lunch box that has a cartoon spaceship on the front.

"Can we upload my picture after school?" Felix asks.

"Sure, we'll do it later—as soon as I get back from London." I don't want to get Felix's hopes up that his terrible digital drawing might be the solution to all our problems, but it doesn't sound like he's going to let it go, and there's no time for a big conversation about it now.

On the family planner, there's a list of all the things the children need on a Monday. Under *Felix*, it says "Football kit (top drawer) and spelling homework (ask him)." After spending ten minutes searching for something I've never even seen, which Felix can only describe as "a book with writing in," Felix remembers he might have left it in Simon Gee's book bag, *whoever the fuck Simon Gee is.*

We're so late now, but as I rush everyone out to the car there's a rumbling sound and the air fills with an ungodly stench.

"Amy's done a poo," Felix says with a heavy sigh.

Amy gives me a wide, toothy grin. *Did she do that on purpose? Can I take her to nursery with a dirty nappy? I imagine it's frowned upon.* But then I've been frowned upon before; I'm happy to take my chances. Sitting in the driver's seat, I let out a long, slow exhale. To think I used to struggle getting to work on time when I only had myself to get dressed and out of the door.

"Good morning, Lucy," says Stanley Tucci. His voice is soothing and sexy, and instantly makes me feel a little less stressed.

"Hi, Stan," I say.

"Are you going to FELIX SCHOOL?" he asks.

"Yes." Though now I'm worried about driving this enormous car. I haven't driven for years, and I never did quite master parallel parking. What if I have to parallel park at the school? But as soon as I press the accelerator, the car silently launches into action, smooth as butter melting off a knife. As I turn left out of the drive, it honestly feels as though the car is driving itself. *Is the car driving itself?*

When we arrive at the school, twenty minutes later, Stanley says, "Have a good day, FELIX."

"Get bent, Stan," says Felix, opening the door.

"Get bent!" Stanley replies cheerfully.

"I taught him that," Felix tells me proudly, then slams the car door and runs across the empty playground.

Stanley navigates us to Amy's nursery, and I'm beginning to think the worst of my day might be over. If I make the nine fifteen train, I can still be at the office by ten fifteen. But when I park and open the passenger door, I discover Amy has managed to get into my handbag, open my expensive cream blusher, and smear it all over her face, and the car seat.

"Amy! How did you do that?" I have nothing to wipe it off with. Trying to rub it off with my hands only makes it worse—her whole face is so flushed, now she just looks extremely embarrassed, which frankly I would be in her position. As I'm handing her over to the nursery worker, I notice her nappy has leaked, and there's a small, light-brown stain seeping through the side of her leggings. *I have plausible deniability—she could have just done that.* Amy clings to me, like a stinky baby koala reluctant to leave her tree.

"It's okay, Amy, I'll be back to get you later. I have to go to work now, sweetie."

As I'm trying to unclench her hands from my hair, her face goes still, and I think she's about to relent. But then she's sick all over my shirt.

"Oh dear," says the nursery worker.

"Agh!" I cry, handing Amy to the woman so I can shake pink vomit off my top. *Now I'll have to go all the way home and change, I'll never make the nine fifteen.*

"She can't come to nursery if she's sick," says the nursery worker, handing her back to me.

"I don't think she's got anything contagious; she just ate my blusher on the way here."

"Sorry, nursery policy. She can't come back for forty-eight hours."

"Forty-eight hours? But how am I supposed to go to work?"

The woman shrugs sympathetically, but I genuinely don't understand. I *need* to go to work. How are parents supposed to hold down jobs? Seriously, how has no one found a solution to this yet? Amy starts crying, and I immediately feel bad for worrying about missing my meeting. Poor little thing probably has a tummy ache, and I don't want to leave her here if she's not feeling well. I hug her blusher-covered face to the dry side of my chest.

"Poor Amy. Let's go home."

Back at the house, I change her nappy and her clothes, but she won't stop crying. I think about calling Sam, but there's nothing he can do from Manchester. He'll just worry I don't have things under control. *I don't have things under control.* Putting a palm against Amy's forehead, I try to gauge if she is hot. My mum used to do that to me, like a human thermometer. Amy feels warm, but maybe it's a normal warm. Where do parents learn this stuff? Is there's a TED Talk I can watch?

Amy sinks into me, closing her eyes. I remember that feeling of simply needing my mum. Something tells me she just needs me to cuddle her in my lap and let her know I'm not going anywhere. So I change my top and that is what we do, until she falls asleep, dribbling on my shoulder. Using my free hand, I manage to text Michael, telling him I've had a childcare emergency and won't make it into London today after all. I'm conscious I'm letting Future Me down. She's left me in charge of her life, her career, her children, and I'm failing on every front. What would she do in this situation? I'll let Amy snooze for ten minutes, then move her onto the sofa, perhaps dial into work remotely. Just . . . ten . . . minutes.

I'm woken by my phone. *Did I fall asleep? What time is it?* Shit, we've both been asleep for two hours! The ringing wakes Amy too, but she smiles up at me with sleepy, contented eyes. She looks so much better, even though she still has residual smears of blusher on her face.

"Mrs. Rutherford, it's Yvonne from Farnham Primary," comes a nasal voice on the phone. "Felix doesn't have his green football jersey. They're wearing green this week because it's an away game. We did remind everyone on the Skoolz app."

There's a pause on the line. "You'll need to drop it off before two if he's going to play in the match."

I don't want to be the reason he doesn't play in the match. Handing Amy a bear that plays music when you press its ears, I run upstairs to look for this green football top. There's nothing in his drawers or on the floor of his room, and after a full search of the house, I eventually find it in the laundry room at the bottom of a pile of washing—covered in mud. *If I do a speed wash, maybe I can get it dry in time.* The space-age washing machine won't turn on without codes for energy efficiency and water usage, but after experimenting with a thousand random number combinations, I finally hear the merciful shooshing sound of water pouring into the drum.

Amy shouts, bored of her toy, and as I go to pick her up, there's a high-pitched repetitive beeping sound from the laundry room. We go to investigate and find ERROR CODE 03 flashing on the washing machine.

"What the bejeezus is Error Code Three?" I ask Amy, and then notice she's picked up a washing powder sheet and is about to put it in her mouth. When I whip it out of her hands, she yells in rage. I can't open the machine, or turn it off, and the beeping noise, coupled with Amy's crying, is torture. If I were a spy and the enemy were interrogating me, five minutes of this and I'd give up all my secrets.

Amy is chewing her fists. Maybe she's hungry? It is lunchtime and she did vomit up most of her breakfast. "Do you want lunch?"

"Blunch!" she squeals.

Then the doorbell rings. Just what I need.

On the doorstep, I find a cheerful-looking man in a smart

green boilersuit. "Mrs. Rutherford?" *I still can't get used to being called that.* "I'm Trevor, I'm here to log your energy meter."

"This really isn't a good time, I'm afraid," I say, jiggling Amy up and down on my hip.

"Right." Trevor shifts his weight between his feet, his smile slipping ever so slightly. "It's just, you'll be charged a call-out fee if you choose to reschedule."

"Fine, come in. But I have amnesia, so I don't remember booking this. Can you find what you need by yourself?"

"Sure." Trevor eyes me warily. "Do you know where your meter is?" I shake my head. "Have you got an appliance cupboard? There's usually a panel."

"Blunch!" squeals Amy, and I put her down for a minute because she's pulling my hair and I need to show Trevor where the utility room is.

When I return, I find that in the thirty seconds I've been away, Amy has managed to take off her nappy and wee all over the hall carpet.

"Amy! No!"

She wails.

"Your panel's not in there," Trevor calls, coming back and grimacing at the mess. "I'll have a scout about for it, shall I? I can see you've got your hands full."

Once I've cleared up the mess in the hall, I head to the kitchen and find a pouch of puree for Amy and a nut-and-seed energy bar for myself. Amy throws the pouch on the floor and snatches the bar out of my hand. The washing machine's beeping feels like a woodpecker tapping at the inside of my skull. What if I can't turn it off? What if we have to live with this sound for the rest of our lives? People will visit us and we'll have to give them earplugs. It will come to define who we are as people.

Trevor's grinning face appears around the kitchen door. "I found the panel," he says triumphantly.

Amy has demolished my nut bar and is now shouting "NANA!" at me.

"Nana's not here, sweetie," I tell her. But she holds out her fists and clenches them open and closed. "NANA!"

"I think she's trying to say 'banana,'" Trevor says. Right. Even Trevor understands my child better than I do. "Do you want me to turn that beeping off?" he offers.

"Yes, please, Trevor! For the love of God, yes."

Trevor looks scared. I find Amy a banana, and she grabs it in delight. Trevor fails to stop the beeping, though he does manage to open the washing machine so I can get Felix's football jersey out.

Ten minutes later, Trevor is gone, and Amy and I are back in the car, with Felix's damp jersey hanging out of my window.

"Baa sheep! Baa sheep!" yells Amy once we're driving.

"Stan, play 'Baa Sheep,'" I try.

"You want to drive to BAARLE-NASSAU in BELGIUM?" Stanley offers.

"No!"

My crush on Stanley Tucci is quickly evaporating. I'm starting to miss Trevor, short as our co-parenting relationship was.

"Baa sheep!" Amy wails insistently. I try singing "Baa Baa Black Sheep" myself, but I can't remember the words, and now I have a pounding headache from all the washing machine beeping and crying and singing and intense multitasking. We lose ten minutes driving in the wrong direction because I realize Stanley *is* trying to take us to Belgium. Eventually, we arrive at the school gates and I unbuckle Amy and run inside with her. My arms are aching from carrying her around all day. *Is this why I have biceps now?*

"Hi, I just wanted to drop off some football kit for Felix Rutherford," I tell the woman at the reception desk, eyeing the clock on the wall, as I try to catch my breath. She gives me a pitying look, and it's only then that I realize what I must look like. I have baby puree in my hair, huge sweat patches on my shirt, and God knows what else because I didn't even look in the mirror before I left the house. Amy looks like a frazzled flamingo.

"What class is he in?" she asks.

"Um. I'm not sure. He's seven."

"You don't know what class he's in?" she asks, narrowing her eyes at me. An older woman with brown curly hair walks through from one of the offices behind and now I feel doubly judged.

"Three C," says the older woman. "Felix Rutherford is in Three C. While you're here, Mrs. Rutherford, I wonder if you have time for a quick chat?"

The receptionist reaches for the football kit and, on feeling it's still slightly damp, gives me a pointed "Tut."

"Maybe you could put it on a radiator for a minute?" I ask in a low voice, before following the older woman into her office. The sign on the door reads Mrs. H. Barclay, Head Teacher.

"Take a seat," she says, picking up a book and handing it to Amy. It's a hardbacked flap book about rabbits, and Amy paws it gleefully. "One of my favorites."

"Excellent," I say, simply for something to say.

"Were you aware that Felix brought nuts onto school property this morning?"

"Nuts?"

"Nuts are not allowed, Mrs. Rutherford. Allergies."

"Oh no, I'm so sorry, that was my fault. Is everyone okay?"

"They were confiscated and disposed of." She pauses. "Felix didn't have the right books this morning either, and he missed roll call."

"Yes, sorry, we were late, we um . . ." I try to think how I can word my excuses. Sam won't be impressed if I'm left in charge for a day and both the children are taken away by social services.

"I just wanted to check everything was okay at home?" she asks, leaning across the desk toward me. "Felix told his teacher you'd disappeared." She pauses, knitting her hands and lowering her eyes. "If there are problems at home, it's always best to let the school know—then we're best able to help your children with any difficult transitions."

"Oh no, nothing like that." I attempt an overly cheerful smile. "Just some, um, health issues." I pause. "I'd rather not discuss the specifics, but they might account for Felix's recent behavior."

"I see." She nods slowly, then frowns as though she doesn't see at all and would like me to elaborate. "He asked his teacher if he could build a space rocket in project time—"

"How ambitious of him."

"—so that he could send his pretend mother back to her alien planet."

A short, sharp laugh escapes my lips, which is met with a frown. "Children have such vivid imaginations, don't they?" I say.

"I don't want to pry," she says, though clearly, she does.

"As long as you have everything under control, and you don't send nuts into school again."

"I do, thank you, Mrs. Barclay. Everything is under control. Got it, no nuts."

At which point Amy throws up a soupy sludge of undigested nuts, all over the head teacher's desk.

21

"SOUNDS LIKE A PRETTY NORMAL DAY IN MOTHERING land to me," says Faye, when I've finished telling her about my disastrous day. I've managed to sneak away from the children for a few minutes to call her, and it's such a relief to hear her friendly nonjudgmental voice. "How's Amy now? Has she been sick again?"

"No, she seems fine. I probably shouldn't have let her have an energy bar for lunch."

"And what's happening with the washing machine? Is it still beeping? Do you want me to come over?"

"No, don't worry, I've wedged all the dirty laundry around the machine and it's muffling the sound." I sniff my top. Even though I've changed, I still smell of vomit. "I feel sticky and sweaty and disgusting. I've failed at everything today."

"Are your children alive?" Faye asks.

"Yes."

"Has the house burned down?"

"No."

"Then you haven't failed."

"Do you think I'm finding this parenting stuff hard because I don't remember how to do it?"

"No, it's just hard sometimes. I imagine doubly hard if you don't remember anything," says Faye. "They can send a man to Mars, but no one's solved the problem of how to get a child dressed, fed, and out of the house without someone losing their shit."

"They sent a man to Mars?" I ask, astounded.

"They did, and a woman, and a gerbil called Spacey McCheeks."

"I haven't even had time to make myself a coffee. I've failed to do any of the washing. I can't even remember if I've been to the loo today. I don't think I have—I don't think I've done a wee in eight hours."

"Lucy, your child is ill, Sam is away, these are the days you just need to survive." Faye pauses. "You're sure you don't want me to come over? I could bring you some lavender tea."

"No, honestly, I just need two minutes to sit down and—" I stop talking, startled by Felix looming over me with a half-empty box of crayons.

"Amy ate my crayons," he says, brow creased in fury.

"Sorry, Faye, I need to go. Crayons have been consumed."

Felix and I stand over Amy in the living room, where she sits in a nest of broken crayons.

"Do you think she'll poop the rainbow now?" Felix asks flatly. His tone makes me laugh, and I see a small smile play at the corner of his mouth. Together we put away all the puzzles and toys Amy has pulled down from the lowest shelf.

"I'm sorry today was so crazy. I'll be better tomorrow. I'll get up *really* early."

Felix shrugs; he seems more annoyed about the crayons than anything else.

"What's the opposite of eating? Is it not-eating, or is it being sick?" he asks me.

"I don't know," I say, confused by this complete non sequitur.

"I think it's being sick. What's that beeping?"

"It's the washing machine. I can't turn it off."

He heads toward the laundry room and I follow with Amy.

"I'm not letting you out of my sight, you little tornado of havoc," I tell her, gently pushing a finger to her nose. She grins up at me angelically.

Felix pulls down the barricade of clothes and shows me a button on the side of the machine. He holds it down for the count of three and finally, silence.

"Wow. That easy, huh?"

Felix gives me an "It was nothing" shrug. I slump down in the monumental pile of laundry.

"I'm not very good at this, am I," I say quietly.

"You're doing okay," Felix says, lowering himself down into the laundry pile beside me. Then I feel his arm around me; Felix is hugging me. *My son is hugging me. I have a son.* The lightness of his small arm around my shoulder stirs something inside me, a new unfiltered affection for him, breaking over me like a wave. I don't want to move or say anything because I don't want him to stop.

"Real Mummy finds it hard too. Sometimes she goes outside and shouts at the vegetables when she doesn't want to shout at us."

I don't know whether this nugget of information is reassuring or disturbing. Passing him my phone, I say, "Come on then, show me these websites you want me to upload your drawing to." A promise is a promise.

Felix takes the phone, his face beaming. He taps away, then hands it back to me. "This is the best one, the site Molly's dad said to use." He points to the website he's opened, Arcadefind .co.uk. "It's for people who collect these machines from the olden days." He hands me back the phone and I scroll through subject headings. Wanted: replacement red joystick for Donkey Kong arcade machine 412. There are some incredibly niche requests on here. Maybe Felix is right. Maybe someone on this site knows where I can find that wishing machine.

It only takes a few minutes for me to create a profile and a post on the site's "looking for" page.

USER: WishingFor26

LOOKING FOR: Vintage Wishing Machine

DESCRIPTION: Coin operated, 10p to flatten and inscribe a 1p coin with "Your wish is granted." Yellow neon lights, plays a tune that sounds like "Camptown Races."

SIGHTINGS: Newsagent's on Baskin Road, South London, sixteen years ago.

Once I've created the post and uploaded Felix's sketch, I show it to him. "It's a long shot. We shouldn't get our hopes up," I tell him firmly. I'm telling myself too.

"Someone will see it," he says confidently. "Someone will know where it is."

At a muffled wail from behind us, we both turn to see Amy with a pair of leggings over her head. Pulling them off, I give Amy a goofy smile. She giggles and reaches for my face, grasping my cheeks like they're Play-Doh.

"What do you think the princess of the laundry room wants for tea?" I ask, getting to my feet and taking Amy with me.

"We both like fish fingers," Felix says, following me out of the laundry room.

"Okay, fish fingers it is. I can probably manage that." Then, because Amy's huge eyes are staring at me expectantly, I cover my face with the leggings. "Oh no, the octopus has got me!" I cry, and Amy squeals with delight as I mime being attacked by the leggings. "Quick, Captain Felix, the princess of the laundry room is in trouble, she needs a boat!"

Amy claps her hands, transfixed. Felix shoots me a confused scowl.

"Captain, we don't have long. The princess can't swim!"

There's a plastic laundry basket behind him, and grudgingly he pushes it toward me with his foot.

"You'll need to do it, Captain, the octopus has got me in its clutches," I yell dramatically, putting Amy down and miming a fight with my legging-clad hand.

Felix walks slowly across to us, picks up Amy, and plonks her in the laundry basket, rolling his eyes at me as he brushes his fringe away from his eyes. But I sense a glimmer of interest, so I step up my performance and go all in, channeling all my drama experience, which consists of playing Sheep Number Five in my primary school nativity play.

"She's safe for now, but to get her home, we need to defeat the evil octopus king"—I wave the leggings in the air—"ascend the waterfall"—I point to the stairs—"then take on the Bath-tub of Many Questions, before reaching the safety of Castle Cot." I pause for dramatic effect. "Are you with me, Captain?"

Felix looks around, embarrassed, perhaps checking to see if anyone is watching us. His eyes flicker with indecision. Amy claps in anticipation, completely invested in whatever this is. "Please, Captain Rutherford, I can't do this without you."

Time stands still, then the urge to play wins. Looking around the room, I grab a pillow from the sofa and throw it to Felix. "Your octopus shield, man." He bangs the pillow to his chest, launches himself at my legging-clad hand, then a fight to the death ensues. Amy stands up in her boat, applauding our performance. Now that Felix is involved, the game notches up a level in complexity. He tells me that before getting up the Waterfall of Seven Fishes, we must take out the octopus's lair in the playroom. He grabs a dressing-gown cord from the laundry pile and ties it onto Amy's boat so we can pull her along as we leap across the furniture. Felix commits to the game with a ferocity I couldn't have predicted. When we're both safe on the living room rug, with Princess Amy moored up in her boat, Felix points to the toy basket at the other side of the room.

"That's the secret lair," he whispers. "Neckie's in there. He's the leader. To get up the waterfall we've got to get him and his goons out of there, distract them so we can get to the button."

"What does the button do?" I ask, genuinely keen to know.

"Antigravity button. It reverses the flow of the water."

"Genius! How do we take out the toys?"

"The goons," he corrects me. "I'll paddle around the back, you distract them at the entrance to the cave. I'll climb in the secret entrance and detonate the"—he looks around, throws a cushion across the floor, then leaps to it so he can reach for a wooden jack-in-the-box from the lower toy shelf—"the bomb."

"Be careful of that. You know how sensitive those are," I say in hushed reverence.

"This isn't my first rodeo, Lieutenant," he tells me with a

cheeky grin, and in that grin, I see a flash of his father, and of this boy at sixteen, at twenty, as a man, and feel a pang of something in my chest, as though my heart has shed some outer shell and now lies open to the elements.

Felix paddles off on the sofa cushion with the bomb tucked carefully beneath his arm.

On my phone, I find "Bad Romance" by Lady Gaga. It starts playing through the speakers in the ceiling and I turn up the volume. For Zoya's sixteenth birthday, we worked out a dance routine for this song and recorded a music video in her parents' living room. It's the only dance routine I know. Felix watches in confusion as I start singing and throwing wild shapes on the rug, Amy squeals in delight and starts rocking her laundry-basket boat back and forth. Felix gives a nod of approval and now that he's near the toy basket he starts tossing soft toys around the room.

"It's working! They're leaving the cave undefended! Don't stop."

I dance like my life depends on it, like my relationship with my son depends on it, like my whole horrible day of failure might be undone by one successful dance routine. Maybe I'm not going to win this little boy's respect by pretending to be the mother he knows, but maybe I'll win it by dancing like a maniac long enough to give him a shot at the antigravity button.

"I can see the button!" Felix roars, diving for the toy basket, and I feel a rush of adrenaline, as though something huge is about to happen.

AN HOUR LATER, Felix and I lie on the upstairs hallway completely spent.

"We did it," he says, reaching out to high-five me.

"We did," I say, glancing into Amy's room, where she's now in her cot ready for bed. Our mission to get to the castle took a detour via the kitchen for hero fuel (fish fingers and chips) and boat fuel (milk), which Amy drank on behalf of the boat. Then we made it up the waterfall to the Bathtub of Many Questions, where Felix had to correctly spell five words to turn on the Taps of Destiny. Amy was delightfully compliant throughout the whole game and was exhausted by the time we finally deposited her in her castle (cot).

"That was one hell of a mission," I say, offering Felix a hand to pull him up to standing. We walk downstairs and through the living room, now scattered with cushions and toys. The laundry pile is halfway across the hall, from when Felix was digging to find a tow rope for the boat. The kitchen is still a disaster zone from Amy's tea . . . and lunch . . . and breakfast. Yet despite the housepocalypse, a new calm confidence has taken hold of me. Maybe I *can* do this parenting thing. I'll put the house to rights, prep all the things I need for tomorrow, get Felix to bed, then lock myself away in the office and email Michael all my show ideas. Then I will try to do it all again tomorrow, only better.

"That was fun," Felix says quietly as I begin to load the dishwasher. "Mummy doesn't do that stuff much anymore. She doesn't play with us, she's always too busy."

"Is she?" I ask, then feel a loyalty toward my future self. "She has a lot on her plate. I'm sure she'd want to play with you more if she could."

"I know. She's a great mummy." He looks up at me, and I sense he wants to tell me he's not being disloyal either. "She does the best birthday parties. Last year she made me this dinosaur cake. All my friends said it was the best cake ever, it had all these teeth made of M&M's."

I hum, biting my lip, feeling a sudden swell of emotion behind my eyes.

"We didn't cook the broccoli," Felix says, pointing to a broccoli head, sitting forgotten on the chopping board.

"Do you want broccoli for dessert?"

"I guess," he says, shrugging.

I fill a pan with water, and Felix picks up a knife to start chopping.

"Wait, can you use a knife?"

"You trust me with a grenade but not with a kitchen knife?" I laugh out loud, and there's that smile again, the one he tries to hide, but he can't disguise his pleasure in making me laugh.

"Hey?" comes a voice from the doorway, and Felix and I both turn to see Sam looking around at the chaos in bemusement.

"Hey, Dad," Felix says, running over to hug his father. *He's home early?* I was going to tidy up before he got back, I was going to do better tomorrow.

Sam looks exhausted, and I have the urge to hug him too, but I'm wary. He's got that "disappointed teacher" look as he surveys the chaos.

"It's not as bad as it looks," I tell him. "We were playing a game in here. I'll tidy it all up."

"It's fine," Sam says, walking through to the living room, picking up sofa cushions and putting them back where they belong. "You should be in bed, buddy," he tells Felix. "It's a school day tomorrow. How about you go brush your teeth and I'll come up and say good night."

Felix gives me a look, conspirator and commiserator, before heading toward the stairs.

"How come you're home early?" I ask.

"Some of the musicians were ill. We couldn't record everything we wanted to. I left you a voice memo . . ."

"Sorry, I've hardly looked at my phone. Maria wasn't well, then Amy was sick. I didn't make it to London."

Sam picks up a cuddly shark and collapses down in an armchair. "I wouldn't have left if I thought you'd be on your own. You should have called me, Lucy."

He's probably right, today has been a complete disaster, just look at this place. But I can't help feeling disappointed that he sees it that way, because playing with Felix and Amy this evening, I finally got a glimpse of another side to parenting—the fun part, the part I might actually be good at.

"I'm going to jump in the shower, the train was a sauna," Sam says. "Then we'll deal with all this, I guess."

As he turns to go up the stairs, I realize he hasn't even kissed me since he came in. How have we gone from our amazing Saturday night to this? Maybe if I make the first move, I can get back to where we were, to the flirting and the teasing and the getting naked. I follow him up the stairs. The shower is already running, so I pull off my clothes in the bedroom. My body aches with tiredness, but as soon as I see Sam's naked body in the shower, a new energy takes hold.

When I wrap a hand around his chest, he flinches, surprised, but then he holds my hand against his and turns around to face me. Water streams down over our bodies; my skin bristles with the coldness of the shower and the anticipation of his touch. Those first few days, lusting after Sam felt like lusting after someone else's husband, but since date night, I've made my peace with the moral ambiguity. Future Me would *want* me to have sex with her husband. I would, if I was her, which

I am. Besides, it would be wrong to let this kind of insane chemistry go to waste. Tilting my head up to kiss him, I feel so small. Every man I've been with before feels like a fumbling boy compared to Sam. As he kisses me back, I let out a moan, and then his hands push me back against the wall of the shower.

"You know, I've never had sex in a shower before," I whisper in his ear. As soon as the words leave my mouth, I feel him freeze, his hands still on my body. I look up at him, eyes wide in surprise, his face full of some undefinable pain. "What? What's wrong?"

He looks down at my left hand, then gets out of the shower and wraps a towel around his waist, ignoring me as he walks back out to the bedroom.

"What? What did I do?" I try again, taking a towel from the rack.

"Why aren't you wearing your wedding ring?" he asks.

"Is that all you're upset about? I'm sorry, I didn't know it was such a big deal."

He turns away from me, and I realize he's shaking. "Who are you? You don't sound like my wife, you don't act like her." He lets out a groan, sits down on the bed, and hangs his head in his hands. He rubs the heels of his palms into his eye sockets and takes a breath. "I'm sorry, I know it's not your fault. It's not that I don't want this, or that I didn't enjoy Saturday. I loved seeing you laugh and let go like you used to. I can't think when you last fell into bed without taking your makeup off, putting your creams on, when you last kissed me in the street, not caring who saw." He looks up at me now, and I see the pain in his eyes. "But I feel bad for liking it. It feels weirdly disloyal, and you acting like this is the first time we've had sex in the shower has just thrown me because we've had sex in there a hundred times. And you never take off your rings, except to sleep. It makes me feel like I'm with someone else, and if you're not my wife, I . . . I don't know where she went."

His words feel like a punch to the sternum.

"I'm not 'acting' anything, Sam," I say slowly, pulling the towel tighter around me, feeling suddenly cold. "This isn't some role play. In case you've forgotten, I don't fucking remember."

He covers his eyes now. "I know, I know, I didn't mean that. I don't know what I mean. I just feel terrible that I left you alone with the children when you're not yourself. Anything could have happened." The torment on his face breaks my heart.

Not yourself. Something in those two words skewers me more than anything else he has said.

"I am myself. I know who I am. You just don't know me," I say coldly.

Then I pick up my clothes and leave the room.

22

WHAT AM I DOING HERE? TRYING TO PLAY HAPPY FAMI-lies with people I don't know, falling all over Sam, embarrass-ing myself. I need to get out of here. I need to get back to London, back to what I know. I need to put on proper clothes, brush my hair, buy eye-wateringly expensive coffee, and be the competent TV producer I know I'm capable of being.

The next morning, Maria is still off sick, but Sam has said he'll stay home with Amy. All I need to do is drive Felix to school on my way to the train station.

"Are you okay, Mummy?" Felix asks me in the car, notic-ing my puffy eyes. It makes me want to cry because it's so sweet of him to ask.

"I'll be fine," I tell him. "Thank you, though."

"What's the opposite of house?" Felix asks, and it's exactly the level of conversation I feel capable of.

"No house," I suggest, and his face takes on a contempla-tive look in the rearview mirror.

"Not field?" he asks.

"Why do you need everything to have an opposite, Felix?"

He gives a slow, exaggerated shrug. "Have you checked for messages on the arcade forum?" he asks. I haven't, so once I've pulled into the school car park, I log in.

"Oh, I have a message," I say in surprise, then read the subject heading. "'I have what you're looking for . . .'"

Felix jumps out of his car seat and cranes across my shoulders to look. Luckily, I click on the link before showing him because it's a full-frontal picture of shriveled male genitalia.

"Eugh."

"What? Let me see," Felix says, reaching for my phone, as I quickly delete the message.

"I'm afraid that was nothing to do with the wishing machine, just a horrible man sending me nasty photos."

"Nasty photos?" Felix looks confused. "What, like of a dog with no eyes?"

"A bit like that, yes."

"Oh," he says, disappointed. I clear my throat, keen to move the conversation on. "Quick question before you go. I'm pitching ideas for kids' TV at work today. What would you want to watch if you could invent your own show?"

"Anything with helicopters," Felix says, "and conger eels, and a chase through a jungle where you get to go on one of those boats with the big fan at the back."

Something tells me *Helicopter Conger Eels* isn't going to be my winning pitch, but I add it to my list anyway.

DRESSED IN A fitted trouser suit and my brand-new ankle boots, I walk into the office feeling confident. *London. TV. Work.* These are the things I know. I've decided I won't tell my colleagues about my memory issues, not if I can avoid it. I don't want to risk losing the only part of my life that feels vaguely normal, that I might have some control over.

"Lucy, how are you?" Michael greets me at the top of the stairs, and Trey and Dominique wave to me from across the office. Callum offers to make me a cup of tea and we exchange a look—pity? Camaraderie? Nope, worse—I think Callum's developed a crush on me. What was I thinking? He is practically a child. I blame Future Me's low tolerance for alcohol.

"I'm so pleased you're finally back," Michael says, beckoning me into his office. "I'll sleep a lot better once we've settled on this idea for Kydz Network." He does look tired. "The team have been brainstorming while you were away, and I know they always appreciate your feedback. Shall we hear a few of their ideas before you hit us with yours?" Michael gives me a nervous smile as Callum arrives with my tea and a delicious-looking tray of pastries.

"Pastry day," he says, blushing slightly as he places one on my desk with a napkin.

"Another thing the pound pinchers at Bamph will no doubt put a stop to," Michael says, reaching for one himself.

"Thanks, Callum," I say, taking a sip of the perfectly brewed tea with just the right amount of milk in it. This is good. I am Badger Boss, Queen of TV, in my serene office with my delightful colleagues, wearing my amazing new boots. No one is crying or biting me or throwing my craft or cooking attempts in the bin. No one is kicking me out of shower sex for saying the wrong thing. Here, I can simply eat croissants and talk to lovely people about my favorite subject—television. I've got a huge list of ideas, so I'm sure one of them is going to fit the bill.

As the team all gather in the boardroom, Trey comes to sit

beside me. He is wearing a red velvet smoking jacket and a silver shirt with huge, pointed lapels.

"I did it," he says quietly. "I proposed to Clare. She said yes."

"Oh, Trey, congratulations, that's wonderful news."

"I spoke to her family too. Her parents were worried about me being freelance, having no job security, how hard it would be for me to get a mortgage, but I told them all about you, about your plans for me."

"My plans?" I ask.

"That when we win this pitch-off, you'll be able to offer me a staff contract," Trey says with a confident grin.

Great, so now Trey's future in-laws are counting on me too.

Dominique is first to pitch her idea. She looks nervous, so I try to encourage her with a thumbs-up. She pitches an animated explorer series, where scientists explore landscapes too small for the human eye to see, like cells on leaves or raindrops in clouds. When Dominique has finished, the room goes quiet, and I realize everyone is looking at me for a response.

"Brilliant, I love it," I say, with a single hand clap. Dominique looks thrilled.

"You don't think it's too similar to *MicroBots*?" Michael asks, tapping a pen against his cheek.

"Hmmm, maybe." I make a note to watch *MicroBots*.

"It's neat, but that kind of world building would be expensive, time-consuming for the turnaround," says Trey.

"With my commissioner head on, it feels at the educational end of the spectrum rather than pure Saturday night entertainment," says Michael. "Maybe we could talk about it for another slot?"

I nod along to Michael's suggestions, tapping my lip to convey "thoughtful listening."

Leon's up next. He pitches a baking show, where teams

would compete to bake cakes for their pets' birthday parties. I'm about to say I love it, who doesn't love baking and pets, but then Trey jumps in. "It's a bit Disney Channel fifteen years ago, isn't it? Sorry, Leon." He gives Leon a cartoon grimace, which elicits a few laughs from others in the room. "Lucy? What do you think?"

"Hmmm. Possibly."

With every pitch, the questions aimed at me get more and more technical. Everything sounds like a good idea, until people bring up practicalities, budget concerns, and shows that I've never heard of. I feel like a fraud because I know nothing, and people start to look disappointed with my evasive answers. Michael is measured, thoughtful; his feedback is positive but practical. Now that I come to think of it, this was often Melanie's role. She knew what questions to ask, she could foresee all potential pitfalls.

"Shall we hear your idea now, Lucy?" Michael suggests, tapping his pen nervously against his writing pad. Standing up, I clap my hands together, trying to summon the confidence I walked in here with. Maybe I'm not great at critiquing other people's ideas, but that doesn't mean I won't be any good at pitching my own.

"I've got loads of ideas, so I'm just going to fire off some toplines?" I say eagerly, looking to Michael, who is now chewing his bottom lip. "Right, so, I'll just kick off then, shall I?" I pause. "I was thinking, what do kids love more than anything? Bouncy castles! How about a game show set in a bouncy castle?" Everyone's looking at me expectantly, so I go on. "There could be all these different rounds, one could be a spelling bee, where you have to bounce while you spell, and then a physical round where you have to grab balloons off the ceiling or something. I'm calling it *The Bounce House*."

People are smiling up at me, but no one says anything.

"So, it's a game show, but bouncy?" Michael asks, slowly, as though he's trying to work out a complex mathematical equation while recalling what he ate for breakfast four days ago.

"Yes," I say.

"I think it would make me feel a bit sick watching people bounce up and down so much," Dominique says with a laugh. She might have a point. It doesn't feel like anyone is bowled over by *The Bounce House,* so I quickly move on. They're bound to like one of these ideas.

"Well, park that one. How about a game show called *Pants on Fire*, where kids compete to tell the most outlandish lies. The player who persuades the most members of the audience wins a huge cash prize."

"I thought you weren't allowed to offer cash prizes to kids anymore," Leon says. "Ever since that boy on *Who Wants to Be a Child Billionaire* got mugged by one of the show's producers."

"It doesn't have to be cash," I say. "It could be anything, sweets, vouchers."

"Sweets?" Trey asks, horrified, as though I've suggested we reward them with class A narcotics.

"Does it feel morally dubious to be rewarding kids for lying?" Dominique asks.

"Okay, forget the lying idea. How about a kids' talent contest? We get a team of children to put on their own circus each week. They'll have to do everything: find all the acts, organize rehearsals, and then every Saturday night is the big live show—it's *The Apprentice* meets *The Greatest Showman*."

"What are those shows? Sorry, I've not heard of them," Trey asks, and I realize these must be very dated references now.

Michael is looking at me in bemusement, as though these are not the kind of ideas he was expecting me to suggest.

"I love talent shows," Callum says, grinning up at me like a loyal Labrador.

"Or, I had this other idea." I decide to just keep talking, throwing everything I've got at the wall, and hoping something sticks. "A fish-out-of-water show, called *Geeks Go to War.* We get the nerdiest, geekiest, least outdoorsy teenagers we can find, and then we send them to train with the marines! Hilarious, huh?"

There's a collective intake of breath around the room.

"What?" I ask, looking down to check my shirt hasn't just popped open.

"Um, I imagine you're using that term ironically," Michael says, "but that kind of marginalizing language would never wash with the channel. Especially in a show aimed at young people."

"As someone who identifies as 'technologically inclined,' it's a little too soon to be reclaiming the pejorative," Leon says, shaking his head. "Geek"? Pejorative? Perhaps I'm out of step with modern sensibilities.

Michael's eyebrows have furrowed into new depths of concern. I'm drowning here, and I need to pull out a surefire winner. Rummaging in my bag, I find the book I brought in, a middle-grade series about space exploration. Future Me had an adaptation proposal saved on her laptop under "New ideas." It's perfect for this time slot.

"So, this book, *Star Gazers,* is ideal for an adaptation—it's informative and exciting . . ." I'm about to go on, but everyone is looking at me warily again, as though not only is my blouse undone, but I've now sprouted a second head.

"You want to repitch *Star Gazers*"—Michael frowns—
"even though Sky didn't go for the pilot?"

*They've already made it. Damn, that detail didn't come up
in any of the notes.* That was my fail-safe big idea. My mind
goes blank, but my mouth keeps talking.

"Right, scrap that then." Here goes nothing. "Three words
for you—helicopters, conger, eels."

Silence. Something tells me this pitch meeting has not
gone well.

"Team, let's rain-check on this," Michael says, pushing
back his chair and standing up. "We'll resume play when Lucy
and I have had a chance to talk strategy a bit more."

The team all shoot one another worried looks as they troop
out. Striding over to the window, I yank it open. "Is it hot in
here?"

Michael shuts the door behind the others before saying,
"Lucy, what's going on?" His voice is full of concern, punctur-
ing my delusion that I could pull this off. I feel myself physically deflate.

"I'm sorry I'm off my game," I say, still facing the window,
bracing myself. I'll have to tell him. "The truth is, the reason I
was off last week, I've been having some memory issues." I
pause, wondering how best to phrase it, but when I turn to
face him, Michael is nodding, as though he's been expecting this.

"Brain fog?" Michael suggests, and I nod. "I suspected it
might be that, what with the hot flashes and the mood swings.
One never wants to presume. Jane went through the same."

"Mood swings?"

"Sorry if I'm overstepping. It was hard not to notice you
came in on Friday an entirely different person. Just like Jane;

she was up and down like a yo-yo. The hormone patches did wonders to level her out, though." He reaches out to squeeze my hand. "I've done my Menopausal Sensitivity Training. Anything you need, Lucy—a longer break, extra support, a desk fan, you just let me know."

"I'm afraid it's a little more than brain fog, Michael. It's—" I pause again, distracted by the sight of Trey through the glass. He's sitting with his head in his hands. *Is he crying?*

"Just like Jane, she was always losing track of what she was saying midsentence."

"No, I don't remember anything. Last week I didn't know your name, I didn't know I worked here, I didn't even know I had a husband and children."

"Just like Jane." Michael puffs out his cheeks, then lowers his voice. "I haven't told you this, but I once found her in bed with a man she met at a bus stop. She was so apologetic, but it was all down to the menopause, she simply forgot she was married."

"Right," I say slowly, unsure about the turn this conversation has taken.

Michael sighs. "It was terrible for her, such an extreme case. All I could do was be supportive."

"Is she okay now?" I ask warily.

"Oh yes. She got patches from the doctor, took up swimming. Her aqua aerobics instructor, Marcus, has been a great help. He has his own line of supplements. I could ask Jane for his number if you like?"

"Thank you, but I think I'm okay. Look, I know whatever it is that's going on with me is terrible timing, what with everyone's jobs being on the line. I'll understand if you want to roll back on the pitch-off. We could tell Gary we changed our mind."

Michael watches me for a moment. He seems disconcertingly calm. "No," he says.

"No?"

"Lucy, do you remember why we set up Badger TV?" Michael continues.

"Not that clearly just now, no."

"We were working together on that documentary about hamster enthusiasts. At the wrap party you said, 'I'll tell you a hundred show ideas better than *Hamsterama*.' And you did. Even though you were three sheets to the wind, most of them were pitchable, several of them brilliant. You can't teach that kind of creativity." He pauses. "You can't forget it either." Michael gesticulates toward the office outside. "We've been a great team all these years, with your ideas and my business brain. I know we've had to make compromises along the way, but I'm so proud of what we've built, of the programs we've made. I know I was nervous about a pitch-off, but you were right—the Cardinals would never accept a merger with the Red Sox. We play together, our way, or we forfeit the whole game."

"I said that?" I ask.

He nods, his fingers fiddling with the buttons on his waistcoat. "You did."

I'm starting to dislike Future Me. She's too persuasive for her own good, manipulating everyone into doing what she wants, selfishly gambling everyone else's jobs on an idea she didn't even write down in a place other people might feasibly be able to find it. She hasn't labeled her files in any logical order or made it clear which shows have already been made and which ones haven't. Crucially, Sam is in love with her, misses her, and I can't possibly compete. I've been trying to make the best of the situation I've found myself in, but now I feel a dawning realization that my best is not going to be good enough.

"We'll think of something," I tell Michael, with all the conviction of a lobster being thrown into a pot to boil.

23

ON THE TRAIN HOME I SEE I HAVE SEVERAL MESSAGES and missed calls from Sam. He says, "We need to talk," and then apologizes for upsetting me. At Farnham station, I can't bring myself to drive home right away. I feel desperately lost, as though I don't belong anywhere—not at work, not at home with Sam, not even in this body. So, I sit in the car, and I call my parents.

"Hello, it's Lucy," I say when Dad picks up.

"Hello, darling, I'm afraid your mother is out. How's it all going?"

"Not great if I'm honest."

"Ah." Dad pauses. "Tricky business, eh?"

"Yes, it is; it's a tricky business," I say, smiling at this familiar turn of phrase.

"Anything I can do, love?"

"Not really, I just wanted to hear a friendly voice. What's happening on your end?"

"Your mother's gone to . . . um . . ." There's a heavy pause on the line. "Well, I can't remember what she said now. Was it this weekend you wanted us to babysit?" He sounds distant on the line.

"No, you're all right." I pause. "What's happening in your veg patch then?"

"Oh, the kale's come through nicely, all my lettuce too, especially since I put that rabbit-proof fence up, best investment I ever made. Now, to an untrained eye the peppers might look like a failure, but I have a few tricks up my sleeve to revive them." And there he is, animated as ever, same old Dad.

We chat for a while longer about nothing of consequence, which is everything to me, and when I say good-bye, I feel calm enough to face driving home, to deal with Sam's disappointment in me.

WHEN I GET back, Sam is sitting up waiting for me. He looks tired, his face drawn. As soon as I'm in the house, he jumps up and strides over to me, pulling me into a hug. At first, I tense, but then I let myself relax into him. After the day I've had, I want nothing more than to be comforted by him, by his strangely familiar smell.

"I'm sorry, I'm so sorry," he says into my hair, and now I feel horrible for not being more sympathetic. I've been mourning my lost life, was in bed for days; of course Sam must be allowed to mourn for his lost wife too.

"It's okay, I understand," I whisper back.

When he lets go of me, he starts pacing the room, talking rapidly. "I know you said you didn't want to hear it all at once, and I didn't want to tell you before because I thought you'd remember soon enough anyway. Then it felt too cruel to bombard you, especially seeing how you reacted to the news of Zoya." I look across at him, but he can't meet my eye now. "But you not knowing . . ." He trails off, shaking his head.

"Something worse than Zoya?" I ask, feeling bile rising in my throat as Sam walks over and takes both my hands in his.

"We had another daughter. Her name was Chloe." *Whatever I was expecting him to say, it was not this.* Sam leads me over to the sofa, his face haunted with emotion.

"Tell me," I say.

"She was born two years after Felix. She was so perfect, Luce. We were both besotted with her. We were with Felix, too, but he had feeding issues, you had a difficult birth, his was a stressful beginning. Chloe came out smiling, this tiny Zen Buddha. But then the doctors said she was too lethargic, wheezing, they thought she wasn't getting enough oxygen." I grip his hands tighter, feeling the pain in every word. "She had a heart defect. It hadn't been picked up on the scans. They wanted to wait to operate, for her to be bigger, stronger. But then suddenly there wasn't any time and it had to happen fast." He pauses. "She was so tiny, Lucy."

We had a baby who died. This feels too surreal. I have no idea what to say, so I just sit beside him and let him go on. "She got an infection after the operation; it was antibiotic resistant. There was nothing they could do."

"I'm so sorry, Sam. How awful," I say, reaching for his hand, but he flinches and I sense I've said the wrong thing. I knew I would say the wrong thing.

"I wanted to tell you at the right time, but there never was one. How do you tell someone the worst thing that's ever happened to them? But then you not knowing, it's been weighing on me in ways I can't really describe."

He walks over to the other chair and picks up a shoebox that's been sitting there, waiting for me. "Chloe" is written on the top in a gold pen. He hands it to me, and I open the lid. It's full of photos of a baby; me and a baby, Sam and a baby, Felix as a toddler, holding the baby in a beige hospital chair, a hospital tag with her name and birth date stapled to the first page. There's a pillowcase, embroidered with the name Chloe, just like the pillows in the playroom that say "Felix" and "Amy." There's also a framed photograph of me holding her.

"That was on the mantelpiece. I moved it."

What can I say? What can I possibly say? I stare down at the photos in my lap, at my own face—tired, with sweaty, lank hair, but eyes full of such joy, holding that tiny baby in my arms. It feels like looking at a long-lost sister I never knew I had. My heart bleeds for her, for Sam too, but that is not me, that is not my child, not my sorrow.

Sam leans forward, an elbow on his knee, then covers his eyes with one hand. It's as though he needs to get it out, but he can't look at me.

"Amy came along, we were both so grateful, but I think about Chloe all the time. It still feels like someone is missing. I'll watch Felix riding his bike and think, Would Chloe be riding a bike by now? Or Amy will fuss about wearing green, because she hates green, and I'll wonder what Chloe's favorite color might have been. I know you had the same kind of thoughts because we often talked about it." Sam takes a long breath, finally dropping his hand. "I don't know how to feel about you not remembering her. It's something we've always carried together." He presses his palms into his eye sockets.

"These last few days, you've got this lightness back, a kind of childlike exuberance, as though nothing bad has ever happened to you. But I feel guilty for enjoying it, for wanting to keep this from you. On Saturday, it felt like we were thirty-one again, having a fun first date, all the heavy stuff, the day-to-day stuff, erased. But I don't want to erase Chloe. I wouldn't want her never to have existed." He pauses. "It changes you, something like that."

He closes his eyes, leaning forward, his face now in his hands. The memory box slipping to the sofa beside me. *I had a child who died, and I don't remember her.* A baby, who grew inside of me, who I birthed and named and held and loved, and it feels impossible not to remember, but there isn't even a glimmer of recollection. Nothing. Even the name is alien to me. Instinctively, I put a hand to my stomach, feeling for some distant echo of a life lived there.

"What's wrong?" A voice at the door, and we both look up to see Felix in his pajamas standing in the doorway.

"We were just thinking about Chloe, buddy."

"Oh," says Felix, and there's so much in that "oh." Felix lost a sister, lived through his parents' grief. I might never come close to understanding what this family has been through.

"It's okay," says Sam, walking over to pull Felix into a hug, then kissing his forehead. "I'm happy and sad when I think about her. Are you okay?"

"I had a bad dream," says Felix.

"Come on, I'll tuck you back in."

Sam gives me a rueful smile as they head back upstairs. He knows he's dropped something huge on me, that there is no answer, no quick fix. No wonder I feel nothing like his wife. The road she has traveled, I can't even begin to imagine.

Opening the box again, I pick up the embroidered pillowcase and lift it to my nose, hoping for the scent to unlock an unconscious memory. *Chloe. Chloe.* There is nothing.

SAM GOES TO sleep in the spare room. It's as though, now that he's told me, he wants to give me space to digest this in private. Does he think I'm going to go back to bed for a week? I can't admit to him that this doesn't feel as sad as losing Zoya. I knew Zoya for half my life; Chloe, I remember nothing about. Though this helps explain Sam's behavior toward me, I don't see how I can fix this. I cannot *be* the wife he misses. Clearly great sex and a few shared stories don't come close to eleven years of lived history.

That night, I struggle to sleep, so I scroll through my phone, back through all the years I've missed, looking for evidence of this child's existence. I find the same photos that were printed out in the memory box. There is just one video, taken in the hospital. Sam must have been filming. I'm holding a tiny bundle of sleeping baby in my arms while lying propped up in a hospital bed.

"So, where's my push present, Sammie?" I ask in the video, my voice teasing. *Do I call him Sammie?*

"What's a push present?" asks Sam's voice.

"You're supposed to buy your wife a present for pushing out a baby. You still owe me one for Felix."

"Isn't your present the baby?" Sam asks, his voice amused.

"No, I will give you my approved list of websites," I say, grinning at the camera, then looking down at the baby in my arms. "Isn't she perfect, though?"

"Just like her mother. Chloe Zoya Rutherford, welcome to

the world," says Sam. *Her middle name was Zoya.* "How am I going to handle having a daughter, Luce? I'm going to be one of those horrible overprotective father types, aren't I?"

"Daddy won't let you have a boyfriend until you're twenty-one," I tell Chloe in a baby voice.

"Twenty-five," says Sam.

That's the end of the video, that's all there is. The sum documentation of Chloe's life and she was asleep the whole time. I watch it again, trying to catch a glimpse of her tiny face, but it is too fleeting.

Scrolling forward, I find other footage of my future self, noting the ways she is different from me—she has better posture, fiddles less with her hair, looks more confident. I examine videos of Sam too, the way he looks at the camera when she is filming him. It is painful and beautiful to see—all the love in his eyes for this alternate version of me.

I don't think I should be watching these videos. Life isn't supposed to be lived in the wrong order like this. These light-hearted hopes and jokes about the future, recorded on camera, now imbued with a bleak foreshadowing.

Staring up at the ceiling, I realize I don't want to sleep alone. Whatever I am to Sam, he is hurting too, and nothing about this situation is his fault. Padding along the corridor to the spare room, I crawl into bed beside him. He is awake and reaches out a hand to me.

"Are you okay?" he asks.

"Yes." I nod.

"I do love you, Lucy," he whispers.

And even though I know these words are not meant for me, I let myself fall asleep with my hand in his, believing that they might be.

24

THE NEXT MORNING AT BREAKFAST, I TRY TO ACT NOR-mally. Sam looks at me across the breakfast table with these huge doleful eyes, as though he's hoping for me to say something, to announce that my memories have come back and I am his real wife again. Unfortunately, I can't do that and I have no idea what to say to him in the meantime. I settle for making him a coffee and a bagel with cream cheese.

Maria arrives for work looking terrible. Her skin is red and raw, her eyelids swollen and bruised. She looks as though she's been in a fight with a meat tenderizer.

"Oh, Maria, you poor thing. Are you okay?" I ask, wincing as I see her face.

"Oh, much better, you should have seen it before," she says cheerfully. "It will look great in a few days." Having assumed Maria was about fifty, I wonder if perhaps she is much older. Her face is alarming me, so I'm worried it's going to scare the children, but Amy only claps in delight to see her.

As I make to leave for the station, Maria intercepts me in the hall. "I get a discount at this place if I recommend a friend. You could get your neck done." She hands me a brochure for something called "Snip 'n' Tuck." Their tagline reads, "Nip and tuck that skin, while your hair gets a trim!" Then there's a picture of a hairdresser wearing doctor's whites, holding two pairs of scissors.

She bounces a hand against her blond bob. "Very easy, very quick, very cheap."

"Thanks, I'll think about it," I say, taking the brochure.

I might not be certain of much in my life right now, but one thing I can be sure of, I will not be booking an appointment at Snip 'n' Tuck.

AFTER A CHALLENGING day at work, sifting through a bulging inbox and racking my brain for this elusive "big idea," I feel completely wiped out. All I want to do is go home, crawl into bed, and watch Poirot alone, but I have promised to go over to Alex and Faye's. Roisin is finally back from America, and they've invited us both over for dinner.

When my cab pulls up to the address, a complex called "the Old Golf Club, Sands," I hardly recognize what's in front of me as housing. The development looks like a series of landscaped mounds, with turf and solar panels covering every inch of their curved surface. Faye appears from a doorway in one of the mounds and waves to me as I get out of the car.

"What is this place?" I ask.

"Ah, you don't remember the eco village," she says. "Come on, I'll give you the tour."

Following her inside a curved wooden entrance, I see that

much of the dwelling we're in has been built down into the ground and is far more spacious than it looked from the outside. As Faye shows me around, I marvel at the tactile surfaces of polished wood, furniture that feels part of the house rather than contents within it. There are living walls of plants, which filter the air; a hydroponic larder; and even a fully insulated living roof. While I've noticed subtle changes everywhere I go— new technology, new buildings, the cars and roads—nothing has felt that radically different. But this? *This* feels radical.

"Faye loves giving people 'the tour,'" Alex tells me, handing me a gin and tonic in a long glass, with two sprigs of mint. "You're really doing her a favor by forgetting you've already had it."

"Hi, Alex," I say, taking the drink and greeting her with a kiss on the cheek, as though we're old friends. "I love the hobbit home."

"Do not let Faye hear you using the H word again," she says in a conspiratorial whisper.

Roisin soon arrives with an overnight bag, wearing impossibly tight white jeans and a gray silk blouse, her hair cut into a sharp red bob. Seeing her in real life, rather than on a screen, I notice that Roisin has aged in a different way from me and Faye—her breasts look perter, her forehead is taut and shiny. I suspect she might have had work done, or maybe it's just the youthful elixir of being child-free. She drops her bag and walks straight over to me, clasping my elbows while looking into my eyes with a serious expression.

"I hope you haven't forgotten that you owe me five hundred quid?" she says, her mouth twitching into a smile.

"Rosh," Faye says, eyeing her with wide, disapproving eyes. "You shouldn't make jokes."

"You had an eleven-hour flight from LA and that's the best you could come up with?" I say, pulling Roisin into a tight hug.

"Eleven? It's only six now. Wow, you do have a lot to catch up on. You know they've worked out the Earth is round now, right?"

"Ha ha."

"Come on then, let's have a drink and hear all about this latest caper of yours," she says.

We gather around the kitchen island while Alex cooks, Faye fixes more drinks, and I fill them all in on the latest episode of "Lucy tries to be a grown-up." Roisin covers her face at all the right moments in my story about the disastrous pitch meeting.

"I can't believe you thought you could just blag it," she says.

"I thought I might be good at it," I say despondently.

"You *are* good at it," says Faye kindly.

"But it took you years to gain that level of expertise," says Roisin. "It's not something that happened overnight."

My eyes dart instinctively to the door, and I realize I am waiting for Zoya to walk in. This is the moment when she would arrive, twenty minutes late and full of excuses as to why the train was delayed or the bus went the wrong way. My stomach clenches, and I shift my chair so I can't watch the door. These last few days, it's been easy to imagine Zoya is simply absent or busy, but being in a room with the others, I can see the gaping hole where she should be.

"You don't think you should just tell your colleagues the truth?" Faye asks, jerking me back to the present.

"I tried, but Michael started talking about perimenopausal brain fog and it threw me off. Besides, when I tell people the truth they look at me with pitying eyes, like the ones you're giving me now."

"Sorry," says Faye, trying to look less sympathetic. "Are we even old enough to be perimenopausal?"

"Yes, no, maybe. It's a broad spectrum," says Alex. "It certainly doesn't cause you to forget half your life. How many years did you say you'd forgotten?" she asks as she feeds onions into a round machine that instantly peels and dices them.

"Sixteen," I say, tapping my glass. "And I know I've forgotten, people keep telling me that I've forgotten, but it *feels* like I skipped those years. I'm still twenty-six inside and I've woken up living someone else's life."

"In my head, I'm still sixteen," Roisin says, pouting her lips and raising one eyebrow at me.

"Do you have to joke about everything?" says Faye, tilting her head in disapproval.

"Well, I'm sorry. It must be confusing and distressing for you and for Sam." Alex leans over to put an arm around me. "Mainly I'm the victim in all this though because you don't even remember me." She lets out a purposefully dramatic wail.

"Okay, joking aside, how are you doing, Luce?" Roisin asks.

"Well, mainly, I feel tired all the time. But I don't know if that's because I'm ill, or because that's what it feels like to be forty-two."

"It's because you've got an eighteen-month-old baby," says Faye.

"Plus, I'm too scared to look at the news in case, beyond my little bubble, it's a dystopian hellscape out there," I go on, "and my nanny thinks I need a face-lift."

"Do *not* go to Snip 'n' Tuck," Roisin says, leaning forward and clutching my arm. "They gave me the worst haircut of my life."

"If it makes you feel better, there's no hellscape," says Alex. "Well, no more than usual."

"Come on, Lucy, it can't all be bad. Of all the people to wake up and be married to, you could do worse than Sam, right? He's pretty feckin' hot," says Roisin, and I give her a wry smile.

"Imagine if Faye forgot the last sixteen years?" says Alex. "She'd need to come out to herself all over again."

"Please no, the drama the first time around." Roisin sighs and Faye gives her a playful pinch. "It would be worse for me. If I forgot the last sixteen years, I'd still be in love with Paul, I'd have forgotten he was a scumbag," says Roisin, rolling her eyes.

"Can I ask what happened?" I ask. "Or is it too much to dredge up?"

"No, dredge away. Life fucks you over, is what happened," she says, taking a swig of wine. "You fall in love, have the Instagram wedding, work your arse off, get promoted, build a beautiful home, but your husband gets jealous of your success and the magic goes. Then one morning you find another woman's underwear in the overnight bag he took on a work trip."

"I'm sorry that happened to you," I say, reaching out a hand to her on the counter, but she pulls it away, toying with an earring.

"It's the cliché I couldn't stand. The cliché of those knickers too—a red lacy thong. Who wears a lacy red thong?"

"I wear lacy red thongs," Alex says, pulling down her trousers slightly to reveal a glimpse of red underwear.

"No, you don't," Faye laughs. "That is not a thong."

"I wore a red thong on our wedding night!" Alex says, grinning mischievously at Faye. "You don't remember?"

"Do you remember what knickers I was wearing?" Faye asks, resting her chin on Alex's shoulder.

"Yes. Cream silk hipster briefs," says Alex, cackling with laughter. Watching them together, I realize I have never seen Faye have this natural, jokey, tactile affection with someone; I realize I have never seen her in love. She looks so at ease, so bubbling with this gentle joy, it gives me a warm, happy feeling just to see it.

"That's love. Perfect pants recall," Rosin says as Alex and Faye kiss. Watching them, I have a sudden flash—a memory of them on their wedding day, both dressed in white, outside a town hall, Faye with purple flowers in her hair. I must have seen a photograph somewhere on the house tour.

"Well, I never liked him, if that helps at all," I tell Roisin. "He had that leg jiggle he was always doing—so annoying. And he was such a coffee snob. I remember you'd spend your weekends hunting out obscure independent coffee shops. Sometimes you just need a Starbucks, Paul."

"He was an Aries," says Faye, as though this is the worst thing she can think of to say about someone.

"Thank you both, I appreciate the sentiment," says Roisin.

"Tell me he got some comeuppance for the red thong situation?" I ask.

"Nope." Roisin shakes her head. "They're getting married next month. She's got family money, and a mansion in St. John's Wood. They're happy as fuckin' clams."

"Comeuppance only happens in fiction and religion," Alex says.

"His comeuppance is, he's a dickhead," says Faye, and

Roisin blows her a kiss across the kitchen island. Faye rarely uses bad language, so it feels very effective when she does.

There's a pause in conversation while Faye tops up everyone's glasses, then she says, "Imagine if we were actually twenty-six again."

"I wouldn't do my twenties again if you paid me," says Roisin. "All men under thirty-five are twats, you're bottom of the pile at work, plus you have to fly everywhere economy."

"The rest of us still fly economy, Roisin," says Faye, rolling her eyes.

"I don't know, I think there's something glorious about being in your twenties, your whole life is ahead of you and everything's a possibility," says Alex, picking up aubergines and peppers to throw into her lethal-looking peeling and cutting machine.

"I will give you alcohol tolerance and skin elasticity, which were both excellent," says Roisin. "What about you, Lucy, would you go back, if you could?"

"Yes," I say, without even hesitating. "I can see the advantages to being this age, but there are things I didn't expect too. Life just feels *so* busy, like there's never any time. The big stuff seems so much bigger, the sad stuff . . . well, it's really fucking sad."

"You're right, in some ways, life only gets more complicated," says Alex. "The older you get, the more you encounter grief, pain, and disappointment. Anyone who hasn't, it is coming for them."

"Amen," says Roisin. "Life is never sorted. It's just an undulating shit storm of problems and pleasure."

"This is all really cheery stuff," I say wryly.

"But"—Alex holds up a hand, she hasn't finished—"maybe

bones need to be broken for you to suck out the marrow of life. We are lucky, we are here, when others are not. I wear the gray in my hair as a badge of honor, the privilege of aging."

We all pause for a moment, glasses still in our hands.

"She'd be so disappointed in us, wouldn't she? Staying in, cooking vegetable risotto, drinking eco wine from a flask," Roisin says, tilting her head to one side.

"She would," I say, my voice breaking.

"To Zoya," says Alex, lifting her wine in the air.

"To Zoya," says Faye, meeting my eye. "Who we miss, every single day."

We raise our glasses, making eye contact with one another, a look that says more than words ever could.

"Sam doesn't think I'm the same person I was a few weeks ago," I say quietly. "Honestly, I was worried you all might find me lacking too."

"What? How could he say that?" says Faye with a frown.

"You're not lacking anything," says Roisin firmly. "Your jokes are still terrible, you still drink too fast, and I see you're clinging on to statement earrings like they didn't go out of style." She pauses. "I don't feel like you've changed at all."

"Maybe that's because we all revert to being teenagers when we're around each other," I say, leaning my head against Roisin's shoulder.

"Or your friends simply know you the best," says Faye.

Sitting down to eat, sinking into this familiar rhythm of conversation, it feels like putting on an old, beloved coat—warm and comforting, embroidered with an indelible history. It refuels me, revives me, and I'm glad I did not go home to watch Poirot alone.

SAM IS AWAKE, reading in the living room, when I get back.

"Hi, how was your night?" he asks.

"Great. It was lovely to see everyone," I tell him. *Everyone.* The word sticks in my mouth because it wasn't everyone.

"Good, I'm glad you went," he says, closing his book, then nodding his head to one side and patting the sofa, inviting me to sit beside him. Once I'm sitting, he pulls my foot into his lap, takes off my shoe, and starts rubbing the sole of my foot. It feels strangely intimate, but I let myself sink into it.

"Where are you at, Luce? I can't tell what you're thinking," he asks gently. "Was I wrong to tell you about Chloe?"

What would Future Me say? What's the mature response? Maybe the truth. Now, suddenly I do know what to say.

"No, I'm glad you told me, I needed to know." I pause. "And I understand why you said that I wasn't your wife, but that didn't make me feel great. It's made me feel like more of an imposter than I already feel."

He stops rubbing my foot and reaches to tilt my chin so that I'm looking him in the eye. "I know, I'm sorry, that came out horribly. You *are* my wife, of course you are. I love you, I will always love you, whatever happens, whatever you do or don't remember."

Sam leans in, his warm, oaky smell so new and yet so familiar. *Is he going to kiss me?* There's a moment that feels electrically charged, before he gently presses his lips to mine, so soft, and then suddenly firmer, deeper. I comb a hand through his messy hair and pull him closer, giddy with the feel of him, relief pulsing through every particle of my body. As I stroke my hand around his back, I have a sudden image of the shirt he's wearing. Breakfast on a beach, him spilling orange juice down it. Is that a memory? *That can't be a photo.* I pull away.

"What's wrong?" he asks.

"Nothing." Less a memory, I reason, more a glimpse, a fragment, maybe something I saw in a video. "You don't need to apologize for feeling weird about all this. *I* feel weird about it too. I guess I don't feel like your wife either."

Sam pulls back, pinching the bridge of his nose. "You're going to remember. You will."

"But what if I don't?"

His hand moves back to my leg and he starts slowly massaging my calf. "Then I will try to fill in the gaps for you."

As we lie on the sofa, he tells me about our life together, the beginning of our story. Our first date, to Borough Market, where I bought so much cheese he had to lend me his backpack so I could carry it home; our first weekend away to the Lake District, where he tried to show off his boating prowess but left us becalmed at the wrong end of lake Windermere. That prompted our first argument. He tells me about the dinner I hosted to introduce him to my friends, how he was so nervous that he spilled gravy all over Roisin's immaculate tablecloth. He tells me about a trip we took to Greece with Zoya and her fiancé, Tarek, where Zoya was painting a mural for a restaurant and thought it was hilarious that she gave Zeus Sam's face. He paints each memory with such vivid details: the color of the sky, the food we ate, my reaction to things, how I laughed at the mural so hard red wine came out of my nose. I'm not sure when I drift off, but his words feel like a balm soothing me to sleep, the details of our life together like brushstrokes, painting their way into my dreams.

25

THE NEXT MORNING, I WAKE WITH A NEW SENSE OF purpose. It's as though falling asleep in Sam's arms has built a new cocoon around me, reminding me of the need to metamorphose. So I've not had instant success. Did I really think I was going to come up with the perfect idea in one evening of research? That I was going to learn how to be a parent in a single day? That I could slot into an eleven-year relationship without any difficulty at all?

Now, as I make breakfast for the children, I pledge I will be more patient. At work, I will try to listen and learn. At home, I will be more empathetic to Sam, give him time to adapt. I will be a calm, composed, ethereal mother. There will be no swearing in front of the children. I will start saying, "Yes, my child," to all questions, like a nun in olden times.

"You have a new message on the forum," says Felix excitedly, holding up my phone at the breakfast table.

"Felix! Don't look at that!" I say, snatching it back, my ethereal, nunlike mothering lasting less than a minute.

"Read it, read it!"

Opening the message cautiously, I check it's nothing pornographic, then, once I'm sure it's not, I show the message to Felix.

TO: WishingFor26

FROM: Crock Pouch

There's a depot under the arches at Battersea Bridge. Guy called Arcade Dave who restores all these vintage machines. Brown door next to the flower stall. If anyone knows about your wishing machine, he will. He's off-grid, no phone, so you'd need to go down there. Tell him Crock Pouch sent you and he'll be more amenable. He can be a bit of a funny fella.

CP

Then beneath his sign-off, there's a quote: "I'm not a player, I'm a gamer."

"We have to go!" says Felix. "It's like a real-life quest, with passwords and everything. Let's go now!"

"We can't go now, I have work, you have school."

"So?"

"So we're not skipping school to go to some random depot to meet a guy called 'Arcade Dave.'"

Felix glares up at me, then turns his attention back to his cereal bowl, filling the air with disgruntled munching.

"Sorry, Felix, I just have a lot of work to do. No one liked any of the ideas I pitched."

"Did you pitch helicopters and conger eels?" he asks.

"Surprisingly, yes." I sigh.

"Did you tell them the conger eels would be *in* the helicopters?" Felix asks.

"Maybe that's where I went wrong."

"What are you two plotting?" Sam asks. He's in a suit, on his way to a recording session in Reading.

"Oh, nothing," I say. Now that Sam and I are on firmer footing, I'm not sure I want to complicate matters by admitting that his son and I are secretly looking for a magical portal to send me back in time. "Felix is just helping me with ideas for work."

"No one's come up with anything yet?" he asks, making himself a coffee to go.

"No. Despite everything, Michael's still confident I can think of the right idea. But I'm not sure how much value I can add. There are too many gaps, too much I don't know."

"There's not a room you could be in and not add value," Sam says, and his sincerity makes me feel as though a tiny cheerleading squad has come out and done a pom-pom routine just for me. "Right, got to run. See you all later." Sam kisses me on the lips, then rushes out of the door. I watch him go through the kitchen window. *Wow, this guy, no wonder I wished for him. He's almost too good to be true.*

"Mummy? Mummy!" Felix says behind me.

"What? Oh, the depot, right. Look, I'll try and find out more. If it's a real thing, maybe I can go this weekend."

"With me?"

"We'll see," I say, beginning to regret going along with all this. Surely it can only end in disappointment. But is it me or Felix that I'm worried about disappointing?

"Can I have more raisins?" Felix asks.

"You don't even like raisins," I say, picking up the raisin jar from the sideboard and passing it to him. Then I stop still. How did I know Felix doesn't like raisins? As I grip the table to get my balance, Felix shoots me a puzzled look.

"No. I like them now, but only on cereal, not on their own." Felix pauses, watching me, then his eyes bulge as he realizes what I'm saying. "You remember something from the in-between?"

"Maybe, I don't know," I say, rubbing my eyes.

"What does it mean—if you start remembering stuff?" Felix asks, flinging his hands in the air, his entire body a frantic jumble of animation. "If you came through a portal, you wouldn't have those memories! Maybe the portal is closing? Maybe the raisins are a *warning*?" He takes a dramatic breath. "Maybe—"

"Forget it, it's probably nothing, your dad must have mentioned the raisins. Come on, Maria will be here any minute, then we need to leave for school."

Clearly, I should not have said anything to Felix. It's hard enough to get everyone fed, dressed, and out of the house as it is, without throwing in a casual debate about the rules of time travel.

FELIX GETS ME thinking though and I'm distracted on the drive to school. If these memories are in there somewhere, does that mean that I didn't jump here? Part of me is holding on to the idea that all this might be temporary. And while I doubt Arcade Dave holds the key to getting me home, I still believe I might simply wake up one morning back where I was. But it has been two weeks now, and if I genuinely do have amnesia, there will be no going back.

"I'll ask Molly what she thinks it means—you remembering about the raisins. She knows loads about time travel," says Felix. "Her dad writes science fiction, but he calls it science fact that hasn't happened yet." He pauses, then says excitedly, "Maybe Molly and her dad could come with us to the depot?"

"Felix!" I say, exasperated. "I am not going to invite Molly and her dad to come on some random outing to find a man in London who may or may not know something about an ancient arcade game that may or may not have magical properties." I take a loud breath. "Can we please just get to school and discuss this later?"

Felix goes quiet, and we drive in silence for a minute.

"I've lost my school library card. Can I look in your bag?" he asks quietly.

"Sure," I say, handing him my handbag from the front seat. "Look, I'm sorry for shouting. I know you're only trying to help." Felix shrugs. "It's just I really need to get my train today."

At the school, Felix holds my eye in the rearview mirror before unbuckling his seat belt. There's a flash of something in his eyes—guilt. What would Felix have to feel guilty about? Maybe he hasn't done his homework, or he's fighting with a friend? Anything could be going on with him, and I wouldn't even know to ask, I'm too consumed in my own drama. It's not just my own life I'm going to need to catch up on, it's the lives of everyone in this family. When I get back from work, I will make time, I will find the right questions to ask.

MY MORNING AT Badger TV is spent trawling through emails, trying to get to grips with a myriad of urgent things I'm apparently now responsible for. The pitch-off itself is just one small cyclone in an endless storm. Michael tells me to delegate but even delegation feels beyond me. Everything requires a level of knowledge I just don't have. My inbox is a torrent of tax code questions, building lease amendments, data protection registration, union petitions, staff training requests, a notification about the expiry of my Bamph retention agreement, commissioner meetings, budget meetings, shooting schedule meetings, pre-meetings, post-meetings, wrap-up meetings. How can one person need to be in quite so many meetings? There's even a meeting scheduled to discuss meeting schedules. I've had to block out my diary with pretend meetings just to stop anyone from putting more meetings in.

Trying to focus on something as frivolous as thinking up new TV shows also feels impossible. My head keeps jumping back to Sam, to the pain in his eyes as he told me about Chloe. That pain must be mine too, lying dormant somewhere. If my memories return, will that grief come back too? I can't even imagine what it must feel like to lose a child. Selfishly, I'm not sure I want to know.

By lunchtime I need to take a break from creating fake meetings, so I nip to Selfridges to try to return all the crazy stuff I bought. Well, most of the crazy stuff; I'm not giving back the boots. Unfortunately, the man at the returns desk won't accept the purple suit. He claims it's been worn, and that the tags have been sellotaped back on. *Outrageous.* And he isn't at all sympathetic when I explain that I didn't know about having to pay for the nanny and the mortgage and the loft cladding and all this other boring grown-up stuff I'm supposed to spend my money on now. It doesn't help my case that, for some reason, I don't have the card I paid for it all with in my wallet. When I lie down on the floor and beg, the manager eventually takes pity on me and offers me 60 percent of the purchase price in store credit, if I'll stop making a spectacle of myself.

Just as I'm wondering whether Maria might agree to be paid in Selfridges vouchers, Sam calls. The thought of speaking to Sam adds a little bounce to my step, but as soon as I answer the call, I know something is wrong.

"Have you heard from Felix?" Sam's voice is stricken with panic.

"What? No. Why?"

"He ran away from school. They don't know where he is." Sam takes an audible intake of breath; he can hardly get the words out. "They wanted to check he hadn't gone home before they called the police. He didn't say anything to you on the drive to school, did he?"

"No, I don't think so," I say. My heart starts pounding in my chest and my lungs contract, leaving no room to breathe. My mind races, trying to remember what Felix and I talked about in the car this morning.

"He doesn't have any money; he can't go anywhere." Sam's voice catches in his throat, as though he's on the verge of screaming.

"Sam, my bank card is missing," I say, with a horrible sinking feeling as I remember Felix going into my purse to look for his library card. "He could have taken it. Where would he have gone?" The thought of Felix, out alone in the world, possibly in danger, causes an animal ache in my gut, followed by a rising tide of panic. What if he's been taken? What if he's hurt? A knot of primal fear tightens in my chest, so overwhelming, it feels like I might pass out.

"The tracker on his iPad," Sam says. "Find My Child. If he has his backpack with him, you might be able to see where he is on your phone."

Keeping Sam on the line, my hand shaking, I search my phone screen for the app. A low hum of dread sits in my stomach, as though this is all my fault. The app opens and I see an icon labeled "Felix's iPad" moving across the map on the screen.

"He's between Aldershot and Ashvale," I tell Sam, but the dot is moving. "He's . . . he's on the train."

"The train?"

"He's coming to London." As I say it, the knot of fear releases an inch.

"Why would he be going to London?" Sam asks.

"I don't know. I'll go now, intercept him at Waterloo."

"I'll call the train line," says Sam, "alert a guard, ask someone to keep him safe until he gets to you." Sam's voice shifts from fear to anger. "I'm going to kill him. What is he thinking?"

"I don't know," I say.

But then maybe I do.

26

AFTER SHOOTING A TEXT TO MICHAEL TO EXPLAIN THAT, yet again, I have a child-related emergency, I reach Waterloo in time to see a red-faced Felix being escorted off the train by a guard. "This one is yours?" he asks me.

"He is."

"This your mum?" the guard asks Felix, and there's the briefest pause as Felix picks something out of his nostril before acknowledging that I am indeed his mother. "All right, my little runaway, off you hop."

Crouching down to his level, I pull Felix into a hug. At this busy station, next to the tall guard, he looks so small, so vulnerable. "We were so worried. What were you thinking?"

"You wouldn't look for the portal," he says, his small brow set in a frown.

"What were you planning to do—wander around London looking for this random depot?" He nods. I'm learning that children are oblivious to both sarcasm and any perceived shame in picking their noses in public. Taking his hand, I start walking toward the main concourse. "Come on, there's a train home in ten minutes."

"Can't we just have a quick look, now that I'm here?" he pleads, tugging on my sleeve.

Looking down at his face, into eyes that look so much like mine, I feel myself relent. He believed in this plan enough to take my bank card, run away from school, and get on a train all by himself.

"It wasn't fair for me to get your hopes up by posting on that forum. I shouldn't have let you believe there's a magical fix for any of this." I pause, pinching my forehead. "You do realize how insane this whole plan is?"

"Yes," he says somberly.

"And if we look for the depot, and we don't find anything, will you drop it—the websites, the hunt for a portal, everything?"

"Yes." He nods his head rapidly up and down, his eyes dancing with delight.

"Fine. I'll call your dad."

Sam answers before the phone even rings. "I've got him."

"Thank God. I'll call the school," Sam says. "What was he doing?"

"He believes there's a portal that brought me here from the past. He thinks if we find it, he can send me back." Sam is silent on the line. "It's my fault, I told him about this wishing machine, the last thing I remember." Turning my back to Felix and lowering my voice, I say, "He knows he's in trouble for running away, but this whole situation has been hard on him too. I think it might be good if I just spent some time with him, one on one."

I'm expecting Sam to object, but he says, "Fine. If you think it will help. He's still in trouble, though. Tell him no screen time for a week—no, two weeks. School will want words with him too."

I turn back to Felix, the phone still to my ear. "Your dad says no screen time for two weeks."

"And tell him I love him and I'm glad he's okay," Sam says, a raw, ragged edge in his voice now.

"Love you too, Dad," Felix calls toward the phone.

"Okay, we'll see you later then. We might be a while."

"I love you," Sam says. Before I can work out how to respond, he's gone.

FELIX AND I get a bus toward Battersea. Traveling past Westminster Bridge, looking out across the Thames, I see the familiar shapes of Big Ben, the Houses of Parliament, and the London Eye. There are new buildings too, changing the skyline I once knew. Twisty columns of steel and stone denote a Parthenon-style building on the south bank. A distinctive conical skyscraper dominates the horizon to the east, and huge curved flood barriers encase both riverbanks. London, old and new, ever evolving, but also somehow intrinsically the same.

Felix pulls a small notebook out of his backpack and hands it to me.

"What's this?"

"It's a logbook. When you go on an expedition, you need to log everything."

"Right."

"If you're on an expedition and an incident occurs, like

someone falls over and cuts their knee or if there's a shark attack, you need to make a log of it."

"Okay, I'll keep a lookout for sharks."

"There aren't going to be any sharks in London, Mummy."

"How did you get out of school this afternoon, Felix?"

He looks sheepish for a moment, picking at a thread on the bus seat in front of him.

"There's a gap in the fence in the playground. You can squeeze out if you really want to."

"And you walked all the way to the station, on your own? That's incredibly dangerous. Promise me you'll never do that again."

"I took my whistle," he says, showing me a small red whistle around his neck.

"What's the whistle going to do?"

"'If anyone tries to steal you, blow your whistle'—that's what you told me, when we went to that music festival." He pauses to inspect his whistle for a moment. "Do you think you would die if you swallowed a whistle?"

"I don't think you'd die. No."

"What about two whistles?"

"I don't know, Felix."

"How many whistles do you think you could swallow and not die?"

"If it got stuck in your windpipe you might die, but . . . why do we need to know the answer to this? Just don't swallow any whistles."

As we get off the bus at Battersea Arches, a teenage boy on a hovering scooter flies along the pavement and nearly crashes into us. Grabbing hold of Felix, I swing him out of the way just in time, then turn to yell, "Watch it, you fucking idiot!" at the teenager, who doesn't even turn to give us a backward glance. Felix looks up at me, his eyes shining with admiration.

"Sorry, I shouldn't have said that," I tell him, biting my lip. "That's a horrible word."

"*That* was an incident," says Felix.

"Was it?"

"Definitely." Felix takes out the logbook. "Can you write it, because my writing's too big? Write the time and then write 'Man on scooter nearly crashes into us. Mummy tells him he's a fucking idiot.'"

"I don't think we need to write the specifics of who said what."

Having located the old rail arches, we wander around looking for a flower stall or a brown door. The place looks uninhabited: boarded-up shops, graffitied walls, and abandoned shopping trolleys. I'm starting to think Crouch Pouch, or whatever his name was, might have been having us on.

"You look lost," says a huge man with an impressive array of body tattoos, working on an upturned motorbike outside a repair shop.

"We're looking for Arcade Dave," Felix says, giving the man a slow wink. The man gives Felix a cold, hard stare, and I'm worried we might be about to put that whistle-swallowing conundrum to the test. But then the man nods over to his left. "Up there, past the flower stall."

Following his directions, we find a small stall selling a few wilting tulips, and just as Crouch Pouch promised, a brown door with a dusty sign that reads Dave's Depot.

"This is it!" Felix says, pushing open the creaking door. On the other side is a metal grate leading to a rusty spiral staircase, heading down into the bowels of London. Felix runs ahead, fearless, and each of his steps echoes with a metallic clack throughout the windowless brick cavern.

"It's a bit dark," I say, nervously following Felix down the winding staircase. "Maybe we should wait." Suddenly, this all seems like a bad idea. What if that website was really a people-trafficking site, and we've been lured here under false pretenses? What if I get Felix kidnapped? Or me kidnapped, for that matter? Just as I'm about to suggest we turn back, Felix shouts, "It's here!" from further below me on the staircase. Hurrying down the final few spirals, I come out on solid ground to see a second set of huge brick rail arches, built beneath the ones at ground level. The cavernous, curved space in front of us is jam-packed with old arcade games and dusty fairground curiosities. It's an awesome sight, like discovering Tutankhamun's tomb (if Tutankhamun had been around in the eighties and obsessed with video games). I pause for a moment to absorb the sheer unexpected spectacle of the place.

"It's going to be here," says Felix, running toward the jumbled aisles of ancient technology.

"Hello?" I call out, worried we might be in trouble for wandering down here uninvited, then remembering the guy from the forum's warning that Arcade Dave "could be a bit of a funny fella." *What does that mean, that he's a comedian or that he's a psychopath?*

A man in filthy overalls with a messy auburn mustache stands up from behind an old Pac-Man machine, eyeing us suspiciously.

"Arcade Dave?" I ask, furnishing him with the best please-don't-be-a-psychopath smile I can muster.

"Who's asking?" he says.

"I'm Lucy and this is Felix. Crouch Pouch sent us."

"It wasn't Crouch Pouch, Mummy, it was Crock Pouch," says Felix, his eyes darting nervously to Arcade Dave.

I imagine this name is going to act as a Masonic handshake in this underground lair, but Arcade Dave simply says, "Don't know 'im," and gets back to work on his machine.

Felix, undeterred, strides over to him.

"We're looking for a wishing machine, it's like a million years old."

"It's not a million years old," I clarify, "it's probably from the seventies or eighties, maybe the fifties. Definitely twentieth century."

"What does it look like?" Dave asks, wiping his nose with an oily rag.

He listens attentively as I tell him everything I can remember, then beckons us to follow him. Felix bounces along behind, unable to contain his excitement. He turns around and mouths to me, "He has it!"

Dave leads us to a machine covered in a sheet, and I brace myself as he reaches to unveil it. *What if this really is it?* But when he pulls off the dust sheet, he reveals a square glass case with a scary-looking genie holding a giant crystal ball. Felix looks at me expectantly, though he knows I never mentioned a genie. I shake my head. "No, that's not it."

"Ain't seen anything else like you're saying," Arcade Dave tells us, shaking his head. "Collectors, are you?"

"Kind of," I tell him, narrowing my eyes at Felix to stop him from launching into a time-travel-themed explanation.

Arcade Dave sneezes on his oily rag, then hands me a greasy business card from his overalls. "Leave your number. I'll ask around. If I hear of anything, I'll let you know."

Perhaps sensing Felix's disappointment, Arcade Dave then

says, "Hey, kid, you want a quick go on a Robotron 2084 that I just got working?"

Felix nods enthusiastically.

WHEN WE FINALLY emerge back into daylight, I can tell Felix is still disappointed.

"I'm sorry it was a dead end," I say, but he shakes his head.

"That was just one stage in the quest. Quests always have multiple stages. Dave has your number now."

"I don't know, it felt like a dead end to me."

Felix shifts his weight between his feet, then looks up at me nervously. "Do you think he knew I thought his game was boring? I didn't want to be rude. I was trying to pretend it was fun."

"Well, you did a good job then. You looked like you were having fun to me," I say, putting an arm around his shoulder.

It's a sunny day and I don't feel like getting back on the bus just yet, so I suggest we walk for a bit. Despite our mission's failure, Felix is surprisingly buoyant and talkative. I am learning that Felix likes everything to have an opposite, and that he is very interested in knowing what might kill you if ingested. When we get to Vauxhall, I ask Felix if he would like to see where I used to live, and he says he would.

"That was your flat?" Felix asks as we sit down on a bench on the opposite side of the street.

"Yup, third floor." I point up to my old window. "I lived up there with my best friend Zoya, and two others, Emily and Julian." I feel the tug of nostalgia, thinking about all the conversations we had sitting up in that window seat; all the cheap wine drunk, the books read, and the dreams shared. Zoya once made Emily, Julian, and me sit up there in the dark beside a propped-up torch, so she could draw silhouettes of our heads. "It was always messy and squashed. We never had loo roll, but we did have a lot of fun."

"Why didn't you have loo roll?" Felix asks.

"Well, we didn't have delivery drones back then," I explain.

"Was Zoya your friend who died?" Felix asks, scuffing his feet against the ground.

"Yes," I say, my eyes still glued to the window ledge.

"And she was your number one best friend?"

"She was."

Felix examines his hands, then says, "Matt Christensen asked if he could be my best friend. I said I'd have to think about it."

"I think at your age, it's nice to be friends with everyone, keep your options open."

"I want a best friend, though." He kicks one foot with the other now. "I asked Molly Greenway to be my best friend. She said girls have to have girls and boys have to have boys."

"That's not true. You can have whoever you like as your best friend."

Felix goes quiet for a moment, as though contemplating this. "Did you choose Zoya, or did she choose you?"

I reach out to hold Felix's hand. "I think we chose each other. We sat next to each other in French, we'd write notes to each other in our own made-up language."

"Made-up language?" Felix asks, bemused.

"Words that sounded funny to us. We were weird kids. I think that's what a best friend is, someone you can show your inner weirdo to."

"I sit next to Molly in Coding Club," Felix tells me. "She's way better at it than me. She's funny too. She made this platform game called Girls Win, Boys in the Bin. You have to put all the boys in the bin to win. And Mrs. Harris wouldn't grade it, she said it was sexist, so then Molly changed all the boys to little Mrs. Harrises and called it Kids Win, Teachers in the Bin." Felix laughs and claps a hand against his thigh.

"I like the sound of Molly."

As we're sitting on the bench, looking at my old flat across the street, the front door opens and Mr. Finkley appears with a bag of recycling. Seeing me, he raises a hand in greeting, and I take Felix's hand to cross the road.

"Felix, this is Mr. Finkley, he lived in the flat above me. Mr. Finkley, this is my son." *My son. Will I ever get used to saying that?*

"What brings you back here?" Mr. Finkley asks. "Still missing a few years, are you?"

"Afraid so. We were just taking a little trip down memory lane."

"Would you like to come up for some ham?" Mr. Finkley asks.

I'm about to politely decline when Felix cries, "I love ham!" and takes a step toward the front door.

"I thought you were super fussy about food," I say, narrowing my eyes at him.

"I'm not fussy about ham," he says, now standing ready and waiting by the front door.

"I guess we're coming up then. If you're sure we wouldn't be an inconvenience?"

"No, no," says Mr. Finkley. "I'm not getting my stamps out, though."

Inside Mr. Finkley's apartment, Felix looks around at the foliage-filled room as though he's just stepped into a secret subterranean world. "Wow, cool house. It's like living in a jungle."

Mr. Finkley's mouth twitches, pleased. "It was your mother here who got me into horticulture."

Of all the things that seem unlikely about the years I've missed, one is that butter boards weren't the short-lived Instagram fad everyone expected them to be, and two is that I, apparently, became a gardening guru.

"Mummy's good at plants," Felix says, puffing out his chest. "Would you like to see my logbook?"

"Felix, I'm sure Mr. Finkley doesn't—"

"I would be honored to see your logbook."

After clearing some space on the sofa for us to sit down, then bringing out a plate of assorted hams, Mr. Finkley settles down to inspect Felix's book. He is an excellent audience, asking all the right questions, and even commenting on the thoroughness of the "incidents" column and the excellent sketch Felix has drawn of Arcade Dave.

"This is the best ham," Felix says as they sit side by side poring over the logbook.

"Smoked. Always smoked," says Mr. Finkley.

"Mummy, can you get smoked next time?"

I nod, making a mental note to ask my car to instruct a flying drone to bring smoked ham to my house, then marvel that this sentence seems entirely normal.

"I could have used a young man like you on one of my boat trips," says Mr. Finkley.

"You had a boat?" I ask, finding it hard to imagine him anywhere other than this apartment.

"Used to. I led research expeditions, took divers and

scientists out to the central Pacific. My wife was an oceanographer."

"You were deep-sea explorers?" asks Felix, his mouth dropping open in awe.

"Not me. I stayed on the boat, but yes, Astrid was." Mr. Finkley nods and sits up a little straighter, his eyes creasing into a smile.

"I didn't know you were married," I say.

"Many moons ago," Mr. Finkley says, standing up and walking across to a wooden bureau that's bursting with books and papers. He pulls out a small brass compass and a folder of old maps. Laying one out on a table, he shows Felix how to chart nautical miles using a compass and ruler. Felix is fascinated and full of questions. I end up leaving them to it, stepping out onto Mr. Finkley's balcony to catch up on messages and work emails.

There's a message from the Bamph CEO's PA asking if I would be willing to move my "F meeting" from the executive suite. It appears I've bumped the quarterly shareholder meeting on the booking portal. Oops, I thought I was only putting that in my own diary. Hopefully no one will be able to crack my cunning fake meeting code.

I also have a message from Michael:

Hope all okay at home. I think best for team morale if we keep your brain fog between us for now. Don't want the team losing confidence in your abilities before the big pitch. Best not put any more fake meetings on the Bamph intranet either . . .

M

P.S. Jane says killer whales go through the menopause too,
so you're in excellent company.

Eventually, I drag Felix away. We need to get our train.
It might not have been great parenting to reward Felix's
running away with such an adventure-filled day, but seeing
him so animated makes me feel it might have been time well
spent.

"You can have this," Mr. Finkley says, handing the small
brass compass to Felix as we leave. "I don't have many places
to navigate to anymore. Better it be in the hands of a real
explorer."

"Oh wow, thank you so much," Felix says, clasping it as
though he's just been gifted the crown jewels.

On the train home, Felix uses the compass to give me con-
stant updates on our direction of travel: "Southwest. West.
South-southwest." It gets annoying quickly, so I try to distract
him by reading back our incident report in a funny, high-
pitched voice. Felix finds it hilarious, then insists I write,
"Mummy reads the incident report in a funny voice," in
the report, which makes him cry with laughter. Watching
him, I feel a warm tug of unfiltered affection for this funny
little boy.

A compact vending machine on wheels trundles along the
carriage toward us, and I ask Felix if he wants anything. He
sits up in his seat and gives me a strange look.

"What?" I ask.

"Mummy never lets us have snacks from the machine."
He raises an eyebrow, as though challenging me to retract the
offer.

"Well, Mummy does now," I say, pulling a goofy face. I

buy two chocolate biscuits from the machine, before it moves away along the carriage.

Felix says in a quiet voice, "Thank you—"

"You're welcome."

"—for letting me look."

"I had fun," I say, then, after a pause, "But you do promise never to run off looking for portals again? I understand your need for this to be fixable, I feel it too, Felix, believe me, but if it isn't . . . well, there are worse things that happen to people. I'm still here, aren't I? I am still your mummy."

He nods solemnly, and as I say it, for the first time, I feel like it could be true.

AS THE TRAIN rattles on through Woking, Felix finishes the last of his biscuit, then says, "You know you're trying to think of a new kids' show. Why don't you pitch one of your games?"

"My games?"

"Like we played the other night all over the house, that was brilliant. You don't even need loads of stuff. Like, for 'the floor is lava' you don't need actual lava."

"Remind me how that game works again?"

"Someone shouts, 'The floor is lava,' and you have to get off the floor or you're dead."

"What, like this?" I ask, jumping up onto the train seat and yelling, "The floor is lava!"

Felix looks up at me in horror or awe, I'm not sure which, then says, "Mummy, we're on a train."

"Okay, sorry, the *train* floor is lava!" I cry, leaping across the aisle to one of the empty seats opposite, giggling as I almost lose my footing because of the motion of the train. Felix covers his face with his hands, then peers out at me through a gap between his fingers. His expression is priceless, but then a gruff voice behind me says, "Ma'am. You'll need to get down from there."

CHAPTER 27

"DON'T TELL YOUR DAD I GOT A FINE," I REMIND FELIX AS I pull the car into the driveway.

"Can I tell Molly at school?" Felix asks, his eyes still gleaming with the adrenaline rush of seeing his mother get a fine for antisocial behavior. "She'll think it's so cool."

"No, you can't tell anyone. What happens on an expedition stays on the expedition."

Through the kitchen window I can see Sam dancing with Amy in his arms. His lips are moving—he's singing to her.

We sit in the car for a few minutes, neither of us making a move to get out. Perhaps Felix remembers he's in trouble, while I'm reluctant for the magic of this afternoon to end, eager to hold on to this new feeling of camaraderie with Felix. Finally, Sam notices us, waves, and now our expedition really is at an end.

In the hall, Sam bends down to wrap Felix in his huge arms, saying muffled words into his shoulder: "Don't you ever do that to us again. You had me so worried."

"I'm sorry, Dad."

"We'll talk about it later. Did you do what you needed to do?" Sam asks, and Felix nods. Then Sam holds out his hand and Felix passes him his iPad.

"I'll need it for school."

"Then you can have it back at school time," says Sam.

I watch as Felix pulls the logbook from his backpack and tucks it into his trouser pocket, shooting me the look of someone who thinks they've gotten away with something.

"There's food on the table," Sam tells him, and Felix heads through to the kitchen.

I nod after him. "He's a great kid, isn't he?"

"He is," says Sam. "They both are."

And then I notice Amy, her eyes wide as pools, crawling toward my leg. She's not crying or biting or smelly, and even though she has a bit of puree on her top, I don't mind picking her up and letting her nuzzle into my neck. I feel a warm hum of pleasure at being loved by this small creature. She doesn't care that I'm failing at work, that I embarrassed myself at the returns desk in Selfridges, or that I just got a fine for jumping on a train seat. She just loves me because I'm her mother, or at least someone who looks and smells a lot like her.

When Felix is out of earshot Sam asks me, "You didn't find this portal back to another world then, I take it?" His face is a picture of skeptical amusement.

"Surprisingly, no," I say, putting Amy down and watching her crawl off toward the kitchen.

"Good. I think I'd miss you if you disappeared into another dimension."

We stand opposite each other in the hall, and I can't quite

meet his eyes. He's looking at me so intently, but I don't know how to be around Sam now. He was so tender toward me last night, saying all the right things, but it doesn't change the facts.

"Do you want the good news or the bad news about what's been happening here?" Sam asks, watching me with smiling eyes.

"Both," I say, clasping my hands behind my back, trying to be normal.

"Well, the bad news is, Amy chewed your favorite pair of shoes."

"And the good news?"

"You probably don't remember which your favorite pair is. They might not be your favorites anymore."

"Ha ha," I say, pushing a hand against his shoulder. He catches it and pulls me into a hug. It feels so normal. I want him to kiss me again, like he did last night. I want him to be Sam from date night, where we get to start at the beginning, not halfway through. I want a *real* second date.

A beam of sunlight shines through the glass on the front door, blinding us both for a moment.

"Let's go out," I say suddenly.

"Out?" Sam asks. "You've only just got in."

"It's such a beautiful evening. I saw bluebells in the park when we drove past. They never last long, if we don't see them now, we might miss them. Let's go—family outing."

Sam looks torn. "That's a nice idea, but the kitchen's a mess, Amy's tired, I need to get her bedding out of the dryer before—"

"Sam. Twenty minutes. Come on." I do a little dance, jigging my thumbs from side to side.

His eyes crinkle in a genuine smile. It feels like a triumph. "Kids, eat up, Mummy says we're going on a family outing."

AT THE PARK, I push Amy in her buggy while Felix shows me his attempt at a wheelie (which isn't a wheelie at all, but Sam and I cheer him on as though he's done something worthy of Cirque du Soleil). In one corner of the park, the grass has been left to grow wild, a haven for bees. A carpet of bluebells spreads out beneath a copse of trees. The evening sun shines through the branches, dappled light landing on the bluebells' stems, which tilt and sway in the gentle breeze. The sweet floral smell transports me to childhood picnics, picking wildflowers for Mum's kitchen table, driving miles to walk in Dad's favorite wood, because the bluebells only bloom for a few short weeks.

Sam gets Amy out and lifts her onto his shoulders, making her squeal in delight as he spins her around and around. Felix yells, "Me! Me!," so Sam puts Amy back in her buggy, then starts to spin Felix, who screams, "Faster, faster!"

When Sam finally puts him down, bent double and out of breath, Felix cries, "Again, again."

"It looks like your father's getting too old to do that," I say with a sly smile. "Look, poor thing's exhausted."

"Is that your way of saying you want a go?" Sam asks, cocking an eyebrow at me.

"No." I grin, but then he starts toward me at a pace, and I turn to run, laughing as Sam chases me across the park. He's too fast for me, and soon wraps me in a bear hug before we both tumble to the ground.

"Who's too old?" he asks, lying on top of me, pinning my hands above my head.

"Not you, not you," I say, laughing, wriggling beneath him. He stops wrestling with me, looks down into my eyes, and I'm suddenly aware of every point where his body is pressed into mine, the glint of intent in his eyes, the effortless way he is pinning my arms with just one hand. "Hmm." *Did I just moan? Oh jeez, we're in public, the kids are right there.* He bites his lip, amused, then releases my arms. I think he might have noticed the moan.

"This was a great idea, Luce," he says, his voice thick with warmth. "I'm glad you suggested it." Before he's done speaking, Felix catches up with us and launches himself onto Sam, crying, "Family pile!" I feel myself blush as I quickly try to dispel the un-PG visuals of Sam and I rolling naked through the bluebells that's just pushed its way into my mind.

As we're walking back to the car, Felix points to us both and says, "Oh look, it's Pocket Day."

"Happy Pocket Day, Felix!" Sam says with a grin.

"Bocket Bay," says Amy.

"What's Pocket Day?" I ask.

"When we're all wearing clothes with pockets, it's Pocket Day," Sam explains. "Felix made it up."

"It's only Pocket Day when it's the whole family!" Felix seems thrilled, showing me the pockets in his little jogging bottoms and pointing to Amy's coat pockets.

"So, what happens on Pocket Day?" I ask.

"Nothing." Felix looks at me as though this is a ridiculous question. "It's just Pocket Day."

"Happy Pocket Day," Sam repeats, taking my hand and swinging it back and forth. Their joy is contagious, and for a moment, I am one of them. But there's no time to savor the feeling, because Felix trips on a stone, flying forward, and then screams as he lands chin first on the gravel path. I should have been watching more carefully; he's fallen here before, on this exact path. The thin scar on his forehead is from where he landed on a sharp rock.

"Are you okay?" I ask, running to put a hand over his bleeding chin. *Did I just imagine that other fall, or do I remember it?* I examine Felix's forehead—there is a narrow scar, just by his hairline.

"People aren't supposed to get hurt on Pocket Day!" Felix wails mournfully.

THAT NIGHT, WHEN we finally crawl into bed, our bed, together, Sam pulls me close. There's that connection again, the spark I felt on date night, only now I am entirely sober. I am probably more tired than I have ever been, but my body still tingles with the anticipation of Sam's touch. I want to tell him about the glimpse I had in the park, but also, I don't, because I don't know what it means.

Sam strokes my cheek with the back of his hand. "Hello, beautiful wife," he says in a low whisper.

"Hello," I whisper back. He leans in to kiss me, slowly, gently, tugging my lower lip into his mouth, running one hand up into my hair. The other strokes up the small of my back, beneath my T-shirt, sweeping around to firmly cup my breast in one exquisite motion. I let out an involuntary moan and then:

"My chin hurts. Can I sleep in bed with you?" a bleary-eyed Felix asks from the doorway.

"Ah . . . sure, buddy," Sam says, moving aside to make room for his son. Felix scrambles between us, like a baby bird returning to a nest. I fall asleep curled around him, my hand entwined in Sam's above his head.

"Love you, Mummy, love you, Dad," he mumbles.

"I love you too, Felix," I say.

Sam squeezes my hand twice, a lovers' Morse code in the dark.

28

THE NEXT MORNING, POOR NIGHT'S SLEEP NEXT TO A sharp-elbowed child be damned, I'm up early and on the seven fifteen train to London. I want to be in before anyone else, I want to be prepared. As my train arrives at Waterloo there's a text from Sam, a photo of a book with a ring of Amy-shaped tooth marks on the corner of the cover: I think your book might have some plot holes. 🤐

The message makes me smile, and I walk to work with a new bounce in my step. I tap out a reply: Amy's book review— "bitingly witty and hole-some."

At work, once the whole team has assembled, I call everyone into the downstairs meeting room. Callum hovers at the door, offering to go and make tea, but I beckon him in.

"Callum, get in here, we can live without tea. Now, I know we're under time pressure," I say. "The pitch is in eleven days and we haven't settled on an idea yet. I'm sorry I haven't been more present in the office, I've had some personal issues to deal with, but I'm here now." I pause, surveying the room. Trey looks exhausted, though he's wearing a cheerful sequined sweater vest, with matching beret. Michael is buttoning and unbuttoning the top button of his waistcoat. Dominique and Leon look up at me with wide-eyed expectation, while Callum just looks thrilled to be here.

"So, I'm counting on you to help me translate this idea into a workable show, but I wanted to tell you about this game I play with my son. It's like the floor is lava but it's not just the floor that's going to get you, it's everything in the house. The airing cupboard is a dragon's lair, a waterfall's coming down the stairs, the kitchen is a cave of killer bats."

"*The House Is Going to Get You*," says Dominique.

"Yes, exactly. I haven't worked out a format, but I like the concept of turning places we know into the location for an adventure, using household objects to defeat monsters. Can you work with that as a jumping-off point?"

The energy in the room slowly shifts as everyone starts talking, all keen to contribute.

"Scene! The office is filling with water," says Leon, jumping onto his chair. "We need a boat, but all we have is . . ." He looks to Dominique, and she hands him an imaginary object.

"This giant stapler." Everyone laughs as he and Dominique mime stapling together a boat out of pieces of paper, climbing into it, and then slowly sinking. They take a bow, then head back to their seats, but Michael says, "No, keep going."

Leon and Dominique carry on their game, imagining disasters befalling the office, which they overcome using office equipment.

"How are they doing this so effortlessly?" I ask.

"They're in an improv troupe together," Michael leans in to tell me. "A talented bunch."

Trey slams a hand on the desk, as though he's just thought of something brilliant.

"We could do 4D VR mapping on the kids' houses. You'd see the monsters right there in hologram, as though they're coming out from under the bed, or the wardrobe or whatever." Trey opens his drawing pad.

"Could we make the monsters the real ones that the kids imagine—if they could draw them for us?" Callum asks nervously.

"I love that idea," I say, and his cheeks flush pink.

"There's this new program—CGH5:8. It could be perfect for something like this," says Trey.

"Can you show us?" I ask, and Trey's fingers dart around his screen at incredible speed.

"This will be rough, but okay, describe a monster to me," he says.

"A disgusting blue blob with an iron for a head, and electric eels for arms," says Leon, grinning.

"Don't make it easy for me, will you, mate," Trey says, shaking his head, but he pulls out his digital pen and sketches what Leon's described. Then, from his tablet, a 3D hologram of the image shines out into the room. It's impressive.

"Wow, that is so gene," says Dominique.

Trey keeps scribbling, and the hologram monster moves its arms up and down. "It will be even better when I have time to prepare," he tells us. "I can do more detailed drawings. With more cameras, we could present it in 4D."

We all clap for Trey and he blushes, then adjusts his beret. As we explore the idea, everyone in the room has something to contribute and a palpable buzz starts to build around the table.

"This is it," I say, looking at Michael.

"This is it," he agrees.

THAT AFTERNOON, TREY asks if he can use my office—it's the only room big enough for him to experiment with this new technology—so I decide to go home early and work from there. Now that we have a concept, I want to write everything up, try to hone the format.

But once I'm set up in my home office, I look down at the picture of Sam on my desk and my mind fills with thoughts of him, of his body, of his hands running up my back last night before we were interrupted. Knowing he is just twenty yards away in his studio proves to be a major distraction. As I'm trying to write a pitch document, my mind wanders to Sam's lips, Sam's hand, Sam's . . . Maybe I'll just go and say hi to him, then I'll be able to focus, *then* I can start to work properly. Yes, that's definitely the mature thing to do.

"Hey, I brought you tea," I say, knocking as I open his studio door.

Sam looks surprised to see me but takes off his earphones and smiles, running a hand through his thick hair. His shirtsleeves are rolled up, exposing his lean, toned forearms and a dark smattering of hair. *What is it about good forearms on men? Like, I want to arm-wrestle him and I want to lose.* With his sharp jawline and ready smile, he's ridiculously attractive. Even though he's tired, his eyes always seem to play somewhere on the edge of mischief. "Sorry, I'm interrupting."

"You're not interrupting," he says, taking the mug from my hands.

"So, I pitched the idea, and everyone loved it. There's plenty to do, but it feels good to have something to work on."

"That's great news, well done." He grins up at me, and I loiter at the door, unable to make myself leave.

"Can I stay and watch you work for a bit, see what it is you do?" I ask him.

"Sure, be my guest," he says, indicating a leather armchair in the corner of the room. Then he pushes his sleeve up and shoots me a bashful look over his shoulder. "I'm self-conscious now."

"Pretend I'm not here."

He turns on a screen and a scene from a movie starts to play. A man and a woman are holding hands, confessing their love for each other beneath a night sky full of dancing green auroras.

"What's this?" I ask.

"*Meet Me in Oslo*, a romantic comedy I'm scoring. This is the climactic scene where the leads confess their feelings for each other. I can't get the tone right."

"I rarely notice the music in movies," I admit. "Is that bad?"

"If you notice it, that usually means the composer hasn't done their job. The score should make you feel, it should add to the emotion of the performances on-screen, not distract from it." He presses a button on the huge dashboard of controls in front of him and the scene from the film restarts. "Sometimes it's understated," he says, playing a few chords on the piano, "then it builds." He keeps playing, developing the music into something bolder, pressing a button to add some strings. "But if you go too big, it's distracting." The music he's playing is now sweeping and dramatic, with heavy, clunking chords. I laugh, because it's changed the mood of the scene so completely, then I shake my head in awe at his ability to improvise like this.

"Wow, you're amazing," I say, and he rubs a palm up his neck, shifting in his chair.

"It's just practice," he says, turning back to the piano. The speaker crackles, and Sam leans across to shift a dial. "Sorry, this speaker's seen better days."

"Can't you get a new one?"

"I was planning to, but then someone spent all our money on strange purple suits." He says it playfully, but I shoot him a grimace.

"Can you make it into a horror movie?" I ask, nodding toward the screen. Sam raises an eyebrow at me before turning back to the piano. He restarts the clip, then plays a dark accompaniment, full of foreboding, and I clap with glee.

"That's so sinister. How do you do that? Ooh, can you do a version where she's an evil creature from outer space, but he's in love with her and doesn't care?"

"What am I, a performing monkey?" he says, pretending to scowl, but the smile lines around his eyes give him away. "I thought you were here to watch me work."

"I thought you were showing me what you can do. Wooing me with your musical dexterity."

"I need to woo you now, do I?"

"Maybe. I don't remember any of the wooing, so . . ."

He pulls a second stool out from beneath the piano and beckons me over. I sit down and he moves his chair in behind me, his hands covering mine on the piano. Gently he guides my fingers to the notes, teaching me a basic set of chords. It feels like there is some muscle memory because my fingers pick it up easily, though I've never learned to play.

"Do I play?" I ask, but my voice wavers, distracted by every point where his body is in contact with mine.

"Yes, I taught you," he says gently, needling his chin into my shoulder. My head tilts toward him, but then he moves back to his side of the keyboard. "Play those notes, whenever the man is talking," he instructs me, then he restarts the clip and hits "record" on his deck of controls. I play my light, flighty chords when the man is talking, while Sam thumps out a more sinister tune whenever the woman does. When the scene ends, we grin at each other, celebrating our mutual accomplishment. Then Sam plays the scene again, with our new musical score.

"He's in love with her and she's a psycho," I laugh.

"Like all the best love stories," Sam says with a wry smile, and I elbow him in the ribs.

"I think this is the version you should go with," I say, standing up. "And now I'm really going to go, let you work in peace." I need to stop distracting him, get back to work myself, but as I turn away, he takes my hand and pulls me back to face him.

"Thank you," he says.

"What for?"

"For coming out here, for taking an interest." He looks so sincere, as though this small exchange between us has been something important. "For reminding me you're still you."

"I am me," I say, then more lightly, "Besides, it's interesting. You're interesting."

"You haven't been out here in over a year," he says.

"Haven't I?"

"Lack of time rather than lack of interest," he says quickly.

"Well, I could listen to you play all day." I start to open the door, but now he's standing behind me, reaching out his hand to cover mine on the doorknob, pushing the door closed, his broad, hot body pressed against mine. My body pulses with longing as he leans in to kiss my neck.

"I thought you had to work," I say, my voice breathy.

"I thought you did too."

Then he turns me around and looks right into my eyes and I feel him looking at me. *Me*. Not whoever I am in the future, or who I might have been before, but who I am in this moment, in this room.

We make love right there against the door, and I know then, whatever plane of the space-time continuum I am living in, right now, there is nowhere else I want to be.

THAT EVENING, SAM goes out to teach a tai chi class. The kids are in bed, and Faye comes over to have a drink with me.

"You know he teaches tai chi to residents at the nursing home? Isn't that the cutest thing?" I tell Faye. "I bet all the little old ladies love him."

"Yes, the little old ladies," Faye says with a smirk.

"Have you heard him compose? He can come up with these arrangements off the top of his head," I say, pouring us both a glass of wine. "It's incredible, he's so talented."

"Yes, very talented," Faye says, smirking again.

"He's so sweet with the kids—"

"You know what's happening here, don't you," Faye says, laughing now.

"What?"

"You're falling in love with him."

"What?"

"This is exactly what you were like when you fell in love with him the first time. All I heard for months was, 'He's so talented, he's so kind, he's so funny.' You had this permanent Sam-induced grin on your face, it was sickening. But also, kind of cute and adorable."

"That's not what this is," I say, shifting back into the sofa, feeling my cheeks burn.

"It is! You don't remember that you love him, so you're falling in love with him all over again." Faye sighs. "It's great, I'm jealous. I would love to fall in love with Alex again, that's the best part."

"Maybe you're right," I say. "But it's confusing. He's often telling me he loves me, but does he love *me*, or does he love old me, Future Me, me who remembers?"

"I wouldn't overthink it," says Faye. "He's always loved you. He loved you before he met you, the promise of you, remember."

"The song?" I ask, and Faye nods. "Was I sure from the start, when I met him?"

"Lucy, you were so sure. That night we met him in the karaoke bar—I remember you saying in the cab home, 'I'm going to marry that man.'"

"I'm sure I was joking, or drunk."

"You were, both." Faye shrugs. "But you'd never said anything like that before. Enjoy it, you deserve to have something good."

"Do I, though? Sometimes I feel guilty, just being handed all this." I wave an arm to indicate the beautiful space we're sitting in.

"Lucy, you didn't get handed anything. Trust me, I was

there, I saw how hard you worked." She sighs, shaking her head. "You took weekend jobs, there were periods where you hardly had time to see any of us. As for Sam, believe me, you put your time in with some frogs before you met your prince." She pauses. "When you lived in New York, you were in love with this guy Toby who completely broke your heart. I didn't think you'd ever trust anyone again after that."

"I lived in New York?" *I always wanted to live in New York.*

"Yes. All I'm saying is, you *have* been on a journey to get here, and it's all connected because if Toby hadn't broken your heart, you might never have come back home, and you wouldn't have met Sam, who is your person." I reach out a hand to Faye, grateful for her unwavering kindness. "You have a strong marriage. But that's taken work too. What you've both been through is not easy."

"I wish I remembered Chloe," I blurt out. "Of all the things I've forgotten, she feels the most significant. It's important to Sam that I remember her."

"I think you will remember, Luce," Faye says gently. "Just enjoy being loved up with Sam before you remember all the things you find annoying about him." Faye laughs, and I throw a sofa cushion at her. I don't admit I can't think of one thing I might ever find annoying about him.

"CAN YOU PASS me a spoon?" I ask Sam as our little family sits down for Saturday breakfast. Sam grabs one from the drawer and hands it to me, his fingers lingering on mine as he does. He shoots me a devilishly loaded look.

"Why thank you," I say, looking up at him beneath lowered lashes.

"Why are you being weird with each other?" Felix demands.

"We're not being weird!" I say, feeling a pulse of heat rising up my neck.

"You are being weird," Felix insists. "You keep looking at each other, for ages, like you're trying to win a staring competition."

Sam clears his throat. "Your mother is a beautiful woman; I like looking at her." He leans in to kiss me, and Felix grimaces.

"Have the aliens hypnotized you?" Felix asks.

"I thought we agreed to knock the alien theory on the head," I say, giving Felix a firm stare.

"Don't call your mother an alien, Felix," Sam says, just as Amy knocks her cereal bowl off her high chair and milk and cornflakes splatter all over the floor. Sam leaps up to get a cloth.

"Chuck it here," I say, already crouching down. Sam throws a damp cloth across the room, and I catch it in one hand without looking.

When I do look up, I see Felix and Sam exchanging glances.

"What?" I ask.

"Nothing," says Sam.

"What are we doing for my birthday on Saturday?" Felix asks out of nowhere, and I wonder if this is the real source of his irritability this morning. Either that, or a few days without access to an iPad. Looking at Sam, I panic that with everything going on, we have overlooked something as important as Felix's birthday.

"What would you like to do, buddy?" Sam asks. "I thought we might just have a family party this year, but you could invite a few mates over. Or I'll take a group of your friends to the VR arcade if you like?"

"Can I have friends here?" Felix asks. "And can I invite Mr. Finkley, Mummy?"

"Who's Mr. Finkley?" Sam asks.

"Mummy's friend from the olden days."

"That's so sweet of you, Felix, but I don't really know Mr. Finkley all that well. He's a little odd and he lives all the way in London."

"I don't think he's odd. I liked him," says Felix.

"Your friend from the olden days," Sam says, giving me an amused look.

"He said he hasn't been invited to a party in twenty years, not since his wife died. He said she was the one people liked, and he doesn't have any friends now," Felix says.

Sam and I exchange a look.

"I don't have his number though, Felix. I don't know how I'd invite him—"

Felix leans forward across the table, imploring me. "You said you know someone's your friend when you like the stuff they like, when you can be weird with them. I felt like that with him." He pauses. "You could take him an invitation when you're in London. He doesn't like the train, though, so we'll have to fetch him in the car."

"Well, if you're sure that's who you'd like to invite, I can ask him," I say.

"That's who I want to invite," says Felix firmly. "And Matt Christensen and Molly Greenway." Sam and I exchange another look.

"Well, if you write the invitations today, we'll deliver them on Monday," Sam suggests. "You could start them now."

"Are you just trying to get me to go upstairs so you can go back to being weird with each other?" Felix asks, narrowing his eyes, then looking back and forth between us.

Sam and I lock eyes and immediately start being weird with each other again. He reaches for my hand across the kitchen table. I can't believe how great this is—to live with someone who you like this much. To have your crush right there, *all the time*. I had this all-consuming crush on this guy Paddy at university, but I only ever saw him in my Monday morning tutorial. I'd look forward to it all week. Living with Sam is like having Monday morning every single day.

"Maybe you could write a song for Felix's birthday," I suggest to Sam once Felix has left the room. His brow furrows and he let's go of my hand.

"I don't write songs like that anymore, Luce."

"But why not? You're so good at it."

When I was stalking my husband online, I found the last song he wrote and sold. It was called "The Pulse of Love," recorded by a band called Neev for their album *Slice*. Of the reviews I found, most said "The Pulse of Love" was the worst thing on the album and not at all Neev's style. Some of the reviews were hard to read, but I can't believe one setback would put Sam off writing anything ever again.

"We've talked about this," Sam says gruffly, standing up to open and then close the fridge door.

"But I don't remember talking about it, do I?" I pause. "I listened to 'The Pulse of Love' and thought it was beautiful. You're so talented, Sam—you should write songs again; you know you should."

"I don't want to talk about it." Sam gives me a sharp look, then turns to leave the room.

"Sam," I call after him, but then I hear the back door slam. I've hit a nerve, but I don't know what or why. Just as I think I'm getting to grips with married life, learning this family's foibles, there's some new curveball. Sam's left the fridge door open, so I get up to close it. He *always* leaves the fridge door open. *Okay, yes!* Now I have one thing to put on my list of things I find annoying about him. That and his inability to share his deepest vulnerabilities about his creative failures. Wow, this might be starting to feel like a real marriage.

29

"COME TO MYKONOS THIS WEEKEND?" ROISIN CALLS ME as I get off the train at Vauxhall. I'm on my way to deliver Mr. Finkley his invitation. "My boss has got an empty villa. It's so lush. We can party all night, soak in the sun all day, sangrias at sundown . . ."

"Mykonos?" My heart skips in my chest. *I always wanted to go to Mykonos.* "I can't," I say. "It's Felix's birthday on Saturday. Maybe another weekend?"

"Sorry, babe, villa's only free this weekend." She pauses, disappointed. "I thought a little holiday might be just what the doctor ordered. Maybe come on Sunday, take a few days off work?"

"I'm sorry, there's just too much going on. I've got this big pitch coming up, I'm still playing catch-up." I let out a sigh. "I just can't. Thank you, though."

Clearly, I'm in no position to go running off to Mykonos with Roisin. But having to say no makes me realize how tethered I am. I can't go anywhere at a moment's notice now. I can't spontaneously jump in a car and head off on a road trip. There were weekends in my twenties where I would wander the London parks for hours, listening to music, just watching life go by. I didn't have to tell anyone where I was going or when I'd be back. Afternoons in the pub could merge into an evening, and entire Sundays could be spent simply "hanging out." I don't think I understood the meaning of the word independence until I had dependents.

"I'd love to do something another time, Rosh, but I might need a little more notice." I pause outside the shop that used to be a Super Way. It's now a florist. How many times did I stop in here to pick up Monster Munch after a night out, or run down in pajamas to get milk? "Do you know why Sam doesn't write songs anymore?" I change the subject and ask Roisin while I have her on the phone.

"I think his last song got panned for being cheesy and generic. You told me it was complicated; you didn't go into detail. Listen, I've got to go, my assistant's messed up and triple-booked my diary. Look at flights, if you change your mind, let me know."

As I hang up, I can't help feeling disappointed. Is that what life is—missing out in your twenties because you have no money, then missing out in your forties because you have no time?

Ringing Mr. Finkley's doorbell, I call into the intercom, "Hello, it's Lucy Young—um, I mean Rutherford." He buzzes me in and I walk up the stairs to the top landing, where I find him dressed in a bathrobe, holding his rusty metal watering can.

"Morning, Mr. Finkley. My son, Felix, wanted to invite

you to his birthday party on Saturday," I tell him, handing over the invitation. "It's in Surrey, and it's not really a party, just the four of us, grandparents, and a couple of school friends. I know you only met him once, so you don't need to feel obligated—"

"Yes," he says, and he looks genuinely thrilled as he opens the hand-drawn envelope. Felix has covered the invitation in drawings of monstrous plants all wearing party hats.

"Oh, okay, great," I say, trying to hide my surprise. "Felix mentioned you don't like the train, so I can drive you if you like?"

He nods, his eyes brimming with emotion as he reads the invitation.

"So, I'll pick you up around midday, shall I?" He doesn't answer, and I wonder if he's heard me. "Mr. Finkley?"

"Leonard. My name is Leonard." He looks up at me and I feel ashamed; ashamed of my first reaction to Felix's wanting to invite this man to tea, ashamed that I lived below him for two and a half years and I never even knew his name.

Walking back toward the tube, I try to console myself with the idea that a kid's party in the garden with my eccentric old neighbor will be just as much fun as a girls' weekend in Mykonos. Okay, so it won't, who am I kidding, but Felix will be thrilled that Mr. Finkley can come, that's the important thing. Looking up at two birds circling each other in the clear blue sky, I find myself wondering what the opposite of bird might be.

THAT EVENING, AS I sit in bed with a book, glancing up at my perfectly plastered ceiling, I reflect how quickly it is possible to adapt to the strangest situations. How can I now be okay with being forty-two, when two weeks ago I could barely catch my breath? Is it because I'm a tiny bit obsessed with my new husband and I'm allowing the experience of falling for him to distract me from the horror of missing all those years? Or am I simply too busy to invest time in the existential crisis I should be having?

"What are you thinking about?" Sam asks, his voice heavy with sleep. He reaches across and presses a thumb to my forehead. "You get a line right here when you're deep in contemplation."

"Nothing," I say softly. It's too much to explain.

Of all the things I have had to adapt to, being loved by this man has been the easiest to accept. I like being his wife, I like sharing a bed with him, knotting hands after sex and knowing I don't have to worry about whether he'll still be there in the morning. And even though objectively I should be less confident in this world-worn shell, the fact that Sam adores every stretch mark, every wrinkle, liberates me from a trap I didn't realize I was caught in.

"Oh, I forgot to tell you, the doctor called me," Sam says. "They want you to go in for another follow-up."

"I don't see the point," I say, leaning over to kiss him.

"Of course there's a point," Sam says, pulling back from me. "There might be a new treatment, more tests they can do."

My body tenses. "You want your old wife back."

"I want you to get better," he says.

"I thought you loved me, just as I am."

"I'll love you whatever happens, for better or for worse, but—" He lets out a moan of frustration. "I don't understand what I've said that's wrong."

For better or for worse. Am I the worse?

"Sorry, I just feel a bit, I don't know—jealous."

"Jealous?"

"Yes. To me, this, us, it feels like a brand-new relationship, and in contrast to all the upsetting parts of this weird situation, it feels great, *you're* great. Whereas you—you're eleven years in, you're already in love with someone I don't even know, who I don't know if I'll ever be again. How do I know you're not just settling for this lesser version?"

"You're not lesser." He looks thoughtful for a moment, sitting up in bed. "Just different in some ways. Honestly, Lucy, even if the memories aren't there, every day you seem a little more like your old self."

I pinch my mouth closed to stop myself from crying. I thought things were fine, I don't know where this emotion is coming from.

"You can't be jealous of yourself," Sam insists.

"I can. I can be jealous of the version of me that got to live eleven years with you, that got to meet you for the first time across a crowded karaoke bar, that got to date you and fall in love with you, not knowing how it would end. The person who got to marry you, who got to see your face when I gave birth to our first child, who got to hold your hand when we lost our second." And now I'm sobbing and he's holding me tight. "Because I missed it all, Sam, I missed my life, I missed *us*."

"You didn't miss it," he says, talking into my hair as he holds my shaking body.

"And that's just the stuff I *know* I missed. There are probably hundreds of life-changing moments I'll never even know about." There's a pause, then Sam lets go of me. He gets out of bed, then reaches a hand to pull me up after him.

"Where are you going?" I ask, confused.

"Come, I want to show you something."

In the hall, Sam grabs a torch, then hands me one of his thick knitted jumpers to throw on over my pajamas.

"Where are we going?" I ask again. But he just slips on some huge green Wellies, then pulls some yellow ones from the hall cupboard for me. The cozy feel of Sam's jumper and the sense of an impending adventure has already taken the edge off my melancholy mood. Wordlessly, I follow him out of the back door into the garden, where the moon is bright and luminous in the sky, and the air has a distinct chill.

"Is this the part where you show me all the bodies you've buried?" I ask playfully.

Sam lets out a "ha," so I keep talking. "Imagine if there were these husband-and-wife serial killers, and one of them got amnesia so their partner had to take them into the basement and be all, 'Hey, honey, you know you forgot about liking Sudoku, well you also forgot about us killing eight people.'"

Sam doesn't laugh like I expected him to, only reaches for my hand and guides me further down the garden path. We stop at a small tree at the end of the garden, planted in a raised bed. He shines the torch onto a carved wooden plaque that reads Chloe Zoya Rutherford. Daughter, sister, and grand-daughter. So little, yet so loved. Then the date of her birth and death, just two weeks between them.

"Oh, shit," I say, slapping a hand over my mouth. Sam turns to face me, but I can't see his expression in the dark. "I am so sorry, I'm an idiot, there's me blathering on about you showing me where the bodies are buried, and you're taking me to see . . . oh fuck."

"It's okay," he says, and I can hear he's smiling. "She's not buried here, it's just a tree."

"Why else would you be taking me outside in the middle of the night," I mutter to myself, then take a deep breath. "I'm so embarrassed."

"Don't be, it's fine." He squeezes my shoulder, then takes off his coat and lays it down beside the tree, beckoning for me to sit next to him on the ground.

"It's because I watch a lot of real-crime shows, that's just where my mind goes—it's not that I think death or murder is funny, it's really *not* funny—"

"Lucy, can we stop talking about serial killers now?"

"Yup." I pinch my lips closed. I'm desperate to keep apologizing, but I don't trust that I won't dig myself into an even deeper hole. I settle for reaching up and squeezing Sam's hand, which is resting on my shoulder. Then there's a rustling in the bushes that makes me jump. "What's that?"

Sam sighs, "Probably just a mouse."

"A mouse!" This is not reassuring.

"Look, I thought this would be a poignant place for me to tell you something important, but maybe we should just go back inside?"

"No, no, here's fine. Sorry." I don't want to ruin the moment any more than I already have so I try to focus on Sam, on the tree, and to ignore the rustling sounds in the hedge.

Sam takes a deep breath, then starts, "So you asked why I don't write songs anymore . . ."

There's a howling noise from somewhere nearby.

"What's that?" I shriek.

"A fox."

"It doesn't sound like a fox."

"Let's go in," Sam says, making to stand up, but I grab his arm.

"No, sorry, please, tell me. I'll ignore the howling."

He pauses, and I wrap my hand tighter around his arm, encouraging him to go on.

He takes another breath and then begins, "I wrote 'The Pulse of Love' for Chloe, before she was even born. No one knows it's about love for an unborn child. Then Chloe was born, and she was sick, and the song came out and everyone hated it." He makes a "hmmm" sound, as though this is hard for him to say. "I don't mind if people don't like my music, but that was the most personal thing I'd ever written. The day Chloe died, I heard it on the radio, and I just couldn't stand it—"

"Oh, Sam, I'm so sorry." I shiver involuntarily, and he rubs my shoulder.

"I never wrote anything real again, which meant I couldn't write anything good, so I stopped trying. Now it's this huge mental block." He shines the torch back onto the plaque at the base of the tree.

"I can understand that," I tell him.

"You once told me that everyone dies twice. Once when your body takes its final breath, then again when someone says your name for the last time. You made me promise we'd keep saying Chloe's name, so part of her would always be here with us. I think that's why you not remembering her feels particularly cruel." He turns to plant a kiss on my head.

"I really do wish I remembered," I tell him.

"When we planted this tree, it was a Sunday afternoon. Felix was sitting over there on a play mat while we dug a hole. We turned our backs for a minute, and he was in the hole, tipping a watering can over himself, grinning from ear to ear. He started flinging mud at me. You walked across to him, I thought you were going to pick him up, but you just grabbed a handful of wet soil and threw it at me too." Sam laughs. "Felix thought it was hilarious, you both did. Whenever I look at this tree now, it's not just Chloe I think about, it's us covered in mud laughing, even through the worst—the absolute worst." He leans into me, and I rub a hand up the back of his neck. "I thought of that when you talked about the small moments—not just the headlines like marriage, birth, and death. I worry I haven't told you enough of the good stuff, even the good bad stuff, if that makes any sense?"

"It does," I say, hugging both my arms around him.

"Now when I see this tree, I'm going to think about serial killers too."

"Oh no, don't!" I say, burying my face in his shoulder.

"In a good way," he says, laughing. "If it's possible to think about serial killers in a good way."

"Maybe we should look at the moon for a minute, try and give the moment a little reverence," I say, half joking, but we both look up, and there is indeed something awe-inspiring about the moon—one side luminous, the other, shadow. It's one sight that doesn't change. As we hold hands in the cold, sitting beneath our daughter's tree, I feel immensely grateful he has shared this with me. Maybe I'm not missing out on as much as I feared. Maybe *this* is one of those small, important moments.

There's another animal cry from somewhere nearby, so Sam gets up and helps me to my feet.

"I don't know if that is a fox, you know," I tell him.

"Oh, it's probably just Bob and Mary, the serial killers who live next door," he deadpans, and we're both laughing childishly as we return to the warmth of the hall.

30

"HAVE YOU REMEMBERED ANYTHING ELSE FROM THE IN-between?" Felix asks later that week while I'm reading him a story before bed.

"Not really, nothing definitive," I tell him. "Small glimpses, maybe."

Felix looks thoughtful. "Molly thinks you're Peter Pan."

"Peter Pan?"

"It's a book."

"Yes, I do know it."

"Molly said he's this boy who can fly, but if he ever starts to doubt he can fly, he won't be able to do it anymore." Felix pauses, pulling his duvet up to his chin. "Do you still believe in the portal, Mummy?"

I'm quiet for a moment, before saying, "Honestly, I don't know. Why?"

Felix shifts on the bed, hugging his cuddly armadillo. "I don't mind if you want to stay, if you like it here now. You'll be my mummy either way. But I think if you stop believing, and start remembering stuff, it might be like Peter Pan not being able to get back to Neverland." Felix bites his lip. "That's what Molly thinks anyway, and she's the smartest person I know."

"Smarter than me?" I say, smiling.

"Yeah, she knows her thirteen-times table and everything."

"Well, she is definitely smarter than me, then," I say, kissing Felix on the head and turning on his night-light. "I think we'll be okay, Felix, whatever happens. Night night."

But as I shut his bedroom door, I feel a nagging pull of panic in my chest. Over the last few days, I haven't thought about going back at all. I haven't even checked the forum recently. I logged out because I was getting too much spam. Is Felix right? Have I stopped believing I can fly?

Sam is out teaching his tai chi class, so I put a wash on, then empty the dishwasher for what seems like the thousandth time this week. I lay out Felix's sports kit for the next day, wipe down all the surfaces in the kitchen, then I really should sit at my desk, do a few hours' work, but first, I take a minute to log in to the arcade game forum. There are no new messages, but even checking reassures me. I have not given up.

ON FRIDAY, I do a trial presentation of *The House Is Going to Get You*. I've spent ages on the pitch, I know it's polished, but when I say it out loud, it feels flat, lacking the magic we all felt when we were brainstorming the idea. Trey's 4D monsters look amazing, but my stilted words aren't doing them justice. Michael tells me I need to be louder, consult my notes less, allow time to pause, but honestly, I'm worse than rusty, I'm completely green.

After the trial presentation, Dominique lingers, pulling me to one side.

"Will you write me a reference, if we don't win?" She gives me a guilty grimace. "I can't be out of work. I owe my tattooist money." She pulls up her sleeve to show me an intricate gold tattoo of a headless mermaid. "I have to get the head done, otherwise it's just a fish with arms."

"Sure," I say, feeling utterly deflated.

Once the team have dispersed, Michael comes to find me in my office.

"I'm not doing it justice, am I?" I say.

He pinches his lips together, then says, "How's the fog?"

"Currently a dense smog," I say, then ask quietly, "Do you think memories make us who we are, Michael?"

"No," he says firmly. "Who we are is our code of morals, the things we stand for, not our ability to recall the past."

Michael has such a calm authority, I find myself saying, "Maybe you should be the one to deliver the pitch?" I can't believe I'm saying this because this is all I ever wanted—to pitch an idea myself—but there's too much at stake for this to depend on me. I'm half expecting Michael to say, "No, you should do it, you'll be great," but he doesn't, he just nods. He must see my face fall because he adds, "It's a team effort, Lucy. It was your idea."

Though I know it's probably the right call, that doesn't stop me from feeling disappointed.

AFTER WORK, I nip up to Selfridges with the vouchers I have thirty days to spend. I walk through the women's clothing floor, go right past the shoes, then straight up to the toy department. Here, I find the perfect present for Felix's birthday. In the tech department, I spend most of the vouchers on new speakers for Sam's studio, arranging to have them delivered to the house. For Amy, I get some new giraffe pajamas, then for Leonard, a shiny new watering can with a particularly long spout, perfect for hanging baskets.

On my way out, I nip down to the Food Hall, where I buy myself a croissant for the train home. Old habits and all that. As I'm paying, I see a mother struggling with both a baby and a toddler. The baby is screaming, the toddler is refusing to walk, and the woman's eyes have the defeated expression of someone close to tears, desperately trying to hold it together. I'm about to leave the shop, but then I turn back.

"Hey, I just wanted to tell you you're doing a great job," I tell the woman.

"She's hungry, that's why she's crying," the woman says, as though I asked her for an explanation. "My boy won't sit still long enough for me to feed her. I shouldn't have come shopping with them both, but it's my mum's birthday and . . ." She takes a breath, and I shake my head; she doesn't need to explain.

"I'm a mum, I get it. Look, I'm not in a rush, why don't you let me distract your son, give you a chance to feed your daughter?"

So that's what we do. I usher the little family over to a booth, then I split my croissant with the boy while his mother breastfeeds his sister. The woman, who I discover is called Greta, starts weeping when I insist on buying her a pastry too.

"I'm sorry. I get emotional when my milk lets down. Don't let me keep you, if you've got somewhere to be," Greta says, wiping her tear-streaked cheek.

"It's okay," I tell her, "I don't need to be anywhere else."
And even though there are a hundred things I could be doing,
even though there is never enough time, right now, it's true.

ON SATURDAY, SAM and I run around getting the house ready
for Felix's party. Sam buys balloons shaped like space aliens,
and I attempt to bake a cake. There's an online tutorial on
how to make the perfect shark cake. It has an "Ace It" rating
of four, which means "not that hard," but I don't know who
these people are baking shark cakes, because they clearly don't
have toddlers pulling on their legs while they do it.

Cake iced, it looks more like a blue log with teeth, so I
write "shark" on the side in white icing, just to clarify what it's
supposed to be. Then I rush up to London to get Leonard.
He's waiting for me outside, holding a book-shaped package,
wrapped in brown paper.

"It's a book on building your own smokehouse, so he can
smoke his own ham," Leonard says, and he's so pleased with
himself, I don't want to point out that an eight-year-old probably won't be able to build his own smokehouse, but then what
do I know, he's a pretty amazing kid. As we start driving,
Leonard opens the glove box and inspects the interior of
my car.

"Is this one of those cyborg cars?" he asks.

"Electric."

"You know the government can track all your movements
in these?"

"Right."

"You need to delete your satnav history and keep lemons
on the dashboard—they disrupt the signals."

By the time we get to Farnham, I've been educated on all the many conspiracy theories Leonard believes: That peanut butter is not made from peanuts, but a genetically modified substitute called Pleanuts, grown in underground labs in America. That JFK was not assassinated but lived to ninety-six in a Florida golfing community. That rather than building space-ships, NASA spends its time spying on the population. As I'm listening to all this, I start to question whether a seventy-something-year-old conspiracy theorist with a criminal record is the sort of person I should be encouraging my child to be friends with. I mean, it's one thing to be neighborly, but quite another to be a negligent parent.

"Leonard, I know it's not polite to ask, but since I'm invit-ing you to my child's birthday party, will you tell me what you went to jail for? It wasn't murder or anything, was it?"

"Ha, no! Impersonating a police officer and fishing with-out a license," he tells me.

"At the same time or two separate incidents?"

Leonard shrugs. "It was a long time ago, you know, I actu-ally don't remember." And now I have to laugh, and Leonard laughs too.

AT THE HOUSE, Felix's school friends Matt and Molly have arrived. Molly has two long black pigtails hanging down over her shoulders and she wears a T-shirt that reads "A girl de-signed you." I don't really understand it as a slogan, but I in-stantly like her vibe.

In the garden I've made a complex assault course. The grass is lava and Hockey Banjo has been taken hostage by the Dread Pirate Lucy (me) and tied to a flagpole erected above Sam's studio door. Felix and his friends must overcome a series of challenges to rescue him. There's a river of sinking sand to cross (the paddling pool full of bubbles and bonus prizes), arrows being fired by a rival pirate gang (my mum and dad firing Nerf guns from the upstairs window), and a terrifying troll bridge to navigate (the vegetable patch), where they must answer questions from a hideous troll before they can pass. Sam does an excellent turn as the troll, until Leonard asks if he can have a go and has us all in stitches with his Oscar-worthy imitation of Gandalf, yelling, "You shall not pass."

The game is a huge success, and as soon as Hockey Banjo has been rescued, Felix insists we play the whole game again. Sam says he doesn't mind being demoted from his role as troll, but as I watch him tug on his earlobe, I suspect he might; that's his classic tell.

"I thought you were a brilliant troll," I say softly into his ear.

When I go inside to get the cake, I find my mum in the utility room putting a wash on.

"Mum, you don't have to do our laundry. Please, just go and relax, enjoy the party."

"It's good to see you back to your old self," she says, still sorting piles of clothes. "You just don't seem very under control with the housework." She looks around in despair at the mountain of washing.

"We're not. But it's okay," I tell her. "Come on, I'm doing the cake."

I've left the candles in a bag in the bedroom. I run upstairs, but once I have them, I pause at the door, beset by an inexplicable feeling that I've forgotten something, that there's something else I need. I go over to the bedside drawer, find my rings, and put them on, exhaling a breath.

As I bring the cake out into the garden, eight candles lit,

everyone starts to sing. It's not a masterpiece by any means, but Felix is delighted with it. "I'm afraid it got overdone on the top, and probably has a soggy bottom," I tell everyone.

"Said the actress to the bishop," says Dad with an exaggerated, slow wink. His words make me hum with joy. Of all the times we've told each other this silly joke, this one might forever be my favorite.

Felix loves the book Leonard gave him and wants to start building a smokehouse immediately. "We might need a little longer than an evening for a project like that," Sam explains, and Felix asks if Leonard can come back next weekend to help. I've never seen anyone look more delighted.

My phone pings: Happy Birthday to Felix. Wish you were here! x R. Then there's a photo of Roisin on a beach, in a bikini with two friends. Surprisingly, I don't even feel too jealous.

Once the birthday cake has been eaten and the presents unwrapped, we say good-bye to the guests. Mum and Dad are the last to leave and they pause at the front door.

"You're sure you're okay to come and stay next week, after my cataracts op?" Mum says. "You've so much on your plate. Can you really afford the time?"

"I will be there," I tell her.

"Lovely party, darling," says Dad. "You always did know how to keep everyone entertained."

As Dad heads to the car, I hold on to Mum's hand and whisper, "How's he doing?"

"We're taking it one day at a time," she says, nodding furiously. "It's all you can do, isn't it?"

WHEN I TAKE Amy up to bed, she drops her head onto my shoulder, exhausted. I inhale the gorgeous smell of her, savor the warm squidge of her podgy limbs. In the hall, I pause for a moment, watching our reflection in the hall mirror. I see a happy mother and a contented baby.

Sam offers to drive Leonard home, and now that the house is quiet and it's just the two of us, I give Felix his present from me.

Unwrapping the parcel, he finds a round, red lava lamp. "Cool," he says, turning it over in his hands. He looks slightly confused, as though wondering why I've chosen this.

"There's a remote, so you can change the settings," I tell him. "It pulses. Like a heart." I take the remote and flick through the settings.

"Oh, Mummy, it's perfect!" His face lights up and my heart swells with pleasure.

We spend the next few hours at the kitchen table trying to make a heart that beats. I've bought some chicken wire, plaster of Paris, and red tissue paper, which we carefully model into shape around the lava lamp.

"Can you . . . ?" Felix asks me, pointing to the top of the wire aorta he's trying to attach, and I reach out to hold it in place, while he tackles it with a glue gun. We're still busy when Sam gets home. He shakes his head, then says he's going to bed.

"Do I have to go up?" Felix asks me.

I look to Sam.

"Mum's call," Sam says.

"I think, since it's your birthday, and the weekend . . ."

BY TEN O'CLOCK, we're finished, and it's spectacular. A work of art. It took a lot of patience, and an obscene amount of glue, but finally, Felix pronounces it complete. With almost religious reverence, he turns on the lava lamp, scrolling through the remote to find the pulse setting. I reach for his hand as we watch it come to life.

"Wow," says Felix. "It's amazing."

"Isn't it?" I whisper. "Is it too late to have it considered for the project fair?"

"All the pieces have been chosen," Felix says.

"We'll take it in on Monday to show your teacher anyway."

"Thanks, Mummy," Felix says, leaning in to hug me.

"Now it really is bedtime," I say, hugging him back.

"Can I keep it on for just a few minutes?"

"Sure, don't touch it too much though, the plaster isn't quite dry."

As I'm walking out of the door, Felix jumps up and throws his arms around me. "That was the best birthday ever. Thanks, Mummy."

"You're welcome, darling boy," I whisper back.

On my way to bed I send Roisin a message and photo of Felix beaming behind his cake: One happy boy! Wish you were here too. x

ON MONDAY MORNING, FELIX AND I ARE AT THE SCHOOL gates waiting for Mrs. Fremantle as soon as she arrives. I'm holding the heart, now dry and pulsing in a cardboard box.

"Mrs. Fremantle, please can I have a quick word?" I ask.

She stops, surprised.

"Felix finally finished his heart assignment. I know it's late but . . ."

Mrs. Fremantle takes her glasses off and peers into the box.

"Felix, you really did this?"

"I helped him put it together, but the design was all his. He spent hours on it." I stare at Mrs. Fremantle, willing her not to disappoint my son.

"It's wonderful, Felix. Highly commendable."

"Can I enter it in the project fair tomorrow?" Felix asks.

"It's a little late, I'm afraid. The entries have all been decided."

My boy looks crestfallen. "And the purpose of the fair, Mrs. Fremantle?" I ask, following her as she walks toward the school, eager to get inside. "On your website it says it's to en-gender a love of creating, of problem solving, a passion for art and science. Well, I've never seen Felix more enthusiastic about coming to school than he was this morning, wanting to show you this."

Please, please, please let him have this.

"Fine." Mrs. Fremantle sighs. "But it needs to be in the school display first thing tomorrow. You'll need to make your own signage; I don't have time to design more."

Once she's gone, Felix and I high-five each other.

I take the model back to the car, to keep it safe for tomor-row. As I'm walking away Felix runs back up to me and says, "Didn't I say you were good at crafting?"

"I guess I am," I say, feeling a swell of pride.

As I get back into the car, an alert goes off on my phone. Ninety minutes until the pitch-off. I need to hurry—if I miss the next train, I'll be late.

THE BAMPH STUDIO is packed. Everyone in the company wants to witness this showdown between me and my Badgers and Coleson and his Ferrets. I didn't register there would be such a big audience and now I'm relieved Michael's doing the pitch rather than me. Coleson looks different from how I re-member him. He's dressed in a sleek black suit, with a turtle-neck, and his hair is slicked back with gel. He looks, in my opinion, ridiculous, like he's turned up for the final exam at Villain School.

"Don't feel bad, Rutherford," he says to me. "I'll give you an internship at Ferret TV, so you can see what it feels like to be on a winning team."

"Coleson, I forgot to tell you, Magneto called, he wants his suit back."

"Magneto? Bit of a dated reference there, Grandma."

Damn. It's hard to make cultural reference jokes when you've missed so much culture. As I'm trying to think of a comeback, Michael arrives and I do a double take. He looks terrible, like he's been up all night drinking vodka and then slept in a skip. Instead of his trademark three-piece suit, he's wearing baggy jeans and a scruffy gray T-shirt. Something is wrong, something is very wrong.

Grabbing his arm, I pull him out of the busy studio and into the hallway.

"What's happened? You look terrible," I say as soon as we're alone.

"It's Jane. I think she's been sleeping with her aqua aerobics instructor."

"Oh no. I'm sorry. What makes you think that?"

"I found them in bed together."

"Did she, um, forget she was married again?" I ask hopefully.

"I don't think so. When I walked in on them, Marcus said, 'Oh shit, it's your husband.' Then Jane said, 'Oh shit,' too."

"That must have been a shock."

He hangs his head. "That's not the worst part." Michael swallows, as though he can hardly get the words out. "This guy, Marcus, he was wearing nothing apart from a baseball glove on his right hand. *My* baseball glove." Michael's face is racked with anguish. "My vintage glove, signed by Ozzie Smith himself. It's a collector's item. Heaven knows what they were doing with it." Michael shakes his head. "How can I ever look at that glove the same way now?" I pull him into a hug as

he starts to sob. "I'm sorry, Lucy, I'm a mess, I don't think I'll
be able to present today."

"It's okay, I'll handle it," I hear myself saying. Michael
nods limply, like a child grateful to be told what to do. Trey
catches my eye as we come back into the room, but there's no
time to explain because Coleson is now taking the stage. His
team all look smug and confident, so I suspect their idea must
be something fiendishly brilliant. A heavy sense of dread settles in my stomach as I realize that without Michael, our pitch
might not be good enough to win this.

Gary Snyder, Bamph's CEO, stands up to address the
room. His face looks pained, as though he's googled "how to
look serious and reverential" but is struggling to make his eyebrows do what he wants them to.

"No one enjoys letting people go." He sighs. "I could have
reinterviewed you all—let you reapply for your jobs, toed the
HR line—but I've witnessed what strong units both the Badger and Ferret teams are. I see the logic in keeping one team
together." Gary looks somber. Amid the strangely gladiatorial
atmosphere, maybe we do need reminding that many of the
people in this room are losing their jobs today. "And to ensure
complete fairness, the decision is not going to be down to me.
Kydz Network's newest commissioner, Melanie Durham, is
going to be the person you're pitching to this morning."

Melanie? Melanie is the new commissioner? We all turn to
see her come in. She looks incredible, like a younger, hotter
Judi Dench with twice the attitude. *Wow, I hope I look that
good when I'm in my sixties.*

"Lucy, Coleson." Melanie nods toward both of us, her
voice smooth as polished marble. "My former runners battling
it out for the top development job, how poetic."

"There are no traffic jams on the extra mile," Coleson says, furnishing Melanie with a grin full of veneers that he certainly didn't have when he was a runner.

"Exactly, Coleson," says Melanie. *Tell me she's not impressed by that? It doesn't even make sense.*

Coleson is up first, so I sit back down, trying to reassure myself that our whole presentation is loaded onto slides, all I need to do is read it. Trey's meticulously prepared graphics will speak for themselves.

"What do children want?" Coleson asks as he opens his presentation with a flick of his wrist. An artful montage of children running in a playground appears on the screen in front of us. "They want to be treated like adults. They don't want to be patronized." More footage of children's faces. "There have been shows where we've put children into adult situations before; we let them survive in the wild, build their own eco home, run a government." *They let kids run a government? Where?* "But what about the area where it really matters—the part of life that means the most to children, that they usually don't get a say in?" Coleson pauses for dramatic effect. "Family." A graphic on the presentation changes to a picture of two children being hugged by a man and a woman.

"Parents separate, and usually the kids don't get to hear about it until someone's moved out."

I scan the room, no idea where this pitch is going. Michael has a fist in his mouth. Coleson has everyone's rapt attention, including Melanie's.

"But that won't be the case on this show. Welcome to . . . *Kids on the Couch.*" Coleson stands back and a clip plays on the screen: a girl of about eight or nine is sitting in an armchair interviewing a couple who sit side by side on a couch. It looks like they built a set for their taster tape; the lighting and editing is slick and professional.

"And why do you think Mummy doesn't like it when you go out with your friends?" the child asks the man on the couch.

"Because she's controlling and doesn't like me having any fun," says the man, and Coleson's team all laugh.

"Because you come back drunk, gunning for a fight," says the woman.

The child consults her notepad. "And how does that make you feel, Mummy?"

"Scared, lonely."

Coleson waves his hand and the screen freezes. "*Kids on the Couch* features kids whose parents are on the brink of separation. Who could be more invested in trying to keep them together than their own children? Now, we're not just throwing them to the wolves here, our kiddie counselors will undergo intensive training from a qualified psychotherapist. We are empowering them to save their own families."

He can't be serious. I shake my head in incomprehension. This is wrong on so many levels. For a child to hear all their parents' problems and then be given the weight of responsibility in trying to fix them—it's a recipe for a lifetime of psychological damage. I look to Melanie but, I can't believe it, she's nodding, writing notes, she looks . . . impressed.

"It's bold, it's original, it's controversial. This is the show journalists will love to hate and hate to love," Coleson says. "It has everything—drama, jeopardy, family, emotion." Someone applauds. *This is not good.*

"But I don't think this idea needs me to sell it," Coleson continues. "I'm going to let the format speak for itself. So, without further ado—I present the pilot episode of *Kids on the Couch.*"

They made a whole pilot. We watch as a young girl, Melody, talks to her mother about her postnatal depression, coaches her father to articulate how it made him feel when her sibling arrived and took all his wife's attention. It's awful and tasteless and yet for some reason, I can't look away. The episode ends with the whole family in tears hugging one another. Someone sniffs, and I look over to see Gary crying. *Gary is crying.* We're screwed.

My palms ache, and I realize my hands have been balled into fists for the entire episode. We're given a five-minute comfort break before it's my turn to take the floor. My armpits are already damp with sweat, even though future deodorant is terrifyingly effective. *Is it normal to be this nervous? I'm sure everyone feels like this before an important, everything-riding-on-it presentation.*

AS I'M ABOUT to walk back in, I get a call on my mobile, a number I don't recognize. I don't have time to answer it, but what if it's Felix's school or Amy's nursery?

"Hello?"

"Hello," says a gruff voice at the other end.

"Who is this?" I ask in confusion.

"Dave, you told me to call if I heard about a machine you're looking for."

My mind scrambles for memory of a Dave. Do I know a Dave? *Shit, Dave!*

"Arcade Dave?" I ask.

"That's right. I found your wishing machine," he says. "Bloke I know says he saw one, just like you described, in a shop on Baskin Place, in Southwark. It's not even far from here. What are the chances of that?"

My heart, which just jumped straight into my mouth, now retreats slowly back down into my throat. It's an old lead.

"I went there," I explain. "It's a building site. That shop is gone."

"Since yesterday? I doubt it," Dave says. "Anyway, it's called Baskin News if you're still interested. Tell 'em I'll take it off their hands at a fair price if it's not what you're looking for."

I mumble my thanks but can't formulate words, because now I realize what he's just said. Baskin Place. Not Baskin Road, Baskin *Place*.

"Lucy?" Gary calls from the meeting room. "It's time."

I need to get down there, I need to leave right now. The wishing machine is still there. I was looking in the wrong place all along.

Glancing around the room, I take in the anxious faces of my team: Michael, who loves three things in this world and just witnessed two of them being desecrated. I can't be responsible for his losing the third too. Trey, who I drunkenly advised to throw caution to the wind and propose to his girlfriend, who's counting on my giving him a permanent position. Dominique, who needs to finish that tattoo—okay, so her concerns might not feel as high-stakes as the others', but everyone on the team works hard, they've all put their livelihoods in my hands. I need to stay and finish this.

As I take the stage, Coleson gives me a thumbs-up, which he quickly turns into a thumbs-down. Mature. However unpalatable an idea *Kids on the Couch* might be, I can't fault Coleson's presentation style. It was slick and confident, perfectly paced; he had everyone's attention. I need to do that, only better. *The machine is still there, the newsagent's is still there. I could go back! You can't think about it now, Lucy. Focus.*

"Lucy?" Gary asks, then coughs. Everyone is waiting for me to start.

"Right, sorry," I say, clearing my throat, which is now drier than sandpaper. "When I think of my own childhood, I think of den building, of make-believe, of hide-and-seek and treasure hunts that my dad used to lay around the house. Simple games, fueled by imagination. Your bed could be a pirate ship, the sofa a rocket flying to outer space." I take a breath; I need to slow down, my heart is beating too loud in my ears. "Children can make a game out of anything, their imaginations can create the fiercest foes. I don't think kids want to be treated like grown-ups, I think kids want to be kids. *I* want them to be kids. As a mum, I know childhood is only too short."

Looking out at all the faces in the crowd, my eyes land on Callum, his eyes so full of faith in me. Then it hits me. Why am I trying to do this alone? We came up with this idea together. If we're the Cardinals, we can't win this with one batsman.

"What were you scared of as a child, Callum?" I ask.

He looks back in surprise, but then he says, "Being sucked down the plughole in the bath by a giant squid." People laugh.

"Dominique?" I ask, finding Dominique in the front row.

"The attic, it was all cold and dusty and full of spiders."

"Melanie? What were you scared of?"

Melanie looks at me blankly, and I'm sure she's going to say "Nothing," but then she says, "The noise of the boiler in the laundry room. It made me imagine a creature made of laundry with huge grinding metal teeth and boiling-hot eyes."

"Okay, Trey, do you think we could create a laundry room monster right now?"

Trey stares at me wide-eyed. He's dressed in a cream jumpsuit today, and in my eyes, he looks like the angel of salvation.

I'm really putting him on the spot here, but I know he can do it. This will be more impressive, showing Melanie *her* monster, rather than the ones we've pre-animated. Trey nods. He quickly sketches the monster Melanie described, then brings it to life right in front of our eyes. There are oohs from the audience, and I see Melanie tilt her head in appreciation.

"We'll give children a chance to beat the demons of their imagination, playing a game only they could come up with. But I'm going to stop talking and let my team show you what we mean. Leon, Dominique, get up here."

This wasn't planned either, but after only a moment's pause, they both jump up, knowing what I'm asking them to do. They start to improvise, walking into an imaginary house, describing what they're scared of: a dark cupboard full of spiders, a sofa that eats people. As fast as they can talk, Trey draws, creating what they're imagining and projecting it for us to see. It creates a far better sense of the game than I could ever describe with words.

"Callum, tell them how the scoring is going to work," I say, beckoning Callum to join us on stage. He devised the scoring; he should be part of this too. Callum explains, stuttering and nervous, but his passion for the project shines, though. The whole presentation is messy and chaotic, but it's fun and real, and it captures the buzz of what we all love about it.

When the demo is finished, Michael starts clapping and punching the air and then the whole room joins in.

"Well, thank you both for those," Melanie says, her voice giving nothing away. "I'll consult with Gary. We'll let you know."

As she leaves the room, Melanie turns and catches my eye, then she gives me the smallest nod. I know that nod; it means

we did it. Once Melanie and Gary have left the room, Coleson
and his Ferrets look on in disdain as my team all run in for a
group hug and start jumping up and down.

"Monsters under the bed, that's really the best you've got?"
Coleson sneers, but he's lost some of his bravado.

"Team, that was masterful," says Michael. "I could watch
you do that all day. That's got to count for something."

"I can't believe I got to explain the scoring," Callum says,
a hand over his mouth to hide his grin. "I wasn't prepared."

Trey pulls me to one side as the others celebrate. "What's
the deal with Michael?" he asks.

"Jane," I say darkly.

"Jane," he says, pushing a fist into his other hand.

I look for Coleson; I want to shake his hand, to make
peace, but he's already gone. Michael has perked up considerably and wants to take the team out for lunch.

"Lucy?" he asks. "You coming?"

"I'm so sorry, I have to run, there's somewhere I need
to be."

Hailing a cab in the street, I ask the driver, "Please, can
you take me to Baskin Place?"

My heart is pounding in my chest, and my hand shakes as
I try to buckle my seat belt. What if Dave is wrong? What if it
isn't there or if it isn't a portal at all? But then a greater anxiety
takes hold—*What if it is?*

CHAPTER 32

IT'S HERE, THE STREET THAT LOOKS IDENTICAL TO BASKIN Road, only here the buildings are all still standing. There, a few doors down, is the newsagent's. It doesn't have the blue and white awning anymore, and the outside has been repainted. It is a completely unremarkable corner shop. I'm not sure I would have recognized it even if I had been on the right street. Thanking the cabdriver, I run in, immediately recognizing the shape of the small rectangular shop, with only two aisles and shelves piled high to the ceiling. There is no one behind the till and no other customers. As I dart around the corner aisle, my heart jumps into my throat, because there it is, the wishing machine, looking exactly as it did all those weeks—years?—ago.

Rushing to touch it, I want to check it's real, not some optical illusion. But then, as my hands curl around the cold metal, I try to temper my excitement. The existence of this machine does not mean that it is a portal to the past.

"I thought I might see you again," comes a voice with a soft Scottish lilt. My head darts sideways to see the old woman. Same white hair, same tartan waistcoat.

"You?"

"Hello, duckie," she says, giving me a broad smile.

"Is this real? Are you real? Is this a figment of my imagination?"

"It's as real as it needs to be," she says, offering me a brown paper bag of green boiled sweets. "Soor ploom?"

"Did I jump through time, or did I lose my memory?" I ask, waving away the brown bag.

She takes one of the sweets herself, sucking on it for a moment before saying, "What do you think, duckie?"

I want to explode that I just want a straight answer, to shake her until she tells me what's going on, but she's so soft-spoken and calm, this little sweet-eating Yoda, that I can't bring myself to raise my voice.

"I jumped," I hear myself saying. Is that what I've thought all along? Or has finding the shop, the machine, her, let me finally believe it?

"And how are you liking this new life of yours, the good part, where everything's sorted?"

"Ha! Life is never sorted." I narrow my eyes at the old woman. "Was that the lesson I was supposed to learn? Because if it was, you could have just told me that, I am very receptive to feedback."

"*You* wished it. So, tell me, is it a grand improvement on before?" she asks calmly, taking a pocket watch out of her waistcoat and checking the time.

"Yes, and no. It's complicated." Then I look down at my wedding ring and say, "But also kind of wonderful."

"It was the best of times, it was the worst of times," the old woman says, still sucking on her sweet. "Maybe you weren't ready."

"Well, there's been a lot to catch up on," I say, relenting and reaching for one of her sweets. "But maybe there aren't any shortcuts in life. Maybe you have to live it all, because it makes you who you are." I pause. "Wait, did I really say that? Wow, I've gone full Elizabeth Gilbert."

"So much wisdom in one so young," the old lady says with a smile.

"Who, Elizabeth Gilbert?"

"No, you, Lucy." And when I turn to look at her, she winks at me. Then she rolls up the top of her paper bag and stows it in a pocket of her waistcoat. "So, do you want to go back?"

"Can I? I don't know how all this works."

"If you *really* want to," she says, tapping the machine, "then you can go back."

"And will everything play out like I've seen? Will I meet Sam and have Felix, Chloe, and Amy? Will I still get to be a part of this family?"

The old lady presses her fingers together and her face grows serious. "Nothing is guaranteed. No one's path is set in stone."

"Would I go back knowing all this, knowing what the future holds?"

"No, duckie. Knowledge changes the path, even if you don't want it to. You wouldn't be able to meet the love of your life, knowing their significance, without it affecting your behavior."

"What about Zoya, Chloe? Can I stop them from dying?"

"Like I said, nothing is set in stone." The old lady turns around and pulls up a stool from behind the till, her forehead creasing in sympathy. "But even if you could go back knowing, no one likes to be told they're going to die, duckie."

Something inside me crumples, as though I've been hollowed out from the inside with an ice cream scoop. I sink to the floor, my back against the wishing machine. She is right—it would be miserable to know what lay ahead.

"So, what choice do I have?" I ask her.

"You can stay here—your memories will no doubt return in time, the gaps filled in—or you can go back, forget all of this."

"But I might not end up here, with the life I've got now?"

She holds my gaze, her eyes glistening. "Our paths are not predestined."

Finally, I understand what she's telling me: stay and remember or go back and forget. If I go back, my life might end up in an entirely different place. It's like *Sophie's Choice* (not that I've ever seen it, but people always seem to mention it when there's an impossible decision to be made). When all this began, I so desperately hoped for the wishing machine to be real, wanted to believe I had skipped forward, because that might mean I could go back. But now, I have fallen in love with the people in this life. I know I could be happy here if I stayed, especially if my memories returned.

"I've been remembering things, from the in-between. What does that mean?"

"When you choose a path, your brain will catch up. If you remember things, you're beginning to choose."

Shifting my body toward the machine, I ask, "So, what is this thing? How does it work? Is it you that's magic?"

The old lady reaches forward and clasps my hands in hers. "'There are more things in heaven and earth, Horatio, than are dreamt of in your philosophy.'"

"Are you Shakespeare?" I ask with a smile, and her eyes light up in amusement.

She drops my hand and holds out her palm. "Are you ready, do you have a coin?"

"What, I need to do it now? Don't I get to say good-bye to people first?"

"No time like the present. Well, no time like the future." She smiles and hands me two coins.

"Could I come back tomorrow, or maybe next week? Just have a few more days here . . . I need to say good-bye to Sam, to give Leonard his watering can, hug the children . . ."

"Lucy, it doesn't sound like your mind is made up at all."

"Oh no, it is, I have to go back. I want my life, I need to see Zoya."

"Then you won't remember this anyway. What good are forgotten good-byes?"

She's right. If I'm going, there's no point in dragging out my departure. Before I can overthink it, I slot the coins into the machine, close my eyes, and wish to go back to my old life, to be twenty-six again, to have all this ahead of me. But when I open my eyes, the lights of the machine are still dull; it sits stubbornly silent.

"Oh dear," she says.

"What do you mean 'oh dear'? Why isn't it working?"

She kicks the machine, trying to jolt it to life.

"Is it broken?"

"I suspected this might happen," she says, bowing her head slightly.

"What? What's happened?"

"You don't want it enough."

"I do. I do want it! I want to go back," I shout at the machine, "I want to go back!"

"It only works if it's with *all* your heart. Some of your heart is here now."

"So I'm stuck?" I ask, panic bubbling in my chest. *I doubted I could fly.*

"Maybe you do need to say your good-byes," she says kindly, but then taps the machine and consults her pocket watch again. "You don't have much time, though. The longer you are here, the harder it will be to leave. When you truly feel this life is yours, more memories will return, and when the blanks have filled in, the window to leave will close."

"What? There's a time limit now! Why is there a time limit?" That seems like a needless plot device to add stress to my already incredibly stressful situation.

"Everyone needs a deadline," she says, clicking and un-clicking a button on her watch. "Go, say your good-byes, but be back and ready to leave before the picture fills in."

Right, so go back home, say good-bye to everyone I love, and then emotionally detach enough to come back here and try again—all before the amnesia wears off and the magic por-tal closes. When I explain all this to Felix, it's going to blow his little mind.

CHAPTER 33

"I KNEW IT!" SAYS FELIX, JUMPING UP AND DOWN ON his bed. "I knew there would be a portal. I can't believe it was there all along."

"I know."

"Do you think I can go through the portal? Do you think I can go to Mars?" Felix asks.

"Why would you want to go to Mars? You'd die, there's no air."

"I could wish for air; I could wish for a whole colony. I could rename Mars 'Felix Is a Badass.' How cool would that be?"

"Felix Is a Badass," I say, smiling. "Something tells me the wishing machine doesn't deal in those kinds of wishes."

Felix nudges his head into me, and I wrap my arm around him. "What will happen here if you go? Will old Mummy come back?"

"I'm not sure. But yes, I imagine everything will carry on like before."

"But if you go back, and you change something, I might never exist—that's what lady Yoda said."

"I know, shit. Why would I change anything, though?"

"Shit happens."

"Don't swear."

"You said it first!"

We grin at each other. "If I stay, she said my memories will come back. I'd be your mummy again."

"You're already my mummy," Felix says, hugging closer into me. "Just messier and swearier."

I blink back tears.

Sam pokes his head around the door. "What's wrong?"

"Mummy's upset because I'm going to be a cosmonaut," says Felix.

Sam shoots me a confused look.

"I'm hormonal," I explain. "Anything will set me off today."

"Will it make you cry if I say dinner's ready?" he asks, and I shake my head, furiously rubbing away tears with my palms.

As I walk down the stairs, I notice the lighting is different. There are candles lit in the hall, and the curtains are drawn. Turning around, I give Sam a questioning look, but he just gives me an enigmatic smile. Something is going on.

Following the candles, I open the door to the kitchen to find the table set for two, a bunch of red roses in the middle of the table.

"What's all this for?"

"It's a restaurant; I'm the waiter," says Felix, pulling out a chair, and I notice he's put an apron on and has a pencil tucked behind his ear.

"I wanted to take you out, but I couldn't get a sitter," says Sam.

As I sit down, I notice a folded piece of paper in front of me
with "Menu" written on the front in Felix's wobbly handwriting. "There's only one thing on the menu," he whispers. "So,
you have to have that."

Inside the menu is written, "Vegetable lasagna—£1000."
"Wow, this is an expensive restaurant," I say.

"Well, I thought I'd push the boat out," says Sam.

"What are we celebrating? It's not an anniversary, is it?" I
ask, feeling myself grinning at Sam.

"No, I just know how hard the last month has been for
you. I want you to know we love you." He pauses. "Whatever
you do or don't remember."

Felix makes a face. "Are you going to get all soppy, Dad?"

"I might, and the waiter is not supposed to comment on the
diners' conversation."

Sam stands up to get wine from the fridge, while Felix
picks up a jug and leans across the table to fill up my water
glass. He then spills it all over the table.

"Oops."

As I jump up to clear up the mess, my phone pings with a
message.

"Mummy, no phones at the table," says Felix. "This is a
smart restaurant."

"Sorry, I'm just waiting to hear from work," I explain.
"Ooh, it's from Gary."

My eyes eagerly scan his message.

Lucy, I won't call this late, but thought you'd want to
know—just got off the phone with Mel Durham. She loved
your pitch, they want to take *The House Is Going to Get
You* to development. Congratulations. Let's have lunch this

week to discuss your new role as head of development for Bamph UK. Big year ahead for you.

Gary Snyder

I squeal, then read the message aloud to Sam and Felix. "I'll forward this to the team; they'll be waiting to hear."

"You clever old thing," says Sam, reaching for my hand across the table, then flashing me a huge smile as he notices I'm wearing my rings. "Now we really are celebrating."

"Well done, Mummy. Can I start waitering now?" Felix asks brightly.

"Yes, go for it."

Felix launches into a long speech about how it's customary to tip your waiter, ideally at least 10 percent of the cost of the meal. He caveats that if we don't have any cash, he's happy to take Lego, and if we don't have any Lego, he's willing to take an IOU.

"Okay, I think it might be the waiter's bedtime," says Sam, pushing back his chair. "Thank you for your help setting this up, Felix."

"No! I haven't told you the specials!" Felix cries as Sam picks him up, throws him over his shoulder, and carries him out of the room, Felix squealing with laughter.

Once our overenthusiastic waiter has been dispatched to bed, Sam serves up a delicious-looking vegetable lasagna, then raises his glass to mine.

"To you and me, Luce, to making new memories," he says, holding my gaze.

"I will drink to that," I say.

For dessert Sam pulls out a smooth mocha gâteau from the

fridge. Something about it looks familiar, and then I realize. "It's just like the one my mum bought me for my tenth birthday."

"I got your mum to dig out a photo, then asked the bakery to copy it."

"That's so thoughtful, Sam, thank you," I say, leaning across the table to kiss him. This evening feels like the perfect way to say good-bye, but at the same time, it's making me realize I don't want this to end.

We stay up far too late, getting drunk on cake, wine, and each other's company. On our way to bed I sneak into Amy's room, to watch her sleeping in the soft glow of her night-light. She looks so cozy and peaceful, her small pink fingers clutching Neckie, her smooth round cheeks glowing rosy pink, the quiet snuffle of her breathing. My heart feels so full of love for this child, I could watch her sleep all night long. Reaching out to tuck a curl of hair behind her ear, I whisper, "Good-bye, little one, I'll see you again. I hope I'll see you again." And then I need to leave, or I'll start crying.

When Sam and I eventually collapse into bed, I feel sated, physically and emotionally.

"Thank you for a lovely evening," I say to Sam.

"I don't want you to get the wrong idea," he says firmly, his eyes glinting in amusement. "I don't usually take you for thousand-pound meals on a weeknight."

"I will temper my expectations," I say, edging closer to him on the bed.

His eyes grow serious. "I don't want you to feel jealous of some alternate version of yourself. You are her, you know that, right?"

"I do," I tell him, and then he pulls me toward him, cocooning me in his arms.

"I heard you talking to Felix earlier," he says quietly, "about leaving."

"Ah."

"Where are you off to?"

I sit up in bed. If this is good-bye, then Sam deserves the truth, whether he believes it or not. "Say, theoretically, I had found the portal, the one Felix thought had transported me here from the past. Say that I don't have amnesia, but I time-traveled here, and now I have the chance to go back." I look into his eyes, waiting for skepticism or laughter, but his face is serious.

"And will this be a permanent departure? Or are you coming back?" he asks, and I shrug.

"If my life works out the same, probably. But nothing is guaranteed."

We sit in silence for a moment. Then Sam says, "Then don't go. Wherever it is you think you're going, don't. I don't want to risk losing you."

"It's sixteen years of my life, Sam."

He cuts me off. "I love you—*you*, not who you were, not who you're going to be, or who you might have been—just you. Please stay with me."

As far as speeches go, it's pretty effective. I am putty in his hands and more confused than ever. He flips me onto my back, then dips his head to kiss my shoulder, my neck, planting light, soft kisses along my jaw. We fit together so perfectly; it feels impossible I could end up anywhere but here. As his mouth finds mine, a familiar giddy feeling courses through me. My hands clasp his broad back, and I close my eyes, succumbing to the heady waves of pleasure. But then he stops, pulls back, and I open my eyes to see what's wrong.

"Look at me," he says. "I want you to look at me."

Now I see with aching clarity—my heart has filled in the gaps, even if my brain has not caught up.

"Sam, I love you." It's the first time I've said it, but as the words leave my mouth, I know it's the truest thing I've ever said.

There is something different between us now, something beyond the physical. We make love slowly, quietly, and I try to seal it deep inside, this exquisite feeling of intimacy.

"What's wrong?" he asks, holding me afterward.

I mustn't cry, I don't want to ruin what could be our last night together.

God, I hope I end up here—please let me end up here, in this life, with this man. Then the thought takes hold that I should stay, that I shouldn't risk this, that I would sacrifice sixteen years to have this. These are not the thoughts that are going to allow me to get back.

As we lie spent in the dark, I whisper, "Thank you."

"For what?"

"For everything—for being you, for loving me through everything, for this life we've made."

"That sounds like a good-bye," Sam says, stroking his fingers gently down my arm. He starts humming softly beside me, murmuring words of a song I haven't heard before.

"You wrote something?" I ask, my eyes welling with tears.

"Just the start of something silly."

"What's it called?" I ask.

"'Stay for All the Pocket Days.' It's not finished, I was just messing around."

"I like the sound of it. You should finish it."

"Okay," he says plainly.

"Okay?"

"Okay."

And then he wraps his arms around me, as though he never wants to let me go, and softly sings me to sleep.

I MUST BE in a deep sleep because I sleep through the alarm. When I wake, Sam is gone, and there's a note on his pillow.

> *Doing the school run, then coming back to work on my new song :) Don't go anywhere, please.*

I bite my lip, feeling myself grin. I love it when he leaves notes on the pillow, like that time on our honeymoon in Italy, where he left me notes in Italian that I couldn't even read.

On our honeymoon. In Italy.

Our honeymoon. In Italy.

Shit. I remember our honeymoon.

CHAPTER 34

AM I TOO LATE? HAVE I MISSED MY CHANCE? THIS MEM-ory is clearer than any of the glimpses I have had before. I re-member Italy, the hotel, the crazy couple in the room next door. I remember all of it. *I have to get to London, now.*

Throwing on my clothes, I run out the door. It's eight thirty, nobody is here. Dashing past Felix's room, I see some-thing that makes me jerk to a halt and retrace my steps. The remote for the lava lamp, for the heart we built—it's on the floor by his desk. He's got the project fair this morning, it won't work without the remote. He'll be so disappointed, like that time he made a spider out of Meccano. *The Meccano spi-der, with only five legs, I can picture it perfectly.*

Grabbing the remote, I run down the corridor, glancing at our wedding photo on the stairs. We had a fruit wedding cake, my mum made it and was offended when everyone was too full to eat it. The photo of Felix on the hall table, it was taken in Crete, after the boat trip where we didn't see any sharks. *I need to stop looking at things, I need to stop remembering—I have to get to London before it's too late.*

Jumping in the car, with nothing but my wallet and the remote for the lava lamp, I speed toward the school. Logic tells me that Felix's project doesn't matter, that if I'm going back, none of this matters. But I can't help feeling that it does. It matters to Felix, right here, right now, in this reality, so it matters to me.

On the drive to school, I see the street where Felix learned to ride a bike. There's the tree he fell out of and broke his wrist. Memories, memories, too many memories. I drive faster. Stan sternly tells me to slow down.

At the school, I park right in front of the steps, leave the engine running, then sprint in.

"Visitors need to scan in, Mrs. Rutherford," the receptionist calls after me.

"I'll only be a minute!" I call back, searching desperately for the main hall. Worryingly, I now know the way.

Bursting through the door, I see I'm just in time, because my son, my beautiful boy, is standing at the front of the room. A crowd of staff and pupils, including Molly Greenway and the headmistress, surrounds his display. He looks pale, as though he's about to burst into tears, because he's realized there is something missing.

"I have it!" I shout, running across the hall to him. "I have it!" His head whips up, the tears vanishing.

Mrs. Barclay, the headmistress, gives me a strange look as I catch my breath, taking in my wild hair and mismatched clothes. If coming here ends up costing me sixteen years, the smile on Felix's face is worth every single day. He presses the button on the remote and the heart beats into life. Pupils ooh and aah in delight and Mrs. Barclay says, "Felix, how on earth did you do that?" as she moves closer to inspect the pulsing sculpture.

I need to go. I wave to Felix as I back out of the classroom, but he runs around the desk to throw his arms around my waist.

"Thank you. I love you," he says, eliciting titters from his classmates, but he doesn't care.

"I love you too, and I'm so proud of you, sweet boy. Good-bye, Felix," I say, and for a moment he won't let go.

Then he looks up at me with tear-stained cheeks. "Good luck, Mummy. Don't worry, I'll see you next time around."

IN THE CAR, I find myself asking Stan for help. "Stanley, please help me, I don't think I'm going to make it in time."

"Lucy, I am here to support you in any way that I can. Would you like some words of affirmation?"

"Yes, yes, please."

"Your goals come to fruition at the right time," says Stanley. "Taking time to rest fuels your creativity and stamina."

Not hugely helpful, but it's enough to distract me from all the new memories vying to push their way in. The tires screech as I pull into the train car park, my vision blurred with tears.

"Good-bye, Stanley, I'm going to miss you," I tell the car, hugging the steering wheel. "Look after everyone for me."

"Have a productive day, Lucy!" says Stan.

Sprinting for the nine fifteen train, I make it by less than a minute. Once, coming back on the last train, I picked a take-away up for Sam from his favorite Mexican in Covent Garden, bringing it all the way back home, then dropping it down the gap between the platform and the carriage. On the train, I hold my head in my hands, trying to distract myself from thinking, to block out the memories that keep coming, unbidden. *Stop. Stop. I need this to stop.* In the next carriage, a tiny baby cries, and with the high-pitched sound a new heaviness envelops me, like metal filings filling my blood, the ground morphing into a giant magnet. A tiny hand curled around my little finger. Cannulas and oxygen tubes, the endless beeping of an incubator. A part of my heart sheared off, forever. Loss. Such overwhelming loss, but steeped in another feeling—love, too big to fathom. *Chloe.*

WHEN I FINALLY reach Southwark, my pace slows. I must be too late. I must be. The rough sketch of this life is being rapidly painted in, making *this* my reality, *this* my present. My feet drag, heavier with every step.

At the bus stop ahead of me I see three women laughing. They are in their twenties, all with matching fringes and heavy eyeliner.

"Becca, you gotta come tonight. It's the last night they're playing," says one girl.

"I'm too tired, look at these bags under my eyes. I need sleep," says another.

I feel like telling this girl she doesn't know the meaning of the word "tired," not until she's lived off three hours' sleep for months on end, dealing with a baby with reflux and a boy with night terrors. She doesn't know the meaning of eye bags either. She is beautiful, so fucking beautiful, but I can see from her posture she doesn't feel it, not fully.

"You can sleep when you're dead," says the third girl, pulling her friend into a messy, long-limbed hug.

That's what Zoya used to say.

Zoya.

I start to run.

The shop is empty, as always, and I call out, "Hello!" as I run through the door. "I'm back!" I pull back the beaded curtain into the back room, but no one is here, though the door was open—the shop unlocked. Whether the Scottish lady is here or not, I have to try, I have to know if I'm out of time.

My hands shake as I look for the coins I put in my purse especially. I slot them into the machine, hold on to its sides, and say aloud this time, "I want to go back. Please, I want to go back. I want to live every messy day—the good ones and the ones that suck—where I don't know what I'm doing, and I don't know where I'm going or how to get there. I want to go on all the shit dates, because then, when I meet the right person I will know how special he is. And when I find him, I don't want to miss a minute. I don't want to miss making him laugh for the first time, I don't want to miss discovering that his eyes look green rather than blue when he wakes up in the morning. I don't want to miss our first kiss, our first fight, our first anything. And I'll take the heartache and the horror and the losses too, the fear of not knowing how it will all come to be, because that is life, in all its glorious, messy Technicolor. And I know I am so lucky to be here, and that every breath I take is the good part." I shake the machine, because nothing is happening, the lettering stays stubbornly dark. "Let me live my life. *Please*, let me live my life."

Then I'm crying, because it isn't working, and I sink to the floor, my head against the machine. Physically and emotionally spent, because I know now, too late, that even if I remember everything, remembering is not the same as living.

Just as I'm about to accept that the window of opportunity to choose has closed, I feel a clunk, and look up to see the old woman kicking the machine.

"Sometimes it needs a wee nudge," she says. "Like me, it's rather old."

The machine bursts into life, illuminating like a Christmas tree; cogs whir, and I see the words pressed onto the copper coin.

Your wish is granted.

TODAY

I WAKE TO THE SMELL OF DAMP. GROANING AT MY alarm, I stare up at the yellow stain on the ceiling. What are the chances of Mr. Finkley ever paying to get that fixed, or our lazy landlord organizing for it to be dried out and replastered? Even though the stain is larger, and the smell is considerably worse, for some reason, this morning, the state of my room doesn't upset me as much as it usually does. As my dad always says, "Worse things happen at sea, love." What these terrible things happening at sea are, I'm not sure, but I imagine interminable dampness is one of them.

Getting out of bed, I draw the curtains, yank open the window, and inhale the sights, scents, and sounds of glorious, sunny London. The cars beeping, the birds tweeting, the smell of the kebab shop's rubbish bins from three doors down. I'm going to wear a proper shirt to work today. Even though yesterday was a disaster—what with Croissantgate and being told my promotion means nothing and that I'm basically still the runner—if I keep on showing up, working hard, and looking extra professional, maybe one day I will be trusted with more.

In the kitchen, Emily and Julian are having breakfast.

"Sorry, I think this is yours. I'll buy you more," says Julian, his spoon full of my cereal freezing in midair.

"It's fine," I say, picking up the box to pour myself a bowl but finding it empty. "Oh."

"I'll make you some toast," says Emily, who is also eating my cereal. "Sorry."

At the end of the corridor, I hear music coming from Zoya's room. "Is Zoya still here? I thought she had an early viewing."

"They canceled last minute," Julian says, then shakes his finger and hunches over as though he's an old man. "Young people today, no sense of commitment."

Walking down the corridor, I knock quietly on Zoya's door.

"Come in!" she calls, and I push the door open but hover in the doorway. Even though I only saw her yesterday, I feel this distance between us—as though it's been far longer.

"Hey. I thought you'd be long gone," I say.

"The viewing was canceled, so . . ." She trails off, and we stand in awkward silence for a moment.

"Zoya, I'm so sorry—" I launch in, but she stops me.

"No, no, *I'm* sorry. I overreacted, I shouldn't have been so prickly. I know it must look to you like I'm selling out, but it's not just about the money. Art school wasn't for me, Luce."

"I know."

"It's not like I'm never going to draw again. This way I'll be able to see the world, paint the world." She grins, walking across the room to pull me into a hug. "Surprisingly, I quite like being an estate agent, but I know you would hate it. You should stick to TV, and I will listen to you whinge about it, because that's what friends do." She pauses before saying, "I think maybe I got upset because I'm slightly jealous. I wish I had your clarity about where I want to be. Maybe I'm too focused on having fun, rather than making plans for where I want to end up."

"I think you're doing just fine. I love you," I say, squeezing her tight. She gives me a suspicious look. "What? I don't think we say it enough. I love you. My life wouldn't be as good without you in it."

"So cheesy. But fine. I fucking love you too." She leans in to give me a big sloppy kiss on the cheek, which I wipe away in mock disgust.

BACK IN THE kitchen, I put the kettle on to make tea for the four of us.

"Right, while we're all here, quick flat meeting," I say, clapping my hands. "I've been thinking, and I propose we have a kitty for basics—put a little cash in each week for the stuff we all use, like cereal, milk, and loo roll."

"I'd be up for that," says Julian.

"Makes sense." Emily shrugs as she sniffs the milk she's about to add to her tea.

"Also, not to be boring, but can we agree not to use the bath for anything but washing? I don't want to find more bones being stewed or clothes being tie-dyed in there."

"Agreed," says Julian. "Em, that last dye job you did turned me purple. Betty thought I had some exotic skin disease."

"Good. That's settled then," I say. "It's payday, so I will buy loo roll and cereal for us all on my way home."

"And since we're having a flat meeting, I have some news," Zoya says. She looks to me and I nod. "I'm going to move out."

"Oh no!" Julian and Emily say in unison.

"Don't break up the four musketeers!" says Julian. "We'd have to change the ZoLu JuEm sign on our buzzer, I love that sign."

"Who will provide the soundtrack to our mornings? The vodka to our evenings?" Emily whines.

"I know, I know, it's just time for a change."

"She's a big-shot grown-up now, and I couldn't be prouder of her," I say, reaching over to muss up Zoya's hair.

"I will still hang out here all the time," Zoya says. "And I will still make excellent playlists and bring half-decent vodka."

"I hate interviewing new flatmates," Julian groans.

"Well, we might not need one immediately," I tell him. "I was thinking, until the damp situation in my room has been fixed, we might be due a rent reduction because it's uninhabitable."

"What's got into you this morning? You're being all Erin Brockovichy. Did you listen to a motivational podcast in your sleep or something?" Emily asks.

"I don't know," I say. "I just woke up feeling good and decided I want to make a few changes."

"Be the change you want to see in the bathroom," says Zoya.

"Exactly."

BEFORE I LEAVE for work, I pick up the two dying plants in my room and tell them, "I'm sorry, I tried, but I'm just not a plant person. You're going to have to go." Maybe one day, if I ever have a garden, I will try to be my father's green-fingered daughter, but for now, there is no shame in admitting defeat.

Outside by the bins, I find Mr. Finkley stuffing a rusty animal cage into an already overflowing green bin.

"Oh, no room for these?" I ask, disappointed.

"No. You'd need to black-bag them anyway," he says, pausing to inspect the plants in my hand. "Why are you throwing them away?"

"I'm not very good at caring for them. They look sad and it was making me feel depressed to watch them wither."

"I called someone about my bathroom floor, they're coming tomorrow," Mr. Finkley says, and I can see he's trying to be amenable.

"Thank you, much appreciated." Then, noticing the curious way he's eyeing up the plants, I say, "Would you like these? Maybe you'll have better luck with them, you might be able to revive them."

"Really?" His eyes light up.

"Of course, I was only going to throw them away anyway."

He takes them from me, hugging one in each arm. "You can come and visit them whenever you like," he offers. "You know, if you ever miss them."

Yeah, right. "I'm good, but thanks." I turn to go, then pause and say, "And, Mr. Finkley, thank you for trying to sort the bathroom, and I'm sorry for shouting at you yesterday. I was just really tired."

He nods, then whispers, "Would you like a drink? I think you would."

As I'm trying to think of a polite way to decline, I realize he is not talking to me, he's talking to the plants, so I run to catch up with Zoya.

"TELLING THE OTHERS went better than expected," she says on our walk to the tube, "and you're sure you really don't mind me moving out?"

"Zoya, I will you miss you terribly, but things can't stay the same forever." I pause. "Please tell me you'll stay south of the river, though?"

She holds my hand and swings it back and forth. "Of course I'll stay south of the river. So, tell me what happened last night. How come you got in so late, and why is there a spring in your step? Did you meet someone?"

"It was a weird night, horrible really. I was miserable after you left, I drank too much, walked all the way home, found myself on a LondonLove date with this flasher called Dale— oh, and then I met this crazy lady in a newsagent's, I have to tell you all about her. But what's strange is that despite my hideous evening, I woke up this morning with this feeling that all was right with the world. Do you ever get that?"

"I do—whenever you start a story with 'I have to tell you about this crazy lady I met . . . '"

FLUSH FROM PAYDAY, I treat us both to a coffee from the café near the tube. A song comes on the radio as we're waiting at the counter; I've never heard it before but something about it grabs my attention.

"What's this song?"

"The new Lex single, 'The Promise of You,'" says Zoya. "Radio One are obsessed, why?"

"Déjà vu. Do you ever get that with songs?"

"All the time. What are you going to do about Melanie?" Zoya asks.

"I'll give it to the end of the series, then start sending my CV out—apply for some proper junior researcher jobs. I think I've been too set on staying at When TV, on proving myself to Melanie."

"Stockholm syndrome," Zoya says, nodding. "Hey, there's a train in four minutes, do you want to run for it?" she asks, checking the transport app on her phone.

"No, let's get the next one. I'm not in a rush."

"Good. I want to hear all the details of your adventure last night."

So we walk slowly, sipping our coffees, soaking in the spring sunshine, and I tell Zoya all about Dale, about walking home with no shoes and going a bit nuts in a newsagent's making a crazy wish on a wishing machine, which of course did not come true.

FIVE YEARS LATER

"WHERE TO NEXT?" ASKS FAYE AS THE FOUR OF US FALL out of a bar on Upper Street.

"You decide, you're the birthday girl," Zoya says, draping an arm around my shoulder. "This gold minidress is really working for you by the way. We should go out-out, we should go dancing."

"Yes! Let's pick up some men," Roisin shouts into the gray night sky.

"Don't let your husband hear you say that," says Faye.

"Not for *me*, for you. I can be your wingwoman."

"Well, Zoya is all loved up, I'm sworn off men for the moment, so that only leaves Lucy," says Faye.

"I'm swearing off men too," I tell them. "Thirty-one is going to be my year of abstinence and sobriety. All the time I would have spent dating and drinking, I'm going to spend reading books and trying new hobbies. I might become amazing at macramé, or roller skating—get ready for a whole new me."

"Well, I'm here for your new me, your old me, whatever me you want to be," says Faye, wrapping an arm around my shoulders.

"Abstinence and sobriety, fuck off, Lucy!" Roisin laughs into the sky.

"Why is she being so shouty?" Faye asks. "Can I vote no for clubbing? I might be up for a bar, but I do need to get *some* sleep this weekend."

"You can sleep when you're dead," Zoya says, suddenly stopping on the street and turning around to face the rest of us. "Let's make a pact right now, that whatever else changes in life—marriage, kids, careers, travel—we'll always have this. We'll always make time for each other. I want us to be having nights out like this in twenty, thirty, fifty years' time."

"I already feel too old for nights like this. Can we do a nice pub lunch for my birthday?" asks Faye. "Maybe a relaxing spa day."

"Fine, it's not about where we go, it's about prioritizing each other, whatever else comes for us in life. Men come and go, but this"—she moves a finger back and forth between us—"this is forever."

"Count me in," I say.

"Me too," says Roisin.

"Me three," says Faye, and we all huddle in for a group hug.

"Right, seriously, Lucy—where are we going? Club, bar, macramé sex dungeon?" Zoya asks.

"Let's find a karaoke bar," I say. "I'm in the mood to sing."

ACKNOWLEDGMENTS

Firstly, I need to acknowledge the multitude of classic films this book takes inspiration from: *Big*, *13 Going on 30*, *The Family Man*, and even *Freaky Friday*. (Wow, the '90s and early 2000s were a great period for cinema, weren't they?) Rewatching these films got me thinking about life leaps—and wondering if the difference between being a young adult and being middle-aged isn't just as marked as the leap from being a child to a grown-up. I have always loved rom-coms with a side of fantasy or magical realism, so once I'd imagined a time leap in the vein of twenty-six going on forty-two, it was an idea that just wouldn't let go. So, thank you to '90s cinema for being so awesome, and yes, I am that woman who sits watching old films while muttering to myself, "They just don't make films like this anymore. *Sigh.*"

I must thank my friends Natalie and Rids, who are always such helpful early readers. I particularly loved the long conversations I had with you, Rids, about the logic of magic portals. It's always good to talk to someone who LOVES time-travel books when writing one, as they will pull you up on *everything*. We talked a lot about what happens in the future timeline when Lucy goes back. I said, "But does it matter?" and Rids said, "Yes, it absolutely matters," and I conceded she was right. *I* had to know, even if Lucy never knows, even if it never appears in the book.

A thank-you to my children, R and B, who inspired much of Felix's conversation. They invented Pocket Day, and we still celebrate it today. Children really do come up with funnier things than I could ever invent, and I could easily have written about fifty more pages of Lucy and Felix chatting. Lucky for you, I didn't. Thanks to my family for their continued support—especially my mother, who still buys everyone she knows my books for Christmas.

Thank you to my editors, Kim Atkins and Kate Dresser, for holding my hand through rewrites and providing such brilliant notes. I love collaborating with you both. To my agent, Clare Wallace, who is not only a fab agent but also an inspiring friend. To all my lovely writer friends, who make this crazy job less lonely and are such an uplifting and supportive community.

Finally, my biggest thank-you must go to you, my wonderful readers—especially if this is the fourth book of mine you are reading. Honestly, your messages and posts about my writing mean the world to me. I know there are SO many great books out there, so a huge, heartfelt thank-you for choosing mine. This is the first book I've written that makes me cry every time I read the ending, so I hope some of that comes through in the reading experience. I also know that all these "live in the moment," "it's all the good part," "value every day" sentiments are easier said than done. So don't beat yourself up if sometimes you just want to eat cheese toasties, watch Netflix, and scroll Instagram. Me too. *Meeee too.*

THE
GOOD
PART

Sophie Cousens

Discussion Guide
And Finally . . .

BOOK
ENDS

PUTNAM
— EST. 1838 —

1. *The Good Part* opens with Lucy despairing about her living situation, her job, and her love life. Despite all the grievances, what are some of the bright spots you think Lucy isn't seeing in her circumstances?

2. Lucy, Faye, Roisin, and Zoya have always been there for one another—from celebrating first jobs to first loves. And despite all the changes with Lucy's leap forward, her connection to them doesn't falter. What role do Lucy's friends play in the novel, and did you relate to any of these characters in particular?

3. Zoya is both Lucy's best friend and her personality opposite. Discuss their similarities and differences. To what extent does Lucy rely on Zoya to make sense of herself?

4. If you woke up sixteen years in the future, how would you react? Did Lucy's reaction make sense to you, or would you have handled the turn of events differently?

5. Some of the most endearing moments in the story include the ways Lucy falls in love with her husband, Sam.

Which was your favorite interaction between them? How do the circumstances of their reunion reinforce their love for each other? Discuss the extent to which you believe their love is fated.

6. One of Lucy's obstacles is coming up with a business pitch that she has no background in. Have you ever had to "fake it 'til you make it"? How did it go?

7. We get glimpses of how the world has changed in sixteen years, with delivery drones, paying via palm scans, and the extortionate price of coffee. How do you think the world will have changed in sixteen years' time?

8. Even after the time jump, Lucy's parents maintain a comforting sense of "Mumness" and "Dadness." How important was it for Lucy to see her parents amid the chaos of her situation? Which of your parents' quirks would you be relieved to see if you found yourself in Lucy's situation?

9. In Lucy's effort to catch up with all that she has missed, she asks Sam to tell her about himself, and he is understandably caught off guard. What opportunity does Lucy's need for recollection offer to those around her? Do you think her loved ones are generally telling the truth or putting a more positive spin on things?

10. Much of the humor in *The Good Part* comes from Lucy's internal reactions to her world. Discuss how author Sophie Cousens uses humor to provide insight into Lucy's struggles. Which reaction did you find the funniest?

11. *The Good Part* pays homage to our past selves, the bittersweetness of life, and what it means to grow up. If you could write a letter to your past self, what would you say? In reference to the title, what does "the good part" mean to you?

12. At the end of the book, Lucy must decide whether to stay in the future or go back to her past life. Do you agree with her decision? What are the risks, and do you agree with how Lucy made her decision?

AND FINALLY . . .

I asked a few friends, "What advice would you give your twenty-six-year-old self?"

"Don't listen to any snipes who tell you twenty-six is 'too old' for anything (and they will). Twenty-six is not too old for anything except starting a career in professional sports, and to be fair, Mhairi, that was never on the cards, darling. This sounds horribly therapy-speak, but act with intention. Make your friends on purpose. Learn things on purpose. Enjoy things on purpose. Work hard on purpose. Have adventures on purpose. You're sort of hunter-gathering for Future You at the same time as reveling in the uncomplicated optimism and strong liver function of being twenty-six. Oh, and get your eyebrows threaded. Don't worry that they'll take too much off; they don't." —Mhairi McFarlane, author

"Don't ever shave your tummy!"
        —Hester Decouz, corporate communications

"You only live once, so this is not a dress rehearsal for life. This is it—so take a risk, have fun, see the world, embrace adventure, shun routine, and honor your friends."
        —Richard Cousens, colonel, retired (Sophie's Dad)

"Do not mistake unbridled passion for proper, I-want-to-sit-on-the-sofa-every-night-with-you love, because that will encourage you to pick the wrong guys. Please, *please* spend less time obsessing about the rounded pouch below your belly button that you hate, because that is literally where your internal organs are and they do a pretty vital job! Never buy shoes that pinch in the shoe shop with the mistaken belief that 'they'll stretch.' Really enjoy this blessed time when your digestive system works. Related: Buy shares in Rennie."   —Sophia Money Coutts, author

"Don't get married until you're forty. Live alone for as long as you can. Trust your gut and meditate if you are torn about what to do. The answer will always come to you and you'll never regret it, because you'll look back and know you made that choice with a clear mind."   —Traci O'Dea, poet

"The advice I'd give myself at twenty-six is probably the same advice I've tried to give myself every day since—unexpected things are going to happen and change is inevitable. The sooner you accept that, the better equipped you'll be to roll with things when they crop up, and trust me, I've spent a lot of money on therapy to figure that out on your behalf. All the things that scared me when I was twenty-six ended up making my life a thousand times better."

—Lindsey Kelk, author

"Enjoy swimming in your bikini—no one is looking at you and you'll never look this good again. Hang out with your parents more. Also, invest in Netflix."

—Antonia, civil servant

"I would have told my twenty-six-year-old self to follow Winston Churchill's maxim: 'Success is the ability to go from failure to failure with no loss of enthusiasm.' If you believe in yourself, then just keep going, and every time you get knocked flat on your back, get up, dust yourself down, and try again. If you want something that badly, one day you will get it." —Peter James, author

"I would tell my younger self to be brave, to put yourself out there creatively. Everyone is winging it to some extent. Let go of people who do not make you feel great. And when you fall in love, be your most authentic self." —Lizzy Dent, author

"Explore more, visit different places—cities, beaches, forests—and walk, because when you have kids, you will crave being alone and exploring without someone asking you for a snack every two minutes/telling you the walk is boring/asking you to carry them. Buy Apple stock. Actually learn how to buy stock." —Cesca Major, author

"Don't worry too much about the romantic love. There are other types of love that are just as important. And even the madly-in-love ones end up arguing about who's taking the bins out in the end. Enjoy drinking while your liver still lets you." —Sarah, writer

"Those worries that seem so enormous right now, they'll be footnotes soon—then not even that. Relax. You're doing great. And there's so much joy ahead of you."
  —Beth O'Leary, author

"Take a moment to enjoy where you are rather than always racing to get to the next exciting thing. Sure, it might feel like you're not quite where you ought to be yet, but I promise if you keep trusting your gut, it will all work out okay! Start wearing sunscreen every day. (It's never too early!) Stop worrying about how much you weigh. Spend all your time and money on making memories and having adventures with your friends and family. It's the best investment you will ever make."   —Kimberley Atkins, editor

"Accept your parents for who they are and just focus on connecting with them. Don't underestimate your health—if you're not well, it can color everything."
                                        —Ridhima Durham, CCO

"You'll never regret a vacation, a night out, a night in, or buying the flowers. Show up for your friends. Wear the red lipstick. Savor the lack of responsibility. Everything will work out as it's meant to, as long as you keep reaching for what you want."   —Kate Dresser, editor

"Stop chasing boys; let them come to you. Instead, take up hobbies: macramé, roller skating, jewelry making, wild swimming, pottery, tai chi, everything, anything! There won't be as much time for hobbies later. Travel. I know you can't afford it, but just do it cheaply—you'll never forget the places you go. Keep writing . . ."   —Sophie Cousens

And perhaps wisest of all . . .

"Play with the children; let the housework go."
—Avril Cousens, occupational therapist, retired
(Sophie's mum)

SOPHIE COUSENS worked as a TV producer in London for more than twelve years and now lives with her family on the island of Jersey, one of the Channel Islands, located off the north coast of France. She balances her writing career with taking care of her two small children, and longs for the day when she might have a dachshund and a writing shed of her own. She is the author of *This Time Next Year*, *Just Haven't Met You Yet*, and *Before I Do*.

Visit Sophie Cousens Online

sophiecousens.com

 SophieCous

Sophie_Cousens

SophieCousensAuthor